Born and raised in New York City, Eric Lustbader graduated from Columbia University in 1969. Lustbader has had a number of fascinating careers. In addition to having written numerous bestselling novels, including *Black Heart*, *The Ninja* and *Angel Eyes*, he introduced Elton John to the American music scene. He spent fifteen years in the music industry in various capacities, including working for both Elektra and CBS Records. He is a former writer for *Cash Box* magazine where he wrote lead stories on new rock acts. In that capacity, he was the first person in the United States to predict the success of Jimi Hendrix, David Bowie and Santana, among many others.

Lustbader has taught in the All-Day Neighborhood School Division of the NYC Public School System and has also taught pre-schoolers in special Early Childhood programmes.

Eric Lustbader, who tr⬛⬛⬛ ⬛⬛⬛⬛ ⬛⬛⬛⬛ in researching his n⬛⬛⬛⬛ ⬛⬛⬛⬛⬛ ⬛⬛⬛⬛ lew York, with ⬛⬛⬛⬛ ⬛⬛⬛⬛ ⬛⬛⬛ rks for the Natu⬛⬛⬛

BY ERIC LUSTBADER

Nicholas Linnear novels

The Ninja
The Miko
White Ninja
The Kaisho
Floating City
Second Skin

China Maroc novels

Jian
Shan

Black Blade
Angel Eyes
French Kiss
Black Heart
Sirens
Zero
Dark Homecoming

The *Sunset Warrior* cycle

The Sunset Warrior
Shallows of Night
Dai-San
Beneath an Opal Moon
Dragons on the Sea of Night

ERIC LUSTBADER

THE SUNSET WARRIOR

Volume 1 of the *Sunset Warrior* Sequence

SHALLOWS OF NIGHT

Volume 2 of the *Sunset Warrior* Sequence

HarperCollins*Publishers*

This omnibus edition published in 1998 by
HarperCollins*Publishers*

HarperCollins*Publishers*
77–85 Fulham Palace Road,
Hammersmith, London W6 8JB

ISBN 0 261 67105 7

Printed and bound in Great Britain by
Clays Ltd, St Ives plc

To R.A.L. and M.H.L.
who were there through the best and,
especially, through the worst.

And

To Henry Steig, more than the master artisan.

To survive is not enough.

– Bujun saying

PART ONE
Echoes

Ronin was dying and he did not know it.

He lay quite still and completely naked on the centre of an elliptical stone slab which occupied roughly the centre of a square, cold chamber. Despite this, tiny beads of sweat glinted in the bristles of his short, black hair. His fine features held no expression whatsoever.

Standing over him, bent, eyes intent, was Stahlig, the Medicine Man. Ronin tried to relax, thinking, This is all a waste of time, as Stahlig's fingers probed and pushed at his chest, moving slowly down towards his ribs on the left side. He tried not to think of it but his muscles had a will of their own and they betrayed him, jumping in pain under the thick fingers.

'Uhm,' Stahlig grunted. 'Very recent.'

Ronin stared at the ceiling; at nothing. What was bothering him? It was merely a fight. *Merely?* His lips curled in distaste. A brawl; rolling in the Corridor like a common – abruptly remembrance blossomed . . .

His bare arms slick with sweat, his thick sword just sheathed, heavy at his side, his hands light after almost a full Spell of Combat practice. Walking alone and distracted out of the Hall of Combat into a knot of people, all at once surrounded by loud voices disclaiming hotly, stupidly, and he paid no attention. Something pushed against him and a voice cut through the din.

'And where are you going?' It was cold and affected and belonged to a tall, thin, blond man who wore the obliquely striped chest bands of the Chondrin. Black and gold: Ronin did not recognize the colours. Behind the blond man on either side stood five or six Bladesmen wearing the same colours. Apparently they had stopped a cluster of Students on their way from practice. He could not think why.

'Answer, Student!' the Chondrin commanded. His thin face was very white, dominated by a waxy nose. His high cheeks were pocked and a scar ran down like a tear from the corner of one eye so that it appeared lower than the other one.

Ronin was momentarily amused. He was a Bladesman and therefore practised with other Bladesmen. But these days he did not have much to do and boredom had led him to practice with the Students also. When he did that, as now, he wore plain clothes and those who did not know him took him for a Student.

'Where I go and what I do is my own affair,' Ronin said blandly. 'What is your business with these Students?'

The Chondrin goggled at him, stretching his neck forward like a reptile about to strike, and two spots of colour appeared high on his cheeks, accentuating the whiteness of the pockmarks.

'Where are your manners, Student?' he said menacingly. 'Speak with deference to your betters. Now answer the question.'

Ronin's hand strayed to the hilt of his sword but he said nothing.

'Well,' sneered the Chondrin, 'it appears this Student is in need of a lesson.' As if the words were a signal, the Bladesmen rushed at Ronin. Too late he realized that he could not draw his sword rapidly within the confines of the crowd. Then they were piling into him, the sheer force of their combined weight bearing him to the ground, and he thought, I do not believe this is happening. Instinctively he kicked out as he was borne under, and had the satisfaction of feeling his boot smash into flesh that gave way. Almost at the same moment, a blow along the side of his head disrupted his enjoyment. Adrenalin spurted and he punched up and out, and even though he was on his back and the leverage was not there, he felt his fist connect as it split open skin, cracked into bone. He heard a brief wail.

Then the boot caught him in the side and a thick gauze came down over his brain. He tried to hit again, could not, struggled with an enormous weight on his chest. His lungs were on fire and he felt ashamed. When the boot hit him again, he passed out . . .

The wave of pain came again but this time he had it under control and there was only the slightest movement. He looked at the wide head bent over him with its shaggy brows, rheumy eyes, and creased forehead.

'Ach!' exclaimed the Medicine Man, as much to himself as to Ronin. 'What have you been up to, ah?' He shook his head and, without looking at

11

Ronin, turned and put a dark, furry cloth against the mouth of an opaque white-glass bottle, and turned it upside down. He applied the cloth to Ronin's side. It was cold and the pain subsided.

'So. Dress and come inside.' He threw the cloth over the back of a hard chair and disappeared through a doorway. Ronin sat up, his side stiff but now without pain, pulled on his leggings and shirt, then his low leather boots. He stood to strap on his sword, then followed in the wake of Stahlig's body into a warmly lighted cubicle in sharp contrast to the starkly geometrical surgery outside.

Here all was a jumble. Shelves of bound papers and tablets rose like wild ivy from floor to ceiling along three walls. Occasionally gaps appeared in the contents of the shelves, or markers stuck out at odd angles. Stahlig's desk was set close to the far wall, and it was covered completely by mounds of papers and tablets, as were the two small chairs set before the desk. Behind the Medicine Man lay glass cases filled with phials and boxes.

Stahlig did not look up from his work as Ronin entered but he reached out behind him and got a clear bottle of amber wine, and from somewhere produced two metal cups, which he blew into perfunctorily before filling them halfway. He looked up then as he held one out. Ronin took it, and Stahlig sat back and waved an arm expansively.

'Sit,' he said.

Ronin had to set his cup down in order to clear away the masses of tablets from the chair. He hesitated with them in his arms.

12

'Oh, drop them anywhere,' said Stahlig with a flick of his thick hand.

Ronin sat and sipped, felt the sweet wine unroll its carpet of warmth along his throat and into his stomach. He took a long swallow.

Stahlig leaned forward, elbows on the masses of tablets, fingers steepled, his thumbs tapping absently at his upper lip. He said: 'Tell me what happened.'

Ronin, swirling the wine slowly in his cup, said nothing. He sat very straight because of his side.

The Medicine Man dropped his eyes, crumpled a sheet of paper, and threw it into a corner apparently without caring where it landed. 'So.' He sighed audibly, and when he spoke again his voice had softened perceptibly. 'You do not wish to speak of it, yet I know something troubles you.' Ronin looked up. 'Oh, yes, the old man still sees and feels.' He hunched forward over the desk again.

He stared at Ronin. 'Tell me, how long do we know each other?' His fingers moved along the desktop. 'Since you were very young, since before your sister dis – ' He stopped abruptly and colour came to his worn cheeks. 'I – '

Ronin shook his head. 'You will not hurt me if you say it,' he said softly. 'I am beyond that.'

Stahlig said quickly, 'Since before her disappearance,' as if, even in speech, it was a terrible thing to linger over. 'A long time we know each other. Yet you will not speak to me of what troubles you.' His hands came together again. 'You will leave here and go and talk to Nirren' – his voice had acquired a hard edge – 'your friend. Ha! He is a Chondrin, Estrille's Chondrin, and what is his first concern? You are without affiliation – you have no Saardin to order you or protect you. He is without feelings, that one. He pretends friendship, for information. That is after all one of his functions.'

Ronin put down his cup. Another time he might have been angry with Stahlig. But, he thought, he truly likes me, watches out for me, he does not realize – yet I must remember that he fears many things, some justly, others not. He is wrong about Nirren.

'No one knows better than I the deviousness of Chondrin,' he said. 'You know this. If Nirren seeks information from me, he is welcome to it.'

'Ach!' Stahlig's fingers flailed the air. 'You are not a political animal.'

Ronin laughed. 'True,' he said. 'Oh, how very true.'

The Medicine Man frowned. 'I do not believe you realize the precariousness of the situation. Politics is what rules the Freehold. There has been much friction among the Saardin recently, and it becomes worse daily. There are elements within the Freehold – very powerful elements – who, I believe, want a war.'

Ronin shrugged. 'I could think of worse things happening.' He sipped his wine. 'At least the boredom will be relieved.'

Stahlig was shocked. 'You do not mean that, I know you better. Perhaps you think you will be unaffected.'

'Perhaps I will be.'

Stahlig shook his head slowly, sadly. 'You talk without thinking because there is little for you to do. But you know as well as I that none shall remain unscathed by an internal war. Within this confined space such a foolhardy action can only have disastrous consequences.'

'Yet I am uninvolved.'

'You are without a Saardin, yes. But you are a Bladesman, and when the time comes you cannot be uninvolved.'

There was a small silence. Within it, Ronin took another swallow of wine. He said, finally: 'I shall tell you what occurred today.'

Stahlig listened to Ronin through half-closed eyes, his blunt thumbs again idly tapping his upper lip. He could have been falling asleep.

'I find it incredible that I should be attacked in such a manner – and by Bladesmen. If I were Downshaft in the Middle Levels – you know the Code as well as I. Fistfights are not for Bladesmen. Any grievances are settled by Combat; it cannot be otherwise. For centuries it has been so. And today I am attacked by Bladesmen led by a Chondrin – as if they were urchins who did not know any better.'

Stahlig sat back now. 'It is as I have said. Tension, and something more, is in the air. A war is certainly coming, and with it a breakdown of all the traditions that have allowed this Freehold, among all other Freeholds, to survive.' He shuddered, just once, a pathetic gesture. 'The victors, whoever they may be, will change the Freehold.

15

Nothing will remain the same.' He gulped his wine, poured more. 'Black and gold, you said. That would be – Dharsit's people. He is one of the relatively new Saardin. A new Order they want; new ideas, new Traditions, so they say. *Their* ideas, *I* say.' He was suddenly vehement, slamming his cup down so hard that the contents flew across his desk, staining the tablets. 'It is power they want!' He jumped up in exasperation, flinging the wet tablets away from him, heedless of where they fell.

'Oh, Chill take it! Ask your friend Nirren,' he said darkly. 'He will know.'

'We do not normally talk of politics.'

'No, of course not,' Stahlig said contemptuously. 'He would not divulge the strategies Estrille thinks upon. But I will wager he gathers Corridor gossip from you.'

'Perhaps.'

'Ah!' Stahlig paused, sitting down once again, and then rushed on as if surprised at having elicited this from Ronin. 'As for this incident today, I trust you are not contemplating a precipitous action.'

'If by that you mean that you are worried I will use this' – he partially withdrew his blade from its scabbard and slammed it home with a whack – 'rest assured I am not interested in being drawn into the world of the Saardin.'

The Medicine Man sighed. 'Good, because I doubt if Security would believe you.'

'What about the Students who witnessed the attack?'

'And jeopardize their chances to be Bladesmen?'

16

Ronin nodded. 'Yes, of course. Well, it is no matter to me. And who knows, sometime I may run into Dharsit's Chondrin at practice.' He grinned. 'He will have cause to remember me then.'

Stahlig laughed then. 'I daresay he will.'

Boots sounded in the surgery and two figures filled the doorway of the inner cubicle as Ronin and Stahlig turned to look. They did not enter the room. They wore identical grey uniforms with three daggers held in scabbards attached to black leather straps buckled obliquely across their chests: Security daggam. Both had short, dark hair and even features; faces one would never look at twice, faces one would have to study closely to remember.

'Stahlig?' said one. He had a crisp, clear voice.

'Yes?'

'Your presence is required. Please pack your healing bag and come with us.' He handed Stahlig a folded sheet. The other one did absolutely nothing except watch them. Both his hands were free. Stahlig read the sheet.

'Freidal himself,' he murmured. 'Most impressive.' He looked up. 'Of course I shall come, but you must tell me something of the nature of the summons. I must know what to bring.'

'Bring everything.' The daggam eyed Ronin suspiciously.

'That is quite impossible,' said Stahlig impatiently.

'I am his assistant. You may speak freely in front

of me,' said Ronin. The daggam's eyes swung darkly upon him, then back to Stahlig.

The Medicine Man nodded. 'Yes, he is helping me.'

'A Magic Man,' the daggam said slowly, reluctantly, 'has gone mad. We have been forced to restrain him – for his own safety as well as the safety of others. He had already wantonly attacked his Teck. But his health seems to be failing, and – '

Stahlig was already busy cramming phials and paraphernalia into a worn leather bag. Seeing this, the daggam stopped, and instead of finishing his thought he stared stonily at Ronin.

'You are no assistant,' he said icily. 'You carry a sword. You are a Bladesman. Explain.'

Stahlig ceased to fill his bag but remained with his back to them. That does not help, Ronin thought.

'Yes, of course I am a Bladesman, but as you can see I am unaffiliated and so have much free time. So I help the Medicine Man from time to time.'

Stahlig finished filling his bag. He turned. 'All set,' he said. 'Lead the way.' He looked at Ronin. 'You had better accompany me.'

Ronin stared at the daggam. 'It would certainly relieve the boredom.'

The Corridor swept away from them in a smooth, gently curving arc. The walls were painted a grey that at one time had been uniform; now, through years of wear and neglect, there were patches made oily and dark by dirt, areas crusty with grime, sections bleached almost white.

Here and there spiderweb cracks extended their fingers like tenacious plants seeking sunlight.

Doorways marched by them on either side at regular intervals. Those with doors were invariably shut. Occasionally an open doorway revealed cubicles dark and musty, debris piled in corners, refuse strewn about the floor. But, beyond the evidence of human detritus, they were empty save for the brief flash of small scurrying bodies: click-click of claw, whip of tail.

Gradually the grey of the walls gave way to a tired lustreless blue. The daggam turned left into a dark passageway in the interior wall of the Corridor and the pair behind them followed. None of them gave a second look at the stalled Lift across the Corridor.

They were on a landing of the Stairwell that ran vertically along the rim of the core of the Freehold. One of the daggam, the one who talked, reached up into a niche in the wall and removed a torch of tarred reeds bound tightly with cord. He held it in front of him while the other daggam produced flint and a tinder box, got a flame going, and touched it to the torch. It flared and crackled as it caught. Sparks jumped in the air and fell blackly at their feet.

Without a backward glance, the daggam proceeded down the concrete steps. Ronin was surprised to find that they were descending rather than ascending. The little he knew of the mysterious Magic Men indicated that they held a lofty position in the hierarchy of the Freehold. Their talents and wisdom were constantly courted by the

Saardin despite their traditional vow for ever to work towards the good of the entire Freehold. But it was possible that they were not immune to politicization. By all rights the Magic Man should be quartered on one of the Freehold's Upper Levels, yet they were descending. Ronin shrugged mentally. No one knew much about them except that they were rumoured to be strange individuals. If one chose to reside on the fringes of the Middle Levels with the Neers it was no concern of his.

Between each Level the Stairwell doubled back on itself at a landing. They traversed the Levels silently, the shivering torchlight distorting their shadows into grotesque parodies of human shapes, shambling things that danced along the walls and low ceilings, expressionless, unthinking, desireless, receding from and approaching their human counterparts disconcertingly.

At length they reached the proper Level and emerged into a Corridor identical to the one they had quit above, save that here the walls were painted a drab green. They waited while the daggam snuffed the torch and placed it in the niche in this landing.

There was more activity on this Level. Men and women passed them going in either direction and the low hum of distant conversations filled the air like a tidal wash. Perhaps two hundred metres from where they emerged, they came upon a door painted dark green. All the others they had seen on this Level were the same colour as the walls. Before the door stood two daggam.

A brief, muffled exchange passed between the

20

four daggam. The shorter of the pair guarding the door nodded curtly, turned, and rapped a peculiar pattern on the door. It was opened by another daggam, and the messengers and Stahlig stepped through. Ronin moved to join them but was stopped short by the palm of one of the guards pressed against his chest. The daggam's jaw jutted. 'Where you goin'?' His voice managed to sound bored and contemptuous at the same time.

'I am with the Medicine Man.' Ronin met his eyes with a steady gaze. He saw a round, jowly face too large for the small, fat nose and close-set eyes the colour of mud. But, thought Ronin, an efficient machine that will respond instantly and unfailingly to orders. I have seen so many.

The square mouth with its thick red lips opened like a reluctant gate. 'Don't know anything 'bout it. Move along 'fore you get into trouble.'

Ronin felt the pressure from the other's hand and stood his ground. Surprise showed briefly in the daggam's eyes: he was used to a certain response to the application of his power. He recognized fear in others easily, loved creating it, seeing it burn before him as if it were a sacrifice. He saw no fear now, and this disturbed him. Anger flared within him, and his fingers plucked at the top dagger strapped across his chest.

Ronin's hand was on the hilt of his sword when a face appeared from around the still partially open door. 'Stahlig, you absentminded – '

The Medicine Man's eyes widened. 'Ronin. Wondered where you were. Come along in.'

Ronin stepped forward but the daggam still

barred his way. The daggam, anger still beating within him, shook his head, and the blade of the dagger gleamed in the Corridor's light.

At that moment Robin saw another face appear. Long and lean with a cleft jaw filled with determination, a very high, narrow forehead topped by coal-black hair so slick and shiny it had blue highlights, it was dominated by wide-apart eyes of a clear piercing blue, whose penetrating gaze appeared to take in everything while giving away nothing.

'*Qieto*, Marcsh. Let the fellow through.' The voice was deep and commanding.

Marcsh heard the words and automatically moved aside, but the anger refused to die, beating ineffectually at the cage of his burly chest. He glared in silent resentment as the figure moved past him, careful that his Saardin should not see, and thus punish him.

Ronin found himself in an antechamber off which he saw two rooms set at angles. The one on his left was furnished starkly and functionally with a large work table and smallish writing desk along one wall, and a narrow bed along the opposite wall. The room was dark but he could make out a figure sprawled on the bed. Battered and scarred cabinets lined the upper areas of three walls. A lone chair squatted empty in the middle of the cubicle.

The room to the right was less utilitarian. Two walls were lined with low couches and cushioned chairs. The daggam, including the two who had been sent for Stahlig, sat on the couch farthest from the door, amid a meal. In the anteroom two more daggam stood flanking Stahlig and the man who commanded the daggam. Ronin thought they must have torn down some walls in order to make these quarters. Two-cubicle quarters were rare enough Upshaft, but Down here –

'Ah, Ronin,' said the Medicine Man. 'This is Freidal, Saardin of Security for the Freehold.'

Freidal inclined his long body from the waist in a gesture that was somehow theatrical. He did not smile, and his eyes were blank beacons that studied Ronin for another brief moment before he returned his gaze to Stahlig. They resumed their discussion.

Freidal was dressed all in deep grey save for the knee-high boots of the Saardin and the oblique chest stripes of the Chondrin, both of which were silver. Ronin wondered at this: overlord and tactician, eyes and ears, all rolled into one.

'Nevertheless,' he was saying now, 'do you take responsibility for this man being here?'

'Ach!' Stahlig rubbed his forehead. 'Do you think he will walk out with Borros? Nonsense.'

Freidal eyed the Medicine Man coldly. 'Sir, there is much here that is of the gravest import to the Freehold.' The brass hilts of his daggers winked in the light as he shifted easily. 'I cannot take unnecessary risks.' He spoke in a curiously formal, almost anachronistic manner. He stood very straight and he was very tall.

'I assure you there is nothing to fear from Ronin's presence,' Stahlig said. 'He is merely observing my techniques, and is here only because I invited him.'

'I trust you are not so foolish as to lie to me. That would lead to dire consequences both for you and your friend.' He glanced briefly at Ronin and the light turned his left eye into a silver dazzle. Ronin started slightly as the Saardin turned back to Stahlig. A reflection, he thought. But it cannot be, not a flash as bright as that. Then he had it, and now, because he was looking for it, he saw that Freidal's left eye did not move in its socket.

Stahlig put up his hands. 'Please, Saardin, you have misunderstood me. I merely thought to reassure – '

'Medicine Man, permit me to make clear my position. I did not wish to summon you. Your presence here disturbs me. Your friend's presence here disturbs me. I am thrust deeply into the midst of a highly volatile Security matter with grave ramifications. Had I my way, no one but my hand-picked daggam would have access to these quarters. However, I am now resigned to the fact that such a course is no longer possible. Borros, the Magic Man, is seriously ill, so my Med advisers tell me. They can no longer help him. They say it is beyond them. Hence, a Medicine Man must be summoned if Borros is to live. I wish him to live. Yet I have little patience with your kind. Please attend to him as quickly as possible and leave.'

Stahlig inclined his head slightly, an acknowledgement of Freidal's authority. 'As you wish,' he said softly. 'However, may I ask you to recount the events immediately prior to Borros's illness?' Ronin bristled inwardly at the Medicine Man's obsequious tone.

'May I ask what for, sir?'

Stahlig sighed and Ronin observed the lines of tiredness in his face. 'Saardin, I would not ask you to defend the Freehold with one arm bound to your side. I ask only that you give me the same courtesy.'

'It is essential, then?'

'The more information I have, the greater the chance of helping the patient.'

'All right.' The Saardin beckoned and a daggam appeared. He had been standing just inside the threshold to the room on the right and they had not noticed him before. A writing tablet lay along the inside of his forearm. In his other hand was a quill with which he drew symbols on the tablet. 'My scribe is never far from me,' said the Saardin. 'He takes down all that I say, and all that is said to me. In this way there can be no – misunderstanding at a later time.' He looked from the Medicine Man to Ronin and back again with a neutral gaze. It was impossible to guess what he was thinking. 'He shall read from the report made to me earlier today.'

'That will be fine,' said Stahlig. 'But let us go in first, so that I may see Borros's condition.'

Freidal bowed stiffly and they moved silently into the shadowy cubicle and over to the cot on which the figure lay. 'I apologize for the lack of light,' Freidal said without a trace of regret. 'The Overheads have recently failed, hence the lamps.'

Two of the familiar clay pots sat on the work table across from the bed, their flames illuminating the room with an uncertain smoky glow.

The figure lay lashed to the bed – an otherwise unremarkable affair consisting of a wooden frame and large, soft pillows – with leather straps around chest and ankles. Both Ronin and Stahlig leaned closer to get a better look in the low light.

In all ways he appeared singular. He was long-waisted with a thick barrel chest and peculiarly narrow hips. His hands had long delicate fingers tipped with protracted, translucent nails. However, most unusual of all was his face. The head, an elongated oval, was entirely without hair, and the skin, drawn tightly over the scalp and high cheekbones, was of a most peculiarly sombre hue with a yellow tinge. His eyes were closed and his breathing was shallow. Stahlig bent at once to examine him.

At that moment the scribe began to recite: '"Recorded on the twenty-seventh Cycle of Sajjit – "'

Freidal raised a hand. 'Just the text, if you please.'

The scribe inclined his head. '"Statement of Mastaad, Teck to Borros, Magic Man. We had been working for many Cycles on the final phases of a Project, the goal of which Borros steadfastly refused to confide in me. I did the mixing and controlling of elements, that is all. For several Cycles Borros had been working nonstop. I would leave him at the end of the sixth Spell and when I returned at second Spell, he would be as I had left him, hunching over his table. Three Cycles ago I arrived to find him immensely agitated. But he would tell me nothing, though I begged him for the sake of his health to – "'

'What are these, Saardin?' Stahlig interrupted. Throughout the scribe's recitation, he had been hard at work probing and listening, trying to ascertain the seriousness of the Magic Man's condition. So he had missed them at first. But he had seen them at last and now he pointed. Ronin bent and saw three small spots, like dark smudges of charcoal, forming a triangle, imprinted on each temple of the hairless head.

Freidal too was looking at the spots, and for the first time Ronin felt a heavy tension fill the room. The Saardin continued to stare at the recumbent body. 'You are the Medicine Man, sir,' he said carefully. 'You tell me.'

Stahlig seemed about to answer, then apparently thought better of it. In the silence, Freidal, looking satisfied, lifted his hand again.

The scribe's voice once more took over: '" – let me let him more fully. He refused, becoming abusive. I withdrew. The next Cycle his agitation had increased. His hands trembled, his voice cracked, and on more than one occasion he found cause to insult me. Second Spell this Cycle, when I arrived, he screamed at me to leave. He said he no longer required a Teck. He began to rant incoherently. I feared for his health. I tried to calm him. He flew into a rage and assaulted me, throwing me into the Corridor. I came directly here to – "'

The Saardin made a brief sign and the scribe was

silent. Stahlig stood up and turned to Freidal. 'Why has this man been restrained?'

The Saardin's good eye blazed. 'Sir, I wish to know if Borros will live and, if so, whether his faculties have been impaired. When I have the answers to these questions I shall entertain your queries.'

Stahlig wiped the back of a hand across his perspiring brow. 'He will live, Saardin. That is, I believe he will. As to his faculties, I cannot tell you until he has regained consciousness and I have had a chance to test his reflexes.'

The Saardin thought about this for a moment. 'Sir, this man was quite violent when my daggam arrived. He fought them although they wished him no harm. They were forced to subdue him and to make certain he would stay that way. It was as much for his protection as for others'.' For the first time Freidal smiled, giving his face the look of a predatory animal. It flashed and was gone, leaving no trace that it had ever been there at all.

Stahlig said: 'It is an inhuman way to treat anyone.'

Freidal shrugged. 'It is necessary.'

He left them abruptly, posting two daggam at the threshold to the room and admonishing them to leave as soon as the Medicine Man had satisfied himself as to Borros's condition. 'If he dies, I hold you personally accountable,' he told Stahlig, and this served as his farewell.

Stahlig hissed softly when they were alone in the room with Borros, the nervous sound of released tension. He sank into the cubicle's lone chair and his shoulders slumped. He clasped his hands in front of him. They trembled slightly. Ronin thought that he looked very frail and very old and he felt pity stir inside him.

'I am a fool.' Fatigue. 'I should never have asked you to come here. I thought for a moment as I thought many years ago, when I was young and foolhardy. I am an old man and I should know better.'

Ronin put a hand on his shoulder. He wanted to say something but no words came to him. Stahlig looked up into his face. 'He has marked you now, do not forget that.' Ronin tried to smile, found he could not. Stahlig rose then, and returned to his ministration of the Magic Man, turning his back on Ronin, who stood, immobile and silent, regarding the dark countenance of the singular man with yellow skin, strapped to the bed, smoky orange light flickering now and again along the considerable lengths of his translucent fingernails, like the traces of some unimaginably mysterious animal.

So it was that when Borros opened his eyes Ronin saw it first, and he called softly to Stahlig, who was at that moment searching his bag.

The eyes were long, that was all he could tell, for they were in deep shadow and Stahlig was bent over him. 'Ah,' the mouth said. 'Ah.' He blinked slowly several times. His eyelids drooped. His lips were dry.

Stahlig lifted a lid, peered at the eye. 'Drugged,' he said very softly.

29

'Ah,' the Magic Man said.

Ronin leaned over so that they could talk without fear of being overheard. 'Why drug him like that?'

'The Saardin would tell us it was to calm him. But I do not believe that was the reason.'

'Why not?'

'Wrong drug, first of all. Borros is semiconscious, but he is still affected by whatever it was they gave him. Had he been sedated, he would either be out completely or awake and wondering what had happened to him.'

'Ah. Ah.'

Stahlig said quite clearly: 'Borros, can you hear me?'

The lips ceased their noises and a tension came over the figure. 'No,' the lips said weakly. 'No, no, no no – ' A bubble of spittle had collected at one corner of the mouth, and now it inflated and deflated with the piteous cry. 'No, no.'

'By the Frost,' breathed Ronin.

The head moved from side to side as the mouth worked. Tendons stood out along his neck and he strained against his bonds. Stahlig reached into his bag and administered something to Borros. Almost at once he quieted. His eyes closed and his breathing became less laboured. Stahlig wiped his sweating brow. Ronin began to say something but the old man stopped him with a hand on his arm.

'Well, I have done all I can now,' he said in a normal tone. He picked up his bag and they left the room. At the door, he left a message for Freidal with one of the daggam. 'Tell your Saardin that I shall return during the seventh Spell to check the condition of the patient.'

'What did you find out?'

The homey clutter was somehow comforting. The dim Overheads threw a dismal light. The clay lamps were in a corner, resting precariously on a pile of tablets, waiting to be used. The crumpled paper lay where it had been tossed. Across the room, the darkness of the surgery filled the open doorway.

Stahlig shook his head. 'I do not wish to involve you further. It is enough that you have encountered the Saardin of Security.'

'But I was the one – '

'I gave the assent.' He was angry at himself. 'Believe me when I tell you that I am going to forget what I have seen. Borros is just another patient in need of treatment.'

'But he is not just another patient,' said Ronin. 'Why will you not tell me what you have learned about him?'

'It is far too dangerous – '

'Chill take that!' Ronin exclaimed. 'I am not a child who needs protection.'

'I did not mean – '

'Did you not, then?'

In the small silence that built itself around the two, Ronin recognized a potential danger. If one of them did not speak soon, they would be irrevocably separated. He did not understand why this was and it bothered him.

Stahlig lowered his eyes and said softly: 'I – have

always thought of you in a certain way. As Medicine Man, many things in life – things that at one time I perhaps wanted for myself – were not allowed me. Both you and – your sister – were very close to me when you were young. And then – there was only you.' He said it in a halting, protracted manner, and it was obvious that it was difficult for him. Yet Ronin could not find it in himself to make it any easier. Or perhaps this was not possible. 'But I understand that you are a Bladesman now. I know what that means. But every once in a while I remember – that child.' He turned and poured himself a drink, swallowed it at once, poured another and one for Ronin, handing him the cup. 'And now,' he said, as if nothing had happened, 'if you insist, I shall tell you what I have learned.'

Stahlig told him that from what he had observed he was sure that Security had had Borros for more than a Cycle. 'Possibly as long as seven Cycles, it is hard to say with that particular drug.' Further, it seemed fairly clear that in defining the drugs used and Borros's reaction to Stahlig's voice, Security had been interrogating him.

'"Interviewing" they call it,' he said. 'One of the effects of this drug is to submerge the will. In other words – '

'They were picking his brain.'

'Attempting to, yes.'

'What do you mean?'

'Well, these things are very tricky and they are certainly not foolproof.'

'But why not just confiscate his notes? Surely that would have been easier.'

The Medicine Man shrugged. 'Perhaps they could not decipher them, who knows? In any event, most of what Freidal told us and allowed us to hear was false.'

'But why go to all that trouble? And if what you say is true, that means Security has deliberately interfered in the work of a Magic Man.'

'Quite so.' Stahlig nodded. 'And then there is the matter of the Dehn spots – ' He stopped abruptly. They both heard soft footfalls in the darkness outside. He said in a louder voice: 'Time is passing. It is near to Sehna.' In an undertone, he added: 'You must be at board. You understand?'

Ronin nodded.

'And tomorrow and tomorrow.' Then louder: 'Good, I shall see you later. I will need to take another look at that bruise.' He flicked his eyes and, with the briefest movement of his head, Ronin again nodded. He rose and left. In the surgery he passed two daggam groping through the dark on their way to see Stahlig.

He passed up the only working Lift in this Sector because the queue was far too long and he lacked the patience to wait. He was hailed several times and he smiled distractedly and raised a hand perfunctorily but he did not stop to greet anyone formally or to talk.

His body went on automatic, as it often did, so that he was only just aware of his surroundings. He was deep in thought but his body knew where to walk to get to the proper Stairwell leading Upshaft to his own Level.

Consequently, he went right by Nirren without seeing him. He was a talk, dark-complexioned man with an aquiline nose and deep-set eyes. He turned, not in the least surprised and, grabbing an arm impulsively, spun Ronin around. Ronin felt the shadow of the approach before the Chondrin had touched him, and there was no resistance in him. He spun with the momentum, and as he did so, he drew his sword with such lightning swiftness that his arm was no more than a blur. The blade was up and ready, light spilling along its width, before he had even seen who had grasped him. Nirren's blade was barely out of its scabbard.

Nirren laughed, showing white, even teeth. 'One day I swear I shall best you.'

Ronin smiled bleakly and sheathed his sword.

'Not a day for one of your tricks.' The smile faded and died.

But the Chondrin was in good humour. His eyes widened and he said in a parody of a whisper: 'Ah, secrets to share with your wise and witty friend.' He put his arm around Ronin. 'Tell all and unending happiness shall be yours.'

Ronin thought fleetingly of Stahlig's admonition and was instantly annoyed with himself. There were questions that puzzled him and Nirren might have the answers to some of them. In any case, he was a friend. My only friend, he thought with a start.

He smiled. 'All right. My quarters?'

They entered the Stairwell and Nirren lit a torch. 'Double practice again today, eh?' He shook his head as they made their way Upshaft. 'When are you going to be sensible and turn your mind to useful activity?'

Ronin grunted. 'Such as?'

The Chondrin grinned. 'Well, it just so happens there is a fine position under Jargiss – '

'I knew it – '

'Now wait, he is really all right, for a Saardin – quick, and a brilliant strategist. I know you would get along. And he knows the meaning of defence, too.' This was a favourite topic of his. He never tired of sketching hypothetical battle plans, outlining tactics for attacker and defender. Given the choice of ground, he would say, the defender will triumph nine out of ten times, even with less men.

'I have never met a Saardin I liked,' Ronin said.

'Tell me, have you ever met Jargiss?'

Ronin shook his head. 'This is like a game with you. No, not to talk to. How many times do you have to hear it?'

Nirren shrugged and grinned. 'I keep believing that one of these times you will ask to meet him.'

Ronin reached out and touched the orange and brown chest bands strapped over the Chondrin's brown shirt. 'I think not,' he said very softly.

'Listen, if it's about the Salamander, you have to expect – '

'That is not it at all.'

'If you do not mind my saying so, I believe it is.'

They were both very still then, regarding each other unwaveringly in the uncertain, sparking light. The reeds of the torch crackled softly and the minute clash of tiny paws on concrete sounded intermittently. The noises were remote, from another world. Somewhere, very far off, boots sounded and then faded. Darkness lapped at their feet.

At last Ronin heard himself say: 'Perhaps you are right.' And the surprise stayed with him long after they emerged on to his Level.

His quarters were actually two cubicles, considerably more space than that of any other Bladesmen. Chondrin were allotted this much room; Saardin had of course quite a bit more.

K'reen was there when they arrived. Her thick, dark hair was up and coiffed for Sehna but she still wore her work clothes: close-fitting leggings, and shirt loose through the torso to de-emphasize the body underneath, with light sleeves. She was tall, fully Ronin's height, with a long, graceful neck, generous mouth, and wide-set, dark eyes. When they came in, she smiled and touched Ronin's hand.

He was momentarily surprised because she should have been either finishing up her work on the Med Training Level or in her own quarters dressing for Sehna.

She breezed past them, on her way out. 'I spent too much time searching for these in my quarters' – she waved silver bracelets at them – 'until I realized I had left them here.' She stuck her tongue out at Nirren and he grinned. 'Unless I run I will never make Sehna on time.' She closed the door behind her.

Ronin crossed to a cabinet, reached out a flagon of wine and goblets, poured them both drink. Already K'reen was gone from his mind.

They sat facing each other on low stools covered with fur. The harsh, white light of the Overheads washed over them, draining the colour from their faces. Nirren sipped at his wine. Ronin's lay untouched at his feet. He told the Chondrin about his meeting with Freidal. The other's eyes flashed briefly.

'What do you think?'

Nirren stood and paced the small room. 'I think I must find out why Freidal is so interested in that Magic Man.'

'They claim he is mad.'

'If that is so, perhaps they made him mad.'

'But the spots.'

Nirren turned. 'What?'

37

'The marks on Borros's head.'

'Ah, yes. The Dehn spots. That could have been it, you see. And all the more reason for me to find out what Freidal is planning as quickly as possible. Few people know of the Dehn. It is a machine of the Ancients. Like so many of the mysterious artifacts that keep us alive here – provide us with air and heat and light, more than three kilometres below the surface of the planet – we know only what it does; the *how* is beyond us.' His voice took on a bitter edge. 'Yet we have knowledge enough to use it. Wires are attached to the head – at the places where you saw the spots – and shocks are delivered to the brain by the same method by which our Overheads function. Do you remember the Neer who opened one up some time ago and touched the wrong wire? He was black when they found him, and he stank. They had a lot of trouble identifying him became his plate had melted.' He sipped his wine and sat down again.

'In any event, the Dehn is very painful, so I am told. Consequently it can be quite reliable in obtaining information from recalcitrants. But there is trouble in controlling it; what can you expect when you are in the dark.' He paused for a moment, lost in thought. 'What *is* Freidal up to?'

Ronin felt something stir within him. He rose. 'Let me understand this. Are you saying that the Saardin of Security has interfered in the work of a Magic Man, has – what, tortured him, to gain information that he will use for himself?'

Nirren stabbed a finger in the air and his eyes sparkled. 'Precisely, my friend. I see there is hope for you yet. The time of battle draws nigh, and when it comes Freidal and Jargiss shall be on opposing sides. We are enemies, he and I.' He grasped Ronin by the shoulders. 'Listen, my friend, the time for neutrality has passed. All shall be affected by the struggle. You must help us. Ask Stahlig to talk to Borros while there is still time. It is the only way, I cannot get at Freidal quickly. And if we gain knowledge of his secret, it will give us much strength.'

'Perhaps Freidal has learned nothing.'

'I cannot afford to think that way.'

Ronin looked at him. 'You do not care what they have done to him. I do not even know whether he will be able to talk coherently after what they have subjected him to.'

There was a warmth in Nirren's eyes. 'Be realistic, my friend. I am talking about something that is larger than any one individual. We are all merely pieces. The Freehold is disintegrating before our eyes because of dissension among the Saardin. You are unaffiliated, so perhaps you are not so aware of it, but believe me when I tell you that much work must be done if we are to survive. But right now, no decisions are being made on behalf of the Freehold. You see? They are all too busy scheming to consolidate their power. This will cause our destruction.'

'Perhaps it will be your battle which causes our destruction,' said Ronin.

Nirren dropped his arms and made a face. 'I will not argue with you. I debate with our people at every Spell. I do not come to you for this.'

He grinned suddenly and gulped down the remainder of his wine. 'Think on what I have said. I will say nothing further on the subject. I have sufficient trust in you. Agreed?'

Ronin smiled and shook his head. He thought: When he grins, his enthusiasm is hard to ignore. He made a mock bow. 'As you wish.'

Nirren laughed and rose. 'Good. Then I will be off. I barely have enough time to change. Until Sehna, then.'

Alone in his quarters, Ronin picked up his untouched wine and sipped it. It was cool and deliciously tart. It could have been brackish water for all he tasted it.

Sehna. The evening meal. A sacred time. So many traditions, Ronin thought as he entered the Great Hall. And how many generations preceded us, lying now in dust, remembered by the traditions they handed down and nothing else.

The heat and noise hit him simultaneously, a vast kinetic wave, startling and bright. Continuous random motion. The Great Hall stretched away, its farthest reaches obscured by a haze of fragrant steam and smoke and heat. Long tables with low-backed benches filled with men and women proliferated in precise rows into the distance. Momentarily his hand strayed to his hip. It felt light and strange without the weight of his sword, but weapons of any kind were forbidden at board.

He moved to the right, then turned and strode down one of the narrow aisles. He wore soft cream-coloured leggings and shirt; no Saardin used that colour. Servers made room for him to pass, lifting huge trays laden with steaming food or tankards of thick ale, flagons of sweet, amber wine. He smelled the mingled aromas of food-stuffs, light perfumes, and thick sweat.

He came at length to his table and took his accustomed place between Nirren and K'reen. She was deep in conversation with a Bladesman next to her, so that he saw only the dark and shining helmet of her hair. He smelled her perfume. Across the table, Telmis lifted a goblet in silent greeting, and next to him G'fand, a very young, blond man, was busy directing a Server.

'Well, how is our Scholar this Spell?' Ronin asked him.

G'fand turned and his blue eyes dropped under Ronin's gaze. 'The same, I expect,' he said softly.

Nirren laughed. 'Now what could be the trouble this Cycle – lost one of your ancient manuscripts?' He laughed again and colour rushed into G'fand's face. By this time K'reen had turned towards them, and, seeing the young man's discomfort, she reached out and covered his hand with hers. 'Pay them no heed, they enjoy teasing you. They think swordsmanship is the most important skill in the Freehold.'

'You have evidence to the contrary, my lady?' Nirren said formally, and grinned. 'If so, I should like to hear it.'

'Quiet, you,' she admonished.

G'fand said rather stiffly, as if no one would hear him: 'It is all right. I expect it from him.'

'And not from me?' Ronin leaned back as a Server filled his plate. He indicated that he wanted wine, not ale.

G'fand said nothing, his eyes still averted.

Ronin began to eat, his mind far away. 'I shall endeavour, in the future, not to tease you.'

At that moment Tomand and Bessat arrived. They were seated amid a great uproar from the table, partly because it amused them to make a fuss over Tomand's corpulence, partly because they felt they must ease the tension. Sehna was a time for relaxation, no matter what else was happening throughout the Freehold.

Slowly the table settled down and the food was served. Noise increased and the heat became oppressive. 'Chill take me,' Nirren said, 'why is it so hot in here?'

Tomand stopped eating momentarily and, wiping his heavy, sweating jowls, gestured for him to lean forward. 'Just between us,' he glanced from Nirren to Ronin, 'we are having problems with the ventilation system.' He took another forkful of food. 'In fact, that is why we were late to Sehna. We were working until the last moment, trying to figure out the cursed thing.'

'With very little success, I notice,' said Nirren.

Tomand grimaced. 'It is simply impossible. We have lost too much knowledge.' He chewed, then continued. 'The most we can do is to try to clean up the mess. I mean how are we supposed to fix something if we don't know how it works? So little of what the Ancients wrote has survived. Only their Machines – '

'No,' interrupted G'fand, 'we could not destroy their Machines without destroying ourselves.'

Tomand paused with a forkful of food halfway to his greasy lips. 'What are you saying?'

'That the writings of the Ancients were deliberately destroyed in the early days of the Freehold.'

Tomand shoved the fork into his mouth, and said around the food: 'What nonsense. Who would wilfully destroy knowledge? Certainly not civilized folk.'

G'fand said carefully: 'The Ancients invented many things. A number of them were quite lethal. And they were inveterate graphologers. It appears that our forefathers had little faith in those who would come after them. In any event, they took no chances. They destroyed the written wisdom of the Ancients. Destroyed it indiscriminately, so that I, a Scholar, cannot learn their history, and you, a Neer, cannot understand the workings of the Air Machines, and the Saardin cannot learn how to destroy each other and the Freehold.'

Tomand wiped his mouth.

Nirren said: 'How came you by this?'

'A fanciful story, that is all it is,' sniffed Tomand. 'A speech to impress us. Everyone knows – '

'What the Frost do you know anyway?' G'fand flared. 'You cannot even perform your job!'

Tomand choked and began to cough. Bessat looked over in alarm as Telmiss thumped him on the back until the coughing subsided somewhat. His face was red and his eyes were tearing. 'How – dare you!' was all he could manage to get out.

G'fand was rigid. 'You fat slug! All you do is eat. You serve no useful function. All you Neers are alike, ineffectual and – '

'Enough!' Ronin said sharply. 'I think you owe Tomand an apology.' He knew it was the wrong approach as soon as he said it.

G'fand turned on him, eyes blazing. 'Who are you to tell me anything!' His voice had risen, overtones of rage and hysteria combining. Cords stood out along his neck. He rose, his arms tense

44

columns, fists tight clumps pressed whitely against the tabletop. 'It is you who owe us an apology. You don't care a bit about us' – his arm swung in a tight arc – '*any* of us. Your training keeps you above all that.' He was spitting the words out, and Ronin could tell without looking that heads at adjoining tables were beginning to turn in their direction. But the myriad minute motions of the Great Hall had faded like a painting exposed to the rays of the sun. The hundreds of conversations and separate lives had ceased to exist.

'G'fand – ' K'reen began, but he swept on without even noticing.

'You're special because the Salamander took you and trained you. For what? To sit here with the likes of us, without the affiliation of a Saardin? He must be sorely disappointed in you!'

Ronin sat impassively, and allowed it to flow past him. Even so, he was abruptly thinking of K'reen, her white skin. And then he saw quite clearly the face of a man strapped to a bed, two smudgy triangles high on his temples. He could hear screaming, a terrible pain-filled noise.

Consequently he did not move fast enough to completely avoid G'fand's mad lunge across the table. Plates and goblets burst apart, sending their contents showering in all directions as they tumbled over backward into the narrow aisle. Servers scattered and people along the adjacent row were sent reeling into their own tables.

G'fand tried to yell but all that came out were grunts as he pummelled the body beneath him. For his part, Ronin was of two minds, as he defended himself. He did not want to hurt the Scholar but neither did he wish to prolong the scuffle and thus risk the intervention of Security daggam. Then, as G'fand shifted, a knee caught him in the side and he felt the lattice of pain lance up into his shoulder. The breath went out of him and he thought, Should have had Stahlig bandage the thing. And the instinct of his training took over. He lashed out with his free hand, slamming his fist into G'fand just below his ear. The Scholar's eyes bulged and his head danced like that of a puppet. Ronin took a breath and, in that instant, felt a searing pain. He twisted his head, saw the hilt of a small dagger protruding from his shoulder, tore it out, cursing, heard dimly the clatter as he dropped it, balled his hand, and swung into G'fand's midriff at the low point of the sternum. He had a momentary glimpse of the other's eyes, open wide, terror burning in them like an uncontrollable fire, before he doubled over. Ronin felt the spurt of adrenalin and he became aware that his fist was raised again. Then he was in control, panting, sweat stinging his eyes, hearing the strange sound of G'fand vomiting on to the floor. He touched him on his bowed back. With that came an understanding of what he had done, and what he had almost done. Then he swung about, searching for the dagger.

Nirren was beside him. 'I had better see about poor G'fand,' he said softly. Ronin nodded. He put his palm up to his shoulder because it was still numb and he would not feel the pain for a while, but he wanted to stop the blood.

Then he felt K'reen behind him, and she knelt and he saw her face. Wisps of hair had come undone so that she looked as if she had been standing in a high wind. Her cheeks were slightly flushed, her lips parted. Down deep in the awful stillness at the core of his being, he felt an inexplicable movement, as if he were a stringed instrument and something he could not see had plucked a thawed chord. He shivered involuntarily and K'reen, misunderstanding, put an arm across his shoulders. He shrugged it off, and she crouched like that, very quickly, so that only he could see, bent her head, flash of pink tongue, and licked at the crack between two of his fingers at the oozing stripe of blood. He stood up then, but not before he had seen her eyes shining.

'Clear away! Clear away!' called a commanding voice. The gaping crowd parted reluctantly and Ronin saw two daggam push their way towards him. Someone at the fringe of the crowd must have summoned them. He cursed silently and wished he knew where G'fand's dagger was. They came up to him. If they found it –

'What caused the disruption?' The one who was not talking stood with his hands free. There was some space around him. Neither of them bothered to look at G'fand as Nirren helped him to his feet.

Ronin took a deep breath, let it go slowly. 'Nothing at all,' he said calmly. 'Just a slight misunderstanding.'

The daggam grunted. 'Huh! Awful lotta people staring at a "slight misunderstanding".'

'You know how people are.'

'Yeh, sure. Listen, you Bladesmen know better than to disrupt the Sehna. You got a problem, go work it out at the Hall of Combat, not here. Get me?'

Ronin nodded. 'Sure.'

The other one had not moved at all. He stood watching Ronin. His eyes looked opaque, as if they had been painted on. 'Names,' said the one who talked, and Ronin gave them while he wrote. Then he took down Ronin's account of the argument.

'What happened to your shoulder?' asked the other one, and the first one looked up.

'I was getting to that,' he said with some annoyance.

'Wanted to make sure, is all,' said the other.

'Well?' The stylus was poised.

'I must have cut it on the edge of a plate when I fell. Quite a lot of them broke.'

'Yeh, so I see.' He turned. 'All right, nothing going on here,' he called to the crowd, and they began to disperse. 'Go on,' he told the other one, and as he turned to leave, he said to Ronin: 'Clean up this mess.'

K'reen stood silently beside Ronin, her hand on his back. He looked at Nirren, who shook his head. 'I can manage.' He still had to support G'fand almost totally. 'Look after yourself.'

Ronin nodded. He turned and saw Tomand, face white and sweaty. Bessat was comforting him as if he were a small child. They came up to him and Tomand said, 'I do not know what to –' He eyed the blood. 'But he had it coming to him.'

'It was about time someone stopped that kind of talk,' said Bessat. 'We are grateful.'

Ronin felt annoyed. 'That is simply what it was. Talk. He meant none of it.'

'He insulted me all right,' whined Tomand. 'But he feels differently about it now, I'll warrant.'

Very softly K'reen said: 'I had better clean you up. Now.'

Ronin looked at her. She had recognized the drift of the conversation.

'Yes.' He sighed. 'I suppose you had better.'

'And no one saw you pick it up?'

'I rather think not. They were all too busy.'

'Yes. I can see that.'

'How far did it go in?'

'To the hilt.'

He sat on the bed, with his shirt off, turning G'fand's dagger over and over in his open palm, staring at the blade with its dark smear. K'reen bent over him, working on the wound. Occasionally she rummaged in an open bag beside her.

They had gone at first to Stahlig's, even though he knew it could have been awkward. But the surgery was dark and the cubicle behind it, and there was no telling where the Medicine Man had gone or when he would return. So they had come to K'reen's quarters because of her bag.

She began to stitch the wound closed, having already cleaned it thoroughly. 'What is wrong with that boy? A weapon at Sehna! What was he thinking of?'

He kept his body very still. 'He is not a boy, firstly,' he said. 'And he takes his work seriously – perhaps too seriously. They do not exactly make it easy for the Scholars, and it affects him. Perhaps.' He forgot and shrugged.

'Keep still.' Her hands were suddenly motionless, then began again.

'I do know that what I said to Tomand is true: he meant none of it.' She finished the stitching and laid a dressing over it.

'But he attacked you.'

'Yes,' said Ronin, 'and that is what bothers me.'

She took cream from the bag and began to massage it on to the bruise over his ribs, which was slightly swollen, with the skin turned dark colours.

'Why?'

He shrugged.

'Do you really care?'

He said nothing. Her fingers felt good against his skin. Along the ridge of swollen flesh she tenderly stroked the inflamed muscles. She wondered what he was thinking about, fancied it was her. She wiped her hands, and unbound her hair so that it fell thick as a forest, long, swirling about her pale face. Traces of the cream glistened in her hair, iridescent and unreal. Her fingers scooped into the bag, came out, set to work again.

'I had never seen you fight before,' she said softly. And something in her voice recalled the image: swift pink tongue on bright scarlet. He flung the dagger from him so that it cartwheeled in a bright arc and stuck in the floor, quivering. He turned his hands over, staring at the backs, fingers clenched, knuckles white. He slammed them together.

'It's all right,' she whispered.

The adrenalin was not quite gone. 'I am trained,' he said slowly and softly, 'to kill and to stay alive. All Bladesmen learn this, some better than others.

51

But those years with the Salamander were different, and now there are times when instinct takes over – very pure and very lethal – because there is no time to think: *Hesitate and you are dead.*' He paused and spread his hands, and, perhaps, at that moment he was not aware of her at all. 'I almost killed him – it was so close. He was defenceless and terrified at what he had done.'

'I know,' she said.

His back arched slightly as he felt her breasts press into him as she leaned over. Her fingers worked. 'To see you in Combat,' she whispered at his ear. 'I want that.' She moved her hands up to the nape of his neck and began a circular motion that drew the tension from his tired muscles. 'I think about that.'

'Somehow I cannot imagine you spending your free time that way.' His body relaxed.

She moved her breasts from side to side against his back. 'I am full of surprises,' she said with a light laugh. Then her fingers moved down along his spine, slowly circling. The stroking became rhythmic. 'Do you win?'

'Yes. All the time.' He was aware that she very much wanted to hear him say it. It was something she already knew.

Her fingers moved lower and again he felt her presence more closely. He breathed her perfume. Strands of her unbound hair brushed lightly against him in concert with her hands. He heard breathing in the silence of their attenuated conversation; became aware that it was his own as well as hers.

Her fingers were at the base of his spine; she touched the tops of his buttocks. Her lips were so near his ear that he could feel her warm breath. 'You fought magnificently. You fought and you bled and through it all I was thinking of only one thing.' Her fingers made wider circles on his body; the pressure more insistent.

He felt his blood pounding. He said nothing.

Her lips touched his ear. They were moist, and she made a sound.

He twisted then, oblivious of his pains, and pulled her into his lap. His hands were lost in the night forest of her hair, clung there. He pressed his lips savagely against hers. Her mouth opened. His hands moved slowly, sinuously down her body, and she moaned into his mouth. And he reached for the fastening of her robe.

They were thin and tall and quite young. The hilts of the triple daggers across their grey shirts shone dully in the cold lights of the Overheads, still in reasonably good condition this far Upshaft. One said: 'Freidal wishes to see you.' He seemed very sure of the identification, although Ronin had seen neither of them before.

He felt a brief worry as he thought of Borros. It was very early, first Spell not half gone, and he was back on his own Level. They had got him as he had walked to his quarters, appearing abruptly from around the far turning, stepping in front of him before he reached his door. Important to remember, he thought, in this Stahlig was right: Freidal is very dangerous.

'At once,' the daggam said.

Security had an entire Sector Upshaft. He had never been there, but for as long as he could remember there had been stories told and retold along the Corridors Up- and Downshaft of the strange and secretive doings there. He had automatically discounted most of that talk; now he was not so sure.

He was surprised, however, to find that the forbidding dull grey exterior, with its massive doors and gates manned by faultlessly garbed daggam, gave way to quarters remarkably bland in appearance. Cubicles that were lit contained daggam pursuing innocuous functions: stacking tablets, desk work, and such. They passed many rooms dark and empty. Some were clearly storage areas, others obviously not, and this was puzzling. A door opened on his right and a daggam emerged. Behind him a glimpse in pale, flickering light of a central table with something pinned on top: scored lines. The door closed swiftly and they moved on. Image remaining: heavy shadows, many daggam. And what was on the table?

'In here.' They went through a doorway into a small cubicle lit by Overheads. 'Wait here.' The daggam left him through a large door. Blank grey walls stared back at him dispassionately. Two chairs, bare floor. Dark shapes moving over the table, pointing. He waited, conscious of fatigue and the dull throbbing in his shoulder. He badly wanted to wash, and he was hungry.

The door opened and a daggam emerged. Eyes the colour of mud regarded him with dull antipathy: Marcsh. Deliberate, Ronin wondered, or is he part of the Saardin's personal staff? Marcsh cocked his thumb at the door. 'In,' he said laconically.

Ronin said, 'What else do you do besides stand at doors?' because he was tired and annoyed.

Marcsh's animal eyes squinted as he made a face. 'Least I got a Saardin.'

Ronin advanced. 'To give you orders.'

''Course. What else?' His jaw clenched. 'Orders is what counts, good orders. An' we got 'em.'

Ronin was very close now. 'That's why we – ' Marcsh's eyes got cunning.

'You what?'

'Nuthin'.' He went sullen. 'Just got my orders. Make sure you behave.'

Is that so. Ronin stepped around him and into the room. The door closed behind him, as Marcsh pulled it shut. It was deep grey with very murky Overheads. No carpet, but two unusual wall hangings in dark, muted colours. An ornate desk cut the cubicle off obliquely. Behind it, in a high-backed chair, sat Freidal. He was dressed as before, in dark grey. Silver chest bands glittered. A large lighted lamp squatted on a low cabinet behind him, so it was difficult to see the features of his face. The Overheads illuminated only the top of his head. He did not look up. Across from him sat the scribe, tablet crooked on arm, quill poised. He seemed oblivious to anything except the spoken word. There was one chair before the desk. Ronin ignored it.

After a time, Freidal shuffled some sheets, put aside a scroll, and raised his head.

'Sir?'

The scribe's left hand moved, a tiny scratching.

'You sent for me,' Ronin said in an even tone.

'Ah yes, so I did.' He did not ask Ronin to sit down. The false eye was white and terrible in the reflected bright light. 'You had better tell me all about it.'

'I do not – '

'You most certainly do,' snapped the Saardin, 'know very well.' The scribe's hand made patterns on the tablet. 'Begin, sir.' Freidal's hands were perfectly still, clasped together on the desktop, white blobs of colour. Except for the unblinking eye, his face was a shadow, unreadable. Ronin thought furiously.

'An argument –'

'I do not believe you, sir.'

But at least he had got it right. 'All right,' he said resignedly. 'I had hoped this would be passed over, but – well, remarks were made about the Salamander, about –'

'One finds it difficult to believe you are so thin-skinned.' A white hand flicked and light caught the polished nails.

What does he want to hear? A bit of the truth, perhaps. 'We – did not part on the best of terms, as you no doubt know.' Sweat had begun to break out on his forehead, and that was good. 'Many think, therefore, that they may insult him, believing that it will please me. But he was my Sensii and I owe him a great deal.'

There was a pause and Ronin knew that the Saardin was referring to the report. 'He made numerous – unhealthy remarks,' Freidal said.

'Who did?'

'The Scholar.'

'I do not –'

'Other people have given witness.'

This is such a minor matter. What is he interested in? 'Under the circumstances, I should think the Saardin would understand.'

'You are defending him?'

57

Careful. 'He is quite harmless, Saardin. He is, after all, a Scholar.'

The papers rustled. 'One cannot be too careful,' the Saardin said pedantically, 'when it comes to Tradition. Such a disturbance at Sehna is cause for an investigation, I am sure you understand that. Order must be maintained at all costs – at any cost. Sehna is the time of obeisance to the Saardin and thus to the Freehold itself. Without the Freehold's structure, we are nothing. Without Tradition, discipline, order, we become barbarians. You understand this clearly, sir?' The hands separated, spread themselves upon the desktop, an implicit threat. 'I am aware that you are without affiliation. Is that one of the principles you were taught Upshaft?' The eye winked out for a moment, shone again. 'One wonders, sir, what the Salamander would think of one of his pupils – pardon me – ex-pupils who was involved in a disturbance at Sehna.' His tongue clicked against the roof of his mouth.

His head turned then, just enough so that Ronin could see that he was smiling. 'I am most apologetic at having to disturb you so early, but' – he shrugged – 'the routines of Security must be maintained.' The white eye winked out as he looked down again. He moved papers off to the side, seemed to be studying something.

'You forgot your sword,' he said.

Ronin almost said something then, but understanding came just in time. He stood very still and stared at the shiny cap of the Saardin's hair. Far off

58

a door slammed, and nearer, booted feet tramped down a hallway, setting a cadence.

'There's a good boy,' said the Saardin. And Ronin knew he was angry, felt some small satisfaction. The sounds of the boots faded, and the silence came again. His shoulder ached.

'That is your own business.' The Saardin's head came up, flash of white light. 'Other things are *my* business.' His voice took on a pedantic tone again. 'Do you know why Security was created, sir? For two reasons. One: to protect the Freehold from invasion from the Outside. Two: to protect the Freehold from those within who would seek to destroy it.' His hands steepled before him, fingers interlaced like white blades. 'Now we are the last. The earth above us is frozen solid and no one can survive there. All other Freeholds perished long ago. Perished because they forsook the Traditions. Perished because they lacked our discipline, sir.

'And so we are the last. And by the Chill, I shall ensure that we remain and flourish.' The hands came apart. 'While there is no one from Above who can harm us, there are still members of the Freehold, hiding among us, who wish us ill.' The hands came down hard on the desktop. 'That I will not tolerate! Do you understand me, sir?' Ronin nodded. 'Good. Very good.'

He turned suddenly in his chair and pointed behind him at a wall hanging. 'You see this? A fine piece of work. Excellent. Better than anything we can do. How old do you estimate it is? Hmm? Two hundred years, three? A millennium. At least. What do you think of that? And we do not have the faintest idea who made it. What kind of people, even. Could have been our forefathers. Perhaps not. No records. Very mysterious, yes?' He turned back. 'There are many mysteries within the Freehold. Most people do not know about them. No time. Would not care about them, if they did. Then there are those few people who cannot resist poking around things they have no business being near. They get hurt that way.'

A small silence built itself in the room and the air seemed to get thick and difficult to breathe. 'I trust you have good sense.'

The white eye went out once more as Freidal returned to his papers. The scratching of the quill had ceased. After a time, the Saardin said, without looking up, 'Sir, I believe you are late for Combat practice.'

Extend the leg twist block thrust forward and down. All in one motion. Return to position. This one will never make it, he thought, as his opponent bent to retrieve the sword he had just flicked out of his hand. No more than a blur.

Not far away Nirren *posted*, a deceptively slow movement, which his opponent reacted to, making him vulnerable to the difficult *solenge*, which Nirren executed with terrifying speed. The point of his blade hooked, bit and thrust, and it was over. Ronin wiped his forehead with the side of his wrist as he watched Nirren step back and bow to his opponent.

Black shadows moving slowly around a table, orange flame flickering, sending shards of light glinting from deadly dagger hilts.

The din of two hundred men boomed off the walls of the Hall of Combat. The place reeked of sweat, hanging heavily on the hazy air. Ronin could not allow himself to miss practice, although he wanted to see Stahlig. He felt instinctively that he must maintain his routine as much as possible. He did not take Freidal's warning lightly.

All eyes on the table in the centre of the room: lines drawn in a familiar pattern. But there had been no time. He had just a split second and he had not been looking directly at the tabletop. The pattern had registered on the periphery of his vision, so that now he could not force it, it would have to surface on its own.

Nirren walking over, very little sweat on him. He grinned. 'How about a real workout?' Ronin smiled, bowed to his opponent, turned to face Nirren. They took up position, searching for an opening.

On the other hand, he had no more doubts as to his course of action. In fact it was the Saardin's warning that had decided him. Not that he had ignored his friend's plea. But in the end it was because this very powerful and dangerous man with the false eye and the smile of a cold animal had warned him away, that he was going to find out all he could about Borros, the mad Magic Man. The authority principle: it rankled.

Nirren found it first, and Ronin, his reaction time down because his mind had been elsewhere, was hard pressed to turn the attack aside: the *faeas*, low thrust, blade extended far forward, flicking up at the last instant, ready to disembowel, and if it was successful, that was the end. Ronin did the only thing he could, turning sideways and plunging his blade straight down just in front of his forward thigh. It was instinct and speed. The inexperienced Bladesman would retreat and that would be it. Attack the *faeas*. Their blades clanged sharply and Ronin swung immediately out and up, attempting to take advantage of Nirren's extension – the drawback of the *faeas* if it does not work – but the Chondrin countered.

By the end of practice, Ronin had disadvantaged

Nirren twice, but, as usual, neither had gained a decisive victory. But then neither was looking for victory. They had been trained differently and thus had vastly individual styles. In practice they learned from each other, keeping their reflexes sharp and their minds ready for the unexpected. Ronin knew many tricks that he simply would not use during a practice; he supposed Nirren had some too.

Into the Corridor and on the way Upshaft, the tarred reeds fitfully illuminating the scarred and cracked concrete walls of the Stairwell. Patterns of lines rippling past him, and he had it, the latent image impressed through the retina on to the brain suddenly giving meaning.

When Nirren had asked him to have a drink after practice he had declined, thinking of Stahlig and Borros. Now he wanted a talk with the Chondrin.

His quarters were much like Ronin's several Levels Upshaft: two sparsely furnished cubicles. 'Sirreg's not in, so we need not worry about what we say,' Nirren told him, reaching out a flagon and goblets from a cabinet. They drank the deep red wine, their sweat drying, muscles relaxing. Ronin sat back in the cushions of the divan, feeling the spreading warmth within him. 'I have never asked you this, but how did you become affiliated?'

Nirren looked at him reflectively and sipped his wine. 'You mean the belief?' He cocked his head. 'Um, so it is not true what they say about you?' He said it with a smile.

'You know perfectly well what is true and what is not.'

'Whatever gave you that idea?' He shook his head. 'My friend, there are many stories – perhaps because you have so few friends, perhaps because you are unaffiliated – they cannot understand that –'

'Neither can you,' said Ronin not unkindly.

'Ah, not true, my friend. Your choice. I respect that, but – well, one must try –'

'If one has the belief.'

Nirren shrugged. 'Or not. Many do not have it, deep down. But the world of the Saardin is all they know. In any event, they fear you – yes, fear is the correct term – because you are a mystery. That and the Salamander, of course. They believe you shun them because of some terrible deed you once committed. Very interesting. But I digress. You asked how I became affiliated.' He refilled the goblets. 'Very well then.

'When I was a Student I had a friend, never mind his name, and he was very ambitious. He dreamed of becoming a Chondrin and thence a Saardin. Now the world is a complex place – you and I understand that now – my friend did not. He craved power but refused to acknowledge the Traditional paths to that end. I saw what was happening, and although I had no clear idea of the world at that time, still I knew down here' – he pointed to his stomach – 'that he was wrong in his approach. I spoke to him but he would not listen. He nodded his head, said, "Yes, that is good advice," and then went out and did the opposite.'

His voice had taken on overtones, the words

64

hanging vividly in the air. He sipped his wine and regarded Ronin. 'And then one Spell we filed into the Hall for practice. We found him spread out on the floor in the shape of a star. Five points in a dark and evil-smelling pool: head, arms and legs. And none of them connected.'

He finished off his wine, poured them both more. It was very quiet in the cubicle; outside, the Corridor was still.

Ronin cleared his throat. 'And then?'

'And then I knew I must affiliate myself as quickly as possible.'

'After what you saw?'

'Precisely that, yes. One moment he was there, full of life and bluff disregard for the Traditions of the world, the next – nothing. A mote of matter. They had gone through him, discarded him as if he were a pile of rubble they had hauled from here to there. The results were public so that we should not mistake his death. They wanted us to know.

'I saw very clearly what I must do. I am a realist, my friend. I understood what he wanted. He was not an evil man. And he was right to want power. Without it we are nothing; worse, we achieve nothing. Power is the link between dream and reality. He understood its nature as do I. But he lacked foresight and patience, and he paid for those deficiencies. I do not mourn for him.

'The world is reality, any fool can see that. One does not have to agree with it, but one must allow oneself to work *within* its structure, do you see. To obtain the power. From there, anything is possible, my friend. Anything.' He was finished and Ronin knew he was waiting for a response.

Nirren rose and went to the cabinet for another flagon. As if divining Ronin's thoughts he said: 'I do not expect anything from you. I want that quite clear.'

'Why say it?'

Nirren smiled then. 'Are you surprised that I should tell you all this?'

Ronin shook his head. 'You know the answer to that.'

The Chondrin laughed. 'My friend, I know you not at all.'

'Because you know nothing of my background. Is that so important?'

'A man is forged by his background, Ronin,' Nirren said with some force. 'And you are only fooling yourself if you believe otherwise.'

'All of us are different.'

'Aye, up to a point.'

'At the centre, I mean. At the core of the being.'

'At the centre all men are linked by their spirit.'

Ronin looked at him with dark eyes. 'Do you really believe that?'

'Yes.'

He said very softly, 'I am not,' and it rushed at him on a chill wind down deep where he feared to go, and knew not why but felt a rushing in his ears and a wetness on his face and body, pinpoints of pressure, and very far off a gasping sound distorted and inexplicably terrifying, and he tried to see but something was in his eyes like mist, so that nothing was clear, and . . .

' – do you know?' Nirren was asking. He leaned over to pour more wine. Ronin cleared his throat again, put his hand over the top of his goblet. 'Enough,' he said thickly.

Nirren laughd. 'Aha, yes. I believe you are right. Too early for more.' He stoppered the flagon, put it away, turned. 'You did not answer.'

'What?'

'Did you know that Jargiss is my second affiliation?'

'No, I – '

'It does not often happen. That is, not many are able to break affiliation and live.'

Wisp of mist, still. 'But you did.'

'Yes, but I was lucky. Jargiss knew of me, my situation, and he approached me.'

'Who was the first?'

'Ah. Dharsit.'

The Chondrin's skin like wax, white scar pulling at one eye, colours of black and gold. He told Nirren of the incident.

'Just like his Saardin. I am not surprised. They treat Combat without respect. They are Freidal's men.'

'But he is such a Traditionalist.'

'Yes, but it does not matter. He uses them only. After he is finished with them – he will use Dharsit's men first in battle, they will make the first assault and they will die – both Saardin and Chondrin will cease to exist.'

'I saw Freidal today,' said Ronin. 'He sent for me.'

Nirren went very still. 'Really.' His tone was

neutral but as Ronin related what had happened he could see that the Chondrin was excited.

Nirren frowned. 'Either he is being overly cautious or he has some interest in you. I do not like it.'

'I saw something while I was at Security. A room filled with daggam studying a large tablet. I only got the briefest glance but I am sure now. They were looking at a map.'

Nirren did not move and his face was lit by a tense concentration. He said: 'You could not be mistaken?'

'No.'

He nodded. 'Very well. Anything else you can remember? Details of the map – '

Ronin shook his head.

The Chondrin sat back for a moment, then stood up. 'Come,' he said. 'We shall go to Jargiss.'

'There are other matters that require my attention.'

They were at the door. Nirren knew better than to press it. 'Later, then.'

'Yes,' said Ronin. 'Later.'

Because of his shoulder wound, he felt confident in approaching Stahlig, even if his visit was reported to Freidal. Sirreg was just coming out of the Medicine Man's quarters when he arrived. His brown and orange shirt was stained and one arm was bandaged near the wrist. 'Ronin. Good to see you.' He was blond with a fine square face and direct dark eyes with long lashes. His face darkened. 'I heard what happened at Sehna.' He shook his head. 'What are we coming to. Brawls at Sehna, really!'

Ronin pointed. 'What happened to you?' He had no wish to discuss the fight, especially in the Corridor.

Sirreg grimaced. 'A souvenir from one of Dharsit's Bladesmen.' He laughed shortly. 'It is nothing, really. You should see what I left with *him*.'

'This happened in Combat?'

'No, in the Corridor – Downshaft. One must get used to these inconveniences now.' He shook his head again. 'But at Sehna! Would that I had seen it. Nirren has all the best of it, being able to sit at any board he chooses, while we Bladesmen are stuck – have you seen him this Spell by chance?'

'He was off to see Jargiss not a few moments ago.'

'Ah. Well, then.' He lifted his good arm and walked off.

A Neer was waiting to see Stahlig when Ronin entered. She was neither attractive nor unattractive, with short brown hair and a lined face like a ripe fruit. She stared at him unashamedly. 'I don't get to see many Bladesmen,' she said in a thin dry voice. 'That's because I'm Downshaft at the eighty-fifth Level.' Ronin had never met anyone who had been that far Downshaft. 'Huge Machines Down there – larger than you can imagine, I'll warrant.' She began to stroke her leg and Ronin saw that the foot and ankle were bandaged. There seemed to be something wrong with the foot's angle to the leg.

She saw where he was looking. 'In one of them,' she said. 'Frost, it hurt!' Her shoulders slumped. 'We were working on one of the Air Machines – the primary ones, you know? – and they tell us first thing when we go Down there to mind the Machine fluids because they're slippery. I guess that's what happened. I stumbled and slid along the hot metal and' – her face screwed up – 'oh, it was awful, the foot in the Machine! It took them almost an entire Spell to decide what to do and get me out.' She stroked the shin above the mangled foot, not looking at it. 'After a while I couldn't feel anything at all, so I didn't care when they talking about sending for a Medicine Man to cut off the foot. They were afraid of damaging the Machine in some way, because we still don't know how it works or even why, only that it does and

70

keeps us alive.' She smiled a beatific smile. 'But in the end they managed to get it out by breaking the ankle and it was all right.'

Stahlig came out to help her into the surgery and she looked back over her shoulder at him for as long as she could. He had never shared the Bladesman's contempt for Neers and Scholars and, of course, the Workers. Frost, it was not their fault, and someone had to –

Stahlig called him. There were several exits from the surgery and, for an obscure reason, Ronin was glad that the Neer had been sent another way. He went through the half-lit deserted surgery, the elliptical stone slab dominating the room. Its polished top and sloping pebbled sides caught the orange lamplight in such a way that for a startling moment it seemed to him to be covered with bright glistening blood, pooling thickly in the slight hollows of the top, running in complex networks down its sides. He blinked and looked again, saw light purple-grey stone marbleized with white striations. He moved slowly past high cases, into the inner cubicle.

If anything the clutter had increased. Stahlig was on the couch, sorting tablets of all sizes. 'Mind those,' he said as Ronin removed a pile from a chair.

'How long have you been treating Neers?'

The Medicine Man waved a hand. 'Ah, they are overworked Downshaft. We – ' He fought to keep the tablets from sliding off his lap, finally gave it up and dropped them to the floor. 'We are expected to handle everything Up here without a word of complaint, otherwise they think we are

71

getting ideas.' He used his hands to brush off his leggings. 'I heard about the mess at Sehna. That is just the kind of notice you do not need now. What happened? Take off your shirt.'

As Ronin told him, Stahlig took apart the bandage and inspected the wound. 'That idiot Scholar!' he said with annoyance. 'Of course he is frustrated. They burned all his books centuries ago.' With great care he worked a cream on to the area. 'Mine too, for that matter, only – Who worked on this for you?' He looked up quickly, then went back to the shoulder. 'Not much for me to do here, just put on a new dressing and in several Cycles you will not even know it is there.'

'K'reen did it.' Why did he have to ask? 'We came by after Sehna but you were not here.'

'Uhm, no. As I have said, they are giving me the overflow, and – ' He shrugged. 'Were the daggam called? At Sehna, I mean.'

'Yes, but it was nothing. They took down a statement.'

He seemed relieved. 'Good. At least Freidal did not summon you.'

Ronin thought: He seems changed. 'But he did summon me – very early, during first Spell.'

Sweat had come out on the Medicine Man's broad forehead. 'I told you! By the Frost you were warned!'

'Calm yourself.' Stahlig was finished with the dressing and Ronin stood up. 'He only wanted me to corroborate the daggam's report. What is the matter with you?'

Stahlig turned and went behind his desk. There

was no colour in his face. 'I want you to forget you ever went with me yesterday.' He stared at Ronin, his rheumy eyes sunken and worn. A tablet slipped off the desk and fell to the floor with a muffled crash. He did not appear to notice. 'It never happened.'

There was silence in the room, but still he was pleading.

'I cannot.'

'Oh, Frost!' Ronin might just as well have hit him. His face crumpled and he collapsed on to the couch. His lips trembled. Ronin went and got some wine, knelt in front of him, made him drink it.

After a while he whispered. 'I know you. I can do no more.' But it was as if he were talking to himself.

'Stahlig,' Ronin said softly. 'You must help me. I want to talk to Borros.'

'How can you ask me to help you to die?' His voice was feeble and there was no resolve behind it.

'I will not die,' Ronin said carefully, because he had to make Stahlig understand. 'And this may be very important for the Freehold. Remember the talk we had?'

He sat up at last and looked into Ronin's eyes. 'Why do you wish to do this?' But it had worked and the answer did not matter now.

Ronin shrugged.

'But you must have a reason!'

'How can I tell you when I do not know what it is myself?'

73

The old man sighed and shook his head. 'I knew,' he said sadly. 'I knew all along.' He stood and turned away. 'Come back after Sehna. I need to look at that shoulder again.'

At that moment he experienced an acute and inexplicable sense of loss. 'Stahlig, I —'

The Medicine Man raised his hand. 'Mind the tablets on the way out.'

'Enter.'

The door remained closed, and the soft knocking came again. He set down his wine, went across the room, and opened it. G'fand stood there, head down. Ronin could see the bandage across his chest under the shirt.

'I – ' He cleared his throat. 'I am not disturbing you?'

'Not at all, I was just thinking of – '

'Because if I am, I can – '

He touched the Scholar. 'Come in.' G'fand seemed rooted to the spot and Ronin had to draw him inside. 'Sit. Please.' He crossed the room and picked up something from the top of a low table. 'I was about to return this to you.' He held it out.

G'fand shrank from it as if it were alive. 'I never want to see that thing again!' he cried.

Ronin set the dagger down next to him. 'Ah, but someday it may save your life.'

G'fand broke down then and sobbed into his hands. Ronin poured him some wine and this too he set beside him. At length G'fand stopped and his hands came away. 'I am so ashamed,' he said.

Ronin sat across from him. 'And I too,' he said quietly.

G'fand's head came up. A light came back to his eyes. 'You? What have you to be ashamed of?'

He held out his hands. 'I am a Bladesman. But, as you pointed out at Sehna, I have studied with the Salamander.' Spots of colour stood out on G'fand's cheeks. 'I learned many skills from him, many techniques few other Bladesmen know. You see, I almost killed you – with these.'

G'fand stared at his hands. 'But I thought Combat is with the sword and the dagger.'

'Combat is very ancient and has many layers.'

'Yes, I see.' G'fand knelt. 'Oh, Ronin, I am so sorry. Please forgive me.'

'Pick up your dagger and put it away.'

The Scholar wiped his face. 'I want you to know what happened.'

'G'fand, I know that you were not attacking me.'

Surprise, relief, puzzlement, all flickered across his face. 'But how? I was not sure myself what I was doing.'

Ronin smiled. 'Yet it was quite apparent to me that you were extremely upset, and not by any of the things you were saying.'

Color crept into his face again. 'I am in your debt.' He was silent for a moment, staring into the depths of his wine. He had not touched it, and now he picked up the goblet and sipped at it. It meant more to him than taking a drink.

'I will tell you something,' he said slowly, 'although it is very difficult for me. I have envied you for a long time, wanting to be a Bladesman and not – not having the chance.' He laughed nervously. 'I suppose I am too small in any event.' He brought the goblet to his lips again, a swift convulsive movement, as if activity were a necessity now. 'I yearn to know how we came to be as a people – and what took place before us. They were a great people, centuries ago, and they built many Machines – huge and awesome.' He put the wine down, gripped himself at the elbows as if he were cold. 'That is all beyond us now. We have lost everything. But I have reached a – I have read all that remains, that meagre pile of knowledge.'

His voice lowered. 'They do not know it, but I have partially deciphered the glyphs of the very ancient writing that comes from the time when all people were surface-dwellers. But it is not nearly enough, just odd fragments – it is nothing, really. I have been able to read just enough to know what an unforgivable thing they did.'

He broke off and wrung his hands. He had not yet said what he had come to say. 'So I thought after all I have chosen to be something that is worthless. Oh, I have grown used to the taunts – I had work to keep me busy. But now I have read everything, so they tell me.'

He took out the dagger, watched light play along its stubby blade. 'So some time ago I went to Combat practice' – he lifted his head, half afraid that Ronin would laugh – 'just like that. The Students joked about it at first and made fun of me, and finally, when I kept coming, wanted to throw me out. But in the end the Instructor came over and gave me this and a short sword and said that since I was trying so hard at least I should have some weapons. And now I work with the

Novices, but' – hs head sunk again – 'I know I will never be a Bladesman.'

'There are other things to be,' said Ronin.

'Nirren says nothing is as important.'

'Nirren enjoys teasing you, but you must not believe everything he says.'

'He is a Chondrin and he does not see!' G'fand blurted suddenly.

'See what?'

'That we are dying! *You* cannot see it? You heard Tomand. He does not know the workings of the Machines, no Neer does. Yet the Great Machines are all that keep us alive. The Instructor talks to us of Traditions, the Code of Combat. But what good are Traditions if the air fails or the food goes or no more water comes to us?'

He stood abruptly. 'I cannot stand it! I do not want to remain here. There is nothing for me, nothing for anyone. And soon – soon the banner of Tradition shall wave over our rotting bones!'

They went to Sehna together and that seemed to settle everything. There was an awkward moment until Tomand stood and said, 'You are forgiven, this is Sehna after all.' Nirren looked at them and smiled to himself, and K'reen squeezed G'fand's hand.

There was much laughter and spirited talk amongst the group, but a lot of it had a hard brittle edge; the topics of conversation were of little consequence. And as the courses came and went and the wine flagon was emptied and refilled, they were gripped by a kind of desperation that caused their laughter to ring louder, as if noise and tumult would keep them safe from their inner thoughts.

Ronin understood this early on, and, while he ate and drank and laughed with the rest because any other course would have been suspect, this knowledge only deepened the gloom that had settled upon him. The Neer's story had started it, he supposed, and he cursed her and then himself. What does it matter to me? he thought angrily. Not my concern.

A Bladesman wearing orange and brown wove his way towards them. He bowed to his Chondrin, whispered briefly in his ear. Nirren nodded and leaned over to Ronin. 'Estrille,' he mouthed silently, rose, and made his excuses to the table.

In some way, although it might have been coincidental, his departure was the signal for even greater revelry. Tomand called to the adjacent tables and soon they were exchanging wine flagons and goblets, talking of inconsequential matters.

The seventh Spell expended itself and the eighth commenced. With it the Great Hall began to empty. Slowly, the tables became less crowded, the heat diminished, and the haze became less dense.

Ronin sat with legs outstretched, swirling the dark dregs of wine in the earthenware goblet, watching the twisting reflections on its opaque surface. The general din of conversation had slackened and the clatter of the Servers clearing the tables could be heard. They hurried along the narrow aisles, huge trays filled now with the remnants of Sehna held high above their heads, out of the way of passing Bladesmen. Ronin was asked if he wished more wine and he shook his head.

He itched to leave but felt the necessity of anonymity: he did not want to depart too soon. It was possible that no one was watching, but in any event he did not want to give the impression that he had somewhere specific to be off to.

Then he saw Nirren approaching and was suddenly glad that he had stayed this long. The Chondrin sat down close to him, pouring himself a drink from the last of the wine still on the table. He smiled and looked about them. There was no one near and plenty of background noise. Still smiling, he said softly, 'I think you will be inter-

80

ested in this. That Teck of the Magic Man's. Maastad? You remember? He works for Freidal.'

Ronin put down his goblet. 'A daggam?'

Nirren sipped his wine slowly, did not look directly at Ronin. 'No. A Teck, all right. But affiliated with Security. They do it all the time. When they are interested in something or some-one, it is sometimes the only way in.' He paused while a Server picked up the empty flagon. 'They tried to affiliate Borros a while ago but he refused. So they sent the Rodent in to learn what he could.'

'Apparently it was not enough.'

'Uhm hmm. Listen, I have been given a special assignment. I have to find a Rodent of my own. I cannot tell you more now, but' – he looked at Ronin, a momentary flicker, and then his eyes were again roaming the Great Hall – 'I may need your help soon, even though you may be reluctant to give it. As for the other matter – ' He smiled and said in a louder voice, 'Later.'

Ronin watched his back as he departed and was lost finally in the vast sea of moving bodies.

A soft snore passed from his open mouth. He lay sprawled on the couch, his legs crossed at the ankles, his arms embracing a pile of tablets. His seamed face was drawn, and pouches of grey skin hung under his eyes. Even in sleep he looks tired, thought Ronin.

He crossed the room, gently shook Stahlig's shoulder. Immediately the eyes flew open, bloodshot but alert. He pulled himself up, heedless of the tumbling tablets, and cleared his throat. 'Uhm, just resting for a moment.'

Ronin turned, hunted for the wine. 'You look like you have lost a lot of sleep.'

'Just' – Stahlig pointed – 'over there behind those tablets.' Ronin poured the wine and he drank gratefully. 'Mm, it's that overload from Downshaft, Frost take it!' His eyes shifted about the room. 'A fine state when there are not enough Medicine Men in the Freehold. We may have to start using promising Students like K'reen.' He finally saw the tablets on the floor. 'Well.' He cleared his throat again.

Flicker.

Down the Corridor and around a turning, very still and silent and watchful, they were caught in the periphery of his vision like rodents in a web.

Flicker: dark shadows against the light.

82

And he did not stop: he moved neither faster nor slower because they had not seen him and he did not want to do anything to attract their attention. Stillness within the organism, not without. Into the darkened surgery as fluid rolls within a jar. Now pause, let eyes adjust, and move again only when all the shadows are in their proper place. Because two daggam stand guard just down the Corridor.

'I shall take you to Borros.' Stahlig drained his cup and stood.

He has not mentioned them, Ronin thought, as they went across the room and into the surgery, aware that Stahlig did not light a light or make a sound.

They stopped at the far wall and the Medicine Man reached out and touched something in the gloom. An opening appeared in the wall, automatic and perfectly silent, and they stepped into the small cubicle and beyond.

It was dimly lit by two lamps, flames flickering in the draught created by the opening. Cabinets lined one side wall, a door cut into the centre of the other. And Ronin had it, the pieces fitting all at once: the daggam, Stahlig's silence, the hidden door. And he looked to the far wall, at the two narrow beds, knew one was filled even before his eyes registered it, knew too that it contained a man with yellow skin, the nexus of an obscure power struggle within the Freehold.

Stahlig's arm waved like a flag. 'Behold,' he whispered. 'Borros.'

'How did you manage it?'

The Medicine Man's eyes lowered. 'It was not – uhm – all that difficult. Borros had not regained consciousness when I returned the last Cycle, and I told Friedal that if he was not brought here immediately he would never again be conscious. Freidal had no choice, really.'

'Would Borros have died?'

Stahlig rubbed his eyes. 'Perhaps. But the important thing is that he has since awakened and talked to me.' He sank on to the empty bed. 'I have not yet told Freidal because I do not understand any of this. What can his value be to Freidal now? He is quite mad. Perhaps at one time – ' He shook his head, and Ronin crossed the room, stood over Borros. 'Such a terrible waste,' Stahlig said wearily. 'Human life means nothing to them. They had him for much too long – his mind is not the same.'

But he did not tell them what they wanted to know, thought Ronin, or Freidal would not care whether he lives or dies now. He must have been a strong man. 'Still, I would talk with him,' Ronin said.

Stahlig shrugged. 'You can learn nothing from him. He is so full of drugs – '

Ronin turned. 'Then how can you tell that he is mad?'

'It is not – '

The sound was tiny but distinct, coming from the anteroom. Stahlig jumped up, his face pale, his eyes wide. 'Oh, Frost,' he whispered hoarsely, 'this was a mistake. I never should have agreed to it. Do not move.' He passed through the doorway to the surgery, and it closed silently behind him.

Ronin stared down at Borros, at the high gleaming pate the colour of old bones, at the long closed eyelids. His breathing was deeper.

The stillness was palpable. Outside he heard the low murmuring of voices. He bent over Borros, gripped the sides of his jaw in his hand. The skin felt smooth and dry. The eyelids fluttered, opened slowly, gazed blankly up at him with unfocused pupils. Still, the eyes were so extraordinary that Ronin almost failed to react to the sound behind him.

He straightened and whirled in time to see Stahlig stepping through the doorway. 'Freidal wants to see me immediately,' he whispered. 'Probably concerned about Borros,' he added needlessly. 'Remain here until I have left with the messenger. I have reminded the daggam outside that their presence in here would be harmful to the patient's health. But even so, you must leave as quickly as possible. Borros has not awakened?'

'No.'

'Good. Better for him to rest. And there is nothing he can tell you. You would be wasting your time.' He turned to go. 'Remember, as soon as you hear us leave – ' He went through the doorway and disappeared into the shadows of the surgery.

Grey they were. But light grey, with golden flecks swimming in their depths like chips of bright metal. The muffled tramp of boots against

85

concrete, diminishing. And then only the soft silence enshrouded them, with its fine susurration of breathing. The world reversed: the figures immobile, the pale flames of the lamps licking at the moving shadows they created. Still the eyes held him.

And then as if through a force of will Ronin moved silently to the closed door to the surgery, put his ear to the cool metal. He could hear nothing moving out there. He returned to the Magic Man, sat on the adjacent bed, elbows on knees. He was aware of the other door, across from him, beyond which the daggam stood guard.

'Borros,' he said quietly. 'Borros, can you hear me?'

There was only the sound of his breathing, lips slightly parted. His eyes stared at the ceiling, seeing nothing.

Ronin repeated the question.

Silence. No movement of the pupils.

Repeat the question: closer, louder, more insistent.

Silent but: eye movement. Blink.

Lips trembling.

'What? What did you say?'

He had to repeat it.

'So blue – '

He had to strain to hear, and thought: No sense, but contact. Repeat.

'Impossible blue. I – know it is there, I – '

Eyes focused now, golden flecks glinting. Breathing rapid. Ronin felt himself sweating, glanced quickly at the door to the Corridor. Had he heard a movement? He wiped his forehead with the back of his wrist, turned back quickly. Too late to get out now. 'Borros, what are you saying?'

'An arch – yes, it – it must look like an arch, so vast, so – ' He jerked as Ronin touched him, head whipping around, eyes bulging. His lips drew back in a laugh that was more an animal snarl, bared teeth gleaming. 'Ahahaha! But there is nothing there, you have nothing no notes and now no more head brain squeezed until it's dry and that's what it is dry so it's no use why don't you st – ' His eyes drooped momentarily, then the lids flew up and he started as if just coming awake. 'No – no more I' – shake of the head – 'do what you want, all usel – ugh!' – he shivered down the length of his body – 'the land brown and rich and plants growing green and free with no tanks and the heat of the bare sun hang – hanging in all that space!'

He stopped there like a mechanism run down and incapable of beginning again. And Ronin thought: It's no good this way, no good at all. He *does* sound like a madman. His words are clear but they have no meaning. He wiped away more sweat, knowing that there was very little time.

Missed something, he thought. But what? Think.

He leaned forward, said urgently: 'The land, Borros, tell me more about the land.' The Magic Man had thought Ronin was one of the Security interrogators. So his approach had been wrong. Get into his mind: what if he was not mad? Only thing to try.

And he saw Borros's mouth working. 'Yes, the land.' The faintest whisper like a dry wind, and Ronin felt a surge of adrenalin. 'The fields, food to eat, great flowing waters, new life for the people but – ' He gasped as if struck by a blow, and Ronin reached out to hold him.

The long eyes were deep pools where golden fish swam frenziedly. 'Oh, Frost, no! Not again!' Eyes popping, face very pale, white lines netting the sides of the mouth, a living skull. As if staring into the face of Death – or a being more terrible.

He strained to sit up but Ronin held him down as gently as he could, feeling the flight of forces within the thin frame. 'Must, must!' Beads of sweat clung to the tight yellow skin of his head. It gathered on his upper lip, ran into his mouth, and the tongue came out, licked at the moisture. Sweat dripped along the sides of Ronin's face as he stared at the twisting, tortured countenance. It rolled along his wrists and on to the backs of his hands, seeping between his fingers, and he tightened his grip. Borros's hands were like claws, the tendons corded and raised just beneath the skin, held out in front of him as if warding off his agony and terror. Then he seized Ronin's arms.

They were locked, immobile, and Ronin, caught in the pull of the grey-and-gold eyes, felt that he had lost volition of independent movement.

'It is coming!'

Bound within the moment, he felt the writhings of Borros's mind –

'I have seen – It – '

– knew with an awful certainty suddenly flooding his being that Something was there –

' – draws closer – the people cannot st – '

– not a presence but merely the threat of a presence, and that was enough to –

'Must go to them – help – hel – '

'Who, Borros, who? We are the only – '

The jaws snapped closed, the eyes saw him, perhaps for the first time, and the terrible ivory grin came again and now Ronin felt as if he faced – what?

'Fool!' hissed Borros. 'They want no one to know. A secret!' And he laughed without humour. '*Their* secret!' The eyes took on a glossy depth, the pupils huge. Veins stood out along his temples where the Dehn spots pulsed as if alive. 'Fool! We are not alone on this world!' Eyes bulging alarmingly, teeth grinding in effort. 'But it – will mean nothing. It comes – comes to destroy everything. Unless – ' His head whipped from side to side, with a spray of sweat. His throat convulsed and it appeared that he cried out, although the sound was low and strangled and seemed barely human. 'Death – death is coming!'

Borros jerked again and went limp, his eyes fluttering closed. Ronin let go of him then, his hands and arms numb. He put his ear to Borros's chest, then quickly pushed rhythmically with his palms. He listened again. Pounded his fist once, twice, over the heart. Listened again.

He wiped his dripping face and stood up. Moving to the doorway to the surgery, he pressed a part of the wall and darkness bloomed before him. He stepped through, out of the light. The door closed. He listened for a moment. His eyes adjusted. All shadows in their place. Then, like Stahlig before him, he disappeared into the shadows.

'What do you know of the Magic Men?'

'What brought that to mind?'

'You are always answering a question with another question – Oh yes! There.' The hand moved, flesh on flesh, orange and light brown in the low guttering lamplight. Black pooled in the hollows.

'Just a peculiar topic to bring up now,' Ronin said softly.

K'reen moved slowly, gently against him. Cascading dark hair, soft and cool, accentuating the heat of their bodies. 'Not at all. They are purported to be – oh! – the saviours of the Freehold, divining ways for us to live in case the Great Machines cease to function. Is that not true?'

Hands moving from orange to black, light to shadow. 'So it is said.' Their lips met and opened.

K'reen licked the sick of his neck. 'With all the political talk going on – the rumours of the Saardin – mmm – it's natural to be thinking of the future.'

'I know very little of them,' he whispered. But the temptation was very strong within him.

She rolled away from him, the lamplight licking at the indentation of her spine, the crease of her buttocks. 'Won't you ever talk to me?' she said in a small voice.

'There is nothing to talk about.' He reached out and she drew away.

'You mean you have nothing to say to me.'

Ronin sat up in the bed and stared at the dark bell of her hair sweeping across the pillows. 'That is not at all what I meant.'

She turned on him, eyes flashing. 'But it is!' she cried.

'You are twisting what I say. Why do you do that?'

'I will not play this game.'

'There is no game.' There was an edge to his voice now.

'I will not let you turn this back on me. You're the one who – '

'K'reen, this is not the time – '

'Not the time?' She sat up too. 'You must be joking! There is nothing more important for us to do.'

'Yes, there is,' he said sharply.

She glared at him for an instant and he felt the charge build within her. She lunged, her open palm striking him across the face with considerable force. 'Chill take you!' she hissed.

He caught her extended arm at the wrist, pulled it forward and down with some violence so that she was suddenly on her back beneath him. He lowered himself. The soft light gleamed off the whites of her eyes. Her breasts heaved under him, the nipples hard, and she brought her knee up into his hip on the edge of the pelvic bone, but he pressed the nerve on the inside of her thigh, numbing it. 'Frost!' she breathed, and pulled his head down to hers, arching her body against him, thighs open.

He made love with a strange kind of desperation, trying, in his confusion and anguish, to lose his mind in his body. And so involved was he in this that he failed to notice a similar despair in K'reen.

He rolled away from her sleeping form, sat on the edge of the bed, and lit the lamp. Its pale flame sent the darkness skittering away in all directions. He kept the light low so as not to wake her. He heard nothing but the white noise of silence in his ears as he stared into the flame and saw again the dream from which he had awakened . . .

He is in the Freehold, yet it is of a different construction from that of the real Freehold. It is under the earth but it is a City, with massive structures that rise through the air to such heights that they almost touch the rock vault above. Dreamscape: suprareal.

He is in one such structure, high up, with K'reen. They are preparing to leave; he cannot think where they are going to. Suddenly the structure trembles heavily. Cracks appear in the walls, and he feels the rumbling in his bones. He looks outside. Structures all around are coming apart and collapsing as the earth continues to heave and split. He hears screaming and sees the red belch of columns of flame.

He cannot find K'reen. He runs out into the Corridor and is met with the choke of smoke and falling rubble; the structure is tearing itself apart.

He calls her name. Over and over. He hears echoes, echoes only. He runs then down the Stairwell, fearing at any moment it will collapse under him.

He reaches the Outside at last and finds – He is in a cool glade of green foliage, dark and moist. A rich, unfamiliar scent comes to him from the earth. His face is wet. And his arms. Drops of water from above hit him all over. Across a river he sees the Freehold disassemble itself and come crashing down amidst huge fires. Bright sparks twist in the air. But he is not there and he wonders at this as he opens his eyes and finds that he is lying beside K'reen in the dark . . .

He sighed now, once, a long inhalation and exhalation of breath, to help rid himself of the last strands of the dream. It had been very vivid. He lay back in bed, put a pillow behind his back, and thought about Borros. For half the length of a Spell he replayed over and over in his mind what the Magic Man had said.

And at the end of that time he thought that perhaps his dream had not after all been dispelled.

Time, Ronin decided, to see the Salamander.

In the Sector the Lift was out, its sliding doors frozen irretrievably half open. Deep parallel lines were scored down one door, as if some large and angry animal had been frustrated by its stasis. The other one was crumpled like an old Bladesman's Combat wound. So he took to the Stairwell and, on the way Upshaft, had time to recall his first meeting with the Salamander.

Combat had always been a game to him. Like every other element in his young life, it was too inconsequential to be taken seriously. On what had come to be known as the Combat Level, the normal Freehold cubicles had, some time before, been scooped out and replaced by a series of large indoor courtyards that now served as training grounds for Combat. Each Cycle at his allotted time, he would file into the Hall of Combat, the largest of these courtyards, along with other Students of his age. Half a Spell of strenuous exercise would eventually give way to a lecture on the art of killing and maiming through ritual moves, after which the Students would be paired off for actual practice.

He had never given much thought to the art one way or another, he was a Student because he had been told to be a Student, therefore he was at best mediocre. Often his mind would wander and his opponent would easily disarm him. This never appeared to bother him, but for the Instructor it was a different matter entirely. Ronin's indifference infuriated him, and it would not be uncommon for the Student to bear the brunt of his wrath in front of the assembled Class.

During one practice, Ronin observed a heavy man, almost gross-looking, stride easily into the Hall. 'Students,' called the Instructor, and the sounds of iron striking iron ceased immediately. He turned to the newcomer, and with a flourish of his hand introduced him. 'Students, the Salamander.' There was a buzz of excited whispering amongst the boys, which the Instructor contrived to ignore. 'As you know – ' He waited impatiently for silence. 'As you know, the Salamander is the Sensii of Arms of the Freehold. He is here to observe your progress.' There was more whispering, and the Instructor was forced to cover another pause by clearing his throat. He looked sternly around the Hall. '*Some* of you may be lucky enough to be chosen to study with the Salamander himself.'

Ronin was aware of the undercurrent of envy that ran now through the Instructor's voice, and he turned to look at the Salamander, but his face, with its heavy jowls, oddly high cheekbones and glossy black eyes, remained impassive. At this moment, the Salamander raised one hand, encrusted with flashing jewels, and in a rich, slightly nasal voice said, 'Pray continue your practising, boys; do let me see what you are made of.'

'Come, come, Students,' called the Instructor nervously, clapping his hands, 'on with it now.' Almost as one, they turned each to his partner, and once again the walls rang with the clash of metal.

Out of the corner of his eye, Ronin tried as best he could to keep the Salamander in sight as he commenced his round of the Hall, the Instructor a pace behind him.

'Listen, you,' growled his practice partner, a huge, brutish Student of mean temperament, 'it was just my ill fortune to be paired with you this Cycle.' He grunted as he swung his sword in a vicious arc at Ronin's stomach. Ronin stepped back, took the brunt of the blow on the edge of his own blade, the force turning it, and there was a sharp scraping sound. A shiver raced up his arm and his fingers went momentarily numb.

'But you will give me a good fight,' the Student said menacingly, 'when the Salamander comes our way. I have been waiting – unngh!' he grunted again as he swung, 'for this chance for a long time.'

Ronin, who had been thinking also of the Salamander, said, 'Korlik, is that his real name?'

Korlik snorted, as close to a laugh as he could come. 'Fool! – unhg! – no one knows.' The blade came whistling at him once again. 'Why don't you ask him – unngh! – when he passes by?' Ronin continued to defend himself against Korlik's pressing attack.

'Haw! – ungh! – I will tell why you won't – unngh! – because you are going to be flat on your back, looking at the bottom – ungh! – of my boot. I mean for him to see me and – uhnn! – take me Upshaft. Understand?'

But Ronin's attention was focused on the approaching figure of the Salamander; only part of himself was given over to the automatic defence of his person. The Sensii was a mountain of flesh garbed in cloth of jet and crimson. How much was muscle, he wondered. And what of his reflexes? His weight must be enormous. Still, he was the Sensii. The Master of Combat.

Korlik growled at him. 'He is coming this way. Chill take you, have you heard what I said? – unhg! Put on a good show, Ronin, I'm warning you – uhnn!'

The two figures were almost abreast of them as Ronin turned his full attention to the Combat. 'Show?' he said. 'There will be no show. Not for you, not for the Salamander.'

Cursing, Korlik bore down upon him and, seeing the Salamander and the Instructor reach them, began to hammer Ronin with blows.

'Now this one, Sensii,' said the Instructor obsequiously, 'is Korlik. Big and strong and he shows fine potential. Unfortunately, he is paired this practice with an inferior Stu – '

'Pray cease,' said the Salamander, lifting a jewelled hand, 'your useless chatter. Do not presume to make judgements for me.' Ronin was pleased to see the Instructor's eyes bulge in his narrow face and his tongue working in his open mouth as he fought to control himself.

During this time Korlik had not lessened his

attack upon Ronin, who neither put up a concerted defence in any of the prescribed ways nor counter-attacked. He preferred to move, using his own blade only when absolutely necessary to turn aside his opponent's sword.

The Instructor, seeing potential disaster for himself in Ronin's refusal to conform to the lessons, made noises for the Salamander to move on. But the Sensii graced him with a momentary glance, frosty and disdainful, and he was silenced.

'Boys,' the Salamander said, 'desist for the moment.' Korlik, sweat rolling down his arms, soaking his shirt, dropped his sword with great reluctance and glowered at Ronin.

The Salamander stroked the end of his long nose between thumb and forefinger, his dark eyes fixed on Ronin. 'And what is your name, dear boy?'

'Ronin.'

'Ronin, *sir*,' corrected the Instructor.

The Salamander's eyes rolled up briefly towards the ceiling. 'Kindly be good enough to take your person across the Hall so that I will not be obliged to suffer your presence.' He said it with a sighing exhalation of breath, not at all forcefully, Ronin thought. Nevertheless, the Instructor stalked off without another word, the muscles at the sides of his jaw working spasmodically.

Around them, the din of practice continued unabated, crashing off the walls and echoing back upon the ear. The acrid stench of sweat and fear hung in the vast Hall, staining the air.

'Sensii,' said Korlik. 'I have waited for this time, working long and hard in the hope that I would please you. It is my greatest wish to be taught by you.'

The eyes of the Salamander, black and hard as chips of stone, turned upon Korlik. 'My boy,' he drawled, 'only the most *special* Students, those who exhibit extraordinary merit, work with me.' The eyes flicked up and down his body. 'Rest assured that you are not one of those. Now pray be still.' Korlik strangled a gasp and ground his teeth in fury, but he remained silent.

The Salamander turned to Ronin and said as if they were in a room alone, 'Tell me why you do Combat in such a manner.'

He wondered what the Salamander wanted; wondered what sort of answer would be best to give. In the end, he told the truth. 'Combat bores me,' he said evenly.

'Then why do you bother with it?'

'I do it because I have to.'

The Salamander rubbed his nose again, the rings on his fingers catching the light. 'Hmm, yes, I suppose you do.' Abruptly he said: 'You think of other matters.'

'Sir?' He was startled.

'When you do Combat,' the Salamander expounded patiently, as if explaining an obvious fact to a child, 'your mind is thinking of other things.'

'Why, yes,' he replied, somewhat surprised. 'Yes, my mind is often elsewhere when I fight.'

'Please.' A pained expression muddied his features momentarily. 'To do Combat is *not* to "fight", dear boy. "Fighting" is done by animals.

Combat is a ritualistic art performed by civilized men.'

'I never gave it much thought,' Ronin said snidely. Because he was growing interested in spite of himself and this perplexed him.

The Salamander was not at all ruffled. 'Ah well, motivation is everything, dear boy. You have natural ability, as any halfwit can see. But motivation – ah! – now that is another matter entirely. What can we do to elicit your interest, hmm? We shall have to attend to that.' So saying, he retreated a pace. His long sword hung at his side, encased in its ornate jet-and-scarlet-lacquered scabbard. 'Yes, we must work on that. Defend yourself, dear boy.'

His hand went not to the hilt of his sword but to the folds of his wide scarlet sash, producing a burnished-metal fan. Ronin could not believe his eyes, but still he put up his sword. The fan wove complex patterns in the air, opening and closing.

The Salamander's attack was over almost before it had commenced, or so it seemed to Ronin. At its swift completion, he was left weaponless, the extended top edge of the fan a bright arc at his throat.

'Hawhawhaw!' Korlik bellowed at his humiliation, but Ronin's thoughts were elsewhere, on the fan's mysterious dances.

Observing the inwardness of Ronin's colourless eyes, the Salamander smiled slightly. He folded the fan and replaced it within his sash. 'Report to my Level in three Cycles' time,' he said briskly. 'Do not bring any personal items.'

He turned on his heel and strode powerfully across the crowded Hall to advise the Instructor of the Students he had chosen, and disappeared down the Corridor in a swirl of jet and crimson, like some elegant and untouchable bird.

He reached the cool Corridor without passing anyone; visitors were rare this far Upshaft. The tan walls arched away from him clean and empty. Here the usual cement floor had been covered in resilient wood planking, enamelled a rich deep brown.

As he walked, the walls lightened until they had reached a cream colour, and he stopped in front of huge double doors with thickly carved panels along their edges. Heavy metal knockers in the likeness of a thin twisting lizard, needle tongue exposed, flames writhing at its feet, were hung in the centre of each door. Tiny ruby eyes glinted in the strong light of the Overheads. He stood in front of the doors and did not touch the knockers.

'Yes?' a flat filtered voice said from nowhere.

He did not stir: he knew the routine. He pronounced his name clearly.

There was nothing for a moment, then the disembodied voice said: 'Former Student?'

'Yes.'

A crackle. A brief hum.

'Enter,' the voice said.

It was large and gave the appearance of being light and airy and open without actually being so; no room in the Freehold could, by definition.

The deliberately rough-finished walls were painted a light blue, the ceiling a soft white. The planking on the floor was lacquered a deep lustrous blue. Low chairs were scattered about the front part of the room. The walls were devoid of any ornamentation. Double doors, the twins of the ones he had just come through, broke up the far wall.

He went across the room and stood in front of a desk that appeared to be very old. Behind it sat a woman with light wavy hair, and a face broad and flat enough to make it interesting. She wore a robe the same colour as the walls.

He looked into her disinterested grey eyes.

'You wished – ?' The cool question hung in the air like a beaded curtain.

'To see the Salamander,' he said.

'Ah.' She said it as if it were a word with meaning. She gazed at him and let the silence stretch itself like a yawn. Her small neat hands fluttered over the desktop, the lacquered nails glistening in the light.

Eventually she said, 'I am afraid he is unavailable at the moment.' There was no trace of regret in her voice.

'Just give him my name, please.'

'Perhaps if you returned during a later Spell.'

'Have you given him my name? Have you told him that I am here?'

The nails scratched their way along the wood. 'He is extremely busy and – '

He leaned over, captured her hands in his,

103

pressed them down. She stared at them as if fascinated, and raised her eyes to his.

'Tell him,' he said softly.

'Still – ' She continued to look at him, searching his face. Her tongue showed briefly between her white teeth like a coral snake.

He released her and she got up and went out through the doors behind her. She left a soft humming and a breeze wafting from a sudden source. Borne upon it was a gentle hint of cloves, and if he had not spent so much time on this Level, he would have supposed that it came from the woman.

She took her time coming back and when she emerged her grey eyes were round, as if she were a bit startled. She held one door open.

'You may go in now,' she said a little breathlessly.

Ronin smiled to himself and, as he passed her, he saw something moving in her eyes, an ambiguous emotion. She stared after him.

'The last door on the right,' she called as if it were an afterthought.

The hallway was painted the lightest blue imaginable over the same rough-textured base. The floor repeated the dark blue. He passed doors on either side at regular intervals.

It ended in a blank wall. Doors to right and left. He rapped with his knuckles. It opened.

The odour of cloves was sharper now. A young man stood in the doorway so that Ronin could not see beyond him. He wore close-fitting breeches and a shirt of a soft tan colour and short dark gleaming boots. He was slim and had unnaturally red cheeks, as if he had just spent a full Spell scrubbing his face. His lips were full and pink. His short curly blond hair shone. Over his heart he wore a jewel-hilted dagger in a scabbard of blood-red leather; another rode on his right hip. He had the appearance of never having done anything in his life.

He stared hard at Ronin and his lips parted slightly. They remained that way for a long moment and then, abruptly, he stood aside and Ronin entered.

It was darker than in the hallway and it took him a moment to adjust. He was in a huge room, panelled in wood. Thick carpets of dark swirling patterns covered the floor. One wall was lined from floor to ceiling with books. Functional leather chairs were grouped casually. A long plush couch was set against one half of the back wall. Open double doors with separate iron-grillwork gates took up the other half. The sounds of water flowing came to him and the scent of cloves came heavily to his nostrils.

There were many men in the room, all dressed, as far as Ronin could tell in the uncertain light, similarly to the man with the red cheeks. They contrived to ignore him with an affected languor.

'Drink?' the red-cheeked man asked, and when Ronin shook his head, he drifted off, looking rather pleased.

Ronin was very interested in the wall of books and he went over to look at them. He ran his fingertips along the rows of spines and thought of G'fand. They were all extremely old, of course, with worn leather bindings. Some, he saw, had required repairs. He opened one at random. The characters were unfamiliar and he tried another. Glyphs: still unreadable. Ah, G'fand, how you would revel in this: an entire world for you. Books! And all they had Downshaft were fragments. A sudden sadness gripped him.

The red-cheeked man beckoned to him, stretched his arm towards the doorway in the far wall. Ronin passed him. He put a delicate forefinger to his lower lip.

It looked to be an open patio, but that was impossible. Even so, it was a square room whose very high ceiling and diffused lighting gave it a tremendously open feeling. He went across the stone flagging while a breeze stirred his hair. Quite suddenly, he was curious. All of this was a part of the Salamander's quarters that he had not seen before.

He heard strange sounds: a small high trilling, a repeated whistling, others he could not isolate. They seemed to emanate from high up in the air.

He passed, in the centre of the room, a square pool of water, which bubbled and gurgled, fed from some hidden source.

On the far side of the pool, some distance away, was the Salamander. He sat on a bare wooden chair with thick arms. A small stone table with crystal flagon and goblets was on his left side. A second chair stood near, empty and waiting.

He was wearing a dull black robe under which he wore jet leggings and loose shirt. His high black boots were polished to a gloss. A scarlet sash banded his ample waist. Just below his throat, like a startling splash of fresh blood, lay an uncurling lizard carved from a single ruby, its body graceful and rich in colour, slightly translucent. Its eyes were of jet, and onyx flames danced around it, arching up into its mouth.

He looked not a moment older than the day Ronin had first met him. Large, squarish face with highly pronounced cheekbones that, had he not heavy jowls, would have given him almost an alien cast. Thick black brows shielded deep-set eyes as jet-black and shiny-hard as those on his brooch. His hair was thick and dark and long, brushed back away from his high forehead to give the impression of small wings.

'My dear, dear boy!' the Salamander exclaimed from his chair. 'How pleasing it is to see you again after all this time!' He smiled his jowly smile, the skin at the corners of his eyes crinkling.

Ronin gazed into the onyx eyes and was not fooled. They were heavy-lidded, the lashes long, but he knew what lay behind that effete exterior.

'Come, come. Do sit down beside me.' With a diffident wave of his thickly ringed fingers he indicated the empty chair. Ronin went up two wide flat steps and sat.

The Salamander reached over to the crystal flagon, but Ronin declined.

'And what do you think of my atrium?' asked the Salamander.

Ronin looked around, said blandly, 'Is that what it is?'

The Salamander laughed deep in his throat; the corners of his eyes crinkled and he showed his white even teeth. But the eyes remained unchanged. 'Many centuries ago, when people lived on the surface of this planet, they built houses, low, separate dwellings, you see, with a central room open to the natural elements: the sun and the rain and the stars, and there they gathered to relax and talk of pleasant matters and smell the fresh air. A marvellous custom, do you not agree?'

He changed tones abruptly. 'My dear Ronin, I have told you a thousand times that you must be more well read.'

'If I may say so, it is quite out of the question without access to a library such as yours. Books are a rarity Downshaft.'

At that moment the red-cheeked man stepped through the far doorway and the Salamander looked over. 'You have met Voss, my Chondrin.' It was not a question.

'He seems quite attracted to doors,' Ronin said.

The Salamander shifted minutely in his chair; the jet eyes were unblinking. 'Dear boy,' he said without inflection, 'one of these times you will make a remark like that to a person without a sense of humour – a person with power – and then you will be in most serious trouble. Voss can do a great many things very well indeed.'

He gestured and the Chondrin dropped to a crouch. Both hands became a blur and Ronin was aware of an angry humming cutting through the

108

background sounds. The brickwork of the wall to the left and behind him crackled and he turned to look. Two very deep incisions had been cut barely a centimetre apart. On the stone floor directly below lay the two jewel-hilted daggers that had, up to a moment before, been sheathed at Voss's heart and hip. A split second was all that he had needed to throw both with deadly accuracy.

Ronin turned back to the Salamander.

'He has no sense of humour.'

Again the big man's deep laugh echoed off the walls. 'You always had peculiar ways of letting me know the people you disapproved of.' He rubbed his nose. 'Which was almost everyone, I might add.' With a flick of his fingers he dismissed the Chondrin, who, after retrieving his weapons, withdrew, closing the gates after him.

The Salamander breathed deeply. 'Ah! Feel that! It is almost like being on the surface three centuries ago. Do you hear the birds? Did you recognize the calls? You are sufficiently knowledgeable to have heard of birds.' He waved, a curiously brusque movement for such a normally expansive gesture. 'All of this is not wasted on you, I trust,' he drawled.

Ronin forced himself to sit completely still and say nothing.

The Salamander's right arm, lying thickly along the arm of his chair, was somehow menacing. 'Let me tell you something. It has been many years since you have been here. Everything has changed.'

He cocked his head to one side as if listening to

a far-off but important conversation. 'How peaceful it is here,' he said after a time, his tone soft and reflective. 'How comfortable, how secure. It took me quite a long time to build this. For instance, this room was under construction when you were last here. It has taken an enormous effort to get all the elements gathered and integrated. The lighting was difficult but, as you can see, not insurmountable. But the birds, the birds, dear boy! For a while I thought I would never hear them in here.' He cocked his head again. Their sweet singing sounded over the music of the water. 'Ah, listen! In the end it was worth it. This place gives me great pleasure.'

There was silence for a time, at least a cessation of human speech, during which a kind of dreamy peacefulness descended upon them.

Broken. 'And you have changed the most, dear boy. You are no longer my Student. You are a Bladesman. That is in itself significant.'

Ronin let out the breath he had been holding. 'Yes?'

'It means that you have been extremely fortunate in not having run across a Saardin without a sense of humour.' Once more he laughed. Ronin thought he liked to hear the sound of it.

The laughter died suddenly. 'Or have you? One hears the most distressing stories. You seem to have put yourself into a somewhat embarrassing position.' One eyebrow arched, giving him a vividly predatory look.

'What have you been told?'

He shifted his bulk in the chair. 'Enough to

110

wonder how much of your training here you still remember. Freidal distrusts you, that is not a good thing.' He looked down at his jewelled hand, then up again. 'He can become quite – um – annoying.'

Ronin sat rather stiffly. 'I did not come to you for that reason.'

'Indeed? But I daresay that you will have to adjust to the fact that you blundered. He has marked you; perhaps he is having you watched. I need only – '

'No.'

'I thought not. It makes no sense, but then – ' He shrugged. 'Perhaps then you will tell me why you came.'

Ronin nodded. 'It is about a Magic Man,' he said.

For a time after he had finished, the Salamander said nothing. He laced his fingers, resting them on his thighs. The scent of cloves came very strong on the air. The 'birds' sang. Along one wall, moss had been encouraged to grow, moist and green. Ronin found it hard to believe that they were underground. He felt isolated, quite disconnected from the world Downshaft, and he recognized this as a form of offering. It was no accident that the Salamander had received him here.

'How do you suppose,' the Salamander said, 'I am able to maintain all of this?' His hands unfolded like a fan.

Ronin thought: So it has been a mistake after all. He got up.

The Salamander's eyes opened wide. 'Ah. What is it?'

'There was a time when this was necessary,' Ronin said angrily. 'Now – '

'Indulge me.'

'As you said, everything has changed.'

'Did I not teach you all explanations in their proper time?'

'I am no longer your Student.'

'You made that quite clear some time ago.'

The onyx eyes were all pupil, black and glittery, locked with Ronin's. An electric charge built itself in the room.

'All right,' the Salamander said finally. 'All right. Sit down. Be assured that I have an answer for you. At least let me reach it at my own pace.'

The gates opened across the room and Voss appeared as if by a signal. He came immediately across to them and stood in front of the Salamander, who said, 'Open the Lens.'

Voss shot Ronin a quick glance, then nodded and went out through a narrow door behind them that Ronin had failed to notice before.

'Now where were we?' The Salamander cocked his head. 'Ah, yes, my not so humble quarters. They are extensive. When you were last here, you saw only what all my Students are allowed to see. You could have – ' He shook his head. 'But old ground is pointless.' He rubbed his hands down the smooth wood of the arms. 'I have an entire Sector, you know.'

Ronin was surprised in spite of himself. 'No, I did not.'

He nodded. 'But that is only part of it, an insignificant part. Decoration, one might say. One

112

impresses those who must be impressed. For the rest, it is all pleasure. And it is only the tip, having it. Getting it, that is what counts. To do that, one needs but one item: Power.' He leaned forward. 'I have it.'

'So it is said.'

The onyx eyes bored into him.

'You do not fear it,' the Salamander said, not without some contempt. 'That is a mistake.'

'I do not worship it.'

'You would do well to heed me.'

'That time – '

'Yes, quite.' The Salamander rose gracefully. 'If you will follow me.'

He crossed to the narrow door and led Ronin into darkness.

Light that bloomed in front of him was dim and faded, the colours smeary and washed out, as if, having been painted quickly and tentatively on canvas, they were now covered in a fine film of dust.

He saw himself as a small child, and everything looked too large for him to use. He was in a room filled with stifled silence. It was very hot and he pulled at the collar of his shirt. It seemed he could not breathe. He wished his sister were here. She was very young, her features still forming, but he loved her. She would come to him when she was sad or lonely or had had a fight, and he would comfort her, help her, protect her. And then she would laugh and hug him around the waist and her happiness would transmit itself to him. She

113

could make him smile. Why isn't she here, why are all these people here, what's wrong? Someone said: 'It is no use, they have called it off.' A figure loomed over him. What's wrong, what's wrong? The figure said: 'Your sister is dead. Can you understand that? Dead.' He began to cry. The figure slapped him hard. Someone said: 'His is too young.' The figure hit him again and again until he stopped.

' – in this room.' It was small, lit only by points of glowing green light, winking like jewels from some far-off city. Ronin rubbed briefly at his eyes.

'Very few people have been in this room,' the Salamander continued. 'Very few people even know of its existence.' Voss was sitting before a metal box, low and wide, from the centre of which an oval cylinder projected perhaps a metre into the air. His hands were busy moving across a complex control panel. 'Do you follow me?' The Salamander moved behind Voss, put a jewelled hand on his shoulder. 'I think that you were wise to stay a while longer.'

He turned and the tiny jet eyes at his throat flashed, reflecting flatly the hard green light. The lizard's body had taken on a dull, dusky hue, like the film on stagnant water. 'This Magic Man, is he sane or mad? You are unsure.'

He lifted his arm, the palm of his hand standing out dead white against the dense black of his robes – even the scarlet sash was turned black by the strange light. 'This is the Lens. We do not know how it works, or even its original purpose, but in a moment you shall see what few men in our lifetime have ever seen. Look. Look upward.' And he squeezed Voss's shoulder.

At first Ronin thought that the ceiling had in some way opened. A swirling opalescent oval lit the darkness. Then he saw that it was a projection from the cylinder of the Lens.

Pearl greys and the lightest of violets swam blurrily above them. Then quite suddenly the scene was sharply delineated. And Ronin stared in awe. This cannot be, he thought. How is it possible?

Thick banks of magenta cloud and pearled, frigid mist whipped by them, forming, and then were gone. The light was diffuse and cold. It seemed infinite.

'Yes,' said the Salamander softly and dramatically, 'we are indeed observing the sky above our planet. This is the outer shell of the world, Ronin.'

Slowly the layers moved upward and out of their field of view as the Lens shifted its focus. They became lighter, finer, shredding before their eyes like gossamer robes.

'We shall now take a look at the surface of the world.'

A whiteness, a terrible frosty barrenness. Sheets of snow and ice picked up by the heavy winds, dragged across the frozen mountains and crevasses, raking the terrain. Ice and snow and rock and not a hint of anything else. It was impossible for anything to live Up there.

'This is the world,' the Salamander intoned. 'Destroyed by the Ancients. Devastated beyond any hope of redemption. A desolate, decaying hulk, useless now. You are seeing what is directly

115

above us, Ronin. This is why we remain encased three kilometres below the surface. To reach the surface is to die. No food, no shelter, no warmth, no one.'

'But is it all this way?' asked Ronin. 'The Magic Man spoke of a land where the ground was brown and green plants grew.'

The Salamander's rings glinted as he squeezed Voss's shoulder again. The scene above them dissolved, shifted, yet all was the same. Ice and snow.

'The range of the Lens is finite. However, for our purposes here, it is more than enough. What you see now is over fifty kilometres distant. And now – ' Dissolve. 'One hundred and fifty kilometres distant.' Dissolve. 'More than five hundred kilometres away. As you can see, it is all the same. Nothing lives on the world, save us. We are the last. The other Freeholds are gone, contact lost many centuries ago. The Magic Man is quite mad. Perhaps his mind snapped from the constant pressure he was under – they are a strange breed. Or perhaps – '

Ronin turned. 'What do you know?'

The Salamander smiled. 'My dear boy, I know as much of this matter as you have seen fit to tell me. But I know Security. And their methods can be somewhat – ah – debilitating at times. It is all according to what Freidal wants.'

'But Security has no right to – '

'Dear boy, wielding power is the only right,' he said sternly, then softening: 'It is all very personal, surely you have learned that by now.'

He removed his hand and the window on to the bleak world above winked out. The green glow came up again.

'In any event, this Magic Man has been known from some while to be most difficult; quite a dissident, at times. But then they all are when time–allotment rolls around.'

The velvet darkness enclosed them snugly. From out of it, Ronin heard the Salamander's voice, soft and reassuring. 'I trust, dear boy, that this extraordinary demonstration has eliminated all your doubts.'

'It is the twenty-ninth Cycle.'

He was wide-shouldered and slightly smaller than average, a fact to which, many believed, he had never quite adjusted. His hair was short and dark, coming low on his forehead, giving him a forbidding countenance which he cultivated and used to full effect. Deep lines scored downward from the corners of his ungenerous mouth even when his face was in repose.

He stood on a small raised platform, dressed in white robes, believing the colour made him appear larger, and addressed his students – Bladesmen who were arrayed before him in precise rows – under the high vault of the Hall of Combat.

'This Cycle, iron strikes iron,' the Instructor continued, in the prescribed manner, his head swivelling on his thin neck. 'For this is the Cycle of the Arm and the Wrist and the Sword. This Cycle we are called by the Horn of Combat.'

His stentorian voice took some time dying away in the vast Hall. In the silence, there was a rustling as the Bladesmen, in perfect cadence, opened a square space in the centre of the Hall. On all four sides they stood rigidly then, facing inward towards the opening, waiting.

There came a note upon the air. Both deep and shrill, it echoed off the walls, seeming to pick up overtones so that it increased in volume before ending. It came again. And a third time.

'It is the twenty-ninth Cycle,' repeated the Instructor. 'The Horn of Combat has been sounded. It is both a reminder and a warning. A reminder of our past, of what we must strive to preserve with our last breath. A warning to all foes present and future that we are ever vigilant in our sacred trust to guard the Freehold from all who would seek her destruction . . .'

The words of Tradition droned on, as they had, Ronin supposed, for centuries. They were meaningless to him now. And he wondered if that had not always been so. The Salamander was correct in one matter: it *was* indeed all personal. Freidal's carefully phrased words of sacred Tradition were as much a fraud as his fabrication of the detention of the mad Magic Man. Yet Ronin was well aware that the Security Saardin's belief in Tradition was unwavering. Personal.

'. . . your pledge that we shall ever remember our sacred duty to the perpetuation of the Freehold above all else.' But for the soft rustle of cloth, the occasional creak of new leather, silence descended on the Hall.

The Instructor's round eyes narrowed and he thrust out his jaw as he scanned the multitude before him. He relished the power he held over the Bladesmen. This was his domain, and for as long as they were within it, they performed as he bade them. His nostrils flared and he delicately sniffed the air. Cutting through the stench of ten score bodies fresh from half a Spell's exercise, as

119

separate, as distinct as if it were the perfume of flowers in full bloom, was the peculiar odour of fear. His nostrils dilated again as he drank in the heady smell, almost dizzying in its intensity. His mouth curled up slightly and he gripped the railing before him.

Ronin, who had been trained to observe faces in his years Upshaft, saw the Instructor's secret smile and felt as if he were spying on something unclean. His mouth curled in distaste and he thought on the complexities of power and how, however much he tried, he could not evade its sphere of influence.

'Ronin,' called the Instructor. 'Step into the Square of Combat.'

Without surprise, Ronin moved from his position within the multitude of Bladesmen into the open Square. He turned and faced the Instructor.

'Bladesmen, are you prepared to do Combat?'

'Instructor, I am.'

The Instructor addressed the Class. 'This Cycle, as a demonstration for you newer Bladesmen as well as the veterans, we are privileged to be allowed a Bladesman from another Class, so that you may observe other techniques and compare them with your own.' He paused to allow the murmuring of the Bladesmen to subside. Ronin was completely alert now. Students generally fought within their own Classes primarily to forestall the creation of grudges that might involve the honour of Classes as a whole. Among Bladesmen, the resolution of quarrels was encouraged through individual Combat matches.

'We have a Bladesman from the eighth-Spell

Class.' The Instructor raised an arm. 'Marcsh, step forward.'

A thick, stolid figure now parted the throng and made its way into the Square. He walked purposefully with just a hint of a swagger, brushing aside Bladesmen too close to him. A smile was tacked on to his square mouth.

Skill at ritualism, thought Ronin, and prepared himself mentally for Combat. One of Nirren's favourite topics was that of coincidence: he rejected the concept completely. Ronin did not share this belief, although it seemed an inarguable point. Yet here, at this moment, he must side with the Chondrin. The Instructor could not possibly have picked Marcsh by chance; it would certainly be dangerous to think along those lines.

Marcsh's greedy close-set eyes stared at him with undisguised malice. Then he turned and faced the Instructor.

'Bladesmen, are you prepared to do Combat?'

'Instructor, I am.'

Ronin wondered what would happen if he asked the Instructor to tell the Class who Marcsh really was. But he did not consider actually doing it because the adrenalin was already rising within him like a great and powerful animal. He wanted this match.

'As a Student of the eighth-Spell Class, do you agreed to be bound by my judgement in this Combat?'

Marcsh was staring again at Ronin. 'I do,' he said.

The Instructor gestured to a thin pale boy on his

right who stood perfectly still beside a small burnished-metal gong. He held a short mallet in his hand. The Instructor addressed both Combatants. 'You will commence when you hear the Tone. You will cease only when the Tone sounds again. Is this acknowledged?'

The Instructor gestured again and the boy swung the mallet in a shallow arc. The crystal tone hung in the air for seconds, refusing to die.

Combat had begun.

Sight, then sound, repeating. And Ronin began to retreat under the frenzied onslaught, first one step, then another. Several. A predatory grin split Marcsh's face as he bore down even harder, grunting and panting with tremendous effort, sensing that the end was near.

As soon as the Tone had sounded, Marcsh had withdrawn his sword and, instead of taking the Position, it had continued its blurred arc out and then down, aimed for the triangular juncture of Ronin's neck and shoulder. But almost simultaneously Ronin was lunging forward, shoulders twisting, and the blade whistled past him so close that he felt its hot wind. Thus extended, he slammed the heavy hilt of his still-sheathed sword into Marcsh's fists. He regained his ground and his blade flashed out.

The Bladesmen shifted in anticipation and excitement, crowding one another, craning their necks to see more clearly. They felt it in the air now, knew this was not an ordinary Combat.

Marcsh had stood, feet wide apart, knees

slightly bent, sword before him. His knuckles were red and slick with blood and he glared at Ronin, hating him even more for the rebuke.

Ronin had faced him with his hip and his shoulder, right foot forward and extended, left behind him. He held his sword out at stomach level, point slightly higher than hilt.

Marcsh had leapt and again the blade flew down and Ronin caught it on the hilt, the heavy shock coursing through them both. They strained against each other, breath hissing through clenched teeth. The veins along Marcsh's thick biceps and inner forearms stood out, pulsing, from the muscles. His face and neck grew red with the effort.

He was extremely powerful, and he used his brute strength to break the deadlock, moving immediately into a series of horizontal thrusts, slashing and cutting. Ronin had parried it all, neither retreating nor advancing. Marcsh's close-set eyes blazed and his mouth opened with the heaving of his chest.

He had turned a horizontal slice into a feint, reversing his motion very rapidly but still having to overcome momentum, his weight working now against him, attempting to use his hilt as Ronin had before. The blade of Ronin's sword glinted and took the force of the attack, and he began a counter but Marcsh retreated. Sweat glistened along Marcsh's arms and down his sides and his shirt clung to him like a loose second skin.

And he had leapt forward, once more on the attack, and his sword lifted and fell, lifted and fell, his full power behind each stroke. The blade was a white blur obscuring the Combatants so that the Bladesmen were obliged to press closer in order to make out the course of Combat.

Still Ronin retreated under the assault, the shocks reverberating even into the first rows of onlookers, so that they imagined they could feel the terrific force being generated and were happy that they were merely watching. Motion blended as the attack resolved itself into the shape of repetition. The heavy blade lifted and fell, lifted and fell. Blue sparks flew upward and the constant clang of metal against metal was deafening. The air was acrid and leaden. Lifted and fell, lifted and fell, and time unravelled.

It was a form of hypnosis and not at all limited to Combat. That was its strength, because one tends to forget under the narrowed concentration of Combat. Narrower still is the deep concentration of the attack, of bringing Combat to its completion. And now Ronin saw it in Marcsh's eyes and he timed the counter perfectly, abruptly holding his ground as Marcsh, intent on the retreat as a gauge for his victory, swung again forward and down with all his strength. He came up on Ronin instantly, sword descending in a blur, eyes just beginning to open in surprise, as Ronin, feet planted firmly, bent into his knees, twisting his torso at the last possible instant. He pivoted his left foot away, and Marcsh, his body made ponderous and overbalanced by momentum, rushed past him. Ronin brought both arms around, following the pivot of his own momentum, using it, locking his elbows so that his arms were rigid with

124

force, and smashed the flat of his sword against the daggam's back.

There came a cracking sound, muffled and thick, as of the rending of a foundation under immense pressure, and Marcsh's body arched horribly, his arms thrust above his head in reflex, as if in supplication. His sword clattered to the floor. The body hit the floor with great force and was still. It lay there, unnatural and ugly, grotesque in its sudden parody of human form, as a great shout went up from the Bladesmen, and the Square of Combat was suddenly filled with milling people.

Ronin did not see the Instructor gesture but he heard over the tumult the clear Tone of the gong that signalled the end of Combat.

He stood and breathed deeply, the still centre of a raging storm. He wiped sweat from his colourless eyes.

As if from far away he heard a voice cry, 'Moment! Moment! I will have silence here!' The din continued. 'Silence, I said!' roared the voice. The shouting died to low murmurings and then ceased altogether.

From his platform the Instructor glowered down at his students. 'Stand silently where you are!' His face was red and his small eyes flashed. 'This conduct is outrageous! Unthinkable! Rank Students would behave better. I shall not tolerate such an outburst in *my Class* again!' he bellowed at them. He pointed to two Bladesmen. 'See to Marcsh.' They bent to their task, trying to lift him gently, but a sound came from him so filled with agony that they left him and ran to fetch a litter.

Seeing this, the Instructor's gathering fury exploded, and he turned upon Ronin. 'You fool!' he screamed, barely in control. 'You have half killed him! How shall I explain that to his Instructor? How shall I explain that to his Saardin!' His voice had become shrill, rising in pitch. 'This will reflect on me! On me! Do you understand what you have done! What gives you the idea you can use your weapon in such a manner?' He shook his fist at Ronin. He was trembling.

'As of this moment you are barred from this Combat Class, and I can assure you that it will be the same for all Classes, because I shall see to that personally. In addition, a full report of your irresponsible behaviour shall be made to the Saardin of Security!'

There was a great tumult in the Hall now, sounds of voices and movement echoing and re-echoing off the walls and ceiling, gaining in volume. Dimly, Ronin was aware of Nirren, somehow miraculously beside him in the crush.

The Instructor's voice rose to peak volume to be heard. 'You will pay for this incident, and pay dearly!'

Ronin, adrenalin still pumping within him, crossed the line. He took a step forward and lifted his sword. 'We will see who shall pay!' he yelled, but it was borne away on the tide of sound.

Nirren gripped him from behind. 'Are you mad? What are you doing?'

Still Ronin advanced through the throng towards the elevated figure of the Instructor. Nirren clung to him, trying to gain a purchase to restrain him, as he fought his way through the tightly pressed, jostling bodies. They clung to Ronin like weights impeding his progress and he was only halfway there when he saw the Instructor, fearful now that he had quite lost control of the situation, wheel off the platform and, with his boy trailing in his wake, stride from the Hall.

Nirren got hold of him at last. The noise had increased and the heat was unbearable. He had to turn his head and stare at Nirren's working mouth before he understood, and even then it took a while. 'Come on! Come on!'

Soon after, the Bladesmen came with the litter and bore Marcsh away.

'They have all miscalculated.'

'How do you know?'

He sighed. 'I do not. It's a feeling.'

'Based on something, surely. All the Saardin could not miss – '

He made a fist. 'But they have, I know it! All they see are their own bits of power – '

'It is personal with them.'

Nirren ceased his pacing long enough to stare at Ronin as he sat on the bed, stripping off his soaked shirt. 'Why, yes, it could be put that way.' He cocked his head quizzically. 'You have been to see him then.'

Ronin threw the shirt over a stool. 'Yes.'

Nirren stood in front of him, frowning. 'But not to go back.'

Ronin laughed humourlessly. 'No, not at all.'

'Were you not even tempted?'

Ronin looked up. 'Well, he did try.'

'Really.'

'No need to worry about it.'

Nirren relaxed somewhat. He looked down at the bruise down Ronin's side. 'I have sent for her,' he said.

Ronin touched the bandage over the wound at his shoulder. There was still some pain. 'That was hardly necessary.'

He flicked a hand. 'Nevertheless it has been done.'

'Where is Stahlig?'

'Ah, attending to Marcsh, I believe,' he said with a thin smile. 'Why did you go then?'

'To see the Salamander?'

'Yes.'

'Advice.'

'From him?' Nirren laughed. 'He is a Saardin. Why should he tell you the truth?'

'There are ties,' Ronin said.

'Yes, and even after – '

'I expect so.' Very quickly.

Nirren shook his head. 'What did he tell you then?'

Ronin sat back on the pillows, resting. 'That Borros is indeed mad.'

'Did he? And how would he know that?'

Ronin took a pillow, wiped the sweat from his body. 'He showed me a kind of proof.' It left dark streaks on the fabric.

'What, exactly?' asked Nirren, his eyes watchful.

'What if I told you that Borros is not mad?'

'Are you?'

'I do not know.'

'What of the Salamander's proof?'

'I talked to Borros myself.'

'You will not tell me.'

'I *am* telling you.'

'Not about what he showed you.'

Ronin threw the pillow from him. 'How do you know he showed me anything?'

'Words would not have been sufficient.'

Ronin nodded. 'Yes.' He went across the room and opened the wardrobe. 'But I am not sure it *is* proof.' He brought out a shirt with loose silk sleeves and no collar. 'What do you think is Up there, above the Freehold?'

'What?' Nirren shrugged. 'Nothing. Nothing worth talking about at least, unless you are partial to the idea of a kilometre of solid ice and snow. Why?'

He put on the shirt. 'Because Borros believes that there is a civilization Up there, living in a land without ice or snow.'

Nirren stared at him. 'This is what he told you?'

'Yes.'

'Did you ask him what he was working on?'

'It did not happen like that. I got what I could. But I am fairly certain of one thing. Freidal does not know much more than we do, otherwise Borros would not have been talking to anyone. Besides, at one point the Magic Man told me that he had not revealed anything of significance.'

Nirren shook his head. 'I can make sense of none of this. Surely nothing lives on the surface – the planet is too cold to sustain life.'

'So it would seem.'

'And where does that leave us?'

'It leaves *you* nowhere.'

'Ah, Ronin – '

'I want no part of any Saardin.'

'But you will try to see Borros again.'

'Yes.' He lifted a hand for a moment. 'But

because *I* wish to do it.' He sat on the pillows again. 'What about your assignment?'

The Chondrin frowned. 'It is a puzzle seemingly without a solution. Perhaps I am closer to my goal, perhaps not. Still, I cannot shake the feeling that – '

Ronin looked up. 'What?'

'That there is more to it than any of us know.' He ran his hand through his hair distractedly. 'Sometimes – sometimes I could almost believe that there is a third force secretly at work – almost waiting for the other Saardins to make the first move.'

'But there are only Saardins. Nothing beyond.'

'Of course. That is what makes it so puzzling.'

'And you have no facts.'

Nirren sighed. 'If I did, I would be with Estrille now.'

'Have you told him?'

'Some.'

'And?'

'He will not act without facts.' He turned. 'K'reen will be here at any moment.'

'What of your Rodent?'

'What?' Nirren momentarily looked startled. 'Oh – that is where I am off to now. Perhaps I am closer to finding him.' He shrugged. 'He is buried quite deep, that is the only fact of which I am certain at the moment. Do not be alarmed if you cannot locate me for a while – wait for me to contact you.' And he was gone.

Ronin lay back on the pillows and waited for K'reen to come.

* * *

131

They came for him after Class, during first Spell, when there were less people about. He went with them without resistance because he was pragmatic enough to know that it had to come sooner or later, that they were just waiting for a valid excuse, because they hated him.

They marched swiftly through the Corridor and perhaps they were surprised that he came so willingly. Into a deserted Stairwell and Upshaft. To the Hall of Combat.

Empty shadows and dusty silence. Grey air hanging in sheets on the dim light, bars of dark and light. The presence of ancestors unseen and forgotten, talking of bygone millennia, the descent into earth, a legacy of – what?

'Draw it,' grated the voice. 'All my plans done in by you.'

Korlik faced him while the others looked on. Perhaps Korlik wanted an audience. More likely they wanted to be here when it happened. He did not think about that.

'I wanted to go Upshaft with him more than anything else. Because of you – ' It was as good as anything else.

Silence.

'Draw it,' Korlik said again, grinding his teeth. 'Come on.' He waved his sword. 'Well, what are you waiting for? Afraid?' He advanced. 'All right, I'll show you what to do with this.' He waved it again as he came on. 'I am going to turn you around and shove this up you!'

Ronin unsheathed his sword and, for the next

quarter Spell, turned aside all Korlik's attacks, standing his ground, refusing to counterattack.

Korlik bellowed in frustration and threw his sword to the stone floor. Perhaps it was a signal, because they all fell upon him then and he went down. Someone tried to step on his neck and he grasped the ankle, twisted it violently until he heard the snap. They pummelled his stomach and tried to turn him over. He lifted his legs, straining against the tangle and the pressure, protecting his groin, and knew that he had to regain his feet now or they would have him pinned with his chest to the cold stone. They could not get a firm grip on his legs, and he did it, all the way up, gasping for air.

He found that Korlik and the others did not matter. He heard a low groan from somewhere near him. Korlik bent and retrieved his sword and, crouched, body shiny, advanced in an arc.

Ronin moved laterally but Korlik kept his sword point and body between Ronin and his weapon, shining dully on the stone, so that there were no more options – it had to be done. And the day-dreaming was gone all at once.

He rushed straight at Korlik, saw the wide blade raised, its size magnified, come whistling down, and knew that it would be all right because it was a vertical blow. He got in, past the point as it came arcing blurrily down, slammed his fist into the side of Korlik's head. And by the time Korlik had regained his balance and turned, he had the sword. He crossed a bar of light and it shone like silver.

But he was overconfident, buoyed by the

success of the tactic, and he misjudged Korlik's recovery time and so was unprepared for the rush. He got his blade up but not enough, and the angle was all wrong, so that Korlik's sword cut through his like fabric. Korlik laughed when he saw the stumpy blade sheared through obliquely.

In truth he obviously did not get a good look at it in the dimness or he would certainly have been more cautious. As it was, he moved in, heedless of the shorn weapon still gripped tightly in Ronin's hand, and was thus surprised to feel it enter his chest.

Ronin had lunged, pushing the truncated blade in to the hilt, the force smashing Korlik against the wall, where he now stood, dark blood running all across him. Still he tried to get at Ronin, lurching up, pushing against the wall with his palm, then jerkily swinging his sword one last time, all co-ordination gone, before he toppled face down on the stone.

They left him there, standing over the corpse in the stillness, not daring to look into his dark and unreadable eyes.

And now he opened his eyes to find K'reen bent over him, face filled with worry. 'I have heard about it,' she said. 'It is all over the Sector.' She looked at him, pushing aside his shirt. 'At least you were not hurt, and the wound has not reopened.' She sat beside him. 'What will happen now?'

He shrugged. 'It is not so serious.'

'But banished from Combat — ?'

He sat up. 'If what Nirren is concerned about happens, it will not matter.'

'I do not – '

'The Saardins.'

'Oh. Yes. What does he say? I so rarely see him now except at Sehna.'

'The two factions appear to be very close to a confrontation – but this is nothing you do not already know.'

'He is with Estrille then.'

'No. He has been given a special assignment.'

She went across the room to the mirror of beaten brass, hanging on the wall at head height, just over the cabinet. 'It is near to Sehna,' she said.

Robin thought: Not enough time to see if Stahlig is through treating Marcsh.

She began to put up her hair, glancing at him from time to time in the mirror. 'What is it that makes you so sad?' she said abruptly.

He sat on the edge of the pillows. 'Why do you ask me such questions?'

'Because – ' Her eyes stole away from his in the mirror and she touched a hand to her face. 'Because I love you.'

He caught the glint of the tears rolling slowly from the corners of her eyes. 'What are you doing?'

She turned away and squeezed her eyes shut. 'Nothing.' Water trembled, glistening along her lashes.

He went across to her and spun her around so that her hair, still unbound on one side, floated in a dark arc, momentarily obscuring her cheek.

'Why are you crying?' he asked with some anger.

With her free hand she wiped under her eyes, and he saw within them a brief hint of – fear? He could not be sure.

'I hate that. Why are you crying?'

Anger flared and the thing within her eyes was gone. 'You mean I am not allowed to cry?' He turned away from her. 'What is it with you?' Her eyes were magnified by the water. 'Does it upset you when I show any emotion? *You* cannot, is that it? Because I accept that. *I* do. Can you understand that? Why must you act like this? I cannot under – Don't you ever feel anything? How is it when we go to bed? Is it just – biological?' She turned back to the mirror, put her head in her arms, leaning on the cabinet.

He went into the other room and began to change his clothes. After a time, K'reen raised her head and stared into the mirror. She wet her fingers with her tongue, wiped away the tear-streaks. Then she finished putting up her hair.

They had to walk farther down the Corridor than was usual because the Stairwell closest to his quarters was newly blocked by a slide of rotting concrete and brittle crusty orange metal. The next one was clear and they began their descent to Sehna, Ronin holding before them the flaming torch. The stairs were cracked and pitted and appeared to be little used. Once or twice they had to jump stumps of stairs that had crumbled or had been sheared away by some force.

136

They did not talk and perhaps that is why they heard the sound. It was very soft and came from somewhere in front of them. Ronin stopped immediately and held K'reen still with his free hand. Slowly he extended the torch in front of them. The stairs stretched downward to the landing where they doubled back on themselves. They were deserted.

There was silence. Dust motes danced in the flickering heat of the torch, writhing as they were consumed by the fire to which they were drawn.

They moved slowly downward and it came again. A low moan, a half-whimper of pain.

They were at the landing. Around the turning, the Stairwell stretched darkly away. She started to say something but he cut her off. He strained his ears, thinking now not about the sound below them but – He heard it again and he was sure. At first he thought that the soft scrabbling noise he had detected at the threshold of hearing was the movement of the small animals that lived in the walls, which everyone heard in the soft silences. But the sound had come again, closer, and he knew it for the patient pad of boots, how many he could not tell, on the stairs above them.

He grabbed K'reen's hand and they fled down into darkness.

Abruptly, the whimpering seemed nearer. Ronin thrust the torch before them and saw that the entire inner wall of the Stairwell had collapsed and, for many Levels, a dark pit yawned vertiginously.

They pressed themselves against the secure

outside wall, and saw a figure below them. Dishevelled and filthy, long hair falling lankly down its back, dressed in rags without colour, it huddled pitifully in a corner away from the pit.

He stepped closer, could now discern a wan face covered with muck and sweat. Haunted, frightened eyes stared back at him, the shivering flame from his torch reflecting in the enormous pupils. The figure shrank from him.

He bent slowly, touched it gently. 'Who are you?' And then, 'We will not harm you.'

He heard the bootsteps on the stairs, nearer, and he stood, turning towards them, ears straining again to gather more information. K'reen had crouched down, close to the figure, trying to talk to it. And he heard her choked gasp.

'Ronin!'

He turned back, lofted the torch, saw that the figure's right arm was a stump, torn and clotted with dried blood and newly forming skin, so it was not as recent as he had at first thought. Shadows danced madly around them, the central pillar of the flame.

Then. In the hollow of the creature's neck a glint of metal. Slowly, carefully, so as not to alarm it, Ronin reached for it: a crusted square on a grimy chain. He rubbed his thumb across the surface and brought it into the light.

'"Korabb; Neer; Ninety-Nine,"' he read.

K'reen said, 'This is a Neer? But how – If she was assigned to the ninety-ninth Level, what is she doing this far Upshaft?'

'And with an arm recently taken off.' He

thought of the Neer in Stahlig's quarters. 'The largest and most complex Machines are on that Level – '

'It's the lowest Level, isn't it?'

'Yes, and only the best Neers work Down there – '

Boots echoed more urgently along the walls, stopped at the landing above them. Ronin thought he could hear the low murmuring of voices.

'Ronin, who – ?'

He put his finger to his lips, turned to the Neer, whispered, 'Korabb, can you understand me?' The figure looked from him to K'reen and back again. It nodded, and at that moment he became aware that the Neer was a female. A combination of the uncertain light, her position, and her filthiness had prevented him from seeing her clearly.

The Neer raised a thin finger, nailless, the end torn and black with blood.

'Ronin. Ronin, you have reached the end!' a cold voice called from above. 'We have come for you!' There came to them the grate of metal on stone, a singular sound that they could not mistake, and K'reen gasped, realizing what Ronin had understood all along: they were on their way to Sehna, and he was weaponless.

He felt something touch his shoulder. The Neer's finger pressed against him urgently. She pointed at him and then K'reen, then down into the pitch of the stairs.

He shook his head and said, 'We cannot leave you; you will surely die here if we do. Do you understand?' She shook her head and her mouth worked soundlessly. It struck him then that something was wrong. Apparently it had occurred to K'reen also, for she reached out and gently opened the Neer's mouth. Her eyes grew round and frightened and she jerked her head, trying to pull away, but K'reen held her firmly.

'Oh, Frost!' she whispered, and involuntarily swallowed. Ronin looked, saw a mouth with teeth and gums and palate and a dark bit of flesh that was trying to move. Where the base of the tongue should have been. And was not.

K'reen let go of the mouth and turned her pale face to Ronin's. 'What could have happened? How could this – '

'Ronin. Ronin, we know the Med is with you!' There was a mocking tone to the voice. 'K'reen? Yes, K'reen, that is her name.' There was scraping again from above as someone shifted. 'Do not delude yourself into believing that you will die quickly and honourably. No Bladesman's death for you, my friend. We shall cut the tendons in the backs of your legs so that you will stay and watch us while we find out what the woman is made of. Cut your eyelids and we will all take turns holding your head so that you get the best view. We would not want you to miss a moment while we see how many of us she can take!' And the voice laughed, high and piercing and unpleasant. 'I mean at a time!' The laughter echoed about them and K'reen shivered.

There was a sudden scuffle of boots and the still air eddied, sending a chill through them. Ronin flipped the torch away from them, down into the pit of the Stairwell. Shadows became visible above them, shuffling and moving. Red light from the torch played far below them but they were wrapped now in darkness.

Hulking shapes advanced down the stairs, the shadows closing in. Ronin counted four and knew that there was little hope. Orange light flashed briefly on an upraised sword and Ronin readied himself for the desperate charge up the stairs.

A thin shadow blurred past him, hurled itself like a bolt, leaping obliquely up the stairs, crashing into the now quickly descending figures. The Neer!

There were shrieks, and for a terrible instant, a clawing mass of arms, legs, and torsos was limned in the shuddering illumination of the dying torch, and it seemed as if the bodies hung suspended in the air. Then they all hurtled into the black well of the pit, gaping and irresistible. He tried to catch a glimpse of a face, any face. The Neer's face. But the mass had dropped out of sight and they heard very loud the sickening wet smacks like giant sacks ripped open far Downshaft, reverberating up the ragged sides of the pit.

K'reen huddled against the outer wall, her body convulsed in long racking sobs.

Ronin turned away from the well.

She came into his arms then and clung to him, trembling. 'I cannot,' she cried through the tears. 'I cannot – ' He stroked her hair and hugged her to him, learning something important about himself.

And in that crumbling twilight world, at the edge of a grinning death, with loss and destruction nearly triumphant, they held each other for a very long time.

The elliptical stone slab, squat and changeless, dominated the darkness. He stood just inside the threshold, waiting for his pupils to dilate. They were still out there, around the sweep of the Corridor: daggam.

And Nirren had not been at Sehna.

Afterward, K'reen had left him to finish her Cycle's work on the Med Level. 'It will be best for me,' she said.

There was no light anywhere, and it was very quiet, so that he would have to be extremely careful in his movements. The surgery looked all right. The back cubicle was deserted.

In the Corridor, G'fand had caught him up.

'Going Upshaft?'

He nodded. 'Back to my quarters.'

'Do you mind if I accompany you part of the way?'

He did not see how he could avoid it. He was thinking only of Borros. Time was suddenly very important. 'Come along then.'

They passed a Stairwell and Ronin thought he could hear the lentitudinous drip of viscous fluid. They took the next one, climbing in silence for a time. There was a fine dust in the air and every now and then they heard small sounds from inside the walls.

G'fand cleared his throat. 'I just – wanted to say that – umm – no one wanted to bring up the subject of Class at board. In case you were wondering.'

'I was thinking on other matters.'

'Oh. Well. Everyone was a bit worried because – you know – of you perhaps being out of Class and – '

'I appreciate your concern.'

'We are *all* concerned,' G'fand said carefully.

Ronin glanced at him and smiled thinly. 'Yes. You can tell them then not to worry.'

'But Combat is your life! I would be inconsolable!'

'You talk about it as if it were a disgrace,' said Ronin. 'I acted honourably. It is others who have bent the Code.'

'But it is what the Instructor says that matters,' G'fand protested, misunderstanding him.

'Only to some people.'

'Yes,' he said bitterly, 'the ones that matter.'

Another shadow; he moved silently and swiftly across the room, touched the wall. The hidden door opened and he stepped through.

The small room was as it had been before: the narrow beds, the low lamps, Borros.

He was sitting up now, staring down at the backs of his hands. The yellow hairless head whipped around on its long neck. The grey eyes were dull and expressionless. He stared again at his hands.

Ronin sat beside him. 'Borros – '

'Go,' said the Magic Man in a tired voice. 'Go

and tell your Saardin that the answer is still no. It can only be no.' The long fingers strayed to his forehead, touched the fading Dehn spots. 'Tell him that there is nothing left worth having. He has tried it all and failed. All the shiny bits gone – I can no longer remember. So his attempt to affiliate me fails, too. I cannot help him, even if I wanted to.' He made a gesture. 'Now go and report on what the Magic Man has said; perhaps he will believe you, he does not believe me.'

'Borros, you must listen to me carefully,' Ronin whispered. 'I am not a daggam; Freidal is not my Saardin. Frost, look at me! I was here last Cycle. You were very ill.'

The grey eyes glanced at him, dull gold in their depths. He laughed grimly. 'That is what they call it now?' The eyes blazed briefly. 'You do not fool me. Deceit without end; I expect it from him. But your time is up. Let him send in the next one; but you can tell him when you leave. It will not work. He has failed.'

This did not sound like the man he had tried to talk to just a Cycle ago; the man whose life he preserved. And now he was worried because Borros no longer sounded like a madman. Freidal would recognize this immediately; perhaps he already had. Ronin himself could see that if the Magic Man had held on this long he would, finally, tell Freidal all that he wanted to know before he went mad, if the Saardin wanted the knowledge badly enough. Freidal could do it, he knew that.

'What can I do to convince you?'

Borros heard the urgency in Ronin's voice and he smiled thinly, secretively. 'All right. I direct it. I ask, you answer. Any hesitation – any hint whatsoever that you are fabricating your answers – and it is over.'

'We have no time for this.' Ronin glanced at the door to the Corridor.

Borros shrugged, his lips curling. 'It is the only way.'

Ronin made a gesture. 'Get on with it then, if it will satisfy you.'

The grey eyes were cold and watchful, perfectly clear. 'I did not say that it would.'

Ronin made an exasperated noise.

'What are you?' Borros said shortly.

'A Bladesman.'

'Who is your Saardin?'

'I have none.'

The eyes narrowed. 'What?'

'I am unaffiliated.'

His hands were like white flowers against the dark fabric of the blanket. 'An interesting response.' His head jerked once, involuntarily. 'Which faction will you side with?'

'Freidal is my enemy.'

'Huh! Is that so.'

'He has already tried twice to have me killed.'

'Do you expect me to believe that?'

There were limits. Ronin grabbed the front of his shirt, jerked him forward until their faces were very close. 'I should have let you die last Cycle. It does not appear to have been worth the effort to save you.'

'Let me go.'

Ronin sat back and the Magic Man pulled at the bottom of his shirt. 'Tell me,' Borros said, 'what happened.'

Ronin recounted the Combat with Marcsh and a wistful smile creased the Magic Man's countenance. 'You broke his back?' he asked. 'Are you sure?'

Ronin shrugged.

The Magic Man closed his eyes briefly. 'Oh, if it were so.' He looked at Ronin. 'Go on.'

Ronin told him how he and K'reen had been forced to take a rarely used Stairwell because of the rubble, which, he believed now, had been planned; how they had found the Neer. 'Her tag was marked "ninety-nine" but I have no idea what she was doing that far Upshaft. She was – mutilated. Perhaps the loss of the arm had been an accident, but not the tongue. She – '

Gold flecks danced in the grey eyes, and the head twitched again. He shivered.

'We could not leave her, and in the end – '

The yellow head whipped from side to side. 'I think I – '

' – she took them with her – '

'It cannot be.'

' – down into the pit.'

'No, it cannot – Her tag, you saw her tag. What was her name?'

'I do not see what – '

'Just do it!' Cold grey boring into him.

'Korabb,' said Ronin. 'Her name was Korabb.'

And abruptly, like a sword being sheathed, the

eyes softened. Then the head turned away. 'Chill take them! What have they done?'

Ronin shook his head. 'I do not understand any of this.'

'Yes,' the Magic Man said in a whisper. 'I believe that.'

'I believe at first they felt that I would never actually get so far as to actually be able to build it,' said Borros quietly. 'After all, Mastaad was there reporting on every step I took. In the beginning I paid him no notice, let him do as little as possible because that is the way I am. But he lacked patience and because of his singlemindedness I became suspicious.

'There are always stories, you know, of Security keeping track of all the Magic Men, but' – he lifted his hands – 'one is never sure what to believe. But once I was sure that the construction was possible I became suspicious of everyone. Then I caught him going through my notes and I was sure. I threw him out and burned the notes.

'He could not read them, of course, but he already knew enough to tell them that I would build it. So they came in directly.'

'But you said that this – Machine you had devised would be able to detect temperature and winds on the surface. Why – ?'

'Why are they so afraid? Because it would have proved that there is life Up there. Human life. They do not want that.'

He sighed. 'The old order is entrenched in its power. Never mind the confrontation. If it hap-

148

pens it will not matter who is victorious. The Saardins are secure in their control over all the peoples of the Freehold. The ancient patterns have been set; they are changeless. If war comes, there will be destruction and loss of life. But then there will be stabilization, and the structure will remain.'

He stared at Ronin. 'Imagine what would happen if people knew that there were men on the surface, that it could support life. There would be a movement to go Up, open the Freehold, live Above. That would blow everything apart, and their power would be gone. Confined here, we have no choice.'

'But we are slowly dying,' Ronin said. 'That surely must be obvious to them.'

Borros nodded. 'Oh, it is. But it is a death by slow attrition. As they view it, death may not truly come for a century, perhaps two. By then –' He shrugged. 'They live in an eternal present.' The hands moved over the dark blanket.

'I have seen the surface,' said Ronin.

'Ah.'

'A Machine called a Lens. The surface is – covered in ice and snow. Completely.'

The Magic Man smiled without warmth. 'Above us, yes. The ice is quite solid for a kilometre or more, I believe, although there is no real way of determining that. But I have learned that the Freehold is located near one end of the planet' – he gestured – 'like this, and we are here, near the top. Ice covers the planet at top and bottom. Millennia ago it was more confined, I believe, now it covers more of the planet. But not all. You see?

Near the centre it is warmer, the land is brown, the sun shines out of a clear sky and heats the land and the people.'

'How do you know this?'

Borros shrugged again. 'It is all pointless, this knowledge, for before long we will all of us – Freehold and surface dweller alike – be destroyed.'

'You spoke of this when you –'

'Yes, you were here, saw the state I was in. I was then more susceptible to the emanations.'

'It was – I felt a kind of presence.'

The Magic Man nodded. 'Entirely possible. There have been Cycles lately when it was certainly strong enough.'

'But what is it?'

'As yet I cannot answer that. I have not the knowledge.'

'It is real.'

'Oh, yes. Just, I believe, a long way off.'

'And now – ?'

'Now we both have a decision to make. I must get to the surface, to the people Above. There is very little chance that this – force can be stopped. But I must try. And so, I believe, must you.' He said it rather smugly. Ronin disliked him, did not trust him, and yet he knew that he was right. It was irksome.

The thin frosty smile came again, unpleasant and inevitable. 'I see that I am correct. All right. It is settled. Now for the second part. Before we attempt to leave, you must go Downshaft.'

The smile dissolved like ice in a hearth. 'You

must go,' he said slowly, 'below the ninety-ninth Level.'

'I have no ink,' he said, pricking it. 'I will give you the best description I can but I am afraid that my knowledge is limited.'

The blood oozed out as he squeezed the finger. 'Still, it is better than nothing.' And he began to draw on the fabric.

Ronin had said, 'But the ninety-ninth is the lowest Level. Below that is the rock foundation of the Freehold.'

'Another deception,' Borros said didactically. 'They are quite expert at it. The remnants of another civilization – the civilization of our ancestors – lies below the Freehold. I am quite sure. I know because Korabb went there.

'She was my wife. They told me she was dead, killed while working on one of the massive Energy Converters. Shredded beyond a hope, they said. That was six Sign ago, and all that time I believed – ' He shook his head. 'I do not know what I believed.'

'But what happened?'

'I shall never know. But my opinion is – Look, ten Cycles before they reported her death, she told me that she had found what she believed to be an entrance to a world below the Freehold on the ninety-ninth Level.

'I was beside myself with excitement. Why, when I thought of the secrets, the knowledge that such a world might contain! They couldn't very well have burned everything – some books and plans that had been brought Up, yes, but not the actual Machines themselves.

'I knew I could never get to that Level myself, so I urged her to do a bit of exploring on her own. She made one brief foray Down there and I knew I had been right.

'I believe now that they must have caught her going Down there a second time. They would have wanted to know what she found. Freidal would want that very much; you saw how much. Perhaps they let her go, afterward.'

There was silence for a while. Ronin watched the Magic Man's movements on the scrap of fabric.

'The answer to what comes is Down there,' Borros said. 'I know it. You must find it and bring it back. Only then can we leave.' He continued to draw. 'It is written on a scroll; written in peculiar glyphs. Here, I am writing glyphs in that mode so that you will recognize them. The scroll will have a heading. Look, this is it. That is all I know. It will tell us much about that which comes, perhaps even describe a method of defence. Who knows?' He shrugged again, and looked up for the last time. 'It is our only hope.' And gave him the scrap of fabric, stiff now with the drying blood.

'And, Ronin,' he said blandly, 'try to get back before they rend me to pieces.'

The panel seemed easy enough to understand; if only it worked.

They heard the sounds of boots, soft voices, indistinct but drawing closer from beyond the Corridor's turning.

Ronin pressed a button and the Lift's massive metal doors slid shut, sealing them in velvet blackness and total silence.

'We are not moving.'

He groped in the darkness, pushed a sphere marked for ninety-five. Close enough. It glowed a cold blue and they began to descend.

He had been in one before and immediately he knew it was all wrong. Instead of the steady humming descent, the Lift plunged in jerks and starts, so that they had trouble keeping their footing and were forced to brace themselves against the walls.

They continued to drop with increasing speed now and the vibrations became more pronounced, the swinging of the Lift more erratic.

They felt the lurch then and their stomachs seemed to rise sickeningly. They felt light. The cable had snapped, he realized. They were hurtling down the Lift shaft at tremendous speed. Their ears blocked, and he heard a moaning beside him.

★　★　★

There was a time when he would not have been able to tell. Certain fundamentals had to be pointed out, explained, and then incorporated so that they became reflexive. And then it was a matter of sharpening the instincts. It took time.

He stood at the threshold of his quarters and knew someone was inside. He realized it as he was reaching for the Overhead panel. He left the rooms dark and, conscious that he was a perfect silhouette in the glow of the Corridor Overheads, went swiftly, silently in.

Across the room, hanging on the wall, was his scabbarded sword. It seemed very far away.

He went across to it and no one stopped him. Slowly he withdrew the blade, keeping the doorway to the rear room in his line of vision.

He came into the rear room very quickly, crossing the threshold and lighting the Overheads simultaneously, his sword above his eyes to shield them from the first bloom of the light.

G'fand blinked at him, squinting. He wore dark leggings and a light shirt of heavy material.

'What are you doing here?' Ronin said with some annoyance, to cover his relief.

The Scholar was pale and drawn, as if he had not slept for some time.

'I came to talk to you. To tell you something.' Despite his obvious tiredness, there seemed a certain resolution about him, perhaps in the way he stood, which Ronin had not seen before.

'Why are you hiding back here then?'

'I heard someone about to come in and I suddenly thought that it might be K'reen.'

Ronin could not help smiling. 'I am quite sure she would have understood.'

G'fand flushed slightly. 'I – it might have been embarrassing.'

Ronin turned and went into the larger room. G'fand followed.

Ronin lit the Overheads and took the scabbard off the wall, strapped it on. 'Tell me what is so important.'

G'fand ran his fingers through his long hair. 'I cannot bear to be here a moment longer. I must leave. I know what you must think! But at least you can understand why I must go. If leaving means freezing on the surface, then I tell you I find that preferable to the living death of the Freehold. At least I shall be free for a time, my own master. Here, I am encased, unable to breathe.'

Unaccountably, Ronin found himself thinking of the Salamander's vast library. Rows and rows of books that G'fand would never have an opportunity to read.

'Calm yourself,' he said. 'I do not think you truly mean that.'

'But I do!' There was a sadness now in the Scholar's voice. 'You are like all the rest. You do not think I am a man. But I have some proficiency with weapons now – I can use sword and dagger –'

'And how will you eat?' Ronin asked, reaching into the high wardrobe and withdrawing a light mailed corselet.

'With these,' G'fand said proudly. From under

155

his shirt he produced two bands wide enough to fit snugly around a man's upper arm.

Ronin paused. 'Food bands. Where did you get those?'

'I stole them. And do not worry, they will not be missed.'

Ronin donned the metal corselet. 'You are serious then?'

G'fand nodded. 'That I am.'

Abruptly something the Scholar had said floated up from the recesses of his mind: *I have partially deciphered the glyphs of the very ancient writing.* It had meant nothing to him at the time, but now –

'A journey is what you need. Is that correct?'

G'fand gave him a puzzled look. 'Ronin, I must get out now – this Spell.'

He took something out of the wardrobe, held it in his hand. 'Come with me instead.'

'With you? But what – ?' The Scholar was staring at the food band Ronin was holding. He watched, fascinated, as Ronin worked it on to his arm.

'What do you say? I leave now.'

'But where – ? I don't – '

'With luck, out of the Freehold. I will explain it on the way. Fetch your weapons.' He reached for his dagger.

The close air was filled with a high keening sound that wavered in tone but built in intensity. The Lift shook as it dropped, trying to shake itself apart.

Ronin pressed the other floor spheres on the

panel in front of him. They lit up in twos and threes as his fingers touched them. The Lift continued its mad flight, their cold blue glow mocking.

He remembered, then. The red sphere at the top of the panel. He hit it.

The Lift slammed to a halt and their legs buckled like fabric. The car hung, quivering, suspended in the shaft, the broken cable above them singing as it snaked on to the top of the Lift. Ronin regained his feet, took several deep breaths. G'fand was still on his haunches, sobbing in great lungfuls of air.

'Ronin, we –'

'No time. We have got to get out of here quickly. I have no idea how long this brake will hold.' His hands worked at the panel but the doors remained shut. He drove his fingers at the centre seam of the doors. 'Come on! We must open it up.'

G'fand was on his knees. He put his hands on his thighs and lifted his head. Sweat had matted his long hair across his forehead and along his cheeks. He looked as if he were bound to the floor.

'We – we almost died –'

'G'fand, the doors!'

'Crushed like vermin – bones to jelly –' His eyes were glazed; he was dazed by the force of his imagination.

Ronin turned and pulled him to his feet, attempting to transmit some of his strength. 'G'fand, we are not dead!' Their faces were very close. 'But we soon may be unless we get out of here! I cannot do this myself. I need your help.'

His eyes focused then. 'Yes. Yes. We will open the doors. The two of us.'

They dug their fingers into the centre seam, both pulling from the same side. They heaved and strained until their arms ached and their stretched shoulder joints burned and the water rolled down their faces and into their eyes, making them sting and clouding their vision. Muscles popped and their legs stiffened with the effort. They clenched their teeth and the cords along their necks stood out.

And minutely they felt the door move. They panted like animals but speech was too much added effort and they pulled with renewed determination. And slowly, slowly, the door slid back.

They stooped when it was open wide enough for them to get through, dropped their arms, which felt as heavy as iron, and gasped at the air. Their mouths were dry.

They looked up then and found that they were between Levels. But they were in luck. Perhaps a metre above them beckoned the open entrance to a Level, the protective doors having been sheared away at some previous time, stumps hanging like rotted teeth.

There came an ominous groaning as of tortured metal, and the Lift lurched sickeningly. Ronin put his hands together and G'fand stepped on to them, launching himself upward until he could grasp the lip of the entrance. The groaning came again and he strained, lifting one knee, finally levering himself up on to the Level.

The Lift lurched again and, below him, Ronin's

ears were filled with a metallic shrieking. The Lift trembled and slid and he saw the walls of the shaft rise as the brake began to give way. The Lift lurched sideways, caught on a protrusion in the shaft, and Ronin coiled his body and leapt. The screaming of hot metal was all that he could hear. His fingers caught the lip of the Level, but one hand, slick with sweat, slid off and he hung for a moment, swinging with unwanted momentum by one arm until G'fand reached down, grasped the free hand, and pulled up. He felt the Lift shudder once again and the top of the car slid down. He pushed with his arms, propelling himself on to the Level, and G'fand pulled him from the lip of the entrance, as with a terrible grinding the Lift plummeted down the shaft, the car's top several centimetres from cutting Ronin in two.

They were assaulted by the combined stench of rotting garbage, excrement, and myriad unwashed bodies. The odour grew as they passed doorways, black and gaping. G'fand peered into one and gasped, choked. Ronin held his breath and pulled him quickly back. Still he caught a glimpse of white bone, a staring human eye, blackness where the other should have been. There was the impression of much movement along the floor, the sounds of soft scuttling.

'Where are we?' G'fand whispered.

Ronin shrugged. 'Far Downshaft, anyway.'

'What do we do now?'

'Find another way Downshaft to the ninety-ninth.' He pointed. 'We will try this way.'

The corridor curved away from them, dim and grimy with disrepair. Ronin thought, Could we be as far Down as the Workers' Levels? The Overheads were going. They glowed dismally, sputtering at spots, completely burned out at others. Apparently they had been dark for some time, because torches crackled and flared in makeshift niches carved crudely into the walls. So what light there was was a bizarre blend of fiery orange and cold blue-white.

They paused once to listen but all they could hear was the background drone of dripping water and tiny scurrying feet.

They went quickly and quietly. The walls here had lost all semblance of colour. Theoretically all Levels were colour coded so that one could tell at a glance what Level one was on. But these walls were covered with a thick coating of filth on to which obscene words and grotesque pictures had been drawn or roughly carved. Their obvious anguish was appalling.

They spied no one. Now and again they passed cracks in the ceiling and walls, extended networks of neglect, the damage once or twice so extensive that the sections on either side no longer matched. Several times they were obliged to clamber over blocks of rubble where parts of the Corridor had collapsed. The light grew perceptibly dimmer.

Ronin paused, extending an arm, holding G'fand back. He peered ahead. They went forward slowly about six metres and stopped abruptly.

It looked as if a gigantic fist had smashed into the Corridor. Something apparently had exploded with tremendous force from the inner Well, tearing open the wall, crumbling the floor for a space of a metre and a half. They peered cautiously into the gaping hole. There appeared to be a fire burning below on what they took to be the next Level.

G'fand wiped at his forehead. 'Frost!' he whispered. 'What is happening?'

Ronin said nothing. He looked across the face of the pit.

'Perhaps we should see if we can help.'

'These Levels appear to be deserted,' Ronin said somewhat distractedly.

'Still – '

'Our problem is how to cross this pit. There is nothing we could do in any event.'

G'fand looked up out of the flickering light. 'Why not retrace our steps and traverse the Corridor from the opposite direction?'

'Too much time lost, and the Corridor might be in worse repair. We press onward here; there is no turning back.'

He stepped into the dark of the blown wall and, after a moment, called to G'fand. He had found a metal beam, set free of its foundations by the collapse. They set to work manoeuvring it through the gap in the wall and setting it down in the Corridor. Then they pushed it across the diameter of the pit, found that it was long enough to reach the floor on the other side. He stood on it, bounced slightly, testing it.

He went first. It was narrow, barely seven

centimetres wide, but it was twisted very little, so that the surface was fairly smooth and even.

The pit blossomed before him, lurid orange light twisting in the darkness like a bloated serpent, alive and deadly, far, far below. Swinging in short arcs, light receding and approaching, forming patterns. And vertigo lapped at the edges of his vision, waves forming. After that he did not look into the depths, but concentrated on his booted feet as they inched along the beam. One step at a time. Centimetre by centimetre, arms outstretched for balance. And at last he was across.

He turned and beckoned to G'fand, who stepped up on the beam and moved out over the pit.

Ronin called to him: 'Concentrate on your movement; feel your feet against the metal. That's right, one at a time. Slowly now. Careful, feel your balance. There. Now.'

G'fand was almost halfway across when his back foot slipped as he put his weight on it and he lurched to one side, over the yawning pit. He fell. And reached up desperately, in reflex, one hand hitting the beam, the fingers finding purchase. He swung dizzyingly in short arcs, his other hand scrabbling to find the beam.

Ronin first thought of pushing himself out on his stomach to get to him, but he did not trust the beam to hold them both and there was no time to find out. 'G'fand,' he called, 'let your legs hang, do not move them, you must stop the swing. All right, now reach up. No, to the left. Yes, more; now stretch.'

G'fand now gripped the beam with both hands, and hung like a vertical bar, arms stretched above him. He looked at Ronin. Hair was in his eyes and he shook his head in an attempt to free his vision, and his slippery hands skidded on the metal. He caught himself just in time.

'Easy, easy,' said Ronin. 'Listen to me, G'fand, and do exactly as I tell you. Put one hand in front of the other. Look up, not down.' The strain showed on the Scholar's face. 'Good. Now again. Think of only the next movement. One at a time. Good. Again.' He spoke to him in a steady stream and in this way G'fand made his painful way across the remaining length of the beam, until, reaching out, Ronin was at last able to pull him up from the edge of the abyss. G'fand's body shook and he turned away from Ronin and was violently sick.

And now dark smoke and choking fumes rose in thin swirling clouds from the Level below. And now the fitful glow appeared brighter through the gaping rent. And now they heard the muffled pounding of running feet, and under it a dry, crackling sound, abnormally distinct and clear on the close air.

Ronin, crouched along one slimy wall, dragged G'fand along the Corridor, well clear of the rubble surrounding the hole. He pulled him off the floor and said, gently, very close to his face, breathing the sour smell, 'I am sorry but we must move on – at once.'

G'fand wiped his mouth and nodded. 'Yes, yes,' he whispered. 'I am all right.'

They moved on as swiftly as they could.

Presently they encountered the first people either of them had seen on this Level. They were all dead. Bodies were strewn about the Corridor as if hurled through the air by some titanic force. They lay burned – some so badly that they could not make out their features – maimed and broken, amid viscous puddles of dark seeping blood.

G'fand stared wide-eyed. 'By the Chill! What has happened here?'

Ronin said nothing, and they plunged on into the murk of the curving Corridor, away and away, over the stinking mounds of the bodies. No Bladesmen here, and Ronin knew that he had been right; they were far Downshaft, among the Workers.

He paused as a small indistinct shape fled from out of a doorway, running at full speed into him. He grabbed hold, almost losing his balance, and looked down to see a small girl struggling in his arms. He picked her up and looked closely at her, the first sign of life they had encountered on this Level. She had thin pinched features visible inter-mittently beneath long lank hair whipping about as she writhed against his grip. She was sobbing, and through her tears Ronin saw that her eyes held a measure of torment that startled him.

'Are you hurt?' he asked, but she would not or could not answer.

G'fand touched Ronin and pointed ahead. A

figure had reeled out of the doorway from which the girl had run. A tall gaunt woman with short hair and a hungry mouth and dull eyes. She saw them.

She ran unsteadily towards them. She screamed, 'What are you doing to her?' She rushed down the Corridor at them. The child cringed and screamed as the woman reached out one long clawlike hand, dirty, the nails broken far down their length. The child clung to Ronin with a strange desperation. Then the woman took her.

She raised her right hand, brandishing a long curved blade, crusty with dried blood. 'Animals! You're not content with me, you take her too – '

'She ran into – ' Ronin began, but the woman was not listening.

'Taking her off to some dark room, were you? Get away!' she screamed, and whirled, pulling the girl behind her back along the Corridor, disappearing through the doorway from which they both had emerged. Ronin still felt the clutch of the girl, felt from far away his lost sister's arms around him.

He began to run, calling, 'Come on!' over his shoulder, and heard G'fand coming after him. Bursting through the doorway.

Dim and smoky. Rooms much smaller than Upshaft. Three rooms to a quarters, two or three families. The rooms were a shambles. Broken furniture, shards of pottery, ripped fabric, the floor slippery-sticky with an indistinguishable amalgam of liquids. Nothing moved here and they went on into the second.

Ronin saw an arm protruding from a pile of refuse. He drew his blade and uncovered the body. It was a Worker, thick chest and arms, squat. By his outstretched hand was a heavy lever, ripped from a Machine, obviously used as a club. He turned the body. The Worker's chest was a pulpy mass and there was so much blood that they could not count the number of times he had been stabbed.

'Frost!' he muttered. 'Have they all gone mad?'

G'fand turned his head away.

They moved into the last room. A lamp burned, hung from the ceiling, swaying slightly so that shadows moved and perspective was shattered.

The woman knelt on a bed at the rear wall. A washstand had been knocked over. The woman grasped the sobbing girl in one hand, and with the other arm, the hand still gripping the blade so hard that the knuckles were white, she held a limp figure to her. Her eyes were wide and staring blankly. A thin line of spittle drooled from a corner of her mouth. They paused just inside the doorway.

'Fiends!' she cried. 'One more step an' you'll get what your friend out there got!'

G'fand stared at her and choked. 'You did that?'

She laughed, a throaty, chilling sound, and her eyes rolled madly in their sockets. The girl struggled to get free. 'Aye, that. Surprised, are ya, well so was he!' Her eyes wavered and dropped for an instant to the head of the small figure she was cradling.

'See,' she wailed. 'Look upon your work! Fiends' work!' And she turned the limp figure, and they saw a thin young boy, perhaps somewhat older than the girl, same dark pinched features. 'See how you have defiled my son! See how you have taken his life!' Her voice rose, and quickly she clutched the boy back to her. Strength seemed to flood into her then, and she drew herself up defiantly. 'You'll get no satisfaction here! Not this time!'

Too late Ronin realized that she had spied his drawn sword. Too late he divined her intent. She pulled the girl to her, the child's eyes round and staring, a high keening coming from her open mouth, and as Ronin leapt she drew the long curving blade across the girl's trembling throat. A gout of blood erupted and the keening became a thick gurgle, and she twisted the body behind her so that he fell atop her.

But the blade was now behind him, out of his line of vision. He dropped his sword to free his hands. He twisted to find the knife before it found him.

He was aware of her arm moving swiftly and then he felt her convulse violently under him, arched and stiffened. A smile came to her face at the same time the trickle of blood did. He looked down to see the knife plunged hilt deep into her side. He tried to withdraw it, but her fist, locked in a death grip, would not give up the hilt. A kind of relief suffused her face. Then he felt a spreading wetness, hot and sickening.

He backed off the bed on his knees. A sudden

dizziness threatened to overwhelm him. Reflexively, he retrieved his sword. G'fand moved to the edge of the bed. 'What – ?' But Ronin waved him wordlessly away. 'Out!' he managed to gasp.

'But – '

'Out!' he bellowed. And they stumbled through the reeking rooms out into the Corridor, raced along its curving length.

They almost overran the familiar bulge of a Lift's doors, and heaving them apart they pitched inside, closing the doors behind them.

In warm darkness they sat, panting, and listened to the soft silence as their pulses slowed and breathing returned to normal. It seemed like a long time.

Presently Ronin heard G'fand stir.

'I have that trapped feeling again, as if the walls are closing in on me. The Freehold is dying, it's all coming apart.' He shifted. 'How far Downshaft are we?'

Ronin stood and moved his fingers over the Lift's control panel. He pressed a sphere and the doors opened, closed again. 'According to the Lift, the seventy-first Level. Perhaps we can take it all the way to the ninety-fifth.'

'Is that all you can think of,' G'fand said accusingly, 'after all we have witnessed. The Lower Levels are going – the Workers murdering one another – total madness!'

There was no response from Ronin. 'By the Chill, you are like ice,' G'fand said bitterly. 'Nothing affects you! We have just seen things that have wrenched my stomach. What flows through your veins? Surely not blood!'

Ronin looked down at him, his colourless eyes barely discernible, and said, 'You are free, as you always were, to return Upshaft, to attempt even to reach the surface.'

G'fand put his head down and would not meet Ronin's gaze. Their harsh breathing was all that could be heard for a while.

When he was certain that G'fand would stay, he punched the sphere marked 'ninety-five'. It glowed and they commenced to sink rapidly and smoothly Downshaft. G'fand stood up. The Lift hummed. Ronin drew his dagger. The Lift sighed to a halt. The doors opened soundlessly.

He had assumed that since no Lift they had been in went as far as the ninety-ninth Level, they would be obliged to take a Stairwell the rest of the way. He saw now that he had been mistaken.

There was no Corridor. They stood instead upon a metal-grillwork scaffold arcing away from them on either side until it was lost to view in the haze.

Space. Where the inner wall of the Corridor should have been was enormous space. Ronin had never seen so much open space. G'fand stared with his mouth partly open.

They moved slowly to the low metal railing that ran around the inner edge of the scaffolding. And looked down.

Immense geometric shapes, some simple, others extremely complex, all stupefying in size, studded the vast gallery below them. And now Ronin knew why the Lifts descended only as far as the ninety-fifth Level. They were peering down into an area four Levels high. Perhaps the sides of the gallery themselves were Machines. The life of the Freehold, he thought. Without these we die.

A deep humming filled the air, permeating it so that it seemed to flutter before their eyes. Soft blue haze hung in the air, trembling minutely. Light came from an unidentifiable source, lost somewhere above them. It was very warm, and a sharp, pungent smell, not at all disagreeable, floated on the air. Over the droning of the Machines they could just make out, now and then, the faint chatter of voices. Oddly, the sound heartened them.

They began to walk along the scaffold and at length they came upon a square opening cut into the outer edge abutting the sheer wall. Ronin looked down. A vertical ladder stretched away into the haze. It appeared clear. They descended, Ronin holding the dagger in his mouth, teeth locked on the hilt. As they went, they passed other scaffolds at regular intervals. They were deserted. He counted seven before they reached the floor of the gallery.

The thrumming was more insistent here, seeping up through the soles of their boots into their legs. The close air smelled of artificial heat and what Ronin knew to be lubricant. He had smelled it enough on Neers. The Machines rose all about them, a lush humid forest, strange and compelling. The light was dimmer, the blue haze thicker.

Off to their left, three Neers stood debating, their voices smeared by the background sounds. The air hung like sheets.

They hunkered down by the purring side of a Machine, aware of its warmth, and Ronin unfolded the crude map the Magic Man had drawn for him. G'fand ate several mouthfuls of food while Ronin studied the piece of fabric.

The trouble was that the map had been drawn assuming that they had come to the ninety-ninth Level via the designated Lift, the one that had failed. Although he knew in which direction they had gone on the seventy-first Level, he had only a rough idea of the distance they had travelled before coming upon the second Lift. The map covered very little of the geography of the ninety-ninth Level. He would have to estimate the difference in their position, a dangerous but necessary action.

G'fand, still chewing, wiped a greasy hand across his mouth and rubbed it on his breeches. He swallowed. 'Do you know where we have to go?'

Ronin pointed away from the group of gesticulating Neers. 'This way. No noise.'

They slipped from Machine to Machine, the bulky shapes looming out of the haze to offer transitory shelter. He took them on a zigzag course out across the floor of the gallery.

Rapidly the walls receded from their view, and G'fand, glancing up, fancied they were adrift in an ephemeral, forbidding world. He felt an odd discomfort without the security of walls about him.

They had covered almost a kilometre and had

begun to sweat profusely in the damp heat, when Ronin brought them to a halt. In the shadow of a squat Machine they stood very still and listened to the voices just ahead of them.

'This is leading nowhere.'

'Don't I know it! We've been here for over a Spell. Are you certain you checked the generator in Block Twelve?'

'Checked and rechecked. If there is any connection it is beyond me.'

'Beyond all of us, I am afraid.'

There came the sounds of metal against metal, a light scraping, and then a sigh.

'I don't know. What if we tried the second Level with *all* the power on?'

'Um, it might work at that. Just make sure – '

The conversation receded as they crept away. Following their short detour around the Neers, they resumed their oblique course across the gallery.

The huge circular Machine stood at the end of a broad area, wider than most of the spaces between the hulking shapes. They dared not approach it directly for fear of being detected either by Neers or by daggam.

They moved cautiously along a narrow aisle parallel to the one leading to the Machine. The heat increased and they had to will themselves not to pant. They were obliged to stop twice to let Security patrols pass them on perpendicular but intersecting routes. Each time Ronin waited long minutes after they had passed before proceeding. Once they almost ran into the back of a daggam

172

who stepped out into their aisle, and they shrank back into the shadows, waiting breathlessly until he moved away.

Crouching low, they made their way, skirting the Machine, until, having seen it from all sides, Ronin judged the way to be clear. Once more he consulted the map, to be certain that they approached it from the right direction. They moved towards it.

It cast its own long shadow, the promise of a haven, a towering structure of incomprehensible function, wider at the bottom than the top, all sharp angles and crenellations. Lights flashed along its summit, smoky in the haze. It seemed to be vibrationless.

They paused in the meagre shadow of a small Machine, about to make the final approach. Ronin held them there. It did not feel right. They sweated.

Three daggam converged on the Machine that was their goal. Their conversation dissipated on the active air. Presently, they split up, went out of his sight. Still he waited.

A black cloud bloomed to their left, the way they had come. A crash filled the air and they felt the floor tremble slightly beneath them. They heard the sound of running feet. They ventured a look. The cloud had ballooned out, staining the haze. Lemon flame licked below it.

'What happened?' G'fand whispered.

Ronin smiled thinly. 'I believe the two Neers we passed knew less about that Machine than they thought.' He saw daggam running towards the fire, and touched G'fand.

They dashed across the open area and into the shadow of the towering Machine marked on the Magic Man's map. Ronin put a palm flat against the metal side. It was still. Perhaps it was the structure's quiescence that had led Korabb to begin her clandestine exploration. They moved along the side.

It did not look like an entrance but then it did not look like much of anything save a wall of metal. There was a wheel to turn, it was that simple. Ronin turned it withershins as far as it would go. A disc approximately a metre and a half wide was now raised from the surface of the Machine. They grasped the right edge of the ellipse and pulled. An opening yawned before them.

Without hesitation Ronin stepped in; G'fand followed. As soon as they were across the threshold, the oval closed of its own accord.

They were in impenetrable blackness.

A vertiginous sense of space, echoing minutely. Silence, almost. A damp rich smell. Far away, a sound: persistent but so very distant that it was indefinable: a kind of seething.

G'fand fumbled out his tinder box, and lit a torch he produced from his belt.

An oval tunnel danced before them, black with age. Underfoot the floor sloped gently downward. They went down into the dark and presently they began to feel a chill breeze on their faces and G'fand was obliged to protect the now-whipping flame from extinguishing. Beads of moisture clung to the walls and fairly soon they encountered cones of what appeared to be ice growing down out of the ceiling. Some were mottled grey but others contained streaks of orange and light green, magenta and deep blue. They became more numerous until Ronin and G'fand had the discomforting sensation of being turned upside down, as if they were walking on the ceiling instead of on the floor.

At first they had paused every so often to listen behind them until Ronin was satisfied that they had not been observed entering the portal and that there was no pursuit. After more than half a Spell, the tunnel commenced to slant more sharply downward and they had to be more careful of their footing. The walls grew slimy and different in texture and Ronin had G'fand bring the light closer to the side. Masses of a grey-blue lichen completely covered the walls, glinting oddly in the light.

Ronin told G'fand to gut the flame. At once they were engulfed in an eerie bluish glow. 'The lichen is phosphorescent,' G'fand exclaimed. 'I have seen the like in some of the food-growing vats. It's thrown away.' They found that they had to get used to the new light. Light colours – G'fand's shirt, for instance, where the fabric showed through the grime and dried sweat – jumped out disconcertingly; other dark colours vanished altogether unless one was very close to them.

The low seething sound that had been with

them since they first entered the tunnel grew more distinct although they were still at a loss to define it.

They paused once to eat and rest, pulling at the tough pressed food from the bands, backs against the cushiony walls, legs stretched out before them. They talked of inconsequential matters, deliberately avoiding certain topics that were all too much on their minds.

They resumed the march and presently the sound increased in volume with such a rush that they felt as if they had opened an unseen door. It washed over them, reverberating down the tunnel, and they perceived a slight change in the light.

Just ahead they found a gigantic aperture in the wall to their right. There was a glow beyond; coloured lights swam. A promontory beckoned to them.

They looked out into a cavern so vast that it seemed to have no end. Streaks of pastel light drew themselves upon the air, and by their uncertain illumination Ronin and G'fand were able to make out the enormous arch of the waterfall thundering out from a rock face, cascading down in a froth of turbid silvery spray into the bed of a snaking river glinting far far below. The echoing boom of the kinetic water reflected back at them like a physical presence enfolding them. They stood transfixed at the sight.

G'fand said something but Ronin could not hear him for the noise. He leaned closer and repeated, 'I never knew such a thing still existed. I had read – it is something out of legend!'

Ronin turned to him. 'Time to go,' he yelled over the roar.

Apparently the glowing lichen needed a great deal of moisture in order to survive, for as they left the waterfall behind them, they noticed that the breeze was now less damp. With that the light became dim and they began to encounter patches of bare wall with increasing frequency until G'fand was forced to relight the torch.

Ronin had estimated that they had descended over a kilometre – although they had actually walked many times that – when he spied something ahead. A lighter patch of darkness. Cautiously but with an increasing sense of anticipation, they approached it. And at last they found themselves standing at the end of the tunnel.

Before them a wide ramp led down to a broad avenue that seemed to be roughly the centre of a dizzying jumble of buildings extending away on all sides, vanishing in the thick air. The structures were bewildering in their construction, each one a complex of styles and shapes apparently mortared together at random. Large windows crowded upon small ones, balconies cut into rooftops of abutting buildings, what they took to be doorways hung suspended five and six storeys above street level.

G'fand gaped. And for an instant Ronin experienced a vertigo so intense that he almost fell. He blinked. And breathed slowly and deeply, exhaling more than he inhaled to empty his system and replenish it.

Beside him, G'fand whispered in an awed voice, 'It is. It must be. The City of Ten Thousand Paths.' Ronin looked at his transfigured face. 'The city of our forefathers, where everything was possible. Ronin, I could have been anything I desired here. They knew – so much, so much.' He shook his head and gripped Ronin's arm. 'You do not know what this means! It is like a dream – all that I wished for and had no hope of obtaining. It is all here!'

Ronin smiled briefly. 'Do you remember when we were young they used to frighten us when we were mischievous with tales of the City of Ten Thousand Paths?'

G'fand could not tear his eyes away from the cityscape. 'Yes.' He nodded. 'They tried to scare me, but I paid them little heed. As a child I was afraid of nothing.'

'And now?'

His breath quickened. His voice was a whisper. 'And now – now I am frightened of a great many things.'

The sweet smell of ancient decay was in the air, and the soft dry tickle at the back of the throat caused by aeons of fine dust floating like gravid spores, cloying, as if they had entered a garden filled with dying flowers.

And they went down the broad ramp into a dense and appalling silence. The creak of their leather, the soft slap of their boots against the rough metal, seemed to be swallowed whole in that vast bowl of quietude.

They tried to use the central avenue but found that, inexplicably, no doorways or windows were to be found on the sides of the buildings facing them. So they were obliged, perforce, to choose at random one of the narrow, twisting streets of which there were a bewildering profusion.

Numerous balconies of all sizes sculpted with decorative cementwork hung above their heads and very little light filtered through the maze of architecture. Yet it was enough to see satisfactorily without the aid of the torch.

And the city was not without an aura, promising a mysteriousness like the aroma of an exotic spice sniffed from far away: powerful, elusive.

The streets were cobbled in stone, slightly rounded down the centre so that it was higher than the sides. They shone dully in the diffused light.

There was no sign of refuse or decay out here although sections of the cobbles appeared to be so dark that it seemed as if dirt had been ground into them for centuries until it was now part of the stone.

They heard it at the same time, their heads lifted, questing. It had sounded like the tail end of a growl. They stopped and listened but the silence had closed down upon them again so that even the sounds of their breathing seemed muffled and peculiar to them. They drew their swords, glint of light on polished metal.

Ronin pointed with the tip of his blade to a small wooden door set in a two-storey building just behind them. G'fand nodded. They moved carefully along the cobbles, aware that they were not used to the surface. G'fand flattened himself against the wall of the building just beyond the door as Ronin inched it open with the toe of his boot and stood back.

The interior was dark. They heard no sound. Ronin made a sign and G'fand nodded again and they went swiftly and silently through the doorway. Ronin immediately stepped to one side so that his body would not be silhouetted by the light from outside. He turned, and shoved G'fand to the side, into the shadows.

The room appeared to be much larger than he had anticipated because it was very deep. He could make out wooden beams set at intervals along the low ceiling and the deep shadows of heavy furniture. Nothing moved.

Then there came a low cough from a corner and

now they could make out two red pinpoints, low, glowing, remote. Outside, the golden light filtered down and the silence hung like a thick winter's shroud. The pinpoints moved and there was another cough, louder, more menacing. The red eyes stared unblinkingly at him, black pupils at their centres very small. They advanced on him. Outside, the silence was a protection against danger, the light spilling like thick honey assuring safe passage. It was part of another world, as remote and unattainable as the Salamander's atrium.

Ronin crouched, turned sideways, gripped his sword with both hands, muscles along his arms and thighs tensing as he heard the soft scraping.

The eyes, half a metre above the floor, were not human, of that he was certain. He moved slowly to the left, attempting to coax the thing into the light from the open doorway, but it kept steadfastly to the darkness. The scraping came again. Ronin was now almost shoulder to shoulder with G'fand.

The thing moved towards them and below the baleful gaze of the eyes a very dim glow of long yellow teeth appeared and then winked out. A soft clicking. The cough came again, and Ronin advanced to meet the shape, moving into the deeper shadows.

'Come back – ' G'fand whispered, but he was cut short by a clear dry laugh.

Light blazed in front of them, illuminating the room: a torch.

'Frost!' breathed G'fand.

Ronin looked first at the little man, because he held the torch. He was on a staircase off to their right, which they had not been able to see before. He walked down the wooden stairs and over to the thing, which crouched two metres in front of them, touching a hand to its back. He had an odd gait.

'Ahahaha! Hynd guards the way,' said the little man in a peculiar raspy voice. He grinned ingenuously.

He was not over a metre in height, his gaunt face belying his thick barrel chest. He had long white hair held in place by a dark leather band and a grizzled beard with more grey than white in it. He had a high forehead and cheekbones, a long thin nose, dark green eyes set wide apart. Ronin was certain that his skin had a yellowish tinge. His mouth split again as he laughed.

The thing, which he now scratched behind its small ears, and to which Ronin now directed his attention, had a different countenance entirely. It had a long wicked-looking snout covered in short brown fur and its large red eyes gleamed from out of a long tapering skull. Its body was perhaps two metres in length, its four legs ending in clawed toes. It had a long thin tail that whipped back and forth like a piece of wire. The body was shiny, covered in a hide ridged and scaly. The whiskers on its snout flicked the air continuously. In all, it partially resembled the rodents that inhabited the Freehold's walls. Except for the size.

'Allow me to introduce myself,' said the little

man. 'I am Bonneduce the Last.' He bowed, then cocked his head quizzically. 'And you are – ?'

Ronin told him.

'And of course you have already met Hynd,' laughed Bonneduce the Last, 'my friend and protector.'

The animal coughed again, and Ronin saw clearly the sharpness of its teeth. The little man bent to its ear. 'Friends.' It was like an exhalation. 'Friends.'

'You take a great deal for granted,' G'fand said. Ronin sheathed his sword.

Bonneduce the Last lifted his thick eyebrows. 'Is that so? You are from up there.' He gestured. 'There is no reason for you to wish me harm. Quite the contrary.'

'Huh,' grunted G'fand. 'You have not met with our Security daggam.'

'How did you know we were from the Freehold?' asked Ronin softly.

'Bones told me,' the little man answered, his head still cocked.

'What!' G'fand sheathed his blade.

'But I have forgotten my manners,' said Bonneduce the Last. 'You must forgive me setting Hynd out. After all, one cannot be too careful; no indeed, not these days.' He sighed, walked to a wall, and set the torch in a blackened metal niche. Ronin saw then that one leg was shorter than the other. 'Times past it was different, oh my, yes. One could walk the paths with no need of protection at all.' He turned back to them. 'But that was a long time ago, a long time' – he shook his head –

'before the Dark Sections. But now – ' He shrugged resignedly. 'Well, times change, bringing with them their own fortunes.'

He waved an arm. 'But come, make yourselves comfortable, for I know that you have travelled hard and far this day. And please, do not be concerned with Hynd.' He touched the animal on the snout and it lay down with a sigh. 'You see, he knows you now – your scent – he will not harm you.'

They sat in wide comfortable chairs while Bonneduce the Last closed the front door and went to fetch wine and food.

The dark panelled walls, the tall heavily carved cabinets, the huge stone fireplace filled with fragrant black wood and white ashes, the massive plush chairs in which they reclined, all exuded age and a singular kind of dignity.

Hynd had put his long snout on his forepaws and was now asleep. From somewhere within the depths of the house they heard a soft precise ticking. G'fand rose and moved about the room, peering at objects of unreflective metal and polished stone, running his fingertips along the edges of the sculpted wood. His face was dark and worried.

Ronin looked at him. 'What troubles you?'

G'fand tapped distractedly at the wood. 'I am ashamed to tell you. I – do not know. You told me what the Magic Man said, about there being people on the surface, people on the planet other than those in the Freehold. You know, to be told all your life that one thing is true, to believe it, even though it is not what you want to believe – oh, this is not making any sense.' He turned to Ronin. 'But now that we have actually met another being, I – ' He glanced quickly at the sleeping animal. 'Can we trust him, do you think?'

'Pull up that chair,' Ronin said softly. 'Now listen carefully to me. This discovery is quite incredible but there are too many ramifications for me to be able to spend any time being shocked. It is true that we know virtually nothing about this man, who he is, where he comes from – although it is certain he is not from here despite the fact that he seems familiar enough with the city. Which is the point. I was sent here to find a manuscript. The Magic Man told me it would be difficult, but Chill take him! he did not explain just *how* difficult it would be. I think he knew precisely how much to tell me in order to keep my interest. This city is so huge that we could spend countless Cycles here and not find the manuscript.' He turned his head momentarily to make sure that they were still alone. 'Now this can be invaluable to us. I know what to look for, where it resides; perhaps he can tell us how to get there. He – '

They heard a small noise, and the subject of their discussion returned carrying an enormous silver tray with finely etched sides loaded with plates of fired clay, glazed and shiny, wooden bowls of food, and skins of wine.

'I trust that I have brought you enough to eat,' he said. 'But there is more inside.' He set the tray down on a low table in front of them.

While they ate hungrily, the little man talked.

He turned to G'fand. 'I perceive that you are still somewhat wary of Hynd. I do not want that, so perhaps an explanation is in order. You see' – he patted his short leg as he walked over to a high wooden stool – 'I cannot move as swiftly as I once did.' He chuckled. 'I disagreed with something that tried to eat me.' He pulled over the stool and sat near them, his short leg swinging back and forth. 'He saved my life – '

'From what?' interrupted G'fand.

The little man's face darkened. 'You would not believe me if I told you.'

'Oh, I would be most in – '

'Do you know what he is?'

'Part rodent,' Ronin said.

Bonneduce the Last nodded, obviously pleased. 'Yes, indeed. Quite correct. But as you can see, he is a hybrid, a cross – '

' – between two different species of animals,' finished G'fand.

The little man raised his eyebrows. 'Aha, we have a scholar in our midst,' he exclaimed, delighted. 'Oh, yes. Hynd is part crocodile, a water creature which I believe died out centuries ago. You see before you the product of millennia of change.' He leaned down and gently stroked the horny back. It rippled slightly and Hynd made a small sound in his sleep. 'Many peoples believed that crocodiles were gods,' he said.

G'fand wiped his hands. 'Will you aid us, we have come in search of – '

'Please.' Bonneduce the Last held up his hands.

'Whatever it is will wait now. You are tired. Rest first. Then we shall talk.'

'But we have little time,' said G'fand.

Bonneduce the Last slipped down off the stool and walked in his odd gait to the front door. 'One does not hurry here.' He slid a thick bolt across the door. 'Darkness is here. It brings things on its heels, things you are better off not encountering.' He turned and went to the fireplace. 'That is why you met Hynd first. I knew of your coming but not when you would arrive.' He knelt and began to light the fire. 'Night was falling as you came and I take no chances, not these days anyway. Had you come in my yesterdays you would have encountered me first.' The flames shot up all at once and the room glowed with light and warmth. They began to feel drowsy with their stomachs full, the heat beside them, and the tensions of the journey finally dissipating. 'But now, we are in a different age, and nightmares stalk the world.'

Ronin, at the edge of sleep, came awake. 'What do you mean?'

Bonneduce the Last stood up with his back to the fire and stretched. 'More anon. Now sleep must come. Blankets are in the cupboard and here is a pitcher of water and a basin. These chairs are large and Hynd is here.' He started up the stairs, then stopped and turned. 'In the morning we shall talk of your purpose in coming to the City and I shall aid you as best I may.' They heard his uneven footsteps climbing the stairs after he was lost to sight.

'What do you think?' G'fand asked as he opened the cupboard and pulled out two woven blankets.

Ronin was splashing water on to his face. He shrugged. 'We have little choice. This seems to be a safer place than we could find on our own.' He removed his corselet and shirt, pouring water over the shirt in an attempt to get out the dried blood that had seeped through the corselet's mesh. 'I cannot see that he means us harm, despite what you may think of the animal. He is right, best to get some sleep. The morning will take care of itself.'

Something reached down and pulled him out of sleep. At first he thought it was a sound and he was at once fully awake. The quiet sonorous ticking, the gentle collapse of ashen logs in the fireplace. Nothing more.

G'fand slept peacefully in the chair across from him. He looked at Hynd. The creature was awake, staring intently at the front door, as if he could see through it. He gave a low cough.

Ronin uncovered himself. The blanket slipped to the floor with barely a rustle. Hynd's ears twitched but he did not turn his head. Ronin grasped the hilt of his sword and stood quietly next to the creature. He strained his ears but could hear nothing outside.

After a time, Hynd's ears twitched twice, then he lowered his head, closed his eyes, and apparently went to sleep. Ronin exhaled a long breath.

His shirt was still wet but he donned his corselet and went back into the recesses of the room. He had it in mind to discover the source of the ticking, but as he passed the foot of the stairs, he heard a tiny sound from above. He paused. Oddly, the sound carried clearly on the heavy air. He turned and silently climbed the stairs.

There were two rooms, roughly the same size, both accessible from a square hallway. Light danced in one room and Ronin went to the doorway, peered in.

Bonneduce the Last knelt on a small rug of intricate and peculiar design with his back to the doorway. 'Come in, Ronin, come in,' he said without turning.

Ronin knelt beside him. The little man held several small objects in his fist. He shook them lightly.

'Did you hear me on the stairs?' asked Ronin.

'I knew you would hear the sounds.' And the white shapes tumbled from his opened palm on to the bare floor. He stared intently at them for long minutes. There were seven in all. Glyphs were etched into their many sides. He scooped them up, shook them again. Ronin heard the tiny rattle.

'I think something was at the door,' Ronin said softly. 'Hynd was up.'

The little man nodded. 'I have no doubt. His hearing is quite keen.' He flung the pieces on to the floor once again.

'Those are the Bones,' Ronin whispered.

Bonneduce the Last studied them with his green eyes but said nothing until he had gathered them up into his hand.

'The Bones, yes,' and his voice was like the

tolling of a far-off bell. 'I roll the Bones.' A sadness came into his eyes, a terrible light shining far back in their recesses, like the agony of ages. 'I am aptly named, you see.' He rolled the Bones upon the floor and their tiny clatter seemed now to echo with tantalizing intimations. He scooped them up.

'They are so ancient that even I cannot trace their lineage. They are used and passed on. It is said that they are fashioned from the ivory teeth of the giant crocodile, a godlike creature that was purported to have lived in a certain valley, along the banks of a wide rich muddy river.' He shrugged. 'It is quite possible. Indeed, they are carved of a singular ivory.'

Very softly Ronin said, 'And what do they tell you, the Bones, when you roll them?'

Bonneduce the Last shook them in his fist and cocked his head to one side. 'Why, I should think that would be obvious,' he answered. 'I see what is to be.'

The Bones rattled in his hand. 'Of course they cannot tell me everything and frequently the outcomes of those occurrences which interest me most are denied me. Some events are clear, others are merely vague outlines.' He shrugged. 'But it is what I do.'

There was a long silence after he had rolled the Bones once more. And then, for the first time, he spoke while they were upon the floor. 'They talk about you,' he said slowly.

Ronin felt a moment of irrational chill. 'It is nonsense,' he said. 'I do not wish to hear it.'

The little man stared at the pieces of ivory. 'You do not fear it,' he said simply. 'Why then?'

The question had such innocence that Ronin was momentarily taken aback. Then something crawled within him again. 'I do not know.' His palm strayed to the gleaming hilt of his sword.

'You do not fear death,' Bonneduce the Last said, with a peculiar intonation. 'That is good, for soon you shall understand its impermanence. Yet deep within you lies a fear which you – '

'Enough!' cried Ronin, lurching to his feet and striking out at the grouping of ivory with his boot. It skittered across the floor. Bonneduce the Last did not move, nor did he speak. He knelt in the same position and did not turn as Ronin angrily strode from the room, even after the sound of his boots could be heard descending the ancient stairs.

Eventually, Bonneduce the Last sighed deeply and got up, made his limping way across the old wooden floorboards. He bent here and there, retrieving the scattered Bones, piece by piece, until he had them all in the palm of his hand. They had never felt so heavy to him, and he gripped them until his knuckles shone as white as the ivory.

He paused then, as if he were to be allowed a choice. He shook his head, and limped slowly back to the rug of intricate and peculiar design, kneeling as before. Very slowly and very deliberately he rolled the Bones upon the floor, and read what their configuration revealed. He wiped the warm sweat from his palms by rubbing them down his breeches.

He scooped up the Bones and rather more quickly now rolled them six more times, so that at length he had rolled them a total of seven times. To see if it would make any difference.

It did not. And he shivered involuntarily.

Golden light streamed down, its slanting rays interrupted and diffused by the ornate structures on all sides. The alleyway was narrow and cramped and mysterious as it wended its meandering way through the bewildering labyrinth of the City.

Dust motes danced in the pale light and the silence had a thickness that he now wore with a grateful intensity. He had gone past the sleeping G'fand and, ignoring Hynd's curious stare, had unbolted the door and strode quickly but at random along the alley until he could no longer see the house.

He stopped at last and sat on an old and dusty wooden keg, outside the open doorway to a shop, its time-beaten sign swinging from a black metal pole above his head. The sign was virtually blank now, scrubbed of all but a few scraps of glyphs, mute but unbroken.

He drew one leg up against his chest, letting the other hand, the heel rapping softly against the side of the keg. It sounded hollow. He closed his eyes and leaned his head back against the small-paned window of the shop. He tried to think of why he had stopped the little man from speaking, but nothing came to him. He thought, At least I should be curious. He was. But –

* * *

'Where is he?'

G'fand looked up and dropped the cold bone from last night's meal into the other remnants of the food that had not been cleared away. He wiped his greasy lips on the back of his sleeve. He shrugged. 'I just got up. I thought perhaps he was upstairs.'

The little man descended the stairs, saw that the bolt was off the door. 'Out then,' he said, and set about gathering up the dishes.

'Is it safe?' asked G'fand, getting up. He put his hands at the small of his back and stretched.

'Oh, perfectly. Hynd will see to him.'

G'fand frowned. 'What does that mean?'

The voice drifted in from the recesses of the house. 'I imagine he is out catching breakfast while keeping an eye on our friend.'

G'fand walked about the room restlessly until the little man returned carrying a fresh skin of wine. 'You seem quite familiar with this city.' He made a sharp gesture at the windows with the edge of his hand. He turned. 'It is the City of Ten Thousand Paths, as Ronin said.'

Bonneduce the Last poured wine for G'fand. 'It is,' he said without pause.

The Scholar crossed the room, looked out of a window. Dust clouded his view. He wiped a small leaded pane with his sleeve but it did little good; the glass, like the cobbles of the streets, seemed ingrained with dirt. 'So ancient.' It was almost a whisper, as quiet as a tear falling. 'Yet you know all about it.'

Bonneduce the Last placed the wine skin on the

low table before him. 'I know many things.' Perhaps too many, he thought.

'Then tell me,' G'fand said with great bitterness, 'how we could evolve from the people who created these wonders.'

'You are a scholar, are you not?'

G'fand's eyes blazed briefly but his voice held a note of despair. 'Now you mock me.'

The little man crossed to him with his peculiar stride. He seemed genuinely grieved. 'No, no, lad. You must not think that.' He touched G'fand, indicated that he should sit. They went back to the middle of the room and G'fand reached compulsively for the wine. 'No, you see, I wanted to be sure.'

The Scholar looked up. 'Of what?'

'That you really did not know.'

'I could have been lying,' G'fand said with some indignation.

The little man's face creased as he laughed. 'I think not.'

Eventually G'fand allowed himself to smile for a moment. 'You will tell me then?'

Just a boy, thought Bonneduce the Last. And he said, 'Yes.' He sat down across from G'fand, the large chair towering over him comically. He crossed his ankles, rubbed his maimed leg along the thigh. 'When the time came,' he began quietly, 'to quit the surface of the world, when there was no other choice but to perish – which many did, by the way – the remnants of the states and nations sent the leading proponents of their cultures to work on the enormous project of carving out a hospitable home beneath the planet's crust.'

G'fand was transfixed by the little man's voice, which held tremendous force despite its softness. He was startled when the voice ceased and Bonneduce the Last cocked his head as if listening to a far-off sound. G'fand listened also but all he could hear was the dark and sonorous ticking from the interior of the house.

After a time, the little man continued. 'The mages and the men of science – you call them Magic Men, I believe . . . were forever at war because, I suppose, the foundations of their work are diametrically opposed. At the time of the city's formation, the mages held sway, and so with the unwilling help of the men of science they created the City of Ten Thousand Paths.' Bonneduce the Last sighed a little and his extraordinary emerald eyes turned inward momentarily. 'It could have been the beginning of dreams; there was room enough for all here. Perhaps they did not work at it, who knows?' He stood abruptly and went to a glass cabinet along the far wall. His hands moved and he returned holding two bits of dull metal. He threw them casually towards G'fand, who caught them instinctively. 'Press them together,' said the little man. And although the bits seemed identical, G'fand could only keep them together by exerting a great deal of pressure; they naturally pushed each other away.

Bonneduce the Last sat once more and gestured with his head. 'Like the metal, the different factions repelled each other. Gradually, the mages began to lose control and the men of science gained ascendancy. In the end, they would have nothing to do with the city their forefathers had helped build under duress, and so they led those that would follow them – a goodly number – upward into the virgin rock above the city because it was fabulously rich in the ores and metals they required, and because it was easier to seal off the city from above. And they constructed the Freehold. And now, over time – ' He shrugged expressively.

There was soft silence for a long time, heavy and lustreless, laden with thoughts of fallen history and forgotten faces.

G'fand shivered involuntarily and got up, leaving the bits of metal apart on the table. Several times he appeared about to say something and each time changed his mind. Finally he said in a choked voice, as if it were difficult for him to articulate, 'We are told that no one lives on the surface of the world. The elements will not allow it.'

The little man, who had been watching him, smiled bleakly. 'So. It depends where you are.' He went and returned the bits of metal to their case. 'The ice reaches farther every day.'

G'fand stared at him, his heart racing. 'Then it's true. Men do walk the surface.'

'Naturally. Did you think I live down here? I must come from time to time – '

'Why did you come this time?'

'To meet some people.'

G'fand leaned forward. 'Who?'

Bonneduce the Last was silent.

The Scholar gave a tiny exclamation of sound, as if he had been hit in the stomach, and he relaxed back into the chair. 'I do not want to know,' he said, his lips barely moving. And he was talking to himself.

Bonneduce the Last was as still as a statue, his eyes lost in shadow beneath his bushy brows.

'What is it like Up there?' The question floated on the air like unused smoke and quite suddenly it was most important that he know.

'Perhaps you will see for yourself soon,' said the little man, knowing that it was not enough.

G'fand stood over him and said in anguish. 'I must know now.'

'This is a desperate time,' said Bonneduce the Last. 'I have not been to the City of Ten Thousand Paths in a long while. In that time, many things have died and many things have come into being. Evil things.' He shook his head.

G'fand knelt before him. 'Look, I want some answers. Is that really so much to ask?'

Bonneduce the Last stared at G'fand for a time and there was a sadness in his eyes that the Scholar did not understand. He looked suddenly older. Around them, the ticking sounded like a constant admonition. At length the little man said, 'I will tell you what I am able.'

G'fand nodded. 'What are you doing here then?'

He spread his hands. 'I will know that only after it is done.'

The Scholar's face twisted. 'You make a fool of me.'

'Believe me, I do not. It is the truth.'

197

'All right. Suppose I can believe that. I am beginning to see that perhaps anything is possible. Tell me then who you are.'

'You do not want to know that.'

G'fand's annoyance grew. 'I just asked you, did I not?'

The sadness came to Bonneduce the Last's eyes again. 'Yes,' he said softly. 'You have asked.'

Ronin's eyes snapped open. He sat very still and inhaled again to make sure of the direction. The sharp smell came from behind him: the interior of the shop. He lowered his leg slowly so that they both were against the side of the keg. He heard movement now, stealthy and difficult to discern.

He drew his sword and leapt to the street, whirling. He heard scufflings, then scratchings and small pantings. He went inside.

It was cool and dark and it took him a moment to adjust and he knew that it was a mistake because anything or anyone smart enough would have attacked him immediately.

Nothing rushed him. There was a heavy snap as of a wooden board being split and then a brief inhuman cry. He moved warily between huge wooden casks. Wine? He pulled cobwebs off his face.

Directly ahead of him he heard a cough. He crouched, sword ready, and saw the red eyes, the long muzzle. The mouth split suddenly, oddly akin to an absurd grin. The long teeth were dark, appeared wet.

Hynd padded up to him and coughed again,

softly. Behind the animal, in the darkness, he could just make out the twisted mass of a broken carcass. He put a hand out, tentatively touched the soft fur of the muzzle.

They went out together into the alleyway and the light, and Ronin saw the blood still dripping from the long snout.

'Well,' he said, walking alongside the creature, in and out of the bars and patches of shadows, 'I trust you have eaten your fill.'

For more than a Spell they followed the little lane as it made its crooked way through the city. For a while dark, narrow alleys led off the lane to right and left – often at peculiar angles. Then abruptly, solid walls lined their path, unbroken, window-less, and doorless. Long narrow balconies with fluted scrollwork ran above their heads, so what illumination they had was thin and watery. The walls were of rough stucco, chipped here and there, discoloured near the bottom, or unglazed brick with pronounced striations, as if they had been manufactured in layers.

The lane was fairly straight, which only increased their uneasiness. Should they encounter any hostile life – according to Bonneduce the Last, there was an abundance of that – they would have no room to manoeuvre and only one path of retreat.

However, nothing approached them, and at last they began again to pass wandering side streets. Sometimes after this they encountered a fork in the lane.

★ ★ ★

'Scrolls?' he had said. 'There are countless scrolls housed in different sections of the city.'

Ronin had reached out the slip of fabric. 'Yes, well, perhaps this will help.' He gave it to the little man, indicating with a finger the glyphs the Magic Man had written.

Bonneduce the Last had nodded, as if to himself, and Ronin had thought he had heard him say, 'It is clear now, yes,' but he could not be sure.

'I was told,' Ronin had said, 'that it would be in a private house and not a library.'

'Quite so,' the little man had said.

'You know the scroll?' G'fand had asked.

'No, no. But I recognize this glyph style. It could only come from Ama-no-mori, an isle I know very little about – I doubt anyone does.'

'Then it does not come from here,' Ronin had said.

'Well, yes and no. The City of Ten Thousand Paths brought with it, when it went below, emissaries from many lands and many cities. Ama-no-mori, the floating world, sent a great magus, dor-Sefrith, who caused to be built a house of glazed green brick in a certain section of the city. Therein, I believe, you will find the scroll. If you can reach it.'

The triangular building directly ahead of them created the fork. Off to the right they could make out a wide street that nevertheless seemed quite cluttered with what looked to be collapsed building materials. Dusty light dappled the ancient cobbles and, perhaps because of the haze, the shadows seemed to shift and waver. To the left, tall arabesqued buildings cast deep shadows into the street for as far as they could see.

As they moved into the mottled shadows of the street on their left, Ronin recalled what the little man had said: 'I shall describe your route but I must warn you that it takes you through a Dark Section. It cannot be avoided if you are to make the journey and return by nightfall. You *must* return by nightfall, it that clear? Too many things abroad at night, too many. Stay to the path I give you and do not falter. Remember, speed is of the essence because the city keeps changing now. I trust this will get you through.'

The cobbled street was cool and they shivered a little. Stone creatures, grotesque and fantastic of visage, leered down at them from cornices and buttresses.

'How I wish there was more time,' lamented G'fand, his eyes moving over the architecture, drinking it in. 'There is so much to learn here.'

'You know we cannot tarry.'

'Yes.' He nodded sadly. 'Bonneduce the Last is right. There is so much danger now.'

Ronin glanced at him, on the point of asking him what had changed his mind about the little man, when the faint susurration reached his ears. One moment the silence seeped sluggishly along the walls of the high buildings, muffling the creaking of their leather, the soft chink of metal on metal from their gear, the next they seemed to be surrounded by sound. It was as if they were hearing, through some trick of architectural acoustics, the combined voices of a multitude. The murmuring as it came upon them, like waves upon a lone and desolate shore, words blurred and indistinct, held overtones, a presence, a super-reality.

They looked in all directions but could make out nothing in the gloom. There was no doorway close to them, no window; the narrow balconies were empty.

'What is it?' G'fand asked.

Ronin said, 'We are in a Dark Section.' His hand strayed to the hilt of his sword.

They moved on, and still the stone carvings regarded them, lips pulled back from bared teeth, and the sea of sound licked along the humped length of the crooked street, increasing in volume.

There was no space between buildings here, although they obviously were separated by walls on the inside, for they passed numerous doors now with individual, excessively carved fronts that seemed somehow unsteady, as if about to give way and expose the bare skeletons of the structures. As they advanced, an increasing number of windows opened on to the street. There appeared to be no order in their placement. They crowded one another in profusion, some just centimetres apart, others overlapping in chaotic riot.

Often, at the periphery of their vision, the pair thought they could detect movement behind the windows, furtive and unnatural, but each time their eyes darted to the spot, it was gone. G'fand particularly seemed disturbed by this.

The muttering continued unabated from all

about them, which, unaccountably, increased the sensation they had of being watched. It occurred to Ronin then that there was a cadence to the sounds and, beyond a rhythm, melody.

They rushed on, almost at a trot, the jangle of metal against metal all but drowned in the pulsing sound. Chanting, Ronin thought. He told G'fand, who listened through his mounting unease, and nodded. But, he said, it was nothing he had ever read about. The words, long meaningless syllables, nevertheless chilled them. And as if one were the cause of the other, the shadows deepened and a cold wind blew along the street.

The chanting was louder now, swelling like an engulfing tide, and Ronin increased their pace until they were running headlong down the lane. The Bladesman in him abhorred this flight; his training was for Combat and his immediate reaction was to turn and find the source of the chanting, which seemed somehow to be affecting their senses.

They were running slowly, too slowly, the dark windows crawling by, the air so gluey and sticking to them that they had to cleave a path through it. And all the while the sound advanced on them from behind, rolling over them heavily.

But through the murk Ronin realized that Combat now was time-consuming and useless. At the back of his brain a tiny voice screamed and screamed: Get out! The trouble was that it was getting softer, and he had to strain to hear it, to remember what it was screaming.

Once or twice G'fand paused, panting, moving

towards the houses, and Ronin, not quite knowing why, pulled him back, set him to running again.

But it was hard, the cobbles slippery and suddenly insubstantial, the breath pounding in their lungs. Small chitterings assailed them, and heavy slitherings from behind them, gruntings and weird moanings, so that the backs of their necks crawled. Tears seemed to be streaming from G'fand's eyes. The street closed in upon them and the stone creatures above their heads proliferated, flocking on the overhanging ledges.

And still they ran, with a dogged singlemindedness now. Shrieks came from behind them, closer now, and the chanting, ritualistic, almost liturgical, reached its peak. Stone walls turned to rubber.

Both of them saw the light of the cross street at the same time, Ronin blinking his eyes to keep the connection so that his pumping legs would know where to go. G'fand began to waver, slowing down, and Ronin reached out blindly, dragging him forward towards the light. Why? he thought. Waves of sound washed over him and his vision went momentarily. Then someone, from very far away, a distant bright land, said: 'Get out!' And his legs dragged themselves forward, one last lunge, the screaming came – what? – ignore, forward to the slitherings, light and . . .

They stood in what appeared to be a wide avenue. Light streamed into their eyes, dusty and golden. G'fand dropped to the cobbles, chest heaving. Ronin turned, peering back into the deep shadows of the narrow lane. Nothing emerged, and – his head lifted – yes, sweet silence descended on to his aching ears.

Old shops lined either side of the avenue, their doorways open, small-paned windows dusty and dim. Above, their signs, of scarred wood and beaten brass, creaked in the warm breeze. Higher still, where one might expect windows to be, were solid walls of fired brick and mortar, broken at regular intervals by deftly carved stonework.

'They are not decorative.'

'What?'

The Scholar pointed. 'The carvings on these buildings. Those are glyphs, very old, but still – '

'Messages?'

'Their history, perhaps. If I only had time – '

The avenue described a turning to the left and they followed this at a fast pace and abruptly found themselves at the edge of a vast plaza. The warm light shone unhindered here and G'fand scanned the vault above them in an attempt to discover the source. Near them now were only low buildings, but in the distance tall structures rose, their outlines blurred in the haze.

As they walked out into the plaza they noted that it was floored with alternating segments of deep brown and light tan stone, the former laced with chips of a mineral that caught the light and threw it back at them in dazzling pinpoints. The stones were precisely cut in shapes roughly like a triangle with its top point cut off so that it formed a four-sided figure, wider at one end. They were larger along the perimeter of the plaza and grew gradually smaller as the pair progressed towards the centre.

They came upon several low wide benches of a textured sandy stone, polished along the seat, grouped in a semicircle around a low oval structure. They sat gratefully down and rested for a time in the heavy molten light.

Ronin took a long pull from the waterpipe and ate some food without really tasting it. G'fand went to inspect the oval in front of them. It was perhaps a metre in height, lidless and hollow. G'fand stooped, found a small piece of rubble, dropped it down. After a long time there came a faint splash.

Ronin got up and joined him.

'A well,' said G'fand. 'But judging by the water level, it has not been of much use lately.'

The walls of the well, constructed from the same sandy stone as the benches, were covered by the same style of carving as they had seen on the avenue. G'fand sat on his haunches to get a better look.

'Can you make anything of it?'

G'fand frowned in concentration. 'Uhm, well, it is quite a sophisticated language – more than our own.' He pointed with a forefinger. 'You see here, judging by the relatively infrequent repetitions, the glyph range must be enormous.' He shook his head sadly. 'Give me, oh, twelve or fourteen Sign and the right texts – although I suppose I could make do without – given more time, and I might be able to read this. Now – ' But he was still excited and would not leave the side of the well until Ronin, deciding that it was time to move on, spoke to him.

He looked up then, reluctantly, and seemed about to say something, when a movement caught his eye and he motioned to Ronin.

Off in the distance, three or four animal-like shapes moved among another grouping of benches. At first Ronin thought that they would move in another direction, but then the breeze freshened and he knew that they were downwind, and if the animals had not noticed them by now, they soon would.

The animals came out from under the benches, started hesitantly towards them. There were five of them, four-legged, long muzzles, dingy yellow fur, matted and dirty. They crept closer, and now he could make them out clearly: long forelimbs, hind legs short and thick with bunched muscles, so that they appeared to be crouching as they moved. Squat necks merged into wide powerful-looking shoulders. Their snouts were all mouth.

As they approached from the far side of the well, they spread in a rough semicircle. G'fand stood. He could see their eyes now, hot lemon circles with tiny black pupils.

Ronin slipped his sword from its scabbard. 'Take the right side.'

At the same instant, they stepped from behind the cover of the well.

Black lips drew back from blood-red gums to reveal long curving fangs, blackened, wet with saliva, set in triple rows. The animal nearest Ronin yawned nervously, its jaws hinging open to an impossible angle. Its mouth snapped shut with a clash, and it licked its lips. The eyes regarded him feverishly.

He moved out to his left, reaching for his dagger, flicking it before him with his left hand, facing the animal with his side.

It blurred before his eyes and he knew it was leaping, but it was coming on his left flank instead of straight on. Impossible! He made a pass with the dagger but too late, and the blur was past him and, simultaneously, a second animal bounded at him from in front. The mistake was in treating them as dumb animals, and as the first one had gone beyond him he had corrected his thinking so that now, at the instant of the dual assault from front and rear, he had his legs far apart, knees bent to help absorb impact, the sideways stance already an enormous advantage because the left hand slashed upward with the dagger while the right arced the double-edged sword. The long blade clove the first animal's skull in twain, spraying bits of yellow brain and shards of bone. Almost at the same time, the second animal was upon him, larger and more massive than the other. He tried vainly to flick it from him but the combination of mass and momentum was too much, and it landed upon his left shoulder, spit on the dagger, howling and shuddering as a great gout of black blood splattered hotly against him, viscous and sticky, the stench of it clinging to his nostrils so that for a moment he had trouble breathing. Staggering under the assault, he tried to avoid the long sinewy forepaws reaching for his eyes, scythelike claws scraping the air, great jaws snapping, eyes rolling. Jerking his left hand, raking the dagger through the thing's insides, knowing his right arm was useless as long as the animal was on him, and still it writhed desperately against him. Then something smashed into his side and all the breath went out of him. Flesh came off in strips and he crashed to the stone tiles of the plaza.

On the right of the well, G'fand faced two animals. Nervousness and exhilaration combined within him. Both hands on his sword hilt, he feinted to his right, swung to the left, catching a beast in mid-spring, opening its chest and deflecting somewhat its body. At the same time, he did his best to keep out of the second animal's way.

Ronin had reflexively let go of the dagger. Still he sprawled in the black blood and slime of the dying animal. Pain raced along his side and dimly he wondered how the blow had got through the mail corselet. He turned on to his back and saw the beast – the third one – poised to smite him again with its powerful forepaw. He struggled to get up as the animal crouched low, recognized that there was no time, and channelled all his energy into a mighty two-handed cut. He did not have the leverage that he would have had on his feet, but it was timing and swinging sword and arms as one, using the pivot of his wide shoulders as the power base. The beast leapt at him, so close that he felt the warm puff of fetid breath as the enormous jaws swung wide, heard the thin whine of the talons ripping the air before his head. He swung from right to left, the blade whistling for an instant before it struck the hide, bit into flesh, and Ronin leaned his torso to the right, using the added leverage as the blade cracked the beast's spine and the carcass danced lazily, black blood pumping in spurts, fluttering in the air like funereal lace. The animal toppled in a twisted heap to the paving.

G'fand could not concentrate on both so he ignored the wounded one, attacking the second beast. He knew it was a mistake when he felt the weight of the first one crash on to his back. He staggered, went to his knees, his vision a blur. Then, miraculously, the thing was off him and he felt lighter than air, springing up and slicing into the neck of the advancing second animal with his bloody blade, oblivious to the impact of its forepaw against his shoulder, swinging again and again even after the creature ceased to twitch.

After a time he was dimly aware of a hand on his shoulder, and he turned, staggering slightly to see Ronin standing over the animal he had wounded and forgotten about, the one that had almost killed him. He saw then that Ronin was grinning and he knew that even through his tiredness, his spent exhilaration, he was returning it.

They wiped their wet weapons on the matted pelts and, leaving the corpses where they had fallen, went across the vast plaza, reluctant in the end to leave it, to plunge back into the midst of narrow streets, dark and confined: the recesses of this enigmatic city.

They worked their way down a crooked alleyway, turned right, then right again. They were in a section of the city containing low rambling houses with some space between them. As a result, this area was divided fairly evenly into square blocks. It was lighter here, though not as light as in the plaza, and for once the streets appeared to run quite straight.

They saw small animals, some looking much like the rodents of the Freehold, others bearing no resemblance to any creature they had encountered before. But all seemed small and likely presented little threat to them.

Occasionally they spotted large slitted eyes peering out at them from a dark doorway or a back alley, but there seemed to be no aggressiveness in the stares, only fright. G'fand commented on this, his spirits high, but Ronin was unaccountably worried by what lurked in those eyes. He tried to shake off the feeling, reasoning that they were now quite near the house of glazed brick. Yet it continued to grow.

Ahead lay the last few turnings. It was deathly still. The small skitterings and occasional chatter of the animals had ceased. In the abrupt absence of sound, he fancied he heard the chanting from the Dark Section. But there was nothing on the air.

They moved around a corner and, at last, caught sight of the house of glazed brick, its canted copper roof glowing in the late light. For a long moment they drank in the sight. G'fand gave a short cheer and Ronin smiled. Then they went down the street, Ronin leading the way.

Ronin, intent on his goal, had just passed a

doorway, oversized and gaping blankly, when he simultaneously smelled a sickly wet stench and felt a wave of coldness at the back of his neck.

He drew his blade, spun, its tip catching the light, saw G'fand slammed against the doorframe as he was whipped into the interior of the building. A muffled scream brought him up short as he hurtled through the doorway.

G'fand had not even had time to withdraw his sword. His arms were pinioned at his side. A huge shape gripped him, its dimensions ill defined. Ronin rushed the shape. He had a flashing glimpse of hooded orange eyes, a protrusion, black and strange underneath, and then his sword swung into the thing.

He grimaced as needles of fire raced up his arms like vibrations. His fingers went numb and only by pulling with his free hand on the hilt was he able to disengage the blade. Immediately, the pain subsided.

He panted, wiping the sweat from his eyes, peered into the gloom. The hulk took on some form. It was at least three metres high, with muscled truncated legs terminating in some form of clawed paw or hoof. The light was too dim for Ronin to be sure. A thick and sinuous tail whipped from the rear of the body. The thing's outline kept changing, pulsing like a heartbeat. Then its head swivelled and he saw its face. His breath was a sharp hiss through clenched teeth. His skin crawled.

It had long slitted eyes with narrow inhuman vertical pupils that pulsed with the creature's outline. Two irregular gashes in the flesh served as nostrils. Underneath yawned a mottled hideous beak, wickedly curved and honed, a stunted rigid tongue throbbing grotesquely.

G'fand still struggled feebly in its terrible embrace. Ronin lunged, slashing with the sword. It sank into the scaly flesh and again he gasped as the agony raced through him. He pulled free, swung again and again. And sound came from that frightful maw, a swift ululation, and he knew that it had not been harmed by his attack. G'fand was limp now within the thing's grasp, and cold sweat broke out on Ronin's face as, heedless of the paralysis weakening his arms, he attacked once again.

Alien orange eyes blasting out of the darkness, and the air became thick with the fetid stench of the thing, clotting in Ronin's throat so that his stomach heaved and his lungs laboured as he put all his strength into the arcing blade that clove the air again and again, ceaselessly, and he was a machine now, a machine of death and destruction, the adrenalin pumping through his veins holding against the pain. He ground his teeth, his muscles jumped as he pushed them to their limits. And still the creature stood before him, the shell of its beak working.

His vision began to blur and he was dimly aware that his reflexes had become slowed. Something thick and heavy was moving towards him; he felt the hot wind of its approach, but the connections refused to work and he could not move away, and it whipped into him, rough and scaly, along the side of his head, and his body was thrown violently forward. He fought desperately for balance, lost, reeled into a wall. Just before unconsciousness came, he thought the creature looked towards the recesses of the interior, then he dropped down an endless stairwell into pitch-blackness.

How beautiful it looked, so far above him. Freed by the distance, floating warm and safe. Watching the pale amber light striking obliquely so far away, his detachment was complete. The stippled patterns wavered in the uncertain light. How nice to be lying here at the bottom of the well, watching the world through the distant oval window, dreamily, drifting. He thought idly of rising up and climbing towards the smoky brightness, but he felt too tired. Alone, adrift.

And then he blinked and it broke apart like a bubble rising through water to the surface. He stared blankly at the circle of amber light thrown against the ceiling. He blinked again and full awareness swept over him.

He tried to sit up. Too fast. Made it halfway before his head pulsed with pain. He edged himself along the floor until he put his back against a wall. He sat like that with his head in his hands, relaxing his muscles through force of will, allowing the ache to flow out of them.

He looked for G'fand, found him stretched out on the floor two metres away, deathly pale. Dragging the body slowly over and it felt like two kilometres. Feeling faint breath still within the chest, unstrapping the waterpipe, feeding him water so that he choked a little and the lungs began working more fully. Only then did Ronin gulp thirstily at the pipe. He felt immediately refreshed and went to retrieve his sword.

When he returned, G'fand was sitting up. He rubbed his palms across his face. 'Frost, I feel like I've been crushed,' he whispered. 'Is that thing gone?'

Ronin helped him to his feet. 'Yes. Are you dizzy?'

G'fand waved away his support. 'No. No.' He walked slightly stiff-legged to the doorway, leaned against it. 'The end of our journey. After all this, I trust that the scroll we seek lies within.'

The house of green-glazed brick beckoned in lazy quietude. It stood at the end of the street, a cul-de-sac, and it was unusual enough in this city of unusual architecture to command the entire area. For one thing, it appeared to be many-sided. For another, the sides sloped inward as they rose, so that the second storey was smaller than the first. The glossy bricks were of singular construction: they showed no age; the house looked as if it might have been built last Cycle for all the wear visible.

There were no windows on the sides that faced them. A giant wooden door banded in thick iron strips dominated the front side of the house. Broad steps of black stone with pink and gold veins running through it, polished to a high sheen, led up to the door, which, they saw now that they were close to it, was in fact a slab of red copper.

Perhaps a trick of the oblique light had caused it to take on the appearance of wood.

A ring of black iron, twisting in an endless circle, formed the handle of the door. Ronin grasped it firmly and, putting his shoulder against the copper slab, pushed inward.

There came a soft dry click, as distinct and close as the sound of an insect in a field of high grass on a quiet summer's day, and the door opened.

The odour of spices greeted them, pungent and ingrained in the air as if someone had lit a fragrant fire of aromatic leaves and green twigs and kept it burning for many Sign.

They were in a long high hallway, the ceiling an arch above them, the floor a narrow path of dark polished wood planks laid straight down the centre. Open spaces, deep and dark, between the floor and the walls on either side, gave them the feeling of being suspended in space.

The hallway terminated in three doors of a peculiar polished wood with deep-red grain, banded in beaten brass. Glyphs were carved into each door. Ronin turned to G'fand. 'Can you make anything of these?'

G'fand studied each door. 'I lack the knowledge to be sure. But – ' He peered again at the glyphs. 'Try the third one.'

Turning the burnished brass handle, Ronin found that it opened easily enough.

The first level consisted of six rooms. Thin, exquisitely woven rugs covered the floors, small dark wooden cabinets stood against the walls, which were hung with tapestries of singular manufacture depicting the hunting of strange and grotesque creatures, the paying of tribute to ornately costumed men and women who appeared to be some kind of Saardin. Upon the carpets were numerous low tables of glass and brass within which resided myriad small treasures of cut jewels, ivory, and faience. There was no sign of age, not even a trace of dust.

Within the fourth room, Ronin found an ornate stairway to the second storey. G'fand was busily moving from glass table to glass table, plainly fascinated by the artefacts. Ronin looked about him. 'Make certain you have seen everything down here,' he called to G'fand. 'Then come upstairs and join me.' So saying, he ascended the stairs.

There were three rooms. One was obviously a sleeping chamber, and one, Ronin surmised, an alchemical chamber of some sort, judging by the equipment. The last room was the one he was searching for. Books lined two walls from floor to ceiling – he saw with some surprise that the room was hexagonal. Another wall contained only a six-sided mirror of beaten and polished silver rimmed in deep-green, black-veined onyx, lustrous, translucent. The adjacent wall was filled with racks of scrolls, some rolled on polished wooden dowels, and he crossed to them at once, searching for the glyph heading the Magic Man had written down.

A quicksilver flash caught the periphery of his vision. He turned his head. It seemed to have come from the mirror, but when he looked around he could find nothing in the room that was likely to cause a reflection.

He went over to the mirror and stared at his face. And the flash came again, like light on moving water, dazzling him momentarily.

He no longer stares at himself, but at a formlessness of light and colour, absorbing and infinite. Motion. Hurtling through the patterns, forward, headlong. He experiences a slight sensation of vertigo, the exhilaration of flying, and he hears a soft rustle, as of a forest of leaves blown on a quickening wind.

Abruptly he is in a cool place made all of richly veined marble, lit warmly but dimly. And vast, for he hears the echoes: perhaps voices, the quiet slap of sandals, the rustle of fabric against flesh, tones of discord and harmony.

From a height he drifts through columnated hallways and high-vaulted chambers and gradually he becomes aware of the molten throb of unfamiliar instruments, pounding skins, trip-rolled and muffled, lazy dark chords under gyring melody, hears the peregrine music unfurling, haunting, electric.

A great night-black bird swoops down upon him, wide wings beating the liquid air, and he tries to cover his face, a reflexive motion, and discovers he has no body. He floats, insubstantial, an essence. And still the bird, long feathers shining, stares at him with unblinking crimson and black eyes. Its talons are enormous. Gripped within one is a writhing lizard. The talons open and the creature drops into a fire burning far below. The bird opens its long beak and human laughter booms out.

He sees K'reen then. Her back is to him as she talks to a dark figure which towers over her, but he recognizes the soft bell of her hair, a forest of texture, the shape of her body, silken of skin, hard of muscle, the orbits of her gestures. The figure screams silently at her, slaps her across the face, again and again. Her head whips from side to side. She turns suddenly and looks up at him, and he starts in shock. She has his face, tearful and saddened.

He is in another place within the marble building. Or perhaps it is another building all of marble. A long hallway. Far away at the other end is a tall figure clothed in black lacquered armour ribbed and banded in sea-green jade and twilight-blue lapis lazuli. Perhaps he wears a helm, for his head is oddly shaped, at once chilling and familiar, although he is too distant and the light is too uncertain to say why. Two swords of unequal length hang from his sides in scabbards so long that they almost touch the marble floor. His hands glitter as the figure looks about as if searching for something. Then he strides from the hallway.

Something cold comes. The incense braziers shudder on their bronze chains. A wind is rising. He feels a presence, very close. A frigid wisp, a seeking tendril – *of what?* – writhes and touches his mind. He recoils, as if seared by a blade burning like ice. Below, in the hallway of eternal marble, frigid fires begin to rage, pale and insatiable. He cannot breathe. He gasps and chokes on the dread

219

creeping into him, washing away all resolve. He feels weak and powerless, a child storm-tossed and alone.

Abruptly, within the chaos of his being, through the terror and desperation, he feels sparks of water against his face and body, and he lifts his head to the roiling of purple clouds. An electric clashing is in his ears, and the surface upon which he stands trembles. White light rings the opening sky. He reaches for the pale hand.

The flash comes again, like light on moving water, dazzling him momentarily.

' – not downstairs,' said G'fand from directly behind him.

He started.

'Say, what are you doing? The scrolls are over here.'

Ronin blinked, licked his dry lips. 'I thought – I saw something in the mirror,' he said thickly.

G'fand stepped closer. 'What mirror?'

Ronin focused and saw a six-sided plate of iron, perfectly plain and unreflective. The onyx border seemed to wink at him in the light. He shook his head. The house of a magus.

Then he shrugged and turned. 'Come,' he said.

They took them systematically, by rows. Once, as he worked, he glanced at the six-sided thing on the wall. And thought of what he had experienced, of what it meant. He was certain, now, that Borros spoke the truth: there was a habitable world on the surface. But why the Salamander should choose to lie to him, he had no idea. However, it was clear to him that he was amid a drama of enormous proportions. He understood its nature not at all, yet he would be a fool to ignore the hints at its scope. Up until now boredom and curiosity and a curious perversity, which he always recognized in himself yet was like quicksilver, his strength, and, he imagined, perhaps his ultimate downfall, had guided him to this strange place. Why else was he here? He gave a mental shrug and got on with the search.

The scroll was not there. It seemed inconceivable to them that they could have come so far, overcome all that they had, for naught. Returning empty-handed was not an eventuality Ronin had spent any time considering. To him it was not a matter of the value of the scroll.

He sent G'fand to search the other rooms on this storey while he looked around here. The floor was bare, the dark wood planks rubbed to a high gloss. Again no dust or wear was evident. Over by the walls of books were a pair of low stools unlike any he had seen before. They were constructed of buffed leather, stiff but worn beneath the polish. They were convex, two sides sloping down, the narrower ends curving up, and were attached to crossed wooden legs by a heavy leather strap with an adjustable brass buckle.

Along the wall most closely opposite the door, several glass cases gleamed dully in the light. He crossed to them, saw there were three. The first was empty, although two indentations on the green felt of the bottom indicated that at one time two objects about the size of a large man's hand had lain there. The second case contained an oversized book, from all appearances quite old, opened midway through. A blue fabric marker ran down one page. Both pages were blank. Ronin moved to the third case, where he saw what seemed to be a replica of a hallway, roofless so that one could easily view the interior. It appeared to be constructed of marble. Twelve columns lined the hallway, tiny metal braziers hung at intervals. The model was extraordinarily detailed, the workmanship superb. Ronin leaned closer and the shock of recognition hit him at once. This was a replica of the hallway in the mirror that was not a mirror! He glanced over his shoulder at its blind face once again.

He turned back to the miniature. Here was where the armoured warrior had stood, and there was the entrance through which the terrible presence had been about to enter. He heard again in his mind the lure of the music. He lifted the glass top. As soon as he did so something caught his eye. A sliver of light yellow from under the marble floor. He stared at it for a moment until it struck him what it must be.

He drew his dagger and slipped the point under the side of the replica, lifting slowly, but it did not give. He tried along one end, and was able, after moments of experimentation, to pry it up.

With mounting excitement, he drew out the sheet, knowing somehow that at the top would be written the line of glyphs for which they had been searching. The miniature fell back into place as he released it, and he called to G'fand, as he stared at the black line of their inscription. Below, the scroll was covered from top to bottom with close-written glyphs.

They clapped each other on the back. G'fand held it as they descended the wide curving staircase. He shook his head. 'It is a language I cannot even begin to understand.'

Ronin took it from him. 'Someone will have to decipher it.' He rolled it into as tight a cylinder as he was able. 'Now that we have it, I shall make sure that we do not lose it.'

The shadows were long, the slanting light deep amber as they went down the black stone steps, the gold veins iridescent. The city seemed peaceful; the dense quiet acquiring a languorous lustre as the day waned. They set off back the way they had come, tired but jubilant at the success of their quest.

Perhaps it was the sounds of their voices or the buoyancy of their mood or the vista of the jumbled city, somehow more familiar, that lay before them bathed in the warm light.

Or perhaps it was something else altogether that caused him to fail to see the movement behind them. It came swiftly. A sharp cloying odour. He whirled and his sword was out in the same motion. But it was too late. He was slammed as if by a giant's fist and he reeled into the gutter, tumbling upon the cobbles. Crimson fire was in his lungs and all the breath went out of him. He tried to inhale, gasped weakly.

Through a haze he saw the creature that had attacked them just before they reached the magus's house. Its thick sinuous tail lashed back and forth continuously as it reached curved talons towards G'fand. He had drawn his sword and was doing his best to defend himself. It was ineffectual.

Ronin tried to rise but it was as if he were paralysed. He lay in the gutter, striving to raise his sword, struggling to breathe, watching the thing close with G'fand. The hideous beak opened and closed spasmodically, and then it took hold of G'fand's sword along the blade. The metal crumbled within the grip of its six-fingered hands.

With a mighty effort Ronin came up on his knees, leaning on his sword, head shaking like that of a wounded animal. He gained his feet, staggered, searched for balance. His sword clanged on to the cobbles. Drawing his dagger, he ran at the creature from behind.

Its talons were at G'fand's throat, squeezing. He looked helpless and stunned. Ronin smelled the awful stench and the coldness just before he slammed into the thing's back. It was like hitting a wall. It ignored him. He climbed upon its back, saw dimly G'fand's legs dangling in the air, his eyes bulging. Then the pain engulfed him. Bolts of fire penetrated his flesh and he fought back a scream. Time shifted.

He was a microbe upon a mountain, climbing hopelessly. The dagger in his hand writhed uncontrollably and he almost let it go, but the sight of G'fand's twisted, pain-filled face was before him, and it drove him on. The pain moved through his body and his lower half began to go numb. His legs and feet still churned for purchase on the scaly hide but he could not feel them, they were parts of someone else's body. Still he clawed upward with his free hand and dagger-filled fist. He gasped at the stinking air, but his lungs would not hold the foulness, and he retched, eyes watering. He concentrated on the shining point of the short blade.

All strength seemed to flow out of him. The numbness began to creep upward. Soon it would be at his brain and he knew he would be finished. Far away in another world he heard a terrible sound, horribly malformed, as if a human voice were being forced through an alien larynx. Far away in another world his body was freezing. Far away into another world he was slipping –

Desperately he forced his eyes open, stared into an infinity of orange coldness, black irises like shards of obsidian, as large as planets. Laughter.

He drew upon his last resources of will, and with a supreme effort, with his final surge of strength, he forced the blade through the air. Pale hand slipping into his at the centre of his being. And he ripped it point first into the gaping maw.

Renewed foulness smote him and he retched violently. Dimly he was aware of a thin screaming like the unbearable tension of a singing wire. He rammed it in with all his power, twisting the blade mightily. Brought both hands on to the hilt.

Abruptly there came a sharp snap, a vibration, and an enormous convulsion, and the howling reached a peak. With that he sank down into a velvet blackness against which he at first tried to struggle, and then from which he was too tired even to return.

* * *

He awoke all at once with the terrible stench of the thing still in his nostrils. He coughed, wiped his mouth. All around him the cobbles were shining and slippery with streaks of crimson and viscous pools of black. There was no sign of the creature but G'fand lay several metres from him. He got up slowly and carefully, went over, knelt beside him. G'fand's eyes bulged and his tongue protruded thickly from his blue lips. There was pink foam on his chin, drying now. His skin held a faint luminescence. His neck was canted at an unnatural angle. His throat had been rent into ribbons of red cartilage.

Ronin's colourless eyes were opaque as he reached out and gently closed the Scholar's eyes. He sat on his haunches amid the offal of the battle and stared at G'fand. Many thoughts ran through his mind but they were as confused and unreachable as a school of darting fish in deep water.

The shadows lengthened slowly, wheeling about the ancient enigmatic buildings, staining the aged cobbles. Far off an animal barked, a short, sharp, startling sound, and close by, small creatures, perhaps attracted by the scent of fresh blood, could be heard, tiny claws skittering along an alleyway.

To all these sounds Ronin was oblivious. He stared, his breathing laboured, at a torn and bloody corpse that had once thought and talked and felt joy and sorrow.

He got up. The ache of his muscles seemed very distant. He bent and gently picked up G'fand's body, eased it over his shoulder. It felt as light as a feather. He went across the glittering cobbles to get his sword. The toe of his boot kicked something that went clattering over the street. The hilt of his dagger, shorn of its blade. He sheathed his sword.

In the plaza the glint of the tiles was dull in the fading light. He found the corpses of the animals they had killed already half-eaten. He looked around, but nothing moved over the broad expanse.

He went to the well and, without pausing for a moment, dropped G'fand's body down the shaft. After a long time, he heard the splash and it seemed to him no louder than the sound the piece of rubble had made.

Darkness was falling, its thick shawl snuffing the last of the long amber shafts of light, the encroaching shadows now dominating the streets, when at last he stood before the scarred door of Bonneduce the Last, and leaned his weary body against the warm wood. He could not remember how he had got there. He heard a snuffling from behind him, near, in the lane. It sounded somehow familiar, as if it had accompanied him for a while, but he was too exhausted to turn his head and look.

Through the door he heard Hynd's low cough, and then it was thrown open and he collapsed at the feet of Bonneduce the Last.

* * *

Bonneduce the Last had already been on his way down the stairs when he heard Hynd's cough. In one hand he held an old leather double shoulder bag. He put something into it and said, 'Almost time.' Then he threw the bag across a chair, crossed the room with remarkable alacrity, his shoulder dipping with each stride of his short leg. He pulled open the front door.

Hynd rushed out into the lane, growling, jaws working. He bit into something, tore away a tremendous chunk of flesh. Bonneduce the Last heard the yelp of pain as he dragged Ronin across the room and settled him into one of the large soft chairs. Hynd trotted in, licking his lips, and used his long muzzle to close the door. Then he lay down and watched the little man minister to Ronin.

By the time he had spent some minutes stripping off Ronin's corselet, the metal blackened and ripped, and removed the tattered remains of his shirt, his eyes had gone cold and hard. The lines on his face seemed to be more pronounced.

'Already the Makkon are abroad,' he said. 'Even here they have come.'

Hynd's head came up, and now he stood at the door, a silent sentinel. The little man pulled his leather bag to him, drew out a packet of ointment, which he applied to Ronin's chest and arms. He spoke to Hynd. 'The Bones can tell me only so much. The young one I knew would not come back.' His hands worked swiftly and surely. 'I am past feeling for them, the Bones have seen to that, else I would have gone mad. It is what I must do.'

Bonneduce the Last went into the interior of the house, returned with a goblet of water. Into this he dropped several grains of a coarse brown powder, which he fed to Ronin as best he could. As much ran down his chin as went into his mouth.

'He will sleep now as his body recovers.' He threw the remains of the liquid into the cold ashes of the fireplace. 'He has suffered much, now. And he will suffer more. Yet it has to be. Out of pain he must be forged.'

He got up then, went briefly again into the interior. When he came back he held a small object of brown onyx and red jade. He slipped it into his bag. 'And now, one thing yet remains to be done before we quit this city.' He reached something out from his leather bag, held it for a moment, feeling its texture with his fingertips. 'Yes,' he said softly, 'it becomes clearer, piece by piece.' He placed the object on the table beside the sleeping Ronin.

He awoke to silence, deep and complete. But it was somehow hollow and empty and he spent some time attempting to determine why. He knew precisely where he was. Then he had it: the ticking was gone.

With that he rose and called out. No one answered. He went across the room and quickly up the stairs, aware that most of the pain had gone from his body. The rooms were bare. It was the same downstairs. No signs remained that either Bonneduce the Last or Hynd had ever been there.

He sat down again in the chair. Morning light was streaming in through the dusty grimed windows, bright and fresh and new. Idly he traced the beams of light, slanting in, and his eyes came to rest on a gauntlet spangled by the light, lying on top of the table next to the chair; the only foreign object in the house.

He picked it up and immediately he was struck by its singularity. It was heavy and there appeared to be no seams except along each fingertip, almost as if the closings of the apertures had been made by shearing off nails. Then two bits of information came to him at once: the scaly texture of the gauntlet and the fact that it had six fingers. It cannot be, he thought with a shock. But the longer he examined it the more convinced he became. He was holding a gauntlet made from the hand of the creature he and G'fand had fought; the thing that had killed the Scholar. Something blazed far back in his eyes. He recalled the trek to the plaza, the small splash of the body, knew that at that precise moment an irrevocable step had been taken. And he had done it.

Without further thought, he pulled on the gauntlet with his left hand, flexing his fingers. The light turned the scales to silver, reflective and brilliant.

He left the house then, and strode down the crooked lane, the air cool and fresh against his face, to start his return to Borros and the Freehold far above him.

They were glittery. Wet-looking yet opaque. They were an entire universe, seeing everything now; seeing nothing. What struck him most deeply, however, were the lines of fear etched into the features. And the red marks. Must it come in such a manner? He was becoming an expert on it: Death.

He stood in the lamplight of the Medicine Man's side room. He had come there to see Borros and had not found him.

He stared down at the body on the bed. The heavy, lined face so frightened in life. The rheumy eyes were glazed. He thought, What have they done to you, Stahlig?

The flame from the sole lamp flickered in the draught. The door to the Corridor opened and Ronin's hand went instinctively to the hilt of his sword.

'I truly wish you would try it,' said Freidal softly. Ronin turned slowly, saw the Security Saardin and three daggam. Freidal went over to the concealed door, opened it. Four more daggam stepped through.

His mouth curled in the parody of a smile. 'Come, come. Where are the heroics that a Blades-man should be famous for?' His voice was silken with subdued triumph. 'Will you not fight your way out? Take us all on?' His good eye stared with intensity. 'Take his weapons,' he barked, and they disarmed him. Freidal had chosen the place well, he thought. No room to manoeuvre in such a small area. No chance.

Freidal's face was a mask. His slick hair glistened. He looked relaxed, almost happy. 'Did you believe for a moment that you could drop from our Levels without my knowledge?' The ghost of a smile played along his thin, white lips. 'Stupid boy!' His tongue clucked reprovingly against the roof of his mouth. 'You were warned. A courtesy which you chose to ignore.' Freidal stepped closer to him, and daggam on either side gripped Ronin's wrists, although he had made no movement.

The Saardin reached out and removed Ronin's corselet, stared at the welts along his chest. 'As I knew you would.' He ran a finger across the bruised flesh. 'You see, I could not get what I wanted from that accursed Magic Man. The fool! But it was purely accidental.' He laughed, a sharp, disquieting sound. 'I knew it would work then, throwing you and Borros together.'

His finger was at Ronin's waist. 'Ah, and what is this?' He grasped Ronin's right arm and the daggam on that side let go. He brought the forearm and hand up. The gauntlet shot silver through the tiny room. Freidal pulled it off Ronin's hand, examining it. 'Could this be it? What he sent you Downshaft to find?' He looked up, into Ronin's face, said sharply, 'Is it?' The false eye flashed. 'It has begun, you know, the struggle for power.'

Ronin thought of Nirren. Where was he now? He had not been able to locate him before he had left, and now this weighed heavily upon him, as if he had violated a trust. But, he told himself, I had no idea it would begin so soon. Could my knowledge of Borros's project have helped him? There was no way to tell now.

Freidal grasped his elbow and swung him around. 'He did not die well. He tried to protect you but his fear won out. He helped.' Ronin recalled his agitation, his warning. The old man had tried to tell him. 'How does that make you feel? And you see what he is now. A piece of meat, stinking and putrefying.' His nostrils dilated and he sniffed delicately. 'Dead things offend me. But Stahlig was put here for a reason. Even a stupid boy like you can see that.' He jerked Ronin around and motioned to two daggam, who removed the corpse. Freidal fondled the scaled gauntlet. 'Be sensible. If you have no interest in power, at least look after your life.' He stroked Ronin's chest with a cold palm. 'It would be a great pity to destroy this body.' He slapped the gauntlet against the side of his leg. 'Can the Machine work?'

Abruptly there was a commotion outside in the dark surgery. Freidal started, as if he had forgotten that beyond these walls, the intimacies of the moment, existed the world of the Freehold. He turned his head, as did Ronin.

They saw that three men in close-fitting breeches and jerkins of a soft tan colour had pushed past the daggam who had just returned from disposing of the body. The man in front was slim, with red cheeks and full lips. The jewel-hilted daggers glittered over his heart and at his hip.

'Saardin,' he said blandly.

'Voss,' Freidal acknowledged coldly. 'What is the meaning of this intrusion?'

Voss saw Ronin. 'Ah, there you are! We have all been quite concerned about you.' He smiled winningly. 'None the worse for your interview with Security, I trust!'

Freidal's good eye flicked in its socket and a muscle spasmed in his cheek. 'This behaviour is inexcusable! Bakka! Turis! See these people out immediately!'

The Chondrin held up his hand. 'One moment, Saardin. The Salamander wishes to see Ronin. He has been distressed over his whereabouts. His safety, you know – '

Two spots of colour burned on Freidal's cheeks. 'What are you saying?' He was trembling with suppressed rage. 'Have you taken leave of your senses? This is strictly a Security matter.'

Voss smiled icily. 'No. I am afraid you are mistaken.'

The good eye blazed at the Chondrin, then Freidal turned abruptly, making a cutting gesture through the air with the edge of one hand. 'Take him then,' he said thickly. 'Take him and get out!'

Voss motioned to one of his men, who took Ronin's weapons from the daggam. Then he stepped up to Freidal and said, 'He will want this too.' He slipped the gauntlet from the Saardin's hand, and the four of them departed.

* * *

The woman with the broad face was gone. A Bladesman sat in her place. They went through the inner double doors and down the hallway. At the end, the Bladesman carrying Ronin's weapons handed them to Voss and he and his fellows disappeared through the door on the right.

Voss opened the opposite door and led Ronin into a low-ceilinged room lit by lamps. There were no Overheads. The walls were dark and bare. Across the room was another door. There was a single wooden chair in the centre of the room. Voss indicated that Ronin should sit. Ronin shrugged. He had no illusions as to why he was here. He had been witness to too many events; and too many people were gone.

The sharp smell of cloves foretold the approach. He had not heard a door open. The Salamander stood over Ronin. He wore black shirt and breeches and gleaming thigh-length boots. A fine mesh vest of red gold winked in the light. He wore a wide crimson leather belt from which a scabbarded sword hung. The ruby lizard was at his throat.

Voss, leaning on Ronin's sword, handed the Salamander the gauntlet. The big man grunted, turning the thing over in his large hands. 'So?'

Voss shrugged. 'Apparently he brought it from Downshaft.'

The Salamander stared at Ronin. 'How far did you go?'

'All the way.'

He glanced at Voss. 'No wonder Freidal was interested.'

Ronin heard a tiny sound behind him, as if someone had slipped into the room, but the Salamander did not turn and he could not twist in the chair. Perhaps it was nothing.

'My dear boy, I hope you appreciate the great service I have done you. Freidal can be most unpleasant when he has a mind to.'

Ronin stared into the eyes like black coals. 'So I noticed. He killed the Medicine Man.'

'Oh?' The Salamander's eyebrows raised. 'What a pity. You knew him a long time.' He spread his hands. 'I am most sorry.'

'The Magic Man too, I imagine.'

'Oh, dear me, no. He could hardly afford to do that. No, Borros is much too valuable. He is being detained several Levels below us.'

'I was not aware that you knew so much about him.'

'Oh, I see.' The Salamander frowned. 'That was careless of me.' Then he shrugged. 'But one hopes, my dear boy, that you can be treated as a friend, an ally – '

'You are as desperate as he is – '

'Not at all, dear boy, not at all. I merely think that you should be back where you belong. There has always been room for you here.'

Voss moved minutely, and Ronin said. 'To be your Chondrin? You already have one. In any event, we have been through this before. What if I should turn you down a second time?'

The Salamander's expression changed. His eyes smouldered and he smote Ronin across the face. 'What an abysmal fool you are. I offered you everything and you spit at me. Did you believe that I could forget?'

'At the time I believed that you would understand – '

'Oh, I understood! I trained you to be the greatest fighting machine in the Freehold. I saw the ability lurking within you. It took a master to bring it out, nurture it, let it blossom. An Instructor could never have accomplished it.'

'You make it seem as if it was all your doing.'

'But it was! You were there and I moulded you. You became what I wished you to become.'

'Not quite.'

The Salamander bristled, and his voice was as smooth as silk. 'I trained you to be my Chondrin; an unbeatable warrior. Did you think that I was wasting my time in picking boys and training them? A reason behind it all. And what was your response? You return the care lavished upon you with insult.'

'There was no – '

'Silence!' the Salamander roared. His face was coloured by rage. His enormous bulk loomed over Ronin, the threat of death. 'Do not presume,' he said quietly, icily, 'to tell me what I already know.' He bent forward and Ronin felt Voss very close at his side and slightly behind him, out of his peripheral vision. 'I should have seen it; you lacked the initiative. It all came so easily to you, you never regarded the mental processes as important. That was a mistake; a fatal mistake.' The stygian eyes were glittery and fever-bright as they stared at Ronin. 'Now Voss has initiative. He – eliminated two other Students of mine in order to ensure his position as Chondrin.' He laughed, a short strange sound. 'I would not trade him for you. What conceit!' He stood up and looked past Ronin's head for a moment before his eyes returned. 'Now we shall see how long it takes for you to tell me what I want to know.' He signalled to Voss. 'Bring the – '

At that moment the door to the hallway was thrown open and a Bladesman came hurriedly in. The Salamander looked up.

'The Magic Man,' the Bladesman said, 'has escaped from Security.'

The Salamander's eyes flicked again behind Ronin, and he heard a slight movement. 'Oh, that fool!' He looked at Voss and threw him the gauntlet. 'You know what to do.' He whirled and followed the man from the room.

'On your feet,' Voss said coldly. He tucked the gauntlet into his leather belt.

He got up and they went out the way they had come in. Six men were in the outer room, two guarding the double doors to the Corridor, and Ronin thought, In that Freidal told the truth: it has begun.

They went out through the doors and Voss prodded him to the right, down the Corridor. He heard a distant clamour, the pounding of boots, the clang of metal, intermittent shouts. He felt the tip of Voss's dagger at his back.

'Where are we headed?' Ronin asked.

'You do not expect an answer to that.'

Ronin shrugged.

'How could you have done it?'

Ronin turned his neck, felt the bite of the iron tip. 'What?'

'Gone away from him.'

'I am what I am.'

'Huh! He is right, you *are* a fool! Did you not realize that you were bound to him?'

Ronin said nothing.

'You had a moral obligation – '

And he almost missed it. The sliver of shadow along the wall ahead of them, around the arc of the Corridor, so that he did not think that Voss had seen it. He kept his pace steady, and thought, Any diversion must be used; he is most vulnerable here in the Corridor. Once we get to a destination, there will be little chance. He thought then of the whirring in the air, angry and hot, cutting through the sounds of the birds, the accuracy of Voss's throws.

A man was in front of them, and Voss still had not seen the small slice of shadow. He must be pressed against the wall, Ronin thought.

'You owe him your life,' Voss said. 'Including your loyalty.'

The figure came out from the wall and Ronin dropped, rolling to the right, across the Corridor, came up with right arm extended to ward off the expected dagger blow. But Voss was not even looking in his direction. He stood facing the figure, his face registering shock.

And Ronin felt the adrenalin pumping. Nirren! Nirren stood before Voss, bright sword unsheathed, held before him.

Voss unfroze. 'What are you doing so far Upshaft?'

Nirren grinned, his mouth a tight line. 'Where were you taking Ronin?'

'That is no business of yours. Out of the way!'

'And if he chooses not to accompany you?'

'The choice is not his to make.'

'I say it is.'

Voss's hands became a blur and simultaneously Nirren lunged like a dancer, extending his front leg very low. The sword shot out as the air hummed. Voss's face held a measure of surprise. His eyes were still looking at the jewel-hilted dagger lodged head-high in the far wall as the blade pierced his chest. He stood that way for a moment, his blood running hotly along Nirren's blade. Then his right hand twitched once and, as Nirren withdrew the sword, he crumpled over as if he were made of fabric.

Nirren touched the face with the toe of his boot, the head turned slackly. He swung to face Ronin and grinned. 'It is too bad. I would have enjoyed seeing you take him.' He shrugged. 'Well, where have you been? And G'fand's gone missing.'

Ronin went across the Corridor, took his weapons from Voss's corpse. He pulled the gauntlet free from the other's belt. 'I have been on a journey Downshaft, for the Magic Man –'

'Then you got through to him!'

'Yes, and I have much to tell you,' Ronin said, strapping on his scabbard. They moved towards a nearby Stairwell. 'But first I must find the Magic Man. He has escaped from Freidal.'

Nirren nodded. 'All right. I am in the midst of following that Rodent. At last I believe I know who it is, fantastic though it may seem – '

Ronin cut him off. 'Listen, fantastic is the word for what I have learned. The Magic Man is correct; we are not alone on this planet – '

'What?'

They both caught the flash at once, but the thing was already in the air. Nirren's jaws swung wide and he threw his hands up in a vain reflexive motion. A gout of blood erupted along his neck. He staggered back and fell clumsily to the floor.

Ronin raced into the Stairwell but the commotion of running feet and raised voices echoing in the Stairwell made it impossible to tell which way the assailant had fled.

He ran back into the Corridor and knelt beside Nirren. The front of his jerkin was soaked in blood. He ripped off a length of the Chondrin's shirt, withdrew the dagger at his neck, his fingers cold on the jewelled hilt. He put the fabric against the wound. White cloth stained red.

Nirren's eyes were still clear and bright with intelligence. Ronin expected him to ask about the Magic Man's project. Instead he said, 'What happened to G'fand? You know.'

There was pain in Ronin's eyes. 'I took him with me. I thought he would be of help with his knowledge of the glyphs.'

'And was he?' The breathing was laboured as the body struggled with the shock.

'Yes.' Ronin looked into his eyes. 'He was killed. He – '

Nirren's body trembled. The cloth at his neck was entirely crimson now. He gripped Ronin's arms and a sadness that Ronin could not understand danced behind his eyes. 'The Rodent,' he managed to get out with difficulty. 'I am sure now, the dagger, go Upshaft, after – ' His head fell and Ronin held it. 'Last time, follow Up – ' He tried to laugh then, choked instead. The light in his eyes was fading; they were opaque, like stones. 'Just thinking – team – what a team.' His eyes closed as if from fatigue. 'All gone now – Ronin, I am sorry.' Then the blood, which he had been holding back with a last effort, came out of his mouth.

Up and up and up. The darkness rushing by and the clamour from below fading, but it was as if a strong wind rushed in his ears and he heard Nirren sighing again, *All gone now*, and knew it was true. The world had collapsed and he was adrift in the dark, directionless. But his legs did not understand. They pumped strongly, up the Stairwell. *Follow Upward*, Nirren had asked, and he would do it now, and he felt the burning within him, the hate growing and pulsing, fed from the secret fires of many events. Surely it was the Rodent who had slain Nirren, for he had been on his trail and had been very close. Closer than he knew. His lungs worked as he raced through the Levels of the Freehold. Upward, ever upward. Once he stared down at his hands, saw with some surprise that he had slipped on the silvered gauntlet and that he clutched the dagger that had killed the Chondrin. Jewels on the hilt? And then Borros came into his mind. Escaped and gone where? Upshaft surely.

He climbed the stairs as far as they would take him. He emerged into a bright Corridor painted a brilliant yellow. Dust lay thickly along the floor, clung to the walls. He looked down. Bootprints in the dust, confused, but certainly more than one pair.

He sprinted down the Corridor and gradually

the colour of the walls deepened. There were no doors. On he ran, the hate a living thing within him now. Existence narrowed.

And the Corridor ended. Here near the summit of the Freehold, the Corridor did not describe a complete circle. He faced the black bulge of a Lift's doors. He stabbed at the black sphere and the doors yawned. He stepped inside. Up, ever up. There was one sphere and he pressed it. He ascended. Eyes like stones. *Ronin, I am sorry*, he said. What had he meant? I am the one who is sorry, Nirren. But death comes and there is no way to stop –

The Lift sighed to a halt and the doors opened. Above him the surface of the planet, so near. Perhaps just steps away? He went into the room before him. It was an ellipse, painted red. In the centre was a black platform from which a metal ladder ran vertically into a round section cut out of the ceiling. Low doors in the solid platform were open, and he saw what looked like neat piles of clothing. One stack had been tipped over. And the thought grew in his mind. Borros –

A tiny whistle in the air, like a tickle at his ear. He drew his sword and spun. The dagger was in his belt. A sword drove into his, scraping down the length of the blade, smashed into the hilt. Slight, deceptive twisting of his wrist and disengagement was accomplished.

He looked at his opponent and a shock ran through him. Blood pounded in his temples and for a split second the scene before him seemed to blur.

She stood before him, in leggings and jerkin of a soft tan colour. Across her chest ran a thin leather strap to which was attached a red leather scabbard that hung between her breasts.

She stood before him in the oblique combat position, legs apart, knees bent, leading with her shoulder to present a narrower target. Her pale hands gripped a sword the same length as Ronin's. The black torrent of her hair was held back from her face by a plain gold band. It had the appearance of a helm.

She stood before him, small beads of sweat glinting at her hairline. Her eyes were unnaturally bright, the pupils contracted so that they seemed to be all iris. She smiled and it was like the coming of the frost. Her white teeth gleamed, small and even. She looked quite deadly.

'K'reen,' he breathed.

She laughed sharply, a bitter sound. 'How I have waited to see you at this moment!' she said in a tight voice. She swung at him and he parried solely by instinct. He felt as if the floor had suddenly become molten. He was sinking into it. He could not move. He could not take his eyes from her. She circled him, and they moved out on to the floor, like slow dancers moving to metalled music. She struck again and he parried.

'A Bladesman,' he said softly. 'Can it be?'

'Come,' she said thickly. 'Come and find out.' She slashed again and again at him, drawing him out, and her eyes flashed coldly, triumphantly as he moved towards her.

He stared at her and realization suddenly flooded

him. Because now she was not beautiful or pretty or any of the other words he would normally associate with her. She was naked to him now, stripped of the layers of femininity. She was at once more and less than she once was, pared and honed and transformed.

She was elemental.

Metal rang against metal in the small oval.

'Here is what I really am!' she said savagely. 'Not what you made me out to be. The Salamander saw the potential in me – to be a Bladesman. He was not afraid to reject Tradition. Years we worked in secret, lest the other Saardin suspect and forbid it.'

They moved around the oval, she advancing, he retreating. She struck at him continuously, testing, probing.

'Why?' asked Ronin. 'Why did he train you?'

She smiled coldly. 'Part of the gathering of power.' Then she sneered. 'Something you would know nothing about.'

But it was not right, somehow, and he heard the Salamander saying, *A reason behind it all*. But there was no time; she swept it away. 'You could have been his Chondrin!' she hissed, striking at him. 'You would have been with him when I came. He would have put us together, and then we could have had everything!'

There was an odd sensation inside him, and he looked at the feral glow in her eyes, the sweat running down her cheeks, her heaving breasts. And he saw what he had not wanted to see before: the jewel-hilted dagger between her breasts. And his gaze moved, as if of its own accord, to her flank, to the scabbard hanging empty there.

'It was you,' he whispered. 'The Rodent. You killed Nirren. Why? He was our friend.'

She shook her head. 'The enemy,' she said deliberately. 'He was the enemy. Just as you are now the enemy – '

'But this makes no sense – '

'You turned your back on him. After he taught you and trained you, you would not serve him. You would not aid him now.'

Still he retreated under her blows. 'I serve no one,' he said softly. 'It is the only fact of which I am certain.' Then, as if suddenly realizing what she had said: 'You were in the room, behind me!'

'Yes!' she hissed. 'Ready to embrace you, if you joined us.' She swung at him. 'He gave you a chance to amend your insult. You mocked him instead.'

Where was the woman he had known? Whence had she fled? Could she have felt any fondness towards him? But the emotions he knew, when they had been there, had been genuine. He recognized the fault within himself. Surely he could have seen this side of her, had he only looked. But he had turned from her too many times, and this, he knew, as much as her training, as much as the purpose set for her by the Salamander, was the cause of this confrontation.'

'But Nirren – '

'He delayed me,' she cut in. 'I had not expected him to be so close.' He wiped the sweat from his forehead, stood his ground. Sparks flew from the meeting of their weapons. 'The delay cost me,' she said bitterly. 'The old man was faster than I had imagined. I missed him by seconds.'

'You mean Borros is on the surface?'

'What is that to you? He will be dead soon enough, frozen and buried under the snow.'

But part of him exulted and he knew now what he must do. He shook his head. 'You are wrong. He will live. And I will follow him.' And he thought, But she is Nirren's killer. In friendship he asked for revenge. *I serve no one.* Sweat rolled along his neck, and he felt a chill. *Ronin, I am sorry.*

She snarled and her teeth looked like those of a small predatory animal. 'Oh, no,' she said. 'This is your tomb.' And she lunged at him, arching her blade with all her might, catching him off guard with the unexpectedly powerful blow, and he realized at once that he had underestimated her cunning. They locked blades, and he twisted again, moving his wrist. But she countered and the blades ground together at a peculiar angle. Her sword snapped abruptly, the released force causing his weapon to jump away. She reached between her breasts, withdrew the jewel-hilted dagger. His palm closed over the hilt of the sister blade and he held it before him. This is what she wants, he realized. She is most proficient with the smaller weapon.

They circled each other in the confined space, judging distances and the switch to lighter blades. He wished his head were clearer, but conflicting emotions darted like lightning in his mind, squirting too fast to catch.

Perhaps she saw a hint of this confusion in his eyes, and perhaps that is why she threw herself against him unexpectedly. They tumbled to the floor, locked together, hand clutching wrist, rolling over and over.

Her hot panting breath was against his face and he smelled her scent as their legs twined and their bodies heaved. They grunted and clung to each other, desperately fighting for position. He stared into her eyes. They were large and deep and liquid and he felt a stirring inside. He thought of what she had done, of what she wanted, and knew the hate was there. He fought to push down the edge of the other emotion. Her enigmatic eyes stared at him and he could not tell whether there was hate or hunger there.

Her heat and her sweat melted into him. Her long hair whipped his face. Her flesh was both hard and soft as it writhed against him. 'I'll kill you,' she hissed. 'I'll kill you.' Her thigh was between his legs, imprisoned. She moved it against him and her other leg came over his hip and her calf pressed his buttocks. Desire rose in him like a great feathered bird gaining the air currents. Her voice was low and thick as she said it again, 'I want to kill you.' But it was almost a moan. Their bodies ground together. He was aware of the press of her breasts against his chest.

Something slammed into the back of his head and a red film clouded his vision as pain lanced through him. He had fetched up hard against the platform at the centre of the oval. Dazed, he still clung tenaciously to her wrist, but using all her strength she wrenched it away from him and the honed blade of the dagger seemed to pulse in the light.

She was panting through her open mouth, the lips pulled back from the pearl teeth, and her thighs gripped him convulsively as she rocked hard against him. He wanted to lie back and embrace her. He shook his head but it would not clear. She began to shudder. 'Kill you,' she choked. 'Kill you.' And with an effort she stopped her eyes from closing. She gripped the dagger, knuckles as white as bone, and she moaned a little as she drove the blade point first towards his throat. Her pelvis ground against him in waves and he looked up to see that her eyes were wet. He saw dimly the terrible flash of light along the moving blade and wondered that he still felt the power of her groin moving against him. He felt suffocated by a great heat and instinctively he put up his hand. As Nirren did; vainly, he thought.

The point of the blade caught his palm. It was his gauntleted hand. The honed tip hit the scales, skidded off harmlessly. Within, his hand never even felt the force of the blow. He shook his head again, and grasped the obliquely moving blade, trying desperately to hold it. But she had both hands on the hilt now and she had the leverage and he had none and she began to force the gleaming point back at him. The cutting edge creased his throat, broke the skin. Blood welled up. But his left hand was free now and it scrabbled along the floor at his side until he found the hilt of the dagger he had dropped. And it was all reflexive now, no thought involved at all. He brought it up very quickly between their bodies, the blade quivering at his throat now, and buried it hilt-deep in her stomach.

Her eyes opened so wide that the whites showed all around the edges, and she grunted thickly, a brief guttural noise that seemed somehow terrible to him. Blood pounded against the back of his eyes and he jerked powerfully on the hilt so that it sliced up between her breasts.

Her head dropped abruptly, as if she had been hit on the back of the neck, and her lips came down over his, warm and soft.

He felt a great hot pool of wetness between them and convulsively he threw her off him and, panting, swayed to his feet.

She lay on her back, eyes still very wide and shiny, with the jewelled hilt protruding obscenely from between her breasts, sending shards of harsh light reflecting in the blood that covered her.

What have I done? he thought, as he stared at her. *All gone now.* It reverberated in his mind. Waves of blackness seemed to reach up, ready to engulf him, but he fought them off. He staggered across the oval to his sword, sheathed it. Then he went back to the platform, reached into one of the open doors. He let the fabric unfurl. It was silvery, slightly iridescent, and it was very light. It was a close-fitting suit of some sort. He believed he knew its purpose. Quickly now he stripped off his tattered clothes and donned the suit. As he had suspected, it fit him snugly and was very warm. It must retain all the body heat, he thought. Pockets

251

along the sides bulged with concealed packets. Food. He strapped on his weapons belt.

He heard a sound and whirled, blade ready. The doors of the Lift hissed open and a whiff of cloves came to him. He tensed. Something moved within the shadows of the Lift and the immense jet figure of the Salamander stood half illumined in the doorway. His hooded eyes scanned the scene before him.

'Come to stop me yourself?' Ronin snarled, flicking the tip of his blade.

The Salamander smiled with the corners of his mouth, almost contentedly. He did not step into the room. 'Oh, no,' he said silkily. 'Others were to have done that. I see that they have been unsuccessful.'

Ronin came forward. 'I am leaving,' he said slowly and deliberately. 'You have lost. You have neither the Magic Man nor the information I possess. Go fight your battle alone.'

The Salamander sighed theatrically. 'You have become a real menace, dear boy, and must be dealt with. But you still have much to learn.' And now he smiled once again. He was delighted with himself. 'You have lost quite as much, in your own way, as I. Perhaps more.'

Ronin stared at him, blinking back the sweat that rolled down his face, and cursed silently. He inched closer. I'll get you yet, he thought. And said thickly, 'Yes, I know.'

From deep within the shadows of the Lift, cloaked in his mantle of jet and crimson, the carved ruby lizard a blood splash duskily visible at his throat, the Salamander laughed long and deep. Then he said, 'Oh, no, dear boy, you do not know. Yet.' His arm extended briefly. 'Look at the face at your feet. What do you see? The woman you slept with – '

'And you trained.' He was closer now.

'Yes, quite. But all for a purpose.' His eyes were dark and unreadable. 'We were close, you and I. Until you – But why bring up old hates?' The Salamander seemed oblivious to Ronin's movement. 'My men found her on the Middle Levels. They had heard rumours, you see, of a child found by the Workers. She was regarded as special, they believed that she sprang from the Freehold itself. They told me of this, not a Sign after you had left. And it occurred to me who she might be. But I dared not believe it. It was too improbable, too wonderful a coincidence. I sent them to fetch her and when I saw her I knew. It had to be, for she was no Worker's child. And her age was right. In secrecy I found her and in secrecy I trained her.' His voice was thick with triumph now and Ronin shivered in spite of himself. 'And then I sent her out. And she was good, very good. She did precisely as I had instructed her. And now she has fulfilled her purpose.' He laughed again. 'Of course she never knew. Never even suspected. And that made it more delicious!' He was gloating now.

Ronin frowned. 'What are you saying?'

'I may not have Borros, or his knowledge. But you,' he said delightedly. 'You, in obtaining your freedom from this place – you have slain your long-lost and beloved sister.' His laughter boomed again, echoing in the oval, as if it had been pent up for centuries.

He tried to reject it but the vision in the Magus's mirror swam up through his mind, and he saw again K'reen turn around to stare at him, turn around with his face. And then small things, minute things, fell into place with the clanging of great metal doors.

He screamed wordlessly and lunged at the Salamander, but his blade scraped along the closed doors and faintly he heard, 'Not now, not now.' And echoes of the laughter came again.

In a frenzy, he pried at the closed doors with blade and fingers until his nails were torn and bloody, but they would not open. And the time for descent had passed.

After a while he turned and eventually he was able to gaze again upon K'reen's face. Something wailed inside him and he sank to his knees beside her. He touched her face. Can you ever forgive me? he thought. Will I ever be able to forgive myself?

Gently, he closed the eyes. Carefully he stepped over the body and commenced to climb the vertical metal ladder that led to the Access Hatch. The entryway, so many centuries unused, to the surface of the planet. He did not look back.

And had anyone been in the oval to see him, they would not have recognized his face.

ERIC LUSTBADER

SHALLOWS OF NIGHT

Volume 2 of the *Sunset Warrior* Sequence

For all the heroes

Contents

1
Ice

Soaring through frigid mists and roiling clouds, he stretches fully his long wings upon the unpredictable currents. Streamers of silvered plumage, running bilaterally across his wings and cresting his majestic questing head, ripple and blur in the wind. He banks and dips. There is a moaning in his ears. His large liquid eyes stare unblinkingly ahead at the immense eye of the setting sun, its face a broad and flattened disc wider at the sides as if caught in a vise of immeasurable proportions. Then thick ribbons of cloud of a metallic grey ride before it like the ghostly remnants of a once vast, victorious army, reaving it.

He banks again, deftly avoiding a treacherous downdraft, and turns his incurious gaze beneath him, through the layers of cloud and mist, to the painful twisting of the earth far below.

High peaks beaten by age and scraped by merciless weather, crowned in bitter frost, sealed in pearl and emerald ice, thrust their humped backs in snaking lines against the whipping winds which, forever swirling, gather layers of fine powdery snow from the mountains' slopes, turning them into rising sheets, hurling them forward, like giants striding across the barren land.

He floats over sheer gorges, frosted thickly in

gleaming sheets of periwinkle ice, plumes of loose snow drifting along their flanks like smoke from a funeral pyre. His keen eyes trace the vertiginous descent from dancing ice crystaled green-turquoise-magenta in the dying light to the violent violet of their yawning and uneasy depths: precipitous chasms sliced out of the land as cleanly as if by a cruel blade of immense size. Powerful wings flutter as out of these depths now is heard the agonized groaning of shifting rock. Ozone and sulphur fill the air as the earth shudders and trembles. Shards of ice shear off in dense clusters with infinite slowness, hanging impossibly in mid-air, crumbling in layers until, with an abrupt and complete swiftness, they explode silently into vast spurts of hyalescent spray high in the sky that turn to rainbow arcs as they catch the last oblique rays of watery light.

He wheels in the coloured, suddenly solid air, unperturbed.

Everywhere is ice and draperies of snow with only the occasional tired fist of granite or twisted schist rising like ancient tombstones in an alien desert, useless punctuation on a blank and crumbling page.

Against this inimical icescape nothing moves.

The bird banks and glides in the sky, his black-irised eyes scanning the dreadful sameness of the land. Into the setting sun he flies, his majestic plumage stained a dilute scarlet and, glancing once more earthward, he sees a dark and tiny shadow limned before the glare of the ice. Muscles respond to the brain's command and the wings dip, their silver plumage losing for a moment the scarlet wash, turning a rich lustrous grey, as he heads southward for a closer look.

Resolution of image comes far too swiftly, for the shadow is huge. Abruptly it moves and, startled, the bird wheels away from the edge of the steep precipice along which he has been flying and, flapping his wings in alarm, speeds westward, rising, gaining the high currents, diminishing into the light of the lowering sun.

Transfixed, Ronin stands at the verge of the high ice ledge staring southward, oblivious to the receding speck in the sky.

Motionless, his body tall and muscular, he appears more a statue erected to the countless legions who, throughout the myriad ages, have fought across the changing faces of this land. For here once grew lush verdant forests of giant fern and slender willow spreading their fans of feathered leaves, building dense jungles of crowding greenery and thick tangles of vines through which cocoa warriors crept and crouched, sweating, listening methodically to the shrill cries of startlingly coloured birds, readying the leap, an uncoiling blur, tan and brown shadow, flickering in the filtering light, the quick silent slash, the gout of bright blood beading the foliage, the dying body of the enemy. And in another age – earlier or later, one cannot be sure – here swelled and sucked fifteen fathoms of green water alive with the riotous growth of the sea. High-booted feet

11

tramped the stained tarred decks of wide-beamed
wooden ships, long oars extending from their high
curving sides, beating through air and water in
hypnotic rhythm. Hoarse shouts filled the sky
heavy with brine and heat as helmed and bearded
warriors prepared themselves for battle.

Layers of hard snow encrust the slippery ice of
the precipice upon which he stands, feet apart and
planted firmly in the frost. Unconsciously he
clenches his left hand, which is covered by a
strange scaled gauntlet, dull and unreflective. The
wind gusts, screaming in his ears, and rushes by
him, unheeded, sucked in by the crevices and piled
hillocks of the plateau tumbling at his back. The
air is dry and chill. The staggering sight at which
he gazes longingly resonates in his mind with the
supravivid impact of an ecstatic dream. And for
this time, the events of the recent past mercifully
dim.

For what lies before and below him, just past
the beetling lip of the high ledge, is a cyclopean
sea of ice. Desolate. Limitless. Awesome and
electrifying.

'An overwhelming sight,' said the voice quite
near and behind him. And he turned slowly, as if
in a dream, to behold Borros, the Magic Man.

'The true wonder is that we have been denied
this sight for all of our lives.' A thin and weary
smile curled Borros' lips.

Wind whipped loose snow against their legs as
they stood atop the ice plateau, strange creatures
garbed in the one-piece foil suits they had found

on the highest Level of the Freehold before each, in his own time and his own way, breached the last metal defense of their subterranean world, cracking the outer hatch, buried in drifting snow. The suits were extremely light, skintight along chest and arms, with filled pockets of hardware and food concentrates, vacuum-sealed, immune to the ravages of time, even a small supply of mineral-enriched fluid to refresh themselves. These pockets ran around the suits' waists and down the outside of each leg, somehow increasing the warmth of the garments.

Ronin stared at Borros, seeing him now as if for the first time, the focus of reality at last forced upon him, and all the raw hate that he had held in abeyance for these long moments flooded back on an inexorable tide. Caught in the slipstream of sewage; shook himself, as if the motion would somehow cleanse him. He knew that he carried now within his depths an anger and a sorrow, that thus was bound to him irrevocably a hideous strength.

The Magic Man had misunderstood the gesture and he grasped Ronin's shoulders.

'Surely you are not cold?'

His fingers moved along the foil to a fold at the back of Ronin's neck. 'Look here.' And he pulled gently upward, the metallic skin stretching to cover Ronin's head, leaving only his eyes and mouth exposed. Borros wrestled his own hood into place.

Borros turned to stare behind them, peering

across the rubble of the frozen waste to the hidden Freehold, the tiny access hatch leading down and down to the world inside, a world at war now, factions struggling for desperate power.

'Do not think me a fool,' the Magic Man said urgently. 'But we must flee from here at once.'

Tears call to Ronin and the mountains melting as he ceases to feel the bite of the wind at his eyes and lips. The sky colourless and the earth with no substance. His feet leaden. His heart pounding as it hit him searingly like the aftershock of a deep wound, the rent cauterized but the nerves still in dysfunction. At first there was no feeling at all. Numb. The body protecting itself. But there is a limit. His consciousness narrowed because he was struggling against it now. All his loves, all his friends, all the people. Gone in a wink of an eye. Just a flutter of time, the space to pull two breaths and lives are snuffed like tapers at first Spell. K'reen and Stahlig and Nirren and G'fand and – the Salamander, the centre of it all, still down there, alive, alive . . .

' – now.'

Slowly, it seemed to him, he became aware of a plucking at his sleeve.

'Ronin, please, we must be off.' He heard the words as if from a great distance. They hung in front of him like lamps, separate and solid, one after another, turning on some unseen axis, their sheen . . .

'Chill take it! Ronin, we mut go now! Before pursuit from below can be organized.'

14

Then the meaning had penetrated and he started as if from a deep slumber.

'Yes,' he said hoarsely, turned to look at Borros. 'Yes, of course we must be off.' His colourless eyes were clear now, their gaze sharp and quick. 'But which way?'

'There,' said the Magic Man. And he lifted his arm in a sweeping gesture outward, over the lip of the precipice to the enormous expanse of the darkling ice sea.

There was nought but the crying of the freezing wind. The ancient rock at his face, rippling, studded with ice in pockets and rivulets, slipped away above him centimetre by centimetre. The sound was like the wailing of the damned. Striations made a constantly changing pattern that held his attention as he searched for foot- and handholds. Following Borros down the immense face of the cliff towards the ice sea far, far below, he felt all too distinctly the void at his back. The magnitude of its emptiness beckoned to him, the wind its siren call, ululating hypnotically, Relax, let go, feel the gentle parting of warm flesh from cold stone, to fall backward, slowly, effortlessly onto the comforting cushion of the wind, turning, to be borne away, tumbling, into the void . . .

An ending he did not wish.

'What, over the edge?' he had said.

A peculiar animation had come to the Magic Man's face, a keen anticipation. 'Yes. Yes! Do you not see?' As if he had waited all his life for this

15

kinetic moment. 'It is the only way down to the ice sea. Our way lies south. South into the land of men.'

And so Ronin had walked with Borros through the crusty snow and treacherous ice to the very edge, entirely free at last of the ties that bind every man at one time to home. Masterless but not directionless.

They went carefully along the lip for perhaps a thousand meters and then Borros slipped over the side. Without a backward glance Ronin too quit the plateau.

Ronin became aware that Borros had stopped below him. He called down but the fluting of the wind made communication impossible at this distance. Carefully he lowered himself to the other's side.

'The way below is blocked,' Borros said in his ear.

Ronin peered down through the intermittent showers of snow. Indeed, directly below them a fresh fall of snow and ice crystals layered the cliff face and it was impossible to determine the nature of the footing. Suicidal to attempt the descent by touch alone, yet it was imperative that they move onward.

Ronin swung his gaze to their right where his peripheral vision had registered a dark area along the rock wall. Now, motioning with his head, he led the Magic Man towards its smudgy outline.

16

They inched along the narrow ledge upon which they had stopped their descent and soon the dark area took on definition. As Ronin had hoped, it was a cave of some considerable size and within its mouth they found a semblance of shelter from the wind and the cold.

Borros sighed deeply as he pulled off his hood. His hairless skull, faintly gleaming in the dim light, seemed peculiarly fitting for this foreign and forbidding place; its singular saffron colour could almost have passed for the patina of age.

Ronin went away from the rough rock walls to the lip of the cave. Below him the cliff dropped precipitously. Beneath the heavy fall of new snow clinging to the rock with an almost sentient tenacity there must be a way down to the ice sea. He could just make out a sliver of its surface sparkling in the lowering light. But from what he could see, there was no way of knowing, therefore no practical way down. Laterally there was only the mean ledge along which they had come. Farther to the right it disappeared into the rock face only meters from where he stood. He kicked at the snow, left plumes arcing out into the wind as he returned to the twilight of the cave.

Borros was agitated. 'What are we to do?' he asked Ronin as he stalked back and forth. 'We must continue the descent. Already men from the Freehold will be searching for us.'

Ronin's mouth moved into the semblance of a brief, chill smile. 'Do you really believe that they would allow anyone onto the Surface? They must think that we shall perish out here.'

The Magic Man's eyes darted from the cave's opening to Ronin's face, back again. 'You do not know Freidal. Or Security. My escape –' His eyes flicked back to the cave's mouth. 'He will kill me if he catches me.' His gaze passed across Ronin's face again like clouds across the face of the sun. 'You also. If he finds me, he finds you.'

'No one is after us,' Ronin said flatly.

Borros pulled his hood up over his bald skull. 'You are wrong but it makes no difference. Even if Freidal was not coming after us, we would still have no choice. We must descend to the ice sea. We cannot survive long here.'

'Better to die on the way down than here in the cave,' Ronin said sardonically.

Borros shrugged. 'Are you coming?'

He did not answer immediately but walked away from the light, into the cave's dank interior, smelling the acrid odour of raw minerals and rock dust, hearing the whistling of the wind diminish. Yet there was sound.

Far back in the cave he dimly heard the Magic Man's strident call but he ignored it. He listened intently, moving purposefully, his pulses quickening. And now he was sure. Excitedly he put his arms out, hands floating through the blackness, feeling along the wall like a blind man's.

He heard Borros calling thinly again, a forlorn and lonely sound, and he went slowly forward so as not to miss it. At last he stopped, his fingers

18

running over the metalwork he had been searching for and his heart soared because he knew now that there was after all a way down to the ice sea. He called out to Borros.

What he had thought was the soughing of the wind had in fact been the distant sound of rushing water. The wind had been in his ears for so long that it was not until he moved farther back into the cave that he had been able to pick up the subtle tonal alteration. Even so, had he not made the long descent from the Freehold to the City of Ten Thousand Paths – the flicker of G'fand's smiling face frozen in his mind's eye, dissolving into the bloody wreck of the Scholar's corpse flung along the dusty cobbles of the ancient street, eyes bulging, throat torn out by the nameless towering thing that Ronin had tried twice to kill and failed, inhuman eyes like crescent moons, a chill more deadly than a coffin of ice and a power – he never would have recognized the new sound as a torrent of water pitching headlong over smooth rock down and down in a frantic cascade. He and G'fand had encountered the immense waterfall on their way to the City of Ten Thousand Paths and its reverberations had been with them for many kilometres. It was the same sound now, merely muffled by distance.

'Borros,' Ronin called again.

They were obviously far from the cataract yet the presence of the sound was a clear indication that this cave was perhaps more than just that. Ronin believed now that they were in the

19

outermost reaches of a tunnel. He thought of Bonneduce the Last, the small, lame man, and his companion, Hynd, a creature that was more than an animal. He and G'fand had encountered the pair in the City of Ten Thousand Paths. Bonneduce the Last had assured them that he and Hynd dwelled on the Surface but had given no indication of how they had come to the City. Could this have been his entrance and egress? Ronin was certain that it was. Given that, the cave must contain a means to descend to the ice sea.

His hand wrapped around the haft.

Borros came up then.

'I have found something,' Ronin told him. 'Do you have tinder?'

The Magic Man reached into one of his pockets, produced tinder and flint. Together they lit the torch.

The flame, tiny at first, sizzled pale yellow and smoked on the damp material so that they choked and, coughing, were forced to turn their heads away. The orange light leapt and quivered and, wiping the water from their eyes, they were for the first time able to see the rough and gritty walls, black ice gleaming like obsidian in the shadowed hollows, the surface streaked ochre and green, silver and pink by the exposed minerals.

Everything they needed was there, hanging by the metalwork of the torch's niche. Long coils of rope of a peculiar material not thick but, as Ronin pulled on them, obviously more than strong enough. Beneath the ropes, small metal hammers with long heads and with these bags filled with metal spikes of unfamiliar manufacture, flattened and broader at the end through which was punched a circular hole large enough for the rope to pass through.

'And so,' said Ronin, 'we descend the cliff after all.'

His head whipped up and his nostrils dilated as the smell came to him. They had worked hard, on their knees driving the spikes into the rock floor of the cave just inside the mouth. They had inserted the ropes and tied double knots, leaning back and pulling hard to test the fastness of their handiwork. The small bags they tied to their suits; the hammers dangled from their wrists by short thongs. Wrapping the ropes about their waists, they had walked to the lip of the cave. Ronin let the rope drop and his fist went to the hilt of his sword.

Before, it had been a stench when the monstrous thing came for them from out of the black shadows through the dry dust and golden dimness, its fearsome visage dominated by the glowing eyes and the curved, wicked beak. His stomach heaved at the thought of its invulnerability, the desperation of his attack as G'fand lay mutilated. The smell was like a living thing then. Now it was far off but, he surmised, reachable; it was getting stronger. He let the anger and fear mingle within him until it became rage. Adrenalin rushed through his body and he clenched his hand within the gauntlet left for him by Bonneduce the Last, cunningly made from the giant claw of one of the hideous creatures. How many of them were there? he wondered fleetingly. He began to withdraw his sword.

And felt the hand on his shoulder, heard the voice crying urgently at his side, 'What are you doing? You fool, we must go now! There is no time to lose!' His hand tightened on the sword hilt. 'Ronin, we must reach the ice sea!'

Instinctively he knew that Borros was correct. Their survival must come first. His battle would have to wait. And perhaps that was for the best. He wanted to be able to pick the time and the place when he would next meet the creature. But more importantly he needed more information about it if he was to have a real chance of killing it and surviving.

He let go the sword and picked up the rope, securing it once more about his waist. He nodded wordlessly to the Magic Man and they crunched backward through the snow. On the ledge the wind bit into the exposed areas of their faces as they went over the edge.

He hung suspended, dangling, the rope biting cruelly into his ankle. Momentum, he thought as warily they circled him, knowing their advantage but fearing him still. He had no weapon and of course that was the point. Because, as he had once told G'fand, learning the art of Combat meant much more than being taught to wield a sword.

His body, near naked and slick with the sweat

22

of exertion and heat, swung along its brief orbit. Keep the body relaxed, the Salamander had told him. Work within as small a space as you feel you can allow without sacrificing the momentum provided by the orbit of the swing. You understand, Ronin, that once inertia takes over you are finished because an opponent will gut you in the time it takes you to overcome it.

Other students in the special Combat class presided over by the Salamander had attempted the *cruol*, that length of rope suspended from the ceiling to which one was tied head down a metre off the floor. Four students attacked with wooden staffs the length of a man's body. No one had survived for long. However, none of the students had been trained by the Salamander as extensively as had Ronin. And none had his skill.

Because it was so terribly difficult, the *cruol* was now used almost exclusively for punishment. Yet Up here on the Salamander's Level it had other uses.

He kept the momentum going, consciously feeding the adrenalin flowing through his body, knowing he would need all that he could produce in the coming moments. A staff came at him, whistling through the air. He twisted his shoulders and felt a burning down his back at the narrowness of the miss. The students fanned out, swinging at him again and again. He used his forearms to block the staffs, while gradually increasing the length of his arcs. Less and less, they found the need to advance towards him in order to make

23

contact; they were too intent on the attack to take notice.

He swung, waiting for a peak, and for a lateral cut. He saw one coming from the left and he knew that it would be close because he was just at the peak of his arc and the student's blow had to be fast or he would lose the advantage of the momentum. But the staff came at him with tremendous force and it was all right because now he was beginning to arc away from the oncoming staff, his momentum picking up, and now, instead of blocking the blow, he reached for the blurred weapon, his tightening fingers slipping along its length in the slick sweat running off him. Palms burning with the friction, a blow from another staff numbing the muscles along his back. Ignore the pain. Concentrate. He used his mounting momentum and, twisting his wrists at the last instant, wrenched the staff from the startled student.

He was moving to his right with great speed now and, taking advantage of the direction of his swing, slammed the staff into the collarbone of a student on that side. He crumpled to the floor as Ronin began to reverse his arc and caught a second adversary in the mid-section so that the student doubled over, retching and gagging.

There was only one now because the one Ronin had disarmed was forbidden to interfere once he had lost his weapon. This one was wary. He would not be trapped as his fellows had been. Ronin noted that he was concentrating on Ronin's

24

weapon. Then he attacked, swinging at the base of Ronin's staff, seeking to bruise his hands. The blows were rapid-fire so that, for every one Ronin blocked, one slammed into his knuckles. They soon turned red and the first spattering of blood appeared as the skin split and tore. The student pressed his advantage, moving in, the bright blood fascinating and irresistible. His concentration narrowed.

It was then that Ronin used his free leg, slamming the sole of his boot against the side of the student's head. The man staggered, off balance. The blow had not been hard enough to knock him down because Ronin lacked the leverage, but it was enough. The staff sang through the air, catching the student on the neck. He gasped hollowly, his face turning white and his mouth hinged open as he fell. There was only the sound of forced breathing then as Ronin dropped his staff, relaxing his body, turning slowly again in his brief orbit.

Suspended in whiteness, his breath fogging the frigid air, descending hand over hand, Borros slightly above him a metre away, Ronin recalled well the lesson of the *cruol*. But now the context had altered, small patterns interlaced with other patterns until, as one steps back to view the configuration, an overall image begins to emerge, different, unexpected.

'My dear boy, of course they hate you.'

The voice was rich and vibrant but with more

than a hint of effete coyness that was as disarming as it was spurious.

'It is quite understandable, really.'

The Salamander, the Senseii, the Weaponsmaster of the Freehold, stood in the doorway of Ronin's spartan cubicle. Not much time had passed since they had cut Ronin down and told him to return to his room.

Ronin moved to stand up but a curt motion, a flash of the Salamander's wide wrist, stopped him.

'Sit, my dear boy, by all means. You have certainly earned the privilege.' The voice flowed thickly, honeyed the air.

The Salamander, an immense figure, was garbed informally in crimson shirt, hung in layers which cunningly concealed the extent of his true bulk, jet-black leggings and high boots of the same colour polished to glossy perfection. His rich black hair was swept back along his skull like the wings of some awesome predatory bird. His thick brows and high cheekbones managed in some unfathomable fashion to accentuate the large onyx eyes, oval, and as hard and opaque as stone.

He moved into the room and it seemed to shrink in size, a diminishing and insignificant background in his presence. He stared unblinkingly at Ronin.

'You are not happy here, my dear boy.' It was not a question. 'Perhaps this is because you feel that you have no friends.'

'Yes,' Ronin said unknowingly. 'All the students hate me.'

The Salamander looked at Ronin with a veiled gaze and smiled without warmth.

'But of course that is true and that should please you greatly. It does me.' Ronin's face was blank with surprise but the Salamander ignored that. 'You are the best, my dear boy; without question the very best student that I have trained. And now no one can touch you, not student, not Bladesman. Oh yes' – he laughed at the expression on Ronin's face – 'that is quite true. You are as far above them as I am above you.' His laughter took on a manic quality.

Ronin was acutely aware of the compliment. It puzzled rather than delighted him. The reaction was quite inexplicable.

The Salamander's fist clenched and his rings caught the light in brief explosions of colour. He bent forward slightly, his voice less oratorical now, more personal.

'They hate you, my dear boy, because you are better than they, you have the talent that they wish they possessed, and they will not rest until they best you in Combat.' His laugh was a bark of emotion. 'Good! For that too serves my purpose. My Bladesmen must be the best in the Freehold.' He touched his chest, a dramatic gesture he nevertheless managed to imbue with a certain grandeur. 'Am I not alone of all the Saardin, Senseii? It is honor. What do the other Saardin know of that?' His voice lowered in volume and gained in intensity. 'They know only to bicker among themselves, vying for power.' He threw his head back and his eyes squeezed shut, then flew open, impaling Ronin with their implacable gaze. 'They do not understand the meaning of the word "power".' He stopped abruptly, realizing that he had revealed more than he had intended. 'It is honour,' he said then, 'that must be upheld always.' He stepped closer to Ronin. 'You must understand this totally.'

He came and sat on the thin bed.

'But you, my dear boy' – a heavy bejeweled hand stroked softly Ronin's arm – 'you also serve my purpose. I have laboured long and hard to make you a Bladesman unmatched by any bound to the Saardin of the Freehold. Tomorrow you will enter the Square of Combat for the last time as a student.' His voice held a quivering note of triumph which he did not bother to conceal. 'You will stun the Instructors who will be there to judge you and then, when you have emerged from Combat a Bladesman, the Freehold's finest Bladesman, while the Instructors and the Saardin are still babbling to each other of your skill, then you will return here to be my Chondrin.'

A stillness eddied in the room, as absolute as a vacuum. For a time it ruled and then, quite slowly, it seemed to Ronin, the tiny background sounds of the Level returned to his ears, drifting male voices, the comforting slap of boot soles against the wooden floor, the distant metal clangour of Combat practice, sounds which had comprised the environmental context of his life for so long.

28

Changed now, these noises came to him as harsh and brittle and without meaning, as if, of a sudden, he found himself in an alien world, wondering just how long he had been there. And looking into the glittery, obsidian eyes so close to his, he saw nothing whatsoever.

They dropped silently into the void, from time to time using hammer and spike to gain footholds along the sheer face of the cliff, or to circumnavigate an otherwise impassable section. It seemed that they had descended for hours, through the mist and the small snowfalls like choking dust storms flung against them by fierce updrafts. They paused neither to rest nor to eat, gulping handfuls of snow occasionally to slake their thirst, to keep them going.

Borros' urgency had become infectious. For Ronin it was perhaps the stench of the monstrous creature, still crawling in his nostrils, which had finally severed the twanging chord of his grief, once as raw and painful as an exposed nerve, and which now allowed him to focus on the reason for this journey. He had gone to the City of Ten Thousand Paths on Borros' urgings. The Magic Man was convinced that a terrifying menace was threatening to engulf the world of man. Perhaps Ronin only half believed him when he first journeyed forth but after encountering Bonneduce the Last and Hynd, after the battles with the thing that killed G'fand, he felt within him a peculiar kind of personal confirmation of what Borros had told him. And the journey had been successful. The Magic Man had sent him on a quest for an ancient scroll, which Ronin had found in the house of dor-Sefrith, purportedly the most famed and feared sorcerer of the legendary isle of Ama-no-mori, now no more than mounds of cracked stone and masonry beneath some far-off sea, Ronin mused. Pity. But I have the scroll now and, as Borros has told me, it is the key to stopping this inhuman menace. He smiled to himself. Despite Freidal's efforts, despite the Salamander's attempted interference. Only I have the scroll. He glanced at the thin face, drawn and haggard with fatigue, the yellow tinge sickly in the failing light. I have yet to tell him. That should bring a smile. And when we find out what it says, we shall return.

Ronin indeed returned from the Square of Combat a Bladesman. He had, as the Salamander had correctly predicted, stunned the Instructors and the Saardin, who had never been seen his like in skill and speed in Combat. Their excited talk sickened him. Yet in one important decision the Salamander would be proven wrong.

Ronin returned Upshaft to the Senseii's Level not in the least elated. He had had no doubts as to his ability and therefore felt no trepidation when it came time for his Trial. On the contrary he felt that the Salamander had dawdled over him, procrastinating, postponing again and again his Trial date. In his own mind, he had been ready many sign ago. Now it seemed to him that the date itself meant more to the Salamander than the Trial itself.

The Salamander was waiting for him in the Hall of Combat. His enormous figure was draped in ceremonial robes of jet. His hair was newly coifed and oiled and the fan that he could wield as dextrously and as fatally as a sword or dagger protruded from his wide scarlet sash. He wore a sword on his left hip, sheathed in a formal scabbard of openwork silver with an ebon tip, intricately carved in the shape of a rampant lizard on a bed of black flame.

On either side of him, dwarfed by his bulk, stood two of his Bladesmen. One held the bands which went obliquely from left shoulder to right hip across the tunic of each Chondrin. These bands were differing colours to identify which Saardin the Chondrin was bound to. The Bladesmen held black on black bands, the Salamander's colours.

The moment Ronin saw the bands, his decision was made. He knew quite clearly what he should do, what he had after all been trained for. He stopped before the Salamander and bowed stiffly, his face a mask, thinking, I know too what I must do. There was a great sadness within him. The Salamander inclined his head solemnly. He was more to Ronin than Combat Instructor, Senseii, Saardin. Yet still Ronin would have no man his master; would have no one now impose his will upon him, that time was surely passed forever. Free at last, he would not enslave himself within the complex political labyrinth of the Freehold society. He had his strength and power; he required nothing more.

'Now you are Bladesman,' the Salamander said formally. Was there a trace of pride in his voice? Oh, surely not from the Salamander. 'You are henceforth my vassal. You obey my commands; are subject to my disciplines, my ordinances, and my will. No other may command your arm or your mind so long as I shall live. In return, you have my protection, the power of my office as Saardin and my power as Senseii of the Freehold. In honor I offer you the bands of the Salamander, Saardin, Senseii of the Freehold, as my Chondrin, to advise, to defend, to command my Bladesmen, to obey me.'

The Bladesman holding the bands stepped forward.

'Do you accept the bands of Chondrin and by doing so pledge your arm and your mind to me?'

'Salamander,' said Ronin hoarsely, 'I cannot.'

'Not much more to go,' Borros said over the crying of the wind. Ronin looked down. The mist and snow had thinned enough for him to see that several hundred meters below them the cliff face ceased its precipitous plunge earthward and became a widening slope upon which they could likely walk downwards the rest of the way to the ice sea.

The expanse was lit now by the wan silver light of the moon, its mottled face hanging large and hungry in a sky of trembling cloud. Ronin stared at the oval, then back again to the ice sea still far below them.

And still they descended, though weariness gripped them like a tightening vise.

In the end it would be his face that stood out in Ronin's memory. For just an instant, a sliver so brief that perhaps only Ronin could have caught it, the seemingly impenetrable façade of the decadent and rather bored Weaponmaster, refined and honed for so many years, appeared to crack and, like the onrush of a spring waterfall, sending rainbows into the light, a score of emotions seemed to dart across his visage. So quickly were they covered that Ronin could not even be sure. Had he seen sadness, shock, anger, hurt? All of them, Ronin surmised. He had been too wrapped up in what he had to do to understand then the larger pattern.

'You cannot!' bellowed the Salamander. 'Cannot? What are you saying, you cannot? You will! You must! It cannot be any other way!' Still impaling Ronin with his furious gaze, he reached out, clutched at the Chondrin's bands, waved them at Ronin. 'You mock this trust! Just as you mock me!' His face was red and spittle flew from the glistening surfaces of his wet lips. He crumpled the bands and threw them in Ronin's face. Ronin felt unable to move or to speak.

The huge face quivered before him. 'You cannot? You do not even understand the meaning of those words.' He raised a huge fist. 'I saw in

you what no one else could, what you yourself
were blind to. It was *my* vision which created you,
my ideas which molded you into the Freehold's
finest Bladesman.' His voice had risen in volume
and force; now his entire frame shook as if within
him a fierce storm raged. 'I trained you, accepted
you, offer you the highest honour!' He advanced
on Ronin. 'And you spit in my face!' The voice
was a shriek now, echoing off the high walls.
Abruptly he swiped with the back of his hand, the
motion so swift that Ronin could not have reacted
if he had wanted to. But he had not wanted to; he
knew with a chilling finality that if he moved at all
he was a dead man.

The blow caught him full on the face, the rings
scouring his cheek. It was a gesture of disdain and
that hurt him more than the enormous force of the
blow, more than the cuts opening up the skin of
his face. Those would heal eventually.

'You do not understand. You know nothing of
honor!' The Salamander hurled the words out as if
they were somehow tainted. Then he hit Ronin
again, and a third time with his hand now a
clenched fist, crying out in rage because Ronin
would not fall, would not retreat, would not
retaliate. 'How dare you! How dare you!' A litany
of humiliation. Pounding at Ronin. Now his
Bladesmen attempted to restrain him. He shook
them off like droplets of water.

'Get away from me!' he screamed. 'Get out of
here! Get out!' And they scrambled obediently
from his presence.

Still he beat Ronin, howling 'Aaahhh!', beyond coherent speech now, staggering, irrational, inhuman.

He reached thick fingers into his sash, grasped the fan, about to draw it forth, spread its lethal edge, a supple guillotine. Then he stopped, his breathing hard and irregular.

'No,' he gasped. 'No. That would be too easy.' His hand came away empty and, turning, he lurched out of the door.

Ronin stood in the centre of the Hall of Combat, hearing the susurration of his harsh breathing like the pounding of wild surf upon a desolate shore, his head and torso aflame with throbbing pain he only dimly felt, and thought, Now we are both shamed.

'What now?!' Borros called to him.

They twisted in the air. Some twenty meters below them beckoned the lower slopes of the cliff. But they were, literally, at the end of their ropes.

'We are short,' said the Magic Man. He kicked at the rock face to stop his twisting; it only made it worse.

'Quit that,' Ronin said. 'Relax your body.'

'I have no strength left,' Borros called pitifully. 'I am exhausted.'

'Then save your breath,' Ronin said reasonably. He peered down again. In the uncertain light, as dense clouds rode across the moon's pale face, he could just make out the blanket of new snow covering the upper slope. But how deep was it? he asked himself. He took the small hammer off his wrist and let it go. It hit the snow and disappeared. He unhooked the bag of spikes and dropped that too. It hit the snow near the spot where the hammer went in and disappeared. Only one thing left to do, he thought. And let go the rope.

He heard a scream and it confused him momentarily and then he was into it, under it, its weight upon him, and he could not breathe and the blackness was a suffocating mass around him, above him but he pushed up, straining and clawing, and broke the surface, inhaling the chilled air in great lungfuls. He felt ice and rock beneath his feet.

The scream came again and he knew that it was Borros.

'All right, Borros,' he shouted, cupping his hands by his mouth. 'I am in the snow below you. Can you hear me?'

The sobbing of the wind.

'Yes.'

'Let yourself drop. The snow will cushion your fall.'

'I am afraid.'

'Close your eyes and let go the rope.'

'Ronin – '

'Chill take you! Do it!'

He heard the crunch against the crisp top layer of snow and was already moving, using sound as well as sight, as fast as he could to the spot. But the deep snow pulled at him and he panted, thinking of the Magic Man's exhaustion, knowing that he would have to pull him free very quickly or he would suffocate.

The undulating expanse of snow was albescent in the moonlight. He waded through it, tired himself, and stumbled, face in the snow, and instinctively pushed up with his hands, sinking deeper into it. Then his brain began to function again and he pushed this time with his feet and knees against the ice and then he was up. He located the darkness of the hole, went to it and dug down hard, shovelling desperately with his fingers, feeling at last the body like a dead weight, and hauled upward now with all his strength, hauling at a weight that seemed inordinately heavy, feeling time slip away beneath him, willing his fingers not to slip.

Borros came up slowly, like an ancient galleon buried beneath a sea reluctant to part with its prize, and as soon as his head came into the open Ronin slapped it. The Magic Man coughed and sputtered and half-melted ice drooled from his slowly working lips. Ronin picked him up.

'All right,' Borros whispered, so softly that it could have been the moaning of the wind. 'I am' – he choked, caught himself, then inhaled his first deep breath – 'quite all right.'

Ronin shoveled snow with his arms, making a shallow depression along the lee of the slope just below the sheer face of the cliff, an implacable wall lifting black shadows, it seemed, into the reaches of the tremulous sky. Deep enough for them to huddle, taking respite from the constant bite of wind and frost while they rested. Borros attempted to rake out several small packets from within his suit but his hands were shaking badly and Ronin had to lift them out, feed Borros as he fed himself.

Across the trackless slope they went dazedly, down, ever down, the wind blowing the drifting snow into their faces mingling with sharp-edged ice crystals as the temperature plummeted. Their lips were frosted and their eyebrows and lashes rimed with ice. Beneath their hoods, their cheeks were already numb. Still they moved painfully onward and when Borros fell Ronin bent and lifted him, the weight as nothing now. He half dragged him, stumbling, along the downward slope, through the drag of the heavy snow, deaf from the wind and then blind in the night, animal instinct alone lifting one foot after another onward, onward . . .

His first thought was the warmth and he recalled a fire leaping and logs crackling and the cheery orange glow. He tried to move closer to the warmth and could not budge. Through a thick haze he understood that something was wrong. One side of his face was warm and – With a start he realized where he was, that he was face down in the snow. With infinite slowness he lifted himself centimetre by centimetre until he was sitting up. He touched the side of his face eventually and discovered that it was numb.

Even then, when it occurred to him within the

context of reality that they might die, he would not give in to it. He went to his hands and knees, saw Borros lying beside him. He was facing the way they had come, away in the distance the solid rock of the awesome, towering cliff down which they had made their descent.

He tried to stand and slipped, sliding downward along his belly. It took him several moments to realize. Then he looked down, oblivious suddenly to the freezing cold and the harsh bite of the wind. He reached out with his hands, felt the ground.

Smooth.

'Borros,' he called in a cracked and dry voice.

Smooth and flat and hard.

'Borros!'

And he turned his face, then his body, until he was facing southward and he beheld the enormous glowing expanse of the ice sea.

'We are here!'

Heat fled up his arms from his finger tips into his shoulders. The image of the flame, dancing lazily from behind the small grating was hypnotic. The gentle bumping, the soft creaking, a soporific. Across from him, Borros was already asleep, his utter fatigue taking him. Ronin felt the swift motion under him, knew sleep was almost here. Almost.

They had lurched, insensate, down the final series of low slopes, to the very edge of the ice sea, without knowing it. There at its banks they had collapsed.

At first Ronin had believed Borros delirious when he had revived him and the Magic Man had told him at last the secret of survival upon the ice sea. Impossible. But already Ronin was learning to ignore that word, for he had been through so many seemingly impossible situations, seen so many startling sights, been forced to readjust to many of the concepts he had originally been taught, this was but a momentary reaction. And too it was their only hope of survival upon the world's forbidding surface; he lost no time in useless queries, he began the search.

It was easier than he could have imagined. Barely a thousand metres from where they had fallen, he found the small headland that Borros had assured him would be there. Mounded in snow many times higher than any area near it, it jutted out into the ice sea. And feverishly now he began to dig.

Moonlight, pale and glittery against the smooth surface of the platinum ice, revealed to him what Borros had told him he would unearth.

Even so it came as a shock, a current like lightning racing through his body momentarily thawing the chill. He began to dig harder now that the outlines had been uncovered and at last he was through and he turned and brought the Magic Man, a muscular arm across his back for support, so that they both could see it together.

The mist had risen, diffusing the monochrome light, but above the moon was riding free, its intermittent cloud cover racing westward. Of this fact they were oblivious as they stood, captivated by the image which loomed before them.

It was sleek. Long and curving, raised on slender runners.

'A felucca,' Borros breathed almost reverently. 'They did not lie.' There were tears standing in the corners of his eyes. 'For years I read and dreamed and, when I was sure, I promised myself that one day – ' He shook his head and the tears flipped to the piled snow of the promontory. 'But now I see that I was not so sure after all, a doubt remained. Until this moment. Oh, Ronin, look at it!'

It was a ship. An ice ship.

Slowly they went on board, explored the high prow and the sweep of its beam all the way to the low stern; they strode along the smooth deck, ran frozen fingers across the top of the low cabin aft rising just above the gunwale.

They went below, finding narrow berths with blankets along the hull, and a black metal oblong in the center of the cabin. Ronin took tinder and flint and, on Borros' instructions, opened the small hinged grate in the front and sparked a flame. The fire came instantly to the interior and Ronin, closing the grate, was too grateful for the warmth to inquire about the fuel source.

He put Borros on a bunk, listened to him talk for a short time, then went on deck. He took the mast from its storage rack along the port sheer-strake and set it in its place just astern of midships. He set the yard, low down on the mast. Then he went over the side and hacked at the metal chocks

41

holding the runners in place. When they were freed, he went aboard and unfurled the high sweeping lateen sail.

Coming down the low slopes, the wind had been off the sea, into their faces. At some point it had turned and, picking up velocity, was now whipping almost due south. Ronin, setting the last of the rigging, thought, Now there is nothing more to do. Borros assures me that we need not stand lookout this night, that there is clear sailing. Does he really know? I wonder.

At that moment there came a powerful lurch and, as the sail caught the wind, the vessel, now standing clear on its runway of ice, was launched upon the ice sea.

Ronin, fatigued and unprepared, fell to the deck. Moving cautiously to the stern, he hauled hard on the wheel and lashed it tight as Borros had instructed him. They flew along the ice due south, the stiff wind billowing the sail, pushing them. He stared ahead for a moment, but the moon had disappeared behind racing clouds and new mist was settling in. Nothing more to do. With a final glance at the fastness of the rigging, he went below.

Sleep.

'Tomorrow night.'

A small squat lamp hanging from a beam in the cabin's low ceiling had been lit. It swung with the ship's motion, shadows fleeing across the bulkheads.

'What?' he said thickly.

Through round crystal portals set in either bulk-head he saw that it was still dark out. It was warm and comfortable here and he closed his eyes, sighing.

'We slept through the night,' said Borros from his berth across the cabin, 'and all of the next day.' He smiled wearily. 'I got up once and it was near sunset, that is how I know. I went on deck and found that the wind had changed slightly. We were running more to the west than I wanted, as close as I could tell – the sun sets only roughly in the west – so I reset the wheel.' He stood up carefully. He looked thin and gaunt. 'Hungry?' Ronin opened his eyes.

They ate voraciously from the stores on ship; concentrates with unsatisfying flavours, but they filled the belly. Abruptly he remembered the frost-bite of his face but, lifting a hand, he could feel no burn or discomfort.

'The ancients anticipated that possibility also,' said the Magic Man. 'You will find a packet of the unguent in one of the pockets of your suit. When I woke yesterday, I fixed us both up at the same time.' He smiled almost apologetically. 'I did not see the need to wake you.' He lay back on his bunk, as if the talk had weakened him.

'Are you all right?' Ronin asked.

The Magic Man lifted a slender hand. 'Only – it will take me somewhat more time than you to recover.' His lips turned up again in a watery smile. 'The disadvantages of age, you understand.'

43

Ronin turned away. 'I have a surprise for you,' he said.

'Ah, good. But first you must tell me of your journey to the City of Ten Thousand Paths.' Ronin looked back at him in time to see the sorrow and regret in his eyes. He shook his head ruefully. 'I am so sorry, Ronin. I sent you on a madman's quest, an impossible – '

'But – '

'They told me about G'fand – '

'Ah.' His heart felt as cold as ice. 'Did they?'

'Yes.' He grimaced. 'It was part of my treatment. Freidal had already subjected me to such prolonged physical torture' – unconsciously his thin fingers sought his forehead, where before Ronin had seen the terrifying marks of the Dehn spots – 'in trying to pry out of me all that I knew of the Surface, that he felt it was time to change tactics. I knew all along that I had sent you down to the City of Ten Thousand Paths and he could have stopped you at any time – '

'He wanted to see what I would return with, since he could not break you.'

But Borros was not listening; he was remembering. 'He was so clever, Chill take him! He came in and told them to stop; gave me water and let me rest. Told me that I had been through it all and had not given in; that it was useless for him to try any more. He – he said that he admired me' – his voice turned to a tremulous fluting – 'that as soon as I had recovered, I was free to go.' He passed a frail hand across his eyes as if the gesture would blot out the nightmare that played in his mind and which, compulsively now, spewed from his mouth.

' "Oh, by the way," he said, as if it were the last thing on his mind, "we have taken Ronin into custody. He has just returned to the Freehold after making an unauthorized exit. We have asked him quite politely where he went, after all it is a Security matter. The safety of the Freehold is at stake; if he can egress, others may gain entrance. So you understand that we must find out where he went and why. It is a matter of utmost importance." Freidal sighed. "But so far he has been most reluctant to accommodate us. He refuses, Borros, to do his duty to the Freehold. You understand what must be done now." I did indeed; he meant to use the Dehn on you. "His disrespectful actions leave me no choice. Oh yes," he said then, "I almost forgot. The young man who accompanied him – a scholar, I believe – G'fand – was killed. Unfortunate, but scholars are hardly essential to the stability of the Freehold." '

Borros shifted uncomfortably on his berth but found no surcease. His eyes were still turned inward. 'Freidal was furious that I did not crumble then, as he had hoped, so he' – the Magic Man's thin frame shuddered – 'he had Stahlig brought in. He had his daggam drag Stahlig in front of me. Someone held my head so that I could not turn away; they hit me when I tried to shut my eyes.' He lifted his head, the narrow skull shining like ancient bone, his eyes lustreless. 'When Stahlig looked at me – I have never seen such terror written upon the face of a human being.' He let go a suspiration then, and it all came out. 'Freidal said to him: "What is it that you fear most, Stahlig? The loss of your feet? Would you care to crawl through the Freehold on your knees? Perhaps your eyes. Do you fear blindness? No? I could break your back then; leave you alive, alive and immobile." And seeing the look in Stahlig's eyes, he continued: "That would be most fitting, would it not? Your friend Ronin left my man Marcsh with a broken back. But you know that; you treated Marcsh. You will be totally helpless; to be fed and wiped like a baby."'

The wind, muffled somewhat by the cabin's bulkheads, moaned mournfully, momentarily drowning out the soft scraping sounds of the runners gliding swiftly over the ice, as if it too was witness to the horror that the Magic Man had conjured.

Borros put his head in his hands. 'In the end,' he whispered so softly that it was like a ghost's breath, 'Stahlig died of fright.'

There was silence for a time save for the moaning and occasional creak of the fittings abovedecks. Ronin lay back on his berth and tried to think of nothing, but his brain was on fire and he got up and went silently up the short vertical companionway.

The small ship shot through the mists of night ever southward. Ronin, on deck, could see nought but the blurred shadows of the ribboning ice as it sped by beneath the vessel. It was a quarter wind which now propelled them and he busied himself learning the fundamentals of tacking into it, working hard at the rigging to keep them on course.

He went aft and freed the wheel, steering manually for a time, letting the vibrations flow from his hands into his body borne away on an imaginary tide. The endless gentle soughing of the runners peeling a thin film of ice below stood by him like a spectral companion.

The wind strained the sail. Already the weather was changing, the air wetter, denser than before and, because of it, the cold seemed fiercer, creeping beneath the skin into flesh and bone. At length Ronin lashed the wheel to and, taking a last deep breath, went below.

Borros lay on his berth staring blankly upward.

'The surprise, Borros,' Ronin said gently. 'I have not told you what it is.'

'Uhm.'

'Do you remember why you sent me to the City of Ten Thousand Paths?'

'Of course, but – ' He sat up so suddenly that he barely missed hitting his head on a beam. Colour had returned to his yellow face. 'You cannot mean – ' At last there was a light kindling his eyes. 'But Freidal had you and – '

'And the Salamander also; his men took me from Security.' A wintry smile broke out on Ronin's face.

The Magic Man's mouth opened soundlessly.

'And?'

Ronin laughed then, for the first time in many cycles. 'And? And? Freidal found nothing, though he was justifiably curious about this' – he lifted his strange gauntlet – 'and the Salamander lacked the time to find anything – '

'Are you telling me that you actually found the scroll? Ronin, you have it?' Borros came excitedly across to him.

Ronin withdrew his sword, grasped the hilt, and twisted it three times. It came away in his hand. From within its hollowed-out recesses Ronin gently pulled forth the scroll of dor-Sefrith. He handed it to the Magic Man, who delicately opened it and stared, breathing, 'You *have* found it. Oh, Ronin – !'

He gave Borros several moments before he said, 'Now you must tell me what it says and why it is so important.'

Borros looked up at him, the flame from the swinging lamp reflecting in his eyes, turning them colourless.

'But you see, Ronin,' he said in a tired voice, 'I do not know.'

There was a time – he could actually force himself to remember that far back in the dim and cloudy past, though he rarely wished to – when Stahlig, the Medicine Man, was not a part of his life.

He had fallen down half a flight of stairs, choked with rubble and debris. Exploring. As he had come to a landing, something had shot across his path, tiny nails clicking industriously, and he had lost his balance, tumbling down the Stairwell.

He might not have been hurt at all if it had been clear. But he had fetched up against a fallen girder, twisted and red, his leg slamming into its side where it lay slashed through a rent in the outer wall. Perhaps he passed out from the pain. Eventually, he got to the Medicine Man on the next Level, limping and crawling because no one was about to help him.

His left leg was broken but he was young and strong and Stahlig knew his business. It was a clean break and with the white end protruding through the torn flesh appeared worse than it in fact was. The bones knit perfectly but that became secondary to him. Stahlig talked to him while he went about setting the leg. That was what interested him, intrigued him, what, ultimately, caused him to return to Stahlig's med rooms whenever he was able. The Medicine Man had no reason to treat Ronin in a special way, yet he did, recognizing somewhere within him a potential others would not.

The two became friends and the reason did not matter at all, at least to either of them. That did not mean that it did not go unnoticed in some quarters of the Freehold, noted, written down, filed away for future use.

We accepted each other, Ronin thought as the ship rocked beneath him. And now you have joined so many others who have known me and because of it have died.

49

Outside, the wind was rising, plucking at the rigging in mournful melody.

'You do not know?' echoed Ronin without emotion. 'What have you done to me?'

Borros put the scroll back into its hiding place in the hilt of Ronin's sword. He rubbed his eyes.

'Sit,' he said, and put his hand on Ronin's shoulder. 'Sit and I will tell you all that I *do* know.'

In ancient times, when the world spun faster upon its axis and the sun burned with energy in the sky, when multitudes of people roamed the surface of all the planet and, beneath their feet, the land turned from dirt and high grass plains as they walked, to fields of rowed food plants green and golden in the sunshine, to arid deserts smeared with low-growing flowers of many hues, to steep windswept steppes and mountain ranges blue with haze, when high-prowed ships from many nations plied the seas in search of trade with new lands, then Ronin, then we were known by another name. We were scientists and then our work was highly empirical, our theorems coming almost exclusively from the forebrain. Are you familiar with the word 'empirical'? Ah, good. Methodology was our watchword, this strict catholicism a firm and supportive base for our work.

But times changed radically and the world of the ancients was disappearing. In that interim period, the world was seized by a progression of natural cataclysms. The continents broke apart and fell away to be replaced by others, rising steamily from beneath the boiling seas. As you may well imagine, many people died but, perhaps more importantly, at the same time the laws that had heretofore governed the world of the ancients were overthrown and destroyed. Others came into being.

The inconceivable had occurred; by what means it is impossible to say, nor is it entirely germane to this account. Still, whatever formal records of that time ever existed are lost now – what remains are but fragments pertaining to the world as it was before.

Naturally, among the living were numerous scientists, yet so tied were they to the bedrock of their empiricism that, though it was clear to many others that the world had irrevocably changed so that the old methodology now worked only sporadically, the scientists refused to listen.

Certain members of these others, born to the new order of things, were able to make, because they had not been trained in the traditional ways of man, the great leap forward in thinking. These then became great mages, as they explored new methods, discovering alchemical, then sorcerous pathways, shining like beacons in the night. So they grew in power, at length banishing the scientists whom they scorned and ridiculed as they threw them down. Then they took upon themselves the mantle of overlords and in so doing lost sight of the original goals of their creation. Irresponsibly, they began to vie with each other for territory and power.

The inevitable holocaust of their quarreling spread throughout the world. The destruction was ghastly; its extent blossoming to unthinkable heights. Many people went underground. The City of Ten Thousand Paths came into being in this way. It was an attempt to form a peaceful society composed of members of all the surviving nations.

But among the populace of the City of Ten Thousand Paths were both mages and scientists, and they were ever at war. It is said that of all the mages only dor-Sefrith of Ama-no-mori remained unmoved and uninvolved though both sides desperately sought his considerable power.

From the time of the holocaust onward, there was of course an attrition of knowledge and each succeeding generation learned less and, eventually, when even dor-Sefrith's long neutrality ceased to maintain the uneasy peace, factions broke away, tunnelling upward through the mineral-rich rock to form our eventual home, the Freehold, only residues of each side's knowledge remained.

We became the Magic Men, not-scientists, not-mages, struggling with but scraps of the methodology of both, learning languages long dead, convoluted equations which we neither understood nor would likely work under our present laws. And even if we grasped the tatters of the ancient concepts, even if we were somehow able to piece together the scattered information to make a coherent whole, we lacked the resources – our Neers so ill trained that they could not even repair the essential machinery of the Freehold, let alone building for us the machines we would require – to accomplish anything.

Most of the Magic Men languished until enterprising Saardin began to see that we had a limited usefulness in the Freehold's power struggle. Then, one by one, the Saardin sought us out for affiliation. It was the end for us. From noble beginnings, we had been reduced to the lowest level, devising projects for the Saardin to increase their power.

I turned my back on them and for many sign would not even step on to their Levels. I spent my time with the remnants of the scholars, on the twenty-seventh Level, studying as best I could the lore of the ancient world, so that I might regain for myself some semblance of my heritage.

But the more I read, the more convinced I became that we were a dying race, strangling in our own mingled blood, indolent, inbred, incestuous.

'G'fand felt the same way,' Borros concluded.

'You knew G'fand?' Ronin asked.

'Oh yes. He helped me quite a bit in deciphering many of the ancient codices. There were revelations each cycle, but everything was in fragments and too often we were only tantalized by the pieces we had managed to decode, discovering afterwards that they were isolated passages, their beginnings and endings lost.'

'I remember,' said Ronin, 'that when we arrived in the City he would stop at every corner to read the glyphs carved into the buildings.'

The Magic Man nodded. 'Yes. I can imagine his excitement. Such a storehouse of knowledge.' He reached into a cupboard under his berth and pulled out food concentrates. He offered some to Ronin, who shook his head, then sat and munched thoughtfully for a time.

'One day,' he said – his voice had a thin far-off quality now – 'we came across a rent manuscript. It was frightfully old and so desiccated that it took us more than three cycles to carefully clean it enough so that we could begin to read the glyphs and restore the missing characters. Then G'fand set about deciphering it and I lost interest as I was involved in a project of my own at the time. Several cycles later he came to me saying that he could make no headway at all; the glyphs were totally alien to him; they bore no resemblance to any language he had studied.

'I laughed. "Well, what can I do?" I said. "You are a far better translator than I." "I do not know," he said, "but come take a look in any case."

'The glyphs which were so baffling to him jumped out at me with such vividness that I had to conceal my surprise, and for once I was grateful for my peculiar training. For this codex was written in one of the forgotten – and I had supposed useless – languages which I had learned as a child.

'The codex foretold of a drastic shift in the presumably immutable laws of our world. "When the foundations of our science are thrown down, then will man tremble before the true power. Conceit is his undoing and he will not heed the

54

coming of his doom until it crushes him. The Dolman, a sorcerous creature of terrifying power beyond man's ken, will come against mankind. The shifting of the laws presages his invasion. Indeed it is his invitation. First his legions, then the Makkon, then The Dolman himself will come to claim the world. With that, annihilation.'"

The wind outside had picked up in intensity, buffeting the ship as it sped across the ice sea. Yet the sound seemed remote to them, unreal, frozen in sticky time. Neither one said anything for a while. Then Borros roused himself and, listening for a moment, made a motion upward.

'The sail.'

If they had left it up any longer it would likely have been torn to shreds. As it was, they managed to reef it just in time. The wind, blowing frantically out of the northwest quarter, tore at their faces, forcing them to gasp for breath and turn their heads from its might. They were blind in the pit of night and only by guesswork did they surmise their direction.

Below, they blew into their cupped hands and shoved them near the fire, trying to warm their faces. Ronin prepared food for himself and before he had eaten his fill Borros was already asleep on his berth. He stretched out and stared at the swinging lamp, thinking long about The Dolman.

He must have dozed, for when he next looked about the cabin the ports were illuminated by a thin milky glow.

55

'Dawn,' breathed Borros, and sat up. 'The sun rises. Soon we can unfurl the sail.'

On deck they got their first real glimpse of the ice sea since setting sail. Ronin saw now why Borros had not been concerned about keeping watch at night. In all directions the ice flew away from them flat and seamless and dark. No high ridges, no steep protrusions marred its surface. And there was a limitless horizon which in all directions held no sight of land.

In the east, the gray clouds had taken on a pale saffron colour as the sun began its quotidian trek across the heavens. The wind came in gusts and Borros was obliged to go aft to reset their course.

Ronin stared southward, watching the shredded clouds pile and tumble, blown across the sky by the high winds aloft. Are there really people out there? he asked himself. Would they look like Bonneduce the Last? He shrugged and busied himself with the rigging, tightening knots which had loosened during the night.

The air became heavier still, leaden despite the strength of the wind, and there was a slight pressure in his ears. He took special care, moving along the rocking deck, remembering his slip the first night and, peering into the wind, he spied the purple and black thunderheads massed just above the horizon on the northwest quadrant that heralded the coming storm.

A shout twisted his head aft, but he could see nothing amiss. He made his way toward Borros, who was already pointing northward.

'What is it?' Ronin asked, coming up to him.

'A ship.' Borros clutched at the wheel. 'Following us.'

Ronin peered aft but could still discern nothing on the expanse of the ice sea.

'Obscured now by the mist.'

'Borros, are you certain – '

'This ship's sister,' the Magic Man hissed. 'Yes, Chill take it! I did see it.'

Ronin turned away, twisted Borros with him. He stared hard into the old man's face and tried to ignore the terror squirming like a serpent there.

'Forget it,' he said reasonably. 'You are still fatigued. You saw what your imagination wished for you to see. You have been through so much but it is over now. Freidal cannot threaten you now. You are free.'

Borros glanced briefly sternward, into the building mist.

'Let us pray so.'

All the day the wind strengthened, a gale now whose great gusts shifted from one quarter to another, hurling them southward at ever increasing speed. It seemed to Ronin, as he worked the rigging, that their runners barely touched the ice, so swiftly did they fly across the frozen wastes. From time to time he caught Borros gazing aft, but he said nothing, keeping his thoughts to himself.

He marvelled at the workmanship of the craft. He watched the small storm sail which they had unfurled when they came on deck at first light. Buffeted by the strong winds, stretched to its limit, it yet would not tear. It was constructed of a different fabric than the woven canvas of the main, lighter, more supple.

For much of the time the pair did not speak. It was essential that the wheel and the sail be manned at all times now because of the sudden unpredictability of the winds. Ronin worked the sail because that took more strength. He spent most of the time hauling on the rigging and staring ahead, one arm about the wooden mast, feeling it tremble, listening to the rhythmic creaking of the fittings, the soughing of the runners against the ice, the desolate call of the wind.

He thought then of nothing; the future would be as it would be. But a peculiar warmth stole over him in those solitary moments against the varnished wood, counterbalancing the pull of the ropes, and he absorbed the transmission of their quivering strength, their pliancy the key to survival upon the ice sea. A bond was slowly forming of which he was not yet perhaps fully aware, as it had inevitably with many men, throughout many ages, on seas too numerous to count. It was an instinct rooted perhaps in some ancestral memories, if such things indeed existed on that world and in that time. It was what allowed him to feel the changing of the wind on his face and pull or slacken the rope immediately so that they continually maintained their course. It was what caused him to pick up a thousand different subtleties of sailing in so short a time.

Just past midday the winds ceased their gusting and steadied enough for the pair to decide to lash wheel and storm sail long enough to go below for food and rest.

While they ate, he told Borros the details of the events which had transpired in the City of Ten Thousand Paths. When he recounted the creature's attack, the Magic Man exclaimed, the sound exploding through his lips. He coughed and swallowed convulsively. Then he had Ronin describe the creature again as best he could.

'The Makkon,' he said then, his face drained of color and looking more than ever like a skull. 'The creatures that are not animal, the four Reavers of The Dolman.' He quivered involuntarily. 'If that is truly what you encountered, then The Dolman is closer than I had suspected.' His eyes closed. 'Is there still time? Oh, Chill, there must be! *There must be!*' He looked up. 'Ronin, we must make all haste southward. Nothing must stop us, nothing, do you understand?'

'Calm yourself, Borros,' Ronin said gently. 'Nothing shall stop us.'

Late in the afternoon the day darkened prematurely and the violent storm which they had been attempting to outrun began to overtake them with an inexorable fury.

The wind shrilled in the rigging like the screams

59

at the gates of the damned and Ronin went to reef the storm sail.

'No!' bellowed Borros, the gale causing his voice to sound muffled. 'Leave it up! We must make all speed no matter what the risk!'

Ronin looked to the sky. The racing purple-black clouds, thick now and lowering menacingly from the west, were gathering themselves. Within them, the storm.

'We may turn over if it does not come down!' He yelled into the wind, the words blown from his mouth like crisp leaves.

Borros' face was mottled in fear.

'I have seen the sister ship again! She is closer! Ronin, she stalks us!' His eyes bulged. 'I will not be caught!'

Ronin began to reef the storm sail.

'You have only seen what you want to see; no one is following us. I want to survive this storm!'

Moments later, slender fingers grasped his arm, tugging feebly. He turned and looked into Borros' rolling eyes, saw the line of sweat freezing along the Magic Man's forehead.

'Please. Please. The ship comes after us. If we slow, it will surely overtake us.' Borros' voice came out in puffs of steam on the chill, dense air. 'Do you see? I cannot go back. I can take no more. Freidal had done what – '

Ronin touched him gently. 'Return to the wheel and guide us,' he said softly. 'The storm sail will stay up.'

Gratefully Borros went again aft and Ronin

retied the knots, vowing to reef the storm sail at the first sign of the gale's full force.

So they raced onward, riding before the gathering wind.

2

Aegir

He has turned from the west, away from the murder of the sun at the grasping hands of the ice plateaus. Frightened now, he flees before the turmoil of the vast sky. He feels, just behind him, the intense excitation of the storm as it bursts open and he is engulfed now by the fierce bite of the high winds, the pressure of the roiling banks of dark cloud, the kinetic scrape of leaping lightning.

Of these elements he is not afraid as he soars upward in a futile attempt to fly above the storm. He has ridden out many a gale, safe on the shifting wind currents, the whirling flurries of snow, the hard pellets of ice affecting him not at all.

The fear is of another kind and he is frantic to escape. His silver plumage a blur, he dips now, the air this high too thin for even his avian lungs, and desperately he tries to find a swift current to take him away from the feel of the living thing behind him, its frozen breath on his spread tail feathers, a pulsing caress of death. For it rolls on at his back, alive and malignant and indefatigable; something beyond life, beneath life. Coming.

He flies like a bolt into lurid purple cloud, out again, his flesh alive with crawling sensation. He tries to call out in his terror, cannot. Down and down he plummets until he sees the surface of the ice sea, dull and flat and comforting. It rushes by beneath him.

It was useless, and worse than that, suicidal. Through the curtains of blinding snow, dense and dark and turbulent, blotting out all else from sight and hearing, Ronin went aft, mindful of the slick layer of ice already forming on the deck.

It had hit with an electric jolt, one moment behind them, the next surrounding them in a frenetic shroud, dancing, swirling, driving. The gale was far too strong; even with both of them gripping the wheel, the ship was being hurled about as if it had abruptly lost all weight. Better by far for them to be belowdecks. He was especially concerned that Borros could be blown overboard.

He skidded once as the ship lurched to port, tilted, trembling in the howling winds, and righted itself. Slowly he unwound his freezing fingers from the rigging and moved now as a mountaineer would, using handholds at every step.

Borros, obsessed now by the thought of the pursuing ship, clung maniacally to the wheel, his blanched face a frozen mask, lips pulled back in a grimace of fear. And Ronin, coming alongside him, was reminded of the visage of the newly dead. Clawlike, Borros' fingers were white bones against the wood. Ronin yelled at him, but his voice was drowned in the mounting shriek of the gale. He seized the Magic Man, chopping at his frail wrists to force him to let go of the wheel, and dragged him, lurching and sliding, to the cabin, thrusting him down the companionway. Then he turned and lashed the wheel firmly in place, went forward and slid along the icy deck, fetching up against the starboard sheer-strake. On hands and knees against the fury of the storm, he crawled to the mast and, pulling himself to his feet, reefed the flapping storm sail. He choked in the crush of whipping hail and frozen snow as it beat at his face and shoulders. He secured it to the yard, doubling the knots.

Only then did he go below.

Borros sat on the cabin's deck shivering in a small pool of water. Ronin sank wordlessly to his berth and thought that perhaps it was after all too much. Too many new situations arising each minute and neither of them yet fully acclimated to the surface. For Ronin, it was not so bad; he was young and strong, with a warrior's body and adaptability. But just as importantly his mind was open and flexible. He could accept. He knew that from his journey to the City of Ten Thousand Paths.

But for Borros, huddled pathetically upon the wooden deck, more concerned with an imaginary ship carrying his all too real tormentor than he was with the realities of the storm hurling itself at their craft, it could not be the same.

The howling outside increased and the ship shuddered and swayed dangerously as it sped within the storm. We live or we die and that is the sum of it, Ronin thought. But, Chill take it, I will not die!

Borros had gotten up and was making his way drunkenly up the companionway to the secured hatch. Ronin caught him.

'What are you doing?'

'The sail,' said the Magic Man, his voice almost a whine. 'I must be sure – that it is up.'

'It *is* up.'

He squirmed in Ronin's grasp. 'I must see for myself. Freidal comes behind us. We must make all speed. If he catches us, he will destroy us.'

Ronin whipped him around so that he could look into the tired eyes. They were clouded with panic and shock. It is too much for him, Ronin thought for the second time.

'Borros, forget Freidal, forget the sister ship. Even if it is following us, the storm will protect us. He cannot find us in this.' The eyes looked blankly back at him, then they turned towards the hatch. Ronin shook him, finally out of patience.

'Fool! The storm is our enemy! There is death out there. It is the sail which will destroy us in this wind!'

'Then you have taken it down!' It was the irrational wail of a disillusioned child.

'Yes, Chill take you, I had no other choice! If I had not, we would be on our side now breaking up.'

Frantically Borros clawed at Ronin. 'Let me go! I must put it up! He will overtake us if I do not!'

Ronin hit him then, a swift blow at the side of

65

the neck, breaking the nerve synapses and blood flow for just an instant, and the Magic Man collapsed, eyes rolling up, his body folding onto the companionway. Ronin put him on his berth and turned away disgusted.

The ship groaned under the onslaught and the hanging lamp swung crazily on its short chain, splashing the bulkheads with bursts of sullen light and geometric shadows.

After a time Ronin reached up and extinguished the flame.

He lay listening to the howling darkness, feeling the felucca shudder and lurch under him, smelling the thin trail of smoke from the doused lamp. The gale tore through the rigging, moaning as if alive, spattering hail against the hull in furious bursts.

The darkness deepened and the sounds modulated subtly downward in pitch, becoming muffled as if heard through layers of viscous fluid. Yet other aspects of the sounds, unnoticed until now, were supraclear. Then the volume altered, increasing and decreasing in a slow rhythm that was comforting. The sounds lengthened, as if stretched out of their original shape by the swell.

He was deep, deep, and the towers of the world rose above him in cyclopean grandeur, steep walls of hard volcanic rock with thick-knuckled ridges of darkly gleaming stone as obdurate as obsidian. Pale fronds and spreading algae partially obscured their faces. The foundations, hewn and sculpted during an age so ancient that Time was but an abstract concept and Law was unknown. An age of great upheaval and movement, when the world was forming and crying out like an infant; when red and yellow molten rock spewed forth in sizzling rivers from the innards of the earth, crawling down new rock edifices, boiling into the violent seas; when land masses arose, glistening and foamy, in the middle of the oceans; when cliffs slid like cataracts into churning waters white with slate and pumice. In an age when all was beginning.

A shadow; he is not alone.

In the awesome canyons of the foundations of the world he feels a presence, diffuse and elemental.

Large it is; unutterably immense so that he does not know whether it moves or is at rest. Perhaps it has features; perhaps it is acephalous or again quite shapeless. There is no way of discerning. Its sides pulse with energy, the source it seems to him of the oceans' very tides. He glides silently over the slippery mountains of its body, a metonymical terrain without end. And he wonders. But in the absolute silence no answers are forthcoming.

He awoke with an enormous thirst and a need to urinate. He ventured on deck. The storm was still raging but the sky appeared somewhat lighter. Dawn, he thought, or just after; impossible to tell in this weather. He relieved himself, then bent and stuffed snow into his mouth, returning to the cabin, shivering.

Borros was still asleep, which was just as well,

Ronin thought, since he would wake with a headache.

Ronin crossed to his berth and, leaning across it, ran his hand experimentally along the outer bulkhead. The craft was obviously built as well as it was designed. He could detect no sign of weakening and, satisfied that it was withstanding the gale's fury, he sat and ate a spare breakfast.

Borros groaned and rolled over but he did not wake up. Ronin saw the blue bruise along his neck. He crossed the cabin and bent over the frail figure. He saw then that the Magic Man was shivering.

Quickly he turned Borros onto his back. He was hot and the skin had a dry, taut look about it. The eyes came open slowly. They were enlarged and abnormally bright.

Ronin reached under the berth and pulled out a woven blanket. He stripped the spare frame of its suit and found that the material was dry but the flesh underneath was damp from the residues of melted snow and fever sweat. The suit was superbly designed to keep out the cold and the damp but conversely, if the body wearing it was wet, the material would not allow it to dry.

The body shook with the force of the fever and Ronin, covering Borros with the blanket, cursed himself for a fool. He should have realized sooner that their enormous differences in physical stamina and mental adaptability would result in the Magic Man's eventual collapse. Because he had been the one to continually urge them onward, Ronin had ignored the signs of utter exhaustion on the other's face. How much did Freidal's terrible probings take out of him? Ronin wondered.

Outside the storm smote the ship in monotonous abandon. From time to time Ronin attempted to cool the Magic Man's face with water. The bare skull, gleaming waxily in the diffuse light of the waning day, seemed a constant reminder of his vulnerability. At sunset the fever appeared stronger. Borros had slept fitfully, eating not at all. Now he was delirious and Ronin felt certain that if it did not break soon Borros would die.

There was nothing he could do and his helplessness vexed him. He had searched the cabin in an attempt to find medicine, but he soon realized that there was no way of knowing what the potions and powders he found were meant for. The wrong choice could kill the Magic Man more effectively than any fever could. So he had left what he had found in the cupboard below the berth, unused, unknown. Borros moaned and the gale shrieked in the rigging.

Abruptly he heard a sharp grinding noise and was sent tumbling as the ship lurched. The motion has changed, he thought as he regained his feet. And then: Chill take it, we have hit something!

It was true. He felt now the slender felucca sliding over the ice at a precarious, oblique angle. If I do not right the ship, our momentum combined with its mass will topple us.

Pulling on his hood, he raced up the companionway, through the hatch, and out into the blinding storm. Needles of ice struck at him and the high winds tore at his torso. Over the screech of the gale he heard a rhythmic heavy flapping and, shading his eyes, peered across the deck. A long strip of rigging had worked loose and was whipping itself against the hull. There was no visibility.

He went aft with the ship trembling as it sped on its oblique and unnatural course. Slowly, he felt the felucca turning broadside into the gale. We shall break up for certain then, he thought. Hand over hand he continued aft, stepping cautiously through the calf-high mixture of ice and snow covering the deck.

A gust of wind tilted the ship and his grip loosened in the slippery iced rigging. He stumbled and skidded along the ice and as his momentum built he knew that he was going over the side. He struggled to regain his balance on the heaving deck, could not, and desperately reached out for the gunwale with his gauntleted hand. He saw with intense clarity the scales of the Makkon hide slide, frictionless, along the slickly iced wood. He tightened his grip, feeling the might of the wind against his body slamming him against the sheerstrake, and he was tossed upward as if weightless over the side, into the howling storm, almost gone, the dark and featureless ice unravelling in a blur below him so close now. His breath caught in his throat and his mouth clogged with flying ice dust. A fire was running along his arm and into his chest as the wind pulled at him, moaning and crying, and he twisted in its fierce grip. And through a haze he thought, Now, now or it will surely claim me.

Calm at the core.

Momentum, he thought. And used it. With the gale tearing at him, he used the last of his strength, concentrating it into his gauntleted hand, exerting the pressure, the scales now biting through the ice, gripping finally. And still the wind battered him.

But now he had a pivot and, using it, he no longer resisted the powerful tug of the storm, but rather relaxed into it, letting it swing his body. At the height of the arc, he pushed. Up came his feet, his legs, his torso and he lunged at the gunwale with his boots, feeling them slide along the icy top. Then he had one boot over and he hooked his leg until the second was over the gunwale, and he was aboard, climbing carefully onto the deck.

He slid gasping along the sheer-strake of the stern, recalling what he had seen as he swung aboard. Just to port of the stern was a long gash in the hull. What did we hit? he wondered.

The thought was thrust aside as he scrambled for the wheel, realizing that he had lost precious time becuase they were still moving broadside. The rope holding the wheel on course had snapped. He gripped the curved wood and leaned against it with all his might. He took deep breaths, seeking to restore his energy, his lungs on fire, and his exhalations made harsh plumes of smoke before him. The wind howled in his face and the felucca juddered as he strove to right its course. He pushed from his feet, hauling at the wheel, using the mass of his body, and heard at last the agonized squeal of metal against ice as the runners fought friction and the storm to turn. Muscles jumped and contracted along his arms and back and thighs.

The craft was frozen in her arc; it no longer swung to starboard. But she was still sliding obliquely and he knew that he could not push the wheel farther, that there was only one chance now before a fierce gust caught the hull across the beam and turned her full broadside to the storm.

Quickly he found another piece of rope and lashed the wheel in place. Then hand over hand he went forward to the mast. His hands moved deftly over the knots, unfurling the storm sail. He pulled at the yard, plucked at the rigging, strung the storm sail.

An ice shower flung itself upon him, heavy clusters, black and jagged as exploded metal, slamming him to his knees, boot soles slithering in the ice. The rigging flew from his hands and the felucca leapt forward, shivering, as the storm sail took the wind.

He tried to get up, sliding in the ice as the gale tore at the ship, and did not attempt it again. Instead he sat, back braced against the port sheerstrake, boot soles buttressed by the base of the mast. He had regained the rigging and was hauling now, hauling to shift the yard into the proper angle.

He became one with the craft. All the creakings and moanings of joints under stress, the trembling of the hull, the incredible singing tension of the mast as it gave in to the wind and thus derived its sleek power, all these were now extensions of his arms and hands and fingers as he fought for the life of the ship.

And slowly the crosstree swayed, moving centimetre by centimetre towards the needed position. It was not a steady process because the storm railed against him, shifted by gusts at odd moments so that he had to be extremely sensitive to the currents.

At first, so minutely that he was not even aware of it, the stern began to swing to port. He thought then that he might fall from exhaustion before he saw any change at all and in that suspended instant of time felt the shift. Like the first long pull of potent wine, a sense of overwhelming exhilaration warmed his chest and new strength flowed into his rigid arms.

At length he lashed the rigging in place and went aft to reset the wheel. Once at the stern, he had time to peer over the side at the gash in the hull. Curious, he thought, the damage is high up. If we had hit a rock outcropping, the mark would have been lower down. What could we have hit? He took another quick look and judged that the damage was not serious. Still, we cannot afford to let that happen again.

Day was done. The purple had deepened, drowning the grey cast of the long afternoon. And now darkness fell with a completeness that was awesome. Still the storm raged and all about him was the dizzying swirl of ice and snow. Just before he went below, he went forward and reefed the storm sail, securing the yard. He was of two minds about it but in the end he felt that it was safer to run the storm without the sail.

'You must tell me.'

'Wait, my friend. Wait.'

'Borros, too many have already been slain over this. I must have answers.'

Dawn, almost. Faint pearled light an incipient glow at the cabin's thick ports. During the night the fever had broken and since then Borros had been breathing easier, the rattle gone from his lungs and throat, the inhalations deeper and more regular. When he awakened after the fever's cresting, he had drunk the warm liquid that Ronin had prepared, gulping greedily and asking for more.

'Later,' Ronin said.

Borros lay back for a time, his energy spent, and drifted off into a deep sleep that his body demanded. Just before dawn he had awakened once more, appearing stronger. His eyes were clear and the colour of his face was near normal.

'How long?'

'A cycle. A day and a night.'

He ran a thin hand across his face. 'Can I have something to drink, do you think?'

'Of course.' Ronin offered him a bowl. 'Not too much.'

The whine and whistle of the wind, the muffled patter of ice crystals against the hull.

'You know,' said Borros after a time, 'I have for so long dreamed of the Surface, imagined what it would be like – in every detail, I mean – wished to be free of the Freehold for so long – and then for my time with Freidal I wished just to die up here – that is why I told him nothing, because I knew that if I did I would die in that hole – and that terrified me more than anything, even' – He shuddered and his eyes closed. He looked bleakly at Ronin. 'Can you understand?'

Ronin nodded. 'Yes. I think I can.'

They had begun talking and, inevitably, the subject of the scroll arose.

'Answers, Borros.'

'Yes, my boy, quite. But I can only tell you what I know.' He sighed deeply. 'The scroll is a key of some sort. The writings spoke of it as a door to the only pathway that could possibly stop The Dolman. He is destined, it said, to return to the world. First the shift in the laws, then the Makkon and the gathering of his legions and, finally, when the four Makkon are all here, they will summon The Dolman. They are his guardians, his outriders, his messengers, his reavers. Of all the creatures at his command, only the Makkon communicate with him directly. Once the four are here, their power multiplies. That is all the writings told me.'

'And where are we bound?'

'Ah, that I can answer with more certainty. We go south; to the continent of man. There I trust we will find those who can translate the scroll of dor-Sefrith.'

'And if not?'

'If not, Ronin, then The Dolman shall indeed claim the world and man shall cease to exist.'

Ronin thought for a time. At length he said, 'Borros, tell me something. If we hit a protrusion on the ice's surface, it would scrape us low on the hull, correct?'

The Magic Man looked puzzled. 'Well, yes, I suppose so. It is hardly likely that the weather would allow any high ice formations to develop. Why?'

'No reason,' said Ronin, turning away. 'No reason at all.'

It was dusk when it came. They had been so long with the background static of the storm that at first they thought that they were going deaf and it was not until the white noise filled their ears completely that they realized what it was. The gale had spent itself, leaving only the uncertain silence of the ice sea.

Ronin helped Borros don his foil suit and together they went on deck. To the east, banks of dark cloud gravid with moisture and lightning scudded against the sky and overhead rolled remnants of thunderheads, the last flutterings of torn banners; but to the west the air was clear, the long horizon virtually unbroken, coloured by a sliver of sun, lowering like a swollen ember in a banked fire. The sky was the colour of cold ash, tinged

76

magenta and pink about the sun's arc. And then it was gone, night stealing over them so swiftly that it seemed as if the sun had never been there at all. Ronin held the image of the sunset in his memory, his heart lightened after so many days of seamless grey and claustrophobic white.

They set about clearing the deck of the debris of the storm. But Borros was still weak and he was forced to stop, moving aft to see to the wheel and their course. While he did this, Ronin stowed the storm sail and set about erecting the larger mainsail to block and tackle along the yard and mast. When he unfurled it, it immediately caught the stiff breeze, billowing out. They shot forward as if fired from a bow. Blue ice flew at the bow.

'Ronin!'

A cry of desperation.

And he knew what it was before he turned his head aft; had known from the moment he had been in the process of swinging back aboard during the gale and had seen it high up on the hull. Too high for any ice, he thought. We did not hit a protrusion. Something hit us. He turned his head then and saw it.

Borros cried out again. Both of them stared sternward. In their wake, in the clearing weather, in the silvered light of the sleeping sun, reflected off the ice, was silhouetted the unmistakable shape of a lateen sail.

'You see!'

Limned for a moment, before it winked out

with the last wisps of light, it appeared to have a sinister cast.

'I told you!'

No time for that now. It was indeed a sister ship to their felucca, now perhaps half a kilometre behind them and closing. Could they have lightened the craft somehow? thought Ronin. And how did they find us in all of the vast ice sea? True, they knew our exact starting point; knew that we would head due south. Yet still it disturbed him. He gazed at the spot where last the sail had been. The storm, he mused. The storm should have made this impossible. It blew us about; it blew them about surely. How could they now be so close; what were the chances . . .? He shrugged resignedly and gave it up. No matter the reason, they are just behind us now.

The Magic Man was clever. Whatever other reading he had done, he had somehow managed to learn a good deal about sailing. That knowledge stood him in good stead now. With the sister ship giving chase, he steered them with the wind so that, with Ronin using his muscle to keep the yard at the proper angle, they caught each gust, using it to its fullest advantage, making top speed. It was all they could do. Here on the limitless expanse of the ice sea, with not even a hint of land on the horizon, evasive maneuvers were useless. But that we do not seem to be doing, thought Ronin as he ran the line through its block so that the yard swung several centimetres to starboard.

'We can outrun them,' Borros called from his position aft at the wheel.

Ronin thought not. How is Freidal managing to sail that ship? he asked himself. Even with his daggam; they have no knowledge of ships? But it was merely another question that had no answer. In any case, he thought savagely, I do not believe I wish to outrun them; I have a score to settle with Freidal. I care not for what Borros said.

'It is not death so much,' said Borros, 'that I fear. It is all that shall come before it.' The fear haunted his eyes, making them appear bulged and glassy. 'You are but one Bladesman; they will cut you down and make you live through it as I have. And I,' he said heavily, 'will have to endure it once again.' His thin lips quivered. 'I cannot. I cannot.'

Unwilling, Borros went below. The night was but half gone but he had almost fallen to the deck and he had no choice, his body betraying him despite the overwhelming fear in his mind.

'Go to sleep,' Ronin had urged him as he helped him to the cabin's companionway. 'You are safe.'

The Magic Man looked at him sardonically.

'You are like all your kind,' he said sharply. 'Every Bladesman thinks himself invincible; until he feels the life streaming out of him.'

Now in the silence of the night, Ronin stood against the trembling mast, oblivious to the delicate shhhing of the runners against the ice, the tiny sounds of the fittings. He stared ahead into the darkness, deep as obsidian, black as basalt, his mind a theatre.

Freidal, you madman, you defend death. The Freehold is no more. The Saardin scheme for greater power, a power as hollow as this vessel. The lower Levels are in chaos, the workers mad and destitute. And you are pledged to uphold the laws of this place.

Freidal, you slayer, you destroyed Stahlig, slowly, joyously crushing the life from him, the terror mounting until the labouring heart burst. You have destroyed Borros too; he still lives but he is not the same man; he lives in total fear of your retribution. And you wanted to destroy me; I saw it in your face, etched as clearly as a stylus shapes warm wax, when you captured me after my return from the City of Ten Thousand Paths. You had already sent your minions after me: on the Stairwell with K'reen, my beloved, my sister; in the Square of Combat with Marcsh. Now you come for us again. Well. I will not run, for it is time we met, you and I, in Combat.

In the pale wash of first light, the sky a feathered shell of mother-of-pearl, Ronin leaned hard on the wheel.

Sunrise flew to starboard as the bow swung round, describing the beginning of its long arc, and shortly it pointed directly at the sail of their sister ship.

Prepare yourself now, Ronin called silently to Freidal. Time has almost run down.

They closed with terrifying swiftness, Ronin guiding his craft from out of the southeast quarter. The contours of the other ship bloomed abruptly from harmless toy size in the strengthening light. The day was overcast, with layers of stratified cloud, white in the sunrise. A strange light fell across the scene, oblique and somehow harsh as the sun crept over the horizon, so that every edge had a sword–blade shadow and all shapes turned angular.

He could discern now dark figures on the deck of the sister ship, dark robes fluttering thickly, white faces staring intently at him. Then there was the briefest flash of cold light, thin as a bolt, and his gaze swung to the tall slender figure at the bow. He knew even without the coalescence of features that it was Freidal. The Security Saardin's false eye had caught the light of the rising sun as it broke momentarily from the grey cloud cover, reflecting it back at him.

Ronin swung farther into the quarter, turning, feeling the adrenalin rising in him now that he was sure that it was Freidal who pursued them, turning until he ran parallel to the other felucca. They sped now across the ice sea linked together more surely than if they were physically one vessel.

Ronin watched, outwardly impassive, as Freidal went slowly aft until he was near midship. The right eye, the real eye, glared at him.

'Of course you were behind this,' Freidal called across the frozen expanse as the ships drifted closer. 'I have come for you, sir; you and the Magic Man. He willfully escaped my custody.' Ronin's eyes roved the other ship. How many? 'You were taken from me but I still have many

81

questions to ask you.' Certainly two daggam. Were there more below? 'The Surface is forbidden to all of the Freehold. I am charged with your return.' They will be the best Bladesmen under his command; he will not underestimate me now. 'The Saardin wish to question you.' Discount the scribe, writing tablet strapped to his wrist, stylus scratching across its face, recording for Freidal. 'Unfortunately, neither of you shall survive the journey back. I am no longer concerned with where you were or what you were doing.' His good eye blinked and burned. 'My daggam are sacrosanct; no one attacks them without being charged with the consequences. You broke Marcsh's back. Now you will pay. Death without honour awaits you, sir!'

Ronin heard a shout aboard ship, saw Borros' head and shoulders emerging from the cabin's hatch.

'Oh, Frost, they have caught us!'

Ronin was fed up. 'Get below!' he yelled. 'And stay there until I come for you!'

The Magic Man stared at the tall figure of the Security Saardin, so close now over the narrowing slice of ice, transfixed with terror at the glowering visage.

'You shall die now, sir!' Freidal called.

'Get below!' Ronin shouted once more and the figure disappeared. The hatch slammed shut.

The twin ships raced on before the wind, and now Freidal motioned to the daggam and they lifted cables with black metal hooks, swung them over their heads, hurled them towards him. They hit the deck and they hauled on the cables, the hooks scraping across the deck until they bit into the wood of the sheer-strake and held.

Now the feluccas were fairly touching and, securing the cables, the daggam leapt to the gunwales. Ronin lashed the wheel in place as they came aboard. Freidal stood silently, his false eye a milky round; the scribe was immobile, stylus poised.

They were tall, with wide shoulders and long arms. They had brutal faces, feral but not unintelligent; one narrow and hatchetlike, the other with a nose wide across the flat planes of his cheeks. Triple brass-hilted daggers were scabbarded in oblique rows across their chests; long swords hung at their hips.

For Ronin it was a moment of delicious hunger, these last still instants before Combat, when the power surged like a flood within him, controlled and channelled. He licked his lips and drew his blade. They advanced upon him. Now the waiting was at an end.

Over the ice they fled, the white spray of their swift passage rainbowed the light, the ships rocking, locked together in an embrace only death could now sunder.

They were a team. They swung at him from different angles, but at the same instant, seeking to confuse him. The blades caught the rising sunlight and, because he was watching their descent, he was blinded momentarily, his eyes watering, and it was instinct that guided his parry, the sword up and twisting broadside on. He got one but missed the other and it sheared into his shoulder, no help for it now. The nerves numbed themselves and the blood began to flow. The daggam grinned and came on.

Everything, said the Salamander, *every thing* that occurs during Combat may be used to your own advantage if you but know how. A strong arm but holds the sword; the mind is the force which guides it. They were more confident now, seeing how easily he was cut, and they swung at him in tandem, with co-ordinated precision, chopping and slashing, moving him backward in an attempt to cut off the number of angles through which he could attack them. They passed the bulk of the cabin as they moved forward along the ship. Let your opponent make the first moves if you are unsure of his skills; in his actions will you find victory.

And so they battered him as he catalogued their offensive strategies, attacking occasionally to gauge their defences. They were excellent Blades-men, with unorthodox styles, and he lacked the space to effectively attack them together.

At midship, he split them, using the yard as a barrier. It was done most swiftly, for they were not stupid and they would counter almost imme-diately. Almost. He had one chance only and he went in fast at hatchet face, slashing a two-handed stroke that slit the daggam's midsection just under the ribs. His innards glistened wetly as they poured upon the deck. The mouth opened in silent protest, so quick had been the blow, and the tongue protruded, quivering. The eyes bulged as the body collapsed, hot blood pumping, congealing on the frigid deck.

But now the second daggam hurled himself under the temporary barrier of the yard, furious at being separated from his partner. Ronin parried his first attack, moving away from the centre of the ship, toward the gunwale across which the hooks had been thrown. The second daggam had glanced briefly at his fallen companion and, noting this, Ronin kept his blows low so that the flat-faced daggam would assume that he was attacking the same spot now. Their blades hammered at each other, sparks flying as they scraped together, then snapped apart, only to clash again in mid-air. Ronin parried again and then, instead of the oblique strike he had been attacking with, swung his blade in a horizontal arc. Too late the daggam brought his own sword up and the flat-faced head, severed now at the neck, flew from the jerking body and landed not a meter from where Freidal stood on the other ship. Ronin heaved at the corpse with its curtaining fount of blood, sent it overboard as he sprinted, gaining his ship's gunwale. He leapt, landing with his soles firmly on the deck of Freidal's vessel.

The rigging vibrated, singing dolefully in the breeze as the Security Saardin turned to face him, the tight cap of his blue-black hair gleaming, his long lean face swivelling like that of a predator's. His hand at his chest; a blur, and if Ronin had had to look, he would have been dead. But he was already turning as the blur came at him, whispering past where he had just stood. And he was off across the deck, sword up, knees bent, searching with his peripheral vision for other daggam. He passed the scribe, solitary and unmoving, stylus poised until words rather than weapons filled the air. His cloak flapped sullenly in the wind; otherwise he could have been carved from rock.

'Ah, sir, you have come to me at last.' Stylus in motion, then he was off, circling in a shallow arc so that he could see the entire length of the ship. 'The corps are unleashed first.' The voice emotionless. 'A basic rule of warfare.' Past the creaking mast, the straining sail. 'Soften the enemy with a preliminary attack.' Mind the yard, swinging. 'Deplete his energy with the soldiers.' Past coils of rope, lashed kegs, the spare mast as on his own craft fixed to the port sheer-strake. 'Then come the elite.' Slick patches of ice near the starboard gunwale. 'To finish the task.' *Shhhhhhh,* the runners peeling the ice below. 'An admirable plan, sir, do you not agree?'

The face closer than expected, white, the thin-lipped mouth, long and cruel, pulled back into a sneer. 'Not too much trouble to kill a traitor!' The two remaining daggers caught the light as they lay nakedly strapped to his chest. Freidal, Saardin and Chondrin in one man. 'The Freehold cannot tolerate your kind. You are a disease that must be

86

cleansed. You see, I cannot allow you to return to the Freehold.' At last he drew his great sword. 'Now I will crush you; with great care and equal skill, paying attention to the finer points.' He twisted sideways until just his right shoulder was presented, leaving Ronin the smallest target to attack. 'Of pain.' He advanced obliquely. 'And fear.'

The first was a downward thrust twisting at the last moment; the second a horizontal slash of enormous power coming from the opposite direction. Ronin parried them both and then Freidal had a dagger in his left hand, holding it before him, point tilted upward.

The scribe observed them impassively as they moved slowly along the deck in a strange and deadly dance. They were just forward of midship when Ronin's booted foot hit something on the deck and he stumbled. At that moment, his eyes still on Freidal's face, he saw the barest flicker of the Saardin's good eye and instead of struggling to regain his footing he relaxed his body and fell to the deck. He heard the angry whine as the dagger buried itself in the wood of the sheer-strake above his head.

Now there was but one yet it would be enough and he had to close immediately before Freidal got to it and he sprang at the tall figure looming over him. The ship shuddered in a heavy gust of wind and the Saardin, shifting to compensate, avoided the full brunt of the blow of Ronin's gauntleted fist. It scraped along his cheek, missing the bone which it would have otherwise shattered, dragging shards of skin as it flayed the flesh, split the corner of his mouth at the end of the arc. His head snapped back, recoiling as Ronin flew by, momentum carrying him into the port gunwale, striking him in the ribs, forcing the breath out of him. He gasped and tried not to double over. Freidal swiped at the blood whipping from his torn face in long droplets and swung a two-handed blow. A haze had descended over Ronin and with only his hearing now, not even fully comprehending what was occurring, he threw up his mailed fist, the scaled hide of the monstrous Makkon his only defence now. The blade hit the gauntlet and its hard peculiar surface rippled with movement. It absorbed much of the force of the blow and the sword slid against the scales as if they were oiled, glanced off, the killing blow turned aside, and it sliced into Ronin's already wounded shoulder. The pain woke him and he pivoted off the gunwale, blood whirling like a crimson scarf about him and, renewing his grip upon the hilt of his sword, staggered away from the sheer-strake while Freidal stared in disbelief at the dull hide of the gauntlet.

His bloody face twisted in fury and he came in low and fast and their blades rang like angry thunder as they met. Ronin kept close to him and now the Saardin attempted to retreat as if he was being forced to give way under Ronin's attack. But Ronin knew it for a ruse, knew that he wished only for room to throw the last dagger. Ronin drove into him, crowding him back against the mast. Freidal gripped the gleaming hilt of the dagger and Ronin's gauntlet closed over it. Their blades locked, scraping edge against edge down their long lengths. Freidal shook himself, twisting lithely, and tore free of Ronin's grasp to withdraw the dagger. They moved at once, as if provoked by the same impulse. The dagger's bright blade came at him and it could not be avoided because Freidal was not throwing it as Ronin had assumed he would, but slashing, and Ronin's momentum took him toward it. Freidal had aimed for the neck and missed, the point hitting Ronin's collar-bone, abrading the flesh. And then Ronin was past him, a dark blur, his sword held now in a reverse grip so that the blade trailed behind him. Plant the feet, breathe in with a long suck, swing the mass of his frame, pushing from his ankles, the sword like living lightning striking backward at the Saardin, who was just turning to face Ronin, the point ramming into his mouth. A bubbling scream choked off. A twist of the blade and Ronin was pivoting, his sword raised above his head for another blow. It was white in the light, darkened near the tip by red rivulets.

Freidal writhed upon the deck, the lower half of his face covered by his hands and arms. Blood was everywhere. Then he was still and Ronin looked up, awaiting more daggam. The deck was clear save for the scribe. He stood watching Ronin approach.

'You have written your last line.'

The stylus dipped to the surface of the tablet,

scrabbled there. Ronin left him, went aft, and threw open the cabin's hatch. Down the companionway and into the cabin. No one.

Across the deck and leapt for the gunwale and, crouching there momentarily, turned. Below him, blurred ice like marble. Freidal was where he had fallen. The scribe had not moved. Ronin scanned for the last time his impassive face, then with one long stride he was aboard his own felucca. With a might sweeping stroke, he severed the cables holding the ships as one. They parted and, helmless, the sister felucca gradually swept away to port, into the east, growing smaller and smaller, a memory now to some.

Borros did not believe him of course, but that was to be expected; it did not concern him.

'He is dead,' said Ronin as he moved about the cabin. 'Believe it or no, as you will.'

The sun was setting dully behind curtains of blank cloud, colourless, featureless; a deflating end to another day. Just before he went below, Ronin had peered into the west, thought he had seen the outlines of land, but he could not be certain. As it turned out, it did not much matter.

'We still have far to go,' Borros said somewhat brusquely when Ronin gave him the news. 'And I do not believe that he is dead.'

'Perhaps you would have us turn around and make sure,' Ronin said acidly.

'If we had but the time, I would insist on it,' the

Magic Man replied obstinately, 'so that I could kick his head in.'

'Of course you would. Now.'

'I do not regret,' he said with a trace of self-righteousness, 'that I lack your zeal for Combat.'

Ronin sat on his berth and, having found a piece of material, began to clean the blade of his sword.

'My zeal for Combat, as you put it, is all the protection you presently have.'

'From the vengeance of the Freehold. Their power is severely limited now that we are on the Surface.'

One edge at a time, upward from the thick middle to the tapered tip.

'You would not have said that this morning.'

'Ronin, you do not yet comprehend. We have been locked away for generations, progress checked, choking on our own detritus.' A nerve in Borros' face began to spasm. 'You are as much a product of that as is Freidal. You are proud to be a Bladesman,' the voice dry and pedantic, 'an artificial life style created by the Freehold.' His hand described a sweeping gesture. 'It is totally useless here.'

'It has not been so far.'

'Yes, by all means mock me. What I mean is that we shall soon reach the continent of man. It will be a civilized society. Man has already learned the bitter lessons of the sorcerous wars – '

Ronin stood up.

'What is it you fear, old man?'

'I?' The grey eyes blazed momentarily. 'I fear

that sword you wield and the arm which wields it. I must speak plainly. I fear that your presence may jeopardize our contact with civilization. I am a man of science and knowledge; I have studied much. They will listen to me but you – you are a barbarian to them. The blood instinct runs strong in you and the chances are quite good that you will misinterpret a movement or a gesture and someone will die.'

'You know me not at all, then.'

'I know only that you are a Bladesman and that is sufficient. You are all alike; you know how to do only one thing.'

'Tell me,' said Ronin, mounting the companion-way, 'how you would have fared on the Surface without me.' And went up into the night.

Its tremulous light spilled like wan petals onto the ice sea, over the flying ship's deck, across Ronin's hunched shoulders. He opened his eyes – lashes, brows, stubble of beard rimed with frost – to the pinks and saffron yellows dimly streaking the south. Still sleep-fogged, still feeling the dream-warmth of K'reen's smooth, supple-muscled body sleekly trembling beneath him, still inhaling the perfume of her hair, tumbling, the last parting of a forest dark before him, he turned his head to behold the ripening spray of red-orange-gold in the east as the sun rose behind low lacquered clouds on the horizon. Above him the vault was cloudless, immense, cerulean and translucent, for the first time open to him.

For long moments he sat transfixed. Then he rose and stretched his knotted muscles, warming them with motion. He crossed to the starboard sheer-strake and watched the land unravel itself perhaps four kilometres away. He withdrew a poignard from his belt and thoughtfully scraped at his whiskers while contemplating the view; it was good to see land again after so much time in the center of nothingness. He breathed deeply. The air was fresh and bright, sparkling with a chill brittleness that was not unpleasant, all the more enjoyable after the oppressiveness of the storm.

'Land at last,' Borros said from behind him.

Ronin turned.

'Here.'

He sheathed the poignard, took the food the Magic Man offered him. The old man appeared to be somehow smaller in the light of the new day, as if his ordeal on the Surface had actually shrivelled him. Ronin thought he could see new lines scored in the taut, yellow-tinged face, under the slender almond eyes, at the corners of the downturned mouth. He was peering at the oblate sun which, having quit its low cloud cover, was rising with the lassitude of age.

'We are farther south than I could have hoped.'

'But we still have ice,' said Ronin, pointing to the low humped shore, covered completely with ice and snow.

'Yes, well, that is to be expected for a while. But the storm propelled us far beyond what would have been possible otherwise. Can you feel that the temperature rises? It does so exceedingly slowly yet there is already a difference. And the ice, too, I believe, has been affected. See there, the difference in colour; its thickness diminishes.'

The wind had slackened somewhat and they ran gently across the ice sea, an occasional gust billowing the sail. Ronin sat against the port sheer-strake, honing the double edges of his sword, feeling the heady beat of the strengthening sunshine.

Borros was near midship, checking the spare mast and yard and clearing the last residue of ice and frozen snow from the deck.

A calmness had crept over them both during the day, a liquid lassitude, dreamy in its warm stillness, which they both welcomed as respite from the kineticism of their journey since descending the ice plateau. Now they were content to drift through the long afternoon without speaking or even thinking.

They ate a cold supper below and then returned to the deck just before sunset. To starboard the cliffs of ice and snow had given way grudgingly to less forbidding rock faces of scarlet and grey. Snow was still plentiful, but for the first time the land appeared to be able to lift itself from beneath the white carpet. Farther off, seeming flat in the dusky haze of evening, a strong line of mountains marched cross the horizon, deep violet, snow-capped, jagged and indomitable, wreathed in mists of mauve and lavender. Abruptly the sun broke onto their summits, light like shards across their peaks, and they lapsed all at once into black paper silhouette with a backdrop of crimson.

Ronin heard it just as the top edge of the swollen sun disappeared behind the mountains. He was near midship and immediately ran to the port gunwale. Borros was at the bow, searching for a spare block to replace one that had cracked during the gale. It was a sound that Ronin did not comprehend, for it had no analogue in his life. It was a dream-sound, as if the world was being split.

It came again. Louder. Longer. Two sounds simultaneously: a deep rumbling roar that vibrated the ship; a high screaming that set the teeth on edge. Borros' head came up.

Then Ronin saw in the lowering light a dark jagged line growing in the ice off the port quarter in front of them. The ice lifted and, in a sledge-hammer blast, flew apart. Chunks of ice were hurled into the air, raining over them. The craft lurched and Ronin reached for the gunwale, hanging on.

He stared awe-struck as, through the widening rent in the sea, a black shape was rising, monstrous and swaying. It rose over them now, blotting out the sapphire twilight, and in a sudden flash of movement Ronin glimpsed a huge eye, baleful and alien, beneath it a narrow ugly jaw. And then it was past him, swooping onto the high stem of the felucca. Shivers ran through the frame and Ronin was hurled into the mast. The runners screeched as the vessel was thrown obliquely across the ice, then shuddered to a halt with an enormous squeal of protest. The deck splintered as the thing lashed itself against the bow for a second time. Fabric tore and Borros screamed. Ronin staggered to his feet and, drawing his sword, scrambled forward, its tip stained crimson in the last of the light.

He heard a violent hissing and inhaled a fetid stench, rotting flesh, slime, and salt and other odours he could not define. It was above him and he felt the chill of the sea depths and the drip of stinking water. Thickets of slimed weed dropped against his face and shoulders. He was in total darkness. Felt rather than saw its presence close to him off the port side and he swung the sword in a vicious two-handed blow. The keen edge cut into scaly hide, into strange flesh. A high keening sound came to his ears as he swung again and again into the thing's side.

It heaved itself away and he caught another glimpse of that terrifying eye, double-lidded, green with black-rimmed iris. He turned and nearly vomited as he confronted the gaping maw of the creature; the stench was overpowering. The jaws were all teeth, enormous and triangular, green with scum and bits of decayed flesh. The head lunged forward and he leapt away, hearing the horrendous snap of the closing mouth.

The head came up and he saw its visage, nightmarish, a great saurian face with a long narrow snout and underslung jaw, blazing filmy eyes on either side of the swaying head and, farther back, rows of crescent slits fluttering along the glistening hide. Then the sight was blotted out as the snout came for him, propelled by a sinuous neck that was the beginning of its great body. Salt spray and seaweed flew at him and he was forced to duck behind the insecure protection of the mast and flapping sail. Too late he realized his mistake. The thing threw itself after him with complete abandon, slicing into the mast and, with a snap and a splintering sound, it collapsed among a forest of shroud and rigging.

The ship rocked under him as he fought his way clear of the clinging tangle to see the dripping jaws hovering over the cowering form of the Magic Man. Ronin raced forward, knowing that he was too far away. His right hand was a blur in the night air as the poignard flew at the thing's head, burying itself just behind the right eye. The terrible head shot forward with incredible acceleration, jaws agape. They snapped shut with a hideous metallic popping. Borros screamed and a geyser of blood and torn viscera showered the air, misting over Ronin as he drove his blade point first into the unblinking eye.

Had he not been as strong, the creature would have jerked the heavy hilt from his hands; but it was his sword and he would not let it go. He was whipped about as the thing writhed in agony. He tried to pull the sword free of the bone into which it had been thrust – an outcropping of skull beneath the destroyed eye. With a grinding sound, he at last pulled it free and dropped to the deck. The saurian head, green viscous blood oozing from the gaping eye socket, quested vainly for its tormentor. Ronin, crawling along the deck, barely missed a blind swipe of the jaws; human blood spattered over him in the thing's wake. Then it reared up and crashed into the ship. The port gunwale near the bow splintered and flew into the air.

It was imperative now that he get to the creature before it tore the ship apart. He had to get it to see him and he moved around so that its good eye stared directly at him. He stood and the head ceased its writhing. It shot at him with alarming speed and he swung at the snout. The blow glanced off the thick scaly hide and he was nearly decapitated by the snapping jaws. He would not attempt that again. But there must be a way.

He turned, searching, and spied the lower half of the mast, the top splintered and sharp. He sheathed his sword and ran aft, the great head following. He ducked another swipe and heaved at the mast. Slowly it pulled up from its mounting. A searing pain scoured his back and he was flung to the deck. Nausea assailed him and his back was on fire. He shook his head and his nostrils dilated at the stench; the head was returning to finish him. Now, he thought through the red haze threatening to engulf him in unconsciousness.

He regained his feet and hauled again on the mast, feeling the thing closing again. Agony shot through him and then he had it and turned to see the glistening jaws. He rammed the broken mast into the gaping maw at an almost vertical angle.

The jaws snapped shut and the mast, braced against the lower jaw, slammed its upper end through the roof of the creature's mouth, through the soft palate and into the brain. The head rose into the night, spurting upward, a scaly fountain, crying.

And then it was gone, slithering back beneath the ice, dying or already dead, drifting languorously down and down with only the cracked surface of the ice sea, the blood and slime coating the deck of the felucca to mark its passage.

Ronin, on his knees, fell forward to the deck, forehead against the coldness. He panted, gulping at the air, clearing now after the creature's descent, then crawled painfully forward.

Borros lay in a pool of blood and rent flesh. His legs were gone and the lower half of his torso was a pulpy mass without recognizable form. Ronin stared blankly. Dead.

Onward, he thought. Onward.

But they were motionless on the ice sea. He tried to stand. A wave of dizziness and pain caught him and his knees buckled. He clung to the port gunwale and waited. Moments later, he was able to stand and, putting the pain into the back of his mind, he went carefully over the side and along the ice until he came to the leading edge of the runners. Chunks of ice, thrown up by the ascent of the creature, blocked the ship's way. He moved off cautiously to port, to the gaping rent in the ice, went down on hands and knees. Too dark to see anything but he listened. A gentle lapping came to him, echoing and distant. Water! The ice was thinning. He raised his head, peering southward. Out there. An end to the ice sea? The beginnings at last of civilization? Men.

And then what? he asked himself. He shook his head like a wounded animal. First things first.

He climbed painfully aboard the stalled ship, went forward and lifted the ruined body of the Magic Man. Down to the black ice, to the slippery edge of the obsidian pit. Home at last, thought Ronin. It slid easily from his arms, a pale, smeary flash in the starlight before it disappeared. Just for a moment the splash broke the rhythmic wash of the subcutaneous waves.

He worked for what seemed an interminable time, clearing the rubble from in front of the runners. His back burned and he was sweating and trembling by the time he had finished.

He went aboard and sat on the deck trying to regain his breath. Moments passed like centuries and he crawled along the length of the ship beneath the cold carpet of stars and in the platinum luminescence broke out the spare mast, fitting it carefully into its mounting, then attached the yard. Ran the rigging through block and tackle while the breeze sighed about him. He attached the sail and went down to his knees, a blackness in his brain, a buzzing in his ears. He pushed himself up and, sitting, raised the sail, lashed the ropes to. It was almost dead calm and the canvas flapped uselessly. He did not care; tried to make it to the warmth of the cabin but fell in a stupor of shock

and exhaustion before he could take two staggering steps.

The pain inside him grew and he weakened.
Sometime during the long night a strong wind
sprang up and the boat lurched uncertainly, then
slithered forward, picking up speed. He awoke
towards dawn but the movement of the vessel
lulled him back to a feverish sleep.

It was night again when he next opened his eyes.
He lay unmoving for long moments, his mind
attempting to retrace the events of the journey. It
was too much. At length his hands went to the
pockets of his foil suit but the last of his food was
gone. His teeth rattled as a dull bassy booming
broke upon him. It took some time for the sound
to penetrate, then he flopped over and crawled
slowly across the deck.

There was a fitful glow to starboard, flickering
smears of reds and oranges lighting the sky. It
appeared to him that in the distance a mountain
was on fire, belching ruby smoke, casting burning
effluvia into the obsidian night. He squinted, fascinated, convinced that he was dreaming. A dense
pressure came to his ears. Great chunks of dark
soapy stone were hurled high into the air and
liquid fire, saffron, pale green, violet, shot from
the summit of the mountain, igniting the air as it
rose, then cascading downward to the earth. Blue
flame, ghostly and luminescent, wrote itself
inscrutably upon the tumultuous darkness while
the land seemed to shiver and shift in a great

upheaval. A roaring vibrated his body, filling him with the incandescence of energy. The entire world was kinetic. He imagined that he heard a mournful wail and the mountain seemed to bleed as rock, white and yellow and crimson, poured steaming and thick down its side, and forests of vapor rolled ponderously into the dulled sky. Then the night and all it held was obscured by a blackness darker even than sleep and Ronin began to choke on the soft dust.

The ship sped southward away, away from the trembling land, the red and onyx sky, over the thinning ice and, when once more the oblate sun cracked the horizon, still steeped in clouds glowing amber from its light, the morning was less chill, promising a day cool, not cold.

Still Ronin lay upon the maimed deck, delirious, the tatters of his foil suit fluttering over his gouged back. Perhaps it was better thus; that he did not see the vast chunks of ice shearing off with great cracks like barks of thunder, floating now out onto the dark green water.

The ship hit the last thin sheet of ice with a noise that was part groan, part splinter. The crust disintegrated under the weight, and at last the ship was afloat. The bow dipped precariously, then righted itself, the stem coming up in a shower. The cascade streamed over the gunwale running aft, eddying around the prone form lying on the deck.

He awoke briefly, snorting salt water from his nostrils, lifting himself weakly, grasping the gunwale, peered over the side. Water! his numbed brain screamed. Water! But he could not think why that was so important. He lifted his head and the sun blinded him. He looked again at the water, blue-green, sun-dazzled golden, and then beneath the surface at – what?

A shadow? Its immense bulk flickered deep beneath the waves without outline or contour. He stared at it for what seemed a long time. Then all that winked back at him were the green waves, tipped with reflected light, chopped into ten thousand minute crescents bobbing and dancing. What? Then he passed out, his body falling limply to the salt-slick deck.

The day turned chill as billowing clouds, dark and gravid, passed before the face of the sun, blotting out its warmth. The sea changed colour, becoming slate grey; and now here and there whitecaps appeared. A heavy, gusty wind sprang up from the northeast and tore at the sail. Moments later, in the gathering gloom, the squall hit with full fury. The seas rose and the ship, unmanned, began to founder. She was turned beam on by the wind, into the troughs of the oncoming waves whose high crests now swept incessantly over the felucca. She began to take on water as she lay heavily in the crashing seas. Rain came in sheets and the day turned grey-green, dark and featureless, filled with the hiss and drum of the downpour.

The ship was sinking and nothing could save her. The wind hit her just as a wave crested broadside and she began to break up. The rain slackened but the wind intensified, as if it knew that the vessel was in the throes of going under.

The deck beneath Ronin's body buckled and collapsed and he was washed unceremoniously into the turbulent sea. He awoke in the water, gasping and choking for air as the sea filled his mouth and throat. He rose to the surface, hearing the grinding roar of the splitting ship all around him. Disoriented, heavy with the weight of his sword, he went under, clutched for a floating piece of the mast, missed, regained the surface, lungs bursting, back a glyph of agony as the salt drenched his wounds, reached again for the mast, felt its slippery length for only an instant before it rolled away from him. He tried to go after it but he had no strength and he knew with a peculiar calmness that he was drowning and there was nothing he could do about it. He went down into the cold green depths, watching the light recede from him, taking with him in his lungs a fast-diminishing piece of the sky.

3

Sha'angh'sei

Even when Rikkagin T'ien looked him full in the face, he was never sure what the stubby man was thinking.

'Tea?'

As now.

'Please.'

What rules him? Ronin wondered not for the first time. Rikkagin T'ien was solid, built low to the ground. His wide shoulders, muscular arms, and short legs made him seem almost other-worldly. Then there was the fact that he was hairless.

'So pleasant to relax every now and then, so?' He lifted the small pot, lacquered in a multicolored wheel pattern. 'You must excuse the lack of a lady,' he continued as he delicately turned the small cups. 'It is most unseemly for a rikkagin to perform this function.' He poured the honey-coloured liquid. It steamed the air. He tilted his head. 'However, war causes us to make do with so many things that we would normally find abhorrent.' He shrugged as if talking to an old friend. His yellowish skin gleamed in the low lamplight, his wide oval head with its small ears, black almond eyes, and smiling mouth seemed almost regal in this atmosphere. The distant sounds of the ship wafted around them like a fragrance, dominated by the rhythmic singing. Rikkagin T'ien ceremoniously presented Ronin with a filled cup. He smiled dazzlingly and sipped at his own cup. He sighed broadly.

'Tea,' he said, 'is truly the gift of the gods.' Then his face fell. This made him appear oddly childlike. 'How strange that your people are ignorant of its existence.' He sipped once more from his cup. 'How tragic.'

They sat cross-legged on opposite sides of a low wooden table lacquered in squares of green and grey.

'You are comfortable in your new clothes?'

Ronin put a hand to his loose shirt, looked at his light pants.

'Yes,' he said. 'Very. But this material is new to me.'

'Ah, it is silk. Cool in the heat, warm when it is cold.' Rikkagin T'ien sipped again at his tea. 'Some things are changeless, so?' He placed his cup precisely in the centre of a green square. 'Now that you are at your ease, please tell me again where you are from and why you are here.'

Something pulled on his feet. His descent was checked. He was cradled, the sea washing over him. Then he rose towards the rippling emerald pool of light, rising from the depths, from the awful liquid silence, from the buoyancy of death, into the clean sweet air, the churning of the waves. Gripped again by gravity, he coughed and retched

sea water, his lungs working like bellows, automatically, independent of his brain, which was still
fogged, in the coruscating quietude of the ocean,
not yet ready to accept the return to life. Then he
rose into the air, a gasping, wounded phoenix.

'So,' Rikkagin T'ien said, nodding. 'A Bladesman
you call yourself.' He stared hard at Ronin; at his
face, at the muscles along his arms, at the deep
chest. 'A soldier you are, a tactician. Well. You
are ill and the injury to your back is quite serious.
My physician informs me that you will carry those
scars for the rest of your life.' He stood up, planted
his bare feet wide apart, bending his knees slightly.
Three men came into the room, swiftly, silently,
all armed, and if he had made a move to summon
them, Ronin had not seen it. 'Yet a soldier knows
one thing. He knows how to fight, so?' He beckoned Ronin to stand. 'Come,' he said in a light
tone that held no overtones, no rancour. 'Come
against me.'

A song in his brain. A song. It dominated his
senses, filling the air with a smoky tang, washing
over him like the sea. It was a singsong tide of
voices, rhythmic, sleepy, and muscular at the same
time.

Slowly, numbly he turned over. Dazed. He had
been drowning, tumbling gracefully down, twisting on the currents. He stretched out his arms.
And now?

He was looking down through the slimy web of

a net within which he lay. Below him, the swell and suck of the sea against long wooden planks. Curved. His eyes travelled upward and a word forced itself into his brain. A ship, he thought dizzily.

Drenched and dripping, he swung perhaps thirty meters above the water. Above him, the ship rose another forty metres. Its immense side sloped outward near the bottom. The hull was painted a deep green from the gunwale until almost fifteen metres from the sea. From there down it was red. From the side of the vessel myriad square ports had been cut and from these jutted long slender staffs, it seemed to Ronin, cleaving the water at an oblique angle. A forest of staffs; on separate levels. Two? Three? Staring upward, the sun struck his eyes and he vomited the last of the sea water before he passed out.

' "Rikkagin," ' said Rikkagin T'ien, after Ronin had for the first time told him the story of the Freehold, 'is a title not dissimilar to that of Saardin, so?'

That had surprised Ronin because at no time since he had been brought aboard had he ever been disarmed, even when he was in the presence of Rikkagin T'ien. Slowly he had come to realize that this was because they did not fear him.

Rikkagin T'ien beckoned to him and these thoughts flew through his mind like doves fleeing before a chill wind. What the little man said to him was true; he was not yet fit. Much of his strength had been sapped by his ordeal and it would be many days before he returned to good health. Yet he was a Bladesman and T'ien was again correct: he would have to prove himself.

He stood and Rikkagin T'ien bowed to him, a curious solemn gesture which he had sense enough to return. Two of the men came forward and, stooping, removed the low table from between them.

Slowly Rikkagin T'ien withdrew his sword, the light gleaming along the single slightly curved edge. Ronin withdrew his blade.

'Ah,' said Rikkagin T'ien as if he had been holding his breath.

Heat. He sensed it even before he opened his eyes. The polyglot odours hit him then: sweat and briny salt, tacky tar baking in the sun and aromatic pitch, fresh fish flopping in the warmth. The singing was in his ears and the deck rolled gently under him to its thudding tempo. Heat. Against his chest and cheek.

He was stretched out on the deck. The burning along his back had somehow lessened. He sensed movement around him. A shadow crossed his face and the heat lessened. He tried to rise. A hand, gentle, firm, stopped him and he obeyed, understanding now that someone was working on his back. He felt weak and drained, not even sure, if he were pressed, what reserves of energy remained within him. The situation was unclear. He had no idea where he was. On a ship. Just a ship. With

109

that came the thought of the mast on the felucca. Bend, he told himself. Bend or you will break. Thus he willed himself to relax in the midst of the unknown. Thus did he survive.

He closed his eyes and let the breath flow out of him completely until his lungs sucked in the air of their own accord. He repeated this, cleansing his respiratory system and energizing himself by oxygenating his blood. His eyes opened. He stared at Rikkagin T'ien. He forced all speculation from his mind.

The curving sword was a blur, flashing upward, and simultaneously Rikkagin T'ien screamed. Ronin parried the blow. Just. The intense sound had surprised him. The clang of the blades echoed off the cabin's bulkheads. The rikkagin whirled and his sword hummed in the air again, the force of the blow stinging Ronin's wrists.

Back burning anew, Ronin lifted his blade; it was as heavy as a drowned corpse. Pain flared in his chest, making him gasp, and his guard dropped. Through the veil of agony, he saw Rikkagin T'ien advancing and, sweat rolling down his head and torso, he attempted to defend himself. Slowly, his sword came up, trembling. The end, he thought.

But instead of striking, Rikkagin T'ien stood as still as a statue, lowered his sword, sheathed it. The deck whirled, seeming to rise towards Ronin, and then he was in the powerful arms of the two men who had stepped behind him. They set him gently on a mat of rushes, carefully sheathed his sword.

Rikkagin T'ien's oval face hovered in Ronin's line of vision. He smiled reassuringly. Ronin struggled to rise.

'Stay still now,' said T'ien. 'I have found out what I needed to know.' He shrugged, a totally pragmatic gesture, free of any theatricality. 'Do not regret your pain, Bladesman.' His face was a great yellow moon planted in the sky. 'You see, we saw your boat break up and your story was most convincing, especially with the evidence of your back. But still' – the moon waned before his eyes, blood pounded in his temples – 'we are at war and I must tell you that my enemies would do anything to discover my plans. Please do not think me melodramatic; it is quite true. And frankly the distinct possibility arose that you were in their employ.' Pain was rippling through his chest, making breathing a labour. The moon smiled benevolently in the cloudless sky. 'Rest now; you have proven your story; you are who you claim to be. Only a lifetime of training would have allowed you to come against me with three broken ribs.' The moon wavered and broke apart. He strained to see it. 'Now my physician is here. He will give you a liquid. Swallow it. He must set the ribs.' Then the moon went out and he was falling, falling.

The passage of the days and nights were as puffs of smoke to him, blooming briefly, evaporating

111

on a jasmine wind as if they had never existed; they were replaced by others, an ephemeral progression blending into a canvas of tonal colours, snatches of sounds, watery whispers of almost heard words. Most of the time he slept deeply, dreamlessly.

When at last he sat up he felt the constriction of the bandages fastened tightly across his chest. Immediately, one of the men in the cabin went out. The other leaned forward and poured tea from a clay pot into a small cup set on a lacquered tray. He held it for Ronin, who sipped gratefully until his thirst was slaked. He sat back and regarded the sailor. He had a sharp aquiline nose and a wide thin mouth. His deep-set eyes were blue. He wore an open shirt and wide-legged trousers. A scabbarded sword hung from his right hip. The cabin's door opened and the physician entered.

'Ah,' he exclaimed, smiling, 'you have had tea already. Good.' He knelt and pushed Ronin gently down onto his back, his fingers moving deftly over the contours of the bandages. He was yellow-skinned as was T'ien, with almond eyes and a wide nose. He clucked to himself, then looked at Ronin. 'It was a very bad fracture, yes. You were hit with great force.' He shook his head as his fingers continued their probing travels. Ronin winced once and the physician said, 'Ah,' quite softly.

'He is better, so?' said Rikkagin T'ien from close by. Ronin had not seen him enter.

'Oh my, yes,' nodded the physician. 'Very. The ribs are knitting faster than I had anticipated. A very fine body. As for the back' – he shrugged almost apologetically – 'it will heal but the scars are forever.' His face brightened. 'Still, not so bad, eh?'

'So,' said Rikkagin T'ien, addressing Ronin. 'When you feel fit enough, you will come on deck. Then we talk.' He turned and left.

'Give him as much tea as he wants. And rice cakes,' instructed the physician before departing. And Ronin was left with the men. Soon he drifted off to sleep.

A dense and smoky tangle, it climbed into the hills. It spread upward and outward from the wide harbour, the shores of the yellow and muddy sea, in a jungle of one- and two-storey buildings of wood, dark paint, brown brick. In many places they seemed set so close together that he could not tell where one ended and another began.

'Sha'angh'sei,' said Rikkagin T'ien.

Ronin could discern movement along the vast front of docks and wharves thrusting out into the slowly lapping waves. Dark masses milled like ants over an earthen mound, they were still too distant for him to pick out individuals. A peculiar haze hovered over the immense city, a component of its clutter and sprawl, obscuring its loftier reaches so that he had no clear idea how high the houses extended.

113

'Welcome to the continent of man.' There was a harsh edge to the laugh.

Ronin tore his eyes away from the domination of the city and looked at the man who stood on the deck beside Rikkagin T'ien. He was tall and muscular with cerulean eyes and short-cropped thick blond hair. An ivory bar was run through the lobe of one ear. He wore a light-coloured, loose-fitting shirt of silk tucked into tight black leggings. A long curving sword hung in a battered leather scabbard on one hip. A wicked dirk of extraordinary length, its hilt studded with rough-cut emeralds, a rather nonchalant statement of their value, was stuck into his sky-blue waist sash. T'ien had introduced him as his second in command: Tuolin.

'It was I who fished you out of the sea,' said the blond man. 'It was reflex, really. Most of the men believed you already drowned; you were under a long time.'

Ronin shook his head. 'I recall sinking, holding my breath, then darkness and a beating silence and then – '

Rikkagin T'ien called out an order and half a dozen men sprang from the deck, racing up the rigging lines. He turned back, observing them both.

'What happened to your back?' asked Tuolin.

'Have you been north?'

Tuolin shook his head, no.

'On the ice sea,' said Ronin softly, 'far enough south so that the water was already coming up on

114

the ice, thinning it, a – some kind of creature broke through the crust and attacked us.' Tuolin's eyes narrowed; he glanced quickly at T'ien, back to Ronin again.

'What kind of creature?'

Ronin shrugged. 'I cannot truthfully say. The world, it seems, is filled with strange and monstrous things. In any event, the light was almost gone. It took us totally by surprise. There was no time for anything save death.' The men in the rigging had reached the highest yards and they began to furl the topsails, using darting rapid motions. 'It tore my friend in two; ate his legs.'

They stood like three statues on the high poop deck, near the stern of the ship. A soft breeze brushed their faces, the tentative touch of a reunited lover.

'You must understand,' Rikkagin T'ien said, 'that death means little to us here in Sha'angh'sei; it is our way of life.' He peered up briefly. The men were returning down the rigging. 'War, Ronin. That is all we have known; all we shall ever know. Death waits for us behind every doorway, beneath every bed, down every dark alley of Sha'angh'sei.' The ship began to slow as the command was given for the rowers to slacken their pace. 'We would have it no other way.'

'We have lost the ability to mourn for our dead,' said Tuolin regretfully. 'Still, I would very much like to know more of this creature of the ice sea.'

'I am sure there is little more I can tell you,' said

Ronin. 'However, I am most curious about this craft's mode of travel. If I could see – '

'The rowers?' said Tuolin. 'I hardly think that you – '

'Tuolin,' interrupted Rikkagin T'ien. 'I do not think that under the circumstances we have much choice. It is a simple exchange of information.' His eyes sparkled. 'By all means, lead us down to the rowers.'

Tuolin's face had set into hard lines and ridges and Ronin wondered what he was missing in this dialogue. He understood only that he dare not interrupt.

It seemed as if there was no air and one had to take short breaths because of the concentrated stench but over all it was cleaner than he would have expected. The men sat along low wooden benches, three to each oar. They were naked to the waist and the ridges of their working muscles along shoulders and backs glistened in the low light. They moved in perfect unison to the cadence of a drum and the rhythmic singing. Three tiers of men along three quarters of the length of the ship. He stopped counting at one hundred. They were dark-haired and swarthy, thick-boned and short, fair-skinned and fair-haired, yellow-hued and almond-eyed; a jumble of humanity, inhabitants of the continent of man.

'You can plainly see,' said T'ien expansively, 'that we refuse to rely solely on the inconsistencies of the weather. Canvas is fine when the wind is up, otherwise – ' He shrugged.

116

They walked slowly down a narrow central aisle between the oarsmen.

'They are continually manned,' T'ien continued. 'The men work in shifts.'

'They do not mind this work?' asked Ronin.

'Mind?' said Tuolin incredulously. 'They are soldiers, bound to Rikkagin T'ien. It is their duty. Just as it is their duty to fight and die if need be for the rikkagin's safety.' He snorted. 'Where is this man from that he does not understand this? He cannot be civilized, surely.'

Rikkagin T'ien smiled somewhat absently as if he were enjoying some private jest. 'He comes from a long way off, Tuolin. Do not judge him so harshly.' Tuolin's eyes blazed and for just an instant Ronin believed that he was going to turn on his rikkagin. 'Teach him if he does not understand our ways,' said T'ien placidly.

'Yes,' said Tuolin, the cold light receding from his eyes, 'patience is its own reward, is it not so?'

T'ien walked on and they followed, a pace or so behind.

'You see,' said Tuolin, 'we carry with us many moral obligations which we are taught to honour virtually from birth.' A dark blur at the corner of Ronin's vision. 'To be bound to a rikkagin has many benefits.' Oblique approach, ballooning. 'One eats well, one is clothed, one has money; one is trained – ' And Tuolin had seen it too because even now he was moving, the long dirk no longer in his waist sash. There was a scream, disturbing the heavy air like a sudden breeze parting a velvet curtain, and the figure was upon them. Tuolin leapt forward, his dirk flashing in a savage thrust. The body, long and thin, sweat-coated, wielded a curving single-edged sword. The face was pinched, the mouth screaming, lips pulled back from rotted stumps of teeth in a rictus, the eyes glassy and bulging fanatically. Then the figure was spitted on the blond man's blurred weapon. The legs kicked violently and then the eyes rolled as the blade ripped through the naked chest, spewing forth blood and bone fragments. The man's sword clattered uselessly to the wooden boards. Rikkagin T'ien watched impassively as Tuolin withdrew the dirk and with a deft economy of motion slit the man's throat. Ronin noted that T'ien had not even drawn his sword.

Now the rikkagin sighed and without looking at either of them said, 'It is best if we return abovedecks.' And stepped nimbly over the crumpled corpse.

Sha'angh'sei loomed over them as they manoeuvred the sea lanes clogged with vessels large and small and eased into the port. The ship ploughed slowly through the thick sea, yellow-brown and clinging, past square-rigged fishing craft and high-sterned cargo vessels. Off to starboard, Ronin thought he could just discern the broad mouth of a river spilling into the sea.

He stood on the high poop drinking in the city while all about him was movement as men raced through the catwalk rigging, reefing the last of the unfurled sail, securing yards and lines, the forest of oars high in the air, dripping and shining, as the rowers prepared to ship them. It lay before him in the inky twilight like a vast fat jewel, dusky and dim with age, smouldering with fitful movement, heaving itself from the spume and effluvia of the land.

The low buildings closest to him appeared to be built on a delta and he looked again for the river's mouth for confirmation but it was lost behind the thick clumps of buildings. Beyond the flat of the delta the city rose like the arched spine of a frightened animal and many of the dwellings in this area seemed to need the aid of wooden columns sunk into the hillside, which supported their jutting balconies, fluted and columnated, dark hardwoods gleaming in the smeary glow as lamps and torches were abruptly lit throughout the city as if by some prearranged signal. The deepening haze, sapphire and mauve, softened the flicker of the flames so that the individual sources blended and blurred and the city seemed to glow with an ethereal incandescence.

Ronin's pulse quickened. By chance he had come to Sha'angh'sei, and it was obviously a major port on the continent of man. Here, he felt confident, he would find someone who could unlock the riddle of the scroll of dor-Sefrith. The wash of light reached out for him as the ship manoeuvred toward the waiting wharf. Perhaps, he mused, Rikkagin T'ien will know of someone.

Men swarmed along the long arm of the wharf

in anticipation of their arrival and Ronin, observing the frenzy of activity, felt the muscles of his stomach contract momentarily as his spirits soared. The continent of man: Borros had been correct all along. So many people here, such a teeming world; even now, though it was before his eyes, it was a shock; so long talked of, it was a dream world that had been an integral ingredient of the fantasy that had kept them alive with a goal as they flew across the featureless platinum ice for endless days and nights with nothing but the cutting wind and cold as their reality. This dream had kept Borros alive until the end, Ronin was sure; his body had been beaten and, save for this land beckoning him on, Borros' mind would have let go in the midst of Freidal's torture within the confines of the Freehold. And now: now I step upon the cluttered foreshore of the continent of man. A dream no more.

There came a brief command and the ship touched the creaking timbers of the long wharf.

There was an electric hum, the live-wire abrasive intensity of rushing bodies, the cacophonous atonality of voices raised in argument, laughter, command, the chunky slap of cargo continually being loaded onto ships ready to sail to other ports, unloaded from just-docked vessels, the brief slam of working doorways, the beckoning cries of vendors, the lilt of hoarse monotonous work songs, the crisp cadence of soldiers' booted feet, the clangour of arms, the tolling of far-off bells, a whiff of mysterious chanting, and, beneath it all, the heavy wash of the yellow sea lapping at the belly of the city, caressing it, washing its soil, eating its bedrock.

He stood on the wharf, an alien island in an ocean of moving bodies. The debarking soldiers passed him in formation, elbowing aside the scurrying workers, bare-chested and barefooted, tattered pants rolled up their legs, sweat streaming down their laden backs, some bent double under their immense loads, others in pairs trotting with crates of foodstuffs suspended from bamboo poles supported on their shoulders. Overseers screaming their instructions, orders being barked, sellers frantically hawking their wares, bodies coming against him like breakers, sounds like waves beating upon the shores of his ears, engulfing him. He breathed deeply and his nostrils flared to the steamy air laden with the fragrances of man, the pungency of fresh spices and syrupy oils, the mingling of exotic perfumes and thick sweat, the briny scent of the sea, rich with the myriad animal flavours of life and death.

Tuolin found him eventually.

'The rikkagin will see you tomorrow in the morning.' Caftans of silk and cotton, tight blouses over firm breasts, long earrings clashing softly. 'He is most anxious to speak with you at length.' Gold rings glinting, a wooden leg with a worn shoe stuck on the end, coloured skirts swirling, armbands dully shining, flash of yellow feathers. 'Now he has many preparations to make and we could both use food and drink.' Carts bumping, green eyes flashing, strange two-wheeled carriages pulled by toiling runners, dark hair floating in the soft scented breeze, music skirling. 'Especially drink, eh?' Faces hidden by veils, faces covered with long beards, greased and curling, the savoury mouth-watering perfume of roasting meat, a black and terribly empty eyeless socket, laughter, mouths gaping wide, black teeth, eyes crinkling, flash of dirk. 'And afterward, a very special place, Ronin. Oh yes.'

Along the sweep of the wharf the crowd thinned momentarily and Ronin was transfixed by a constellation of bobbing lights along the waterfront. Low, wide boats, some with makeshift shelters, most without, rocked gently on the evening tide. Lanterns were hung, illuminating the occupants. Families crowded the vessels, men, women, scrambling children and screaming infants, old ones still as statues, all assembled now for the meal at day's end; sitting with cracked shallow bowls of rice close to their faces, eating with long sticks, throats working as if they were famished.

'Home for many people,' said Tuolin. 'Generations have worked on land and have lived on the tasstans.' Bodies closed over the view in an unwashed tide, blotting out all but the sea lanterns' mobile glow reflecting off the restless water. They began walking again. 'There is no room for them in Sha'angh'sei.' Shouts and the sounds of running feet. 'There never was.'

'Yet they work here, do they not?'

'Oh yes.' A scuffle beside them; coarse curses, receding, drowned in the sea of bodies. 'There is always work from dawn until dusk: for a copper coin which the merchants take at the end of the day, for the mildewed rice that they must eat. There is always work in Sha'angh'sei for a strong back, day or night. But nowhere to live.' Tuolin laughed abruptly and clapped Ronin on the back. 'But no more talk now. I have been too long from this city.' He guided them skilfully through the jostling throng, moving at an increasing pace.

'Come,' he called as he moved ahead. 'We go to Iron Street.'

Night lights flared along every street they took; black iron lanterns, wrought in openwork grills, the flames within licking smokily at the darkness. The packed street were cobbled, lined with buildings variously assigned as apartments or shops without any discernible pattern. Men, thin and fat, lolled in open doorways, picking at their teeth or smoking pipes with long curving stems and tiny bowls, squatting against grimy wooden and chipped brick walls, talking or dozing. Off these thoroughfares were ubiquitous narrow twisting alleys, blacker than the night, down which people would sometimes wander, disappearing within instants, leaving behind only a dissipating breath of sweet smoke.

They passed many soldiers, of differing types and obviously bound to various rikkagin. They seemed to be the only people in these noisome streets not in a hurry. Ronin was pleased to be able to walk; it gave him a chance to test his body. His back had ceased to pain him days ago and the wound in his shoulder was almost healed but he knew his ribs needed more time to mend. His chest was stiff and sore but most of the sharp pain had left him and this exercise was invigorating, not tiring.

On Iron Street, two men threw a set of five dice against the side of a wall, talking softly to each other, intent on the faces of the cubes. A woman in filthy clothes sat in the dust of the street, a bawling baby in the crook of one arm. She held a grimy hand, nails torn and black with dirt, palm upward.

'Please,' she called in a pitifully weak voice. 'Please.'

Her sad eyes caught Ronin's and they were filled with pain.

'Ignore her,' Tuolin said, noting the direction of Ronin's gaze.

'But surely you can spare something for her.'

Tuolin shook his head.

'Please,' the woman called.

'The baby is crying,' said Ronin. 'It is hungry.'

Swiftly Tuolin crossed the crowded street and, thrusting aside the folds of the woman's robe, grasped the hidden wrist and Ronin saw that she held a dirk which she had been digging into the baby to make it cry. Her almond eyes flashed angrily and she wrenched her wrist from his grip, lunging at him with the blade's point. Tuolin

124

stepped back out of harm's way and they resumed their walk along Iron Street.

'A lesson of Sha'angh'sei,' he said.

Ronin glanced back through the crowds of people. The woman sat, palm outstretched, the other hand hidden. Her lips moved; her eyes searched the passing faces. The baby cried.

'War is the reason Sha'angh'sei was built and it was built in a day.'

'Surely you are not serious.'

'Perhaps I exagggerate just a bit.'

'How long?'

'To build the city?'

'No. How long has the war been on?'

'It is endless. I do not remember. No one can.'

'Who is fighting whom?'

'Everyone against everybody.'

'That is not an answer.'

'Yet it is the truth.'

They were sitting in a low-ceilinged tavern, at a plank table located along the back wall which ran almost the entire width of the establishment. A wide wooden stairway to the second storey took up the remainder of the wall.

The air was thick with smoke and grease and burning tallow. Before them lay platters of broiled meat and steamed fish, raw vegetables and the inevitable rice. Cups of a clear rice wine, hot and potent, were constantly refilled as they ate using the long sticks. The men aboard ship had taught Ronin how to use these peculiar eating utensils.

'All the races of man are here, I think,' said Tuolin between mouthfuls, 'in differing strengths. And they have never gotten along.'

'Borros, the man I travelled with over the ice sea, believed that the sorcerous wars had ended all conflict.'

Tuolin smiled as he swallowed but his eyes showed that he was not amused; they were as coldly blue as ice. 'Man will never learn, Ronin. He is eternally at war with himself.' He shrugged. 'There is no help for it, I am afraid.'

Six soldiers in dusty uniforms came into the tavern, pulling up chairs around a table near the door. They ordered wine and began to drink, laughing loudly and pounding on the table. Their long swords scraped against the floor boards.

'This city is composed of factions,' said Tuolin, 'all of them mistrusting the others because the war allows you to make much money if you are shrewd.'

In the far corner two cloaked men, tall and light-haired, sat with arms around a pair of sloe-eyed women, slight, with high-cheekboned, flat-nosed faces, long black hair falling sleekly to the middle of their backs.

'The city is filled with many, many hongs – merchants – who are rich and fat from the war.'

'They live here?'

One of the couples was kissing now, a long and passionate embrace.

'Hardly,' Tuolin snorted. He gulped at his wine.

126

'They live on the upper reaches.' He refilled his cup. 'In the walled city.'

'Another city?'

'Yes and no.' He took more meat with his sticks. 'It is still Sha'angh'sei.'

Along the opposite wall a woman with long eyes and a curiously simian face whispered to three men in dark cloaks. She wore her shiny hair piled upon her narrow head and long earrings of a green stone spun as she moved her head.

'What about the war?'

'It is everywhere. It is why we returned to Sha'angh'sei. An army of bandits have massed to the north and west.' Three children ran in from the street, thin and filthy and hollow-eyed. The tavernmaster called to them as they clattered up the stairs. He shouted and the tallest one returned and laid a number of dull coins in the man's hand. The tavernmaster slapped the boy so hard that his frame shook. The boy dug a dirty hand into a pocket and extracted several more coins, then he ran up the stairs after the others. 'The hongs are paying us to protect their interests before the bandits become a nuisance by descending on the city itself.'

Even to Ronin, so short a time with these people, it seemed an implausible story; however, he could not guess why Tuolin should lie to him.

'Then you will be leaving Sha'angh'sei?' he asked.

The simian-faced woman was gesturing now with narrow bony hands. Her long nails were lacquered green and, Ronin saw with some surprise, her teeth were black.

'Yes. The day after tomorrow. It is a three-day march to Kamado, the fortress in the north.'

One of the men got up and walked out. The remaining two resumed talking to the simian-faced woman with increased animation. Her teeth gleamed darkly.

Ronin was about to say something but Tuolin's hand on his arm stopped him. He followed the blond man's gaze.

Two men stod in the doorway. They wore dark baggy pants and black cloaks over silk shirts. They were almond-eyed with flat wide faces. Their long hair was waxed and bound in queues. An errant gust of wind plucked at their cloaks and Ronin caught a glimpse of short-hafted axes thrust into their sashes.

'Keep still,' whispered Tuolin, his eyes drifting slowly away from the tall figures. His voice carried a peculiar note, of fear perhaps? He looked at Ronin and said in a more normal tone, 'The rikkagin will require you at a specific hour tomorrow. Until that time, he requested me to be your guide around the city.' Ronin stared at him. 'Sha'angh'sei is a most complex and at times bewildering city. The rikkagin does not wish for you to get lost.'

The men were still in the doorway, their black eyes sweeping the room. The tavernmaster glanced up from serving a table and, wiping his hands on his apron, hurried across the room. He drew from some inner pocket a small leather sack which he handed to one of the men. The other said something to him and laughed. The tavern-master bowed. Then the two were gone without a sound.

'Who were they?' asked Ronin.

'The Greens,' said Tuolin as if that were all the answer needed. He drained the last of his wine. 'I have had my fill of this place. What say you, Ronin, shall we move on?'

Tuolin paid for their meal. The green stone earrings of the simian-faced woman danced as she spoke.

Outside in the fragrant air, there seemed less people about than earlier in the evening. Tuolin looked both ways along the street, then he seemed to relax, stretching.

'Now,' he said, 'the evening begins.'

The gold plaque said 'Tenchō.' It was fixed with golden spikes to the brown brickwork to the left of the high yellow double doors at the head of a curving iron stairway on Okan Street.

Twice he had caught Tuolin glancing behind them as if he thought they were being followed. However, it seemed quite impossible to tell among all the bodies darting in every direction.

Tuolin knocked on the yellow doors and after a moment they opened inward.

'Matsu,' he breathed, smiling.

She stood between the two armed men, her slender frame appearing smaller for their presence.

She had an oval face with long almond eyes and thick black hair which she wore straight and loose so that one eye was continually blanketed by its cascade. She wore a silver robe with a high neck and flaring sleeves, embroidered with grey doves. Her skin was very white; her lips were unpainted. The oval lapis pin at her throat was the only relief from black, grey, and white.

She smiled at Tuolin, then gazed for a long moment at Ronin. Then she murmured to the guards, who relaxed somewhat.

She led them wordlessly through a narrow foyer. Strips of thin carpeting covered the wooden floors; a tall gold-framed mirror briefly disclosed the small procession. They went through open doors on the left from which yellow light wavered and danced.

They were in a wide, deep room with blond wood panelling long the walls to a height of an average man's waist. Above this, the walls were painted a muted yellow. The high ceiling was bone white. From its centre hung an immense oval lamp constructed of faceted topaz; perhaps five hundred crystals had been cunningly mounted so that the lamp's myriad small flames, set in its centre, shone through the facets. It was this singular light which gave the room its tawny aspect.

Scattered about the lacquered wooden floor were small intimate couches and groups of plush chairs upon which sat the most diverse assortment of women that Ronin had ever seen. Some were with men, drinking and smoking, others were in small groups talking languidly among themselves, turning their exquisite faces to the prowling men like petals of a flower following the path of the sun. Young girls in quilted jackets and wide silk pants of pastel colours moved between these groups, ships in the indeterminate voids separating these trembling constellations.

Matsu left them, crossing the room to a group of two men and a woman. After several moments the woman detached herself and approached them. She wore a floor-length saffron silk dress, slit up one side so that with every step she took Ronin could see the length of one naked leg. The dress was embroidered in patterns of fantastic flowers in the palest green. Like Matsu's, the dress was wide-sleeved and high-necked and this style managed somehow to highlight her figure.

But it was her face that was most extraordinary. She had long dark eyes, the upper lids dusky and sensual without seeming to be painted. Her face was narrow at the chin, accentuating her high cheekbones. Her lips were painted deep scarlet; glossy, half opened. Her hair was so violently dark that it appeared blue-black; she wore it very long and brushed to fall delicately across her left shoulder and breast.

She smiled with small white teeth and lifted her hands, pressing them together.

'Ah, Tuolin,' she said. 'How good it is to see you again.' Her voice had the tonality of a bell, far away, lilting. She dropped her hands. They were small and white with delicate fingers and long nails lacquered yellow. She wore topaz earrings in the shape of a flower.

Her head turned slowly and she gazed at Ronin and at that precise moment he had the peculiar sensation of seeing double.

'Kiri, this is Ronin,' said Tuolin. 'He is a warrior from a land far to the north. This is his first night in Sha'angh'sei.'

'And you brought him here,' she said with a musical laugh. 'How very flattering.'

A young girl in a light blue quilted jacket and pants came up to them.

'Liy will take you to bathe. And when you return, you shall decide.' The dark eyes regarded him.

The girl led them across the room of topaz light, through a wide teakwood door into a short passageway of rough-hewn stone. The contrast was absolute.

They went down a narrow stairway lit by smoky braziers set high up along the walls. The stone steps were damp and somewhere, not far off, Ronin could discern the soft slap of water. The stairs gave out into a wide room with rock walls and a low wooden ceiling, lamplit, warm. Into one wall had been hewn an immense fireplace within which hung an equally enormous cauldron steaming as the fire boiled its contents.

The room itself was dominated by two large square wooden tubs set upon raised wooden slats; one of the tubs was half filled with water. Four women, dark-haired, almond-eyed, naked to the

132

waist, stood as if waiting for their arrival. Water steamed and gurgled.

'Come on,' Tuolin called happily, stripping off his dirty sea clothes and hanging his weapons on one of a line of wooden pegs set into one wall. Ronin followed suit and the women directed them to the empty tub. As they climbed in, the women drew up buckets of hot water, filling the tub. Then they climbed in and, taking soft brushes and fragrant soap, began to wash each man thoroughly.

Tuolin snorted and blew water from his mouth.

'Well, Ronin, what do you think of this? Was home ever so pleasant?'

The hands were soft and gentle and the hot soapy water against his skin felt delicious. The women murmured to each other when they saw his back, the scars long and livid and newly healed, and they took great care in cleansing that part of him so that he felt no discomfort, only pleasure. They stroked his chest, gently massaging his muscles almost as if they knew of his recently broken ribs. They murmured to him and he and Tuolin moved, creators now of their own waves, commanders of tides and currents, to the second tub to which clean hot water was added. Two of the women began to clean the first tub while the other two gathered up the pair's dirty clothes and went out.

Ronin lay back, stretching out his legs, letting the heat slowly soak into his body. Gradually, his muscles loosened and much of the tension drained out of him. He closed his eyes.

How unexpected this all was. How utterly different were the circumstances than what Borros had pictured. How – Abruptly the realization came that he had had no idea of where he might be headed or even if he could survive when he had ascended onto the surface from the Freehold's forbidden access hatch. He had followed Borros blindly, not caring, wanting to escape from the Freehold as much as he had wanted to solve the mystery of the scroll of dor-Sefrith. The heat climbed into him like the presence of a naked woman close beside him.

And with that the barriers which he had so painstakingly erected folded in upon themselves and he thought of her. Oh, K'reen, how you must have been tortured. He destroyed you day by day with the poison he fed you. The lies!

The water rippled and Ronin looked up, into the present. One of the women had climbed in beside Tuolin.

'Do you want the other one? It is perfectly all right but you must ask.'

Ronin smiled wanly. 'Not just now. The water is enough.'

The blond man shrugged and splashed the woman, using his cupped hand. She giggled.

Strange. The Freehold seems like so long ago; as distant as another lifetime. But she does not. She is still with me and there is nothing, Chill take him, that the Salamander can do about that.

He glanced at his great sword, swinging a small arc, brushed by one of the women as she slipped out of the room. Within it was the scroll and perhaps, if Borros was right about this, the key to man's survival. And he could no longer doubt the Magic Man. He had already grappled with the Makkon; felt its awesome power. And instinctively he had known that such a creature was not of this world; it held its own kind of monsters.

Of this he was certain: at least one Makkon was already here. If the scroll has not been deciphered by the time the four converge, they will summon The Dolman and mankind will surely be doomed.

'Ready?' asked Tuolin.

They both stood up, dripping.

'Let me look at you.'

The scarlet lips opened. The tiny pink tongue brushed the even white teeth.

She laughed. 'She is always so clever about these things.'

He wore a silk robe of a colour that could have been light green or brown or blue or any one of a dozen colours. Yet it was none of these but perhaps a subtle blend to cause the finished cloth to appear colourless. Along the body and arms were fierce dragons, rampant, eyes seething, taloned limbs seeking, embroidered in gilt thread so that their hides seemed molten. Tuolin was clothed in a robe of deep blue with white herons on front and back.

'Ah, Tuolin, you must have brought me a remarkable man.' Kiri directed her eyes to Ronin's. 'You know, I will not say this to all who come to Tenchō, but Matsu chooses the robes to fit each person who enters here. She is rarely wrong in her matching.'

'And what does this mean, then?' asked Ronin, glancing down at the glittering dragons.

'Why, I am sure I do not know yet,' she said with a small smile. 'I have never seen that particular pattern before.'

She turned to Tuolin then and took his arm. Her perfume came to Ronin, rich and subtle, musky and light. The three of them strolled across the room of topaz light, stopping momentarily as one of the girls offered them tea and rice wine, and Kiri introduced them one by one to the women who were not already engaged with men. All were beautiful; all were different. They smiled and stroked the air with their ornamental paper fans. At length, Tuolin made his choice, a tall slender woman with light eyes and hair and a generous mouth.

Kiri nodded and turned to Ronin.

'And you,' she said softly. 'Whom do you wish?'

Ronin looked again at all the women, the jutting landscape of femaleness, and he came back to her black dusky eyes.

'It is you,' he said slowly, 'that I wish.'

★　★　★

When the organism does not comprehend, sight and sound become meaningless. The light-haired woman therefore looked strange to him as she opened her mouth wide and emitted a sound.

She gasped, then half giggled, stifling it with a swallow as the three others stood quite still watching her. Around them the movements continued, the languid flutters of a fan, the flashes of naked legs, the sweet smell of smoke curling, the steaming of hot tea and spiced rice wine, like the slow immense wheel of the stars.

There came then the chink of a cup being set down on a lacquered tray, as separate and distinct a sound as a crack of thunder on a rain-washed night.

Tuolin said: 'But that is im – '

Kiri's delicately upraised hand halted him in mid-sentence.

'He is,' she said, 'from another land. That is what you told me, Tuolin, yes?' The yellow nails were like slender torches in the light. 'I asked and he replied as he wished.' Now she was gazing into Ronin's eyes but she spoke to the blond man. 'You have selected Sa, as *you* wished. Take her then.'

'But – '

'Think no more upon it, lest your harmony be broken and this house become worthless. I take no offense.' The yellow nails moved fractionally, spilling light. 'I shall take care of Ronin. And he shall take care of me.'

'What happened?' asked Ronin after Tuolin and Sa had departed.

She took his arm and laughed softly. They began to walk in the room of topaz light. 'Death,' she said lightly and without any trace of coyness. 'It is death to ask for me, foreigner.'

A tiny girl in a pink quilted jacket came up to them to offer rice wine.

'Please,' Kiri said and he handed her a cup, took one for himself. He sipped at the wine; it was quite different from the rice wine of the tavern. The spices added a tang and sweetness that he appreciated.

'I will choose another then.'

There was muted laughter and the sinuous rustle of fabric against scented skin. The sweet smoke was heavier now.

'Is that what you wish?'

'No.'

'You told me what you desired.'

He stopped and looked at her. 'Yes, but – '

'Hmmm?' The scarlet lips opened and curled in a smile.

'I wish also to abide by the rules of your people.'

She urged him to begin walking again.

'The one thing you must remember about Sha'angh'sei, the only thing worth remembering, is that there are no laws here.'

'But you just told me – '

'That it is death to ask for me, yes.'

The yellow nails traced the gilt dragons of his robe, over flaring nostrils, open mouth, and snake tongue, down the serpentine body, across the rampant claws, following the sinuous tail.

138

'But everything is yours for the taking. The factions of this city bind themselves in codes and unwritten rules.' Her eyes were huge and mysterious; he felt the pressure of her nails through the cloth. Her voice was a whisper now: 'Who dwells in Sha'angh'sei but the dominators and the dominated?' He drew towards her. 'Yet law is unknown here.'

It was less dense in the room of topaz light as the couples began to disperse. The girls were cleaning up in perfect silence and soon its tawny splendour was left to them alone.

'No,' she said, and when she shook her head her hair was like a forest in the night, 'you are not from Sha'angh'sei or anywhere close. You are totally untouched by the city.'

'Is that so important?'

'Yes,' she whispered. 'Oh yes.'

'Tell me again why you have come to Sha'angh'sei.'

'You have heard it before.'

'Yes, but this time I wish Tuolin to hear it.'

'I had never heard of the city until you told me of it.'

'Of course,' he said, not unkindly.

Rikkagin T'ien sat cross-legged behind a green lacquered table on which stood a fired clay teapot, a cup showing the dregs of many fillings in its bottom, an inkwell, and a quill pen. He put aside the sheaf of rice papers upon which he had been writing a vertical list of figures.

'Begin, please.'

Ronin told the story of the scroll of dor-Sefrith, the gathering of the Makkon, the coming of The Dolman.

There was silence in the room when he had finished. Yellow light streamed obliquely through the leaded glass panes beyond which, one story below, lay Double Bass Street where the rikkagin and his men were quartered and from which they would depart at dawn tomorrow for the long march to Kamado.

He saw T'ien glancing at Tuolin, who stood, hands clasped behind him, facing away from the windows. With the light at his back, his face was in deep shadow. It occurred to him then that they did not believe him; that, despite Rikkagin T'ien's words to the contrary, they perhaps thought him still an enemy. Nevertheless, I must ask.

'Perhaps you could help.'

'What?' T'ien had been pulled from some deep thought. 'Help in what way?'

'By deciphering the scroll.'

The rikkagin smiled somewhat sadly. 'I am afraid that is quite impossible.'

'Perhaps the Council could aid him,' said Tuolin.

Rikkagin T'ien looked bewildered for a moment and he stared at the blond man as if he were a statue which had just spoken. Then he said, 'Yes, now that you have brought it up, that might be the answer.' He seemed lost in thought again.

'You see,' said Tuolin, 'the city is governed by

140

a Municipal Council: nine members with the major factions represented and the minor ones currying favours through taels of silver and other commodities. If any in this city possess the knowledge you seek, they would.'

'Where does the Council meet?'

'In the walled city, on the mountain above us. But you will have to wait until tomorrow; I do not believe there is a council session today. Is that not correct, Rikkagin?' Tuolin smiled.

'Hmm? Oh yes, quite so,' T'ien said, but his mind still seemed preoccupied with other matters.

In the small silence, the soft clatter of the rikkagin's men attending to their preparations drifted lazily through the open windows.

There came a knock on the door and Tuolin crossed the room before T'ien had a chance to say anything. A soldier bowed his way in, handing Tuolin a slip of folded rice paper. The blond man opened it and read its contents, his brows furrowing in concentration or anxiety. He shook his head at the soldier, who immediately departed. Then Tuolin crossed the room and laid the paper open in front of the rikkagin. While T'ien read it, he said, 'I am afraid that a number of last-minute administrative problems have arisen and they will require the attention of the rikkagin and myself for the remainder of the day. Please feel free to see the city but we should like it if you would return here and take the evening meal with us.' The smile came again.

T'ien looked up. 'Ask one of the men downstairs

for directions. They have been instructed to give you a bag of coins. You cannot get anything in Sha'angh'sei without paying for it.'

Ouside, he turned left and then right, walking down a street of some incline. The day was overcast and a yellow mist was still rising. He caught himself thinking of T'ien and Tuolin. Again he had the feeling that he had missed something vital in their exchange, yet the answer remained elusive. He shrugged and put the problem out of his mind.

He came to a broad avenue after several minutes and the noise of the city welled up at him. Rows of stalls lined the crowded street. One sold fowl. They were hung by their necks, cooked and varnished with a shiny vermilion sauce so that they looked wooden and unreal. As he watched, people stopped, putting down a few coins. The stall's owner brought out bowls of rice and sticks and commenced to cut up pieces of a cooked bird into the rice. The people ate standing up. For another coin they received a small cup of green tea to wash down the meal.

Elsewhere, a tailor of leather worked, making boots and cloaks. And at a busy intersection a fat man with a thin drooping moustache sat within a square metal cage, lending money at the day's going rate, which, Ronin surmised, was somewhat higher than yesterday's.

He heard the cadence of boots and a group of

soldiers tramped by, moving disdainfully through the clouds of people.

He walked the city's twisting fluid streets, caught up in the rapid pulse, repeating and changing, flashes of colour, a riot of sound, aromatic spices drifting across his meandering path.

He observed transactions of all kinds, handled in quick sharp movements; he watched people who seemed to do nothing but watch other people, standing by shop windows or sitting along the sides of buildings.

He was staring at a line of six barrel-chested birds on a thick wooden perch, preening their long saffron feathers, when it came to him, strained through the myriad sounds of the city, yet perfectly clear as it gyred in the wind. Following his ears, the sound pulling him in like a net, through the turnings of broken streets and dank alleyways until at length he stood before a stone wall and listened to the tolling of the bells, colouring the air. An ancient wooden door was set into the stone wall. Without thinking, he opened it and went through.

The tonal wash of the city faded as he crossed the threshold and he heard the bells more clearly now although their source seemed still far away.

Across a sudden background of misty silence he heard a horn sound once.

The bells tolled sweetly once again, in the garden, neat, precise, beautiful. Glistening flowers of white and yellow and pink were arranged amid rocks and furry moss and feathery ferns in exquisite patterns.

Water burbled and farther on he found a tiny waterfall and a pool filled with small fat fish with long silver fins fanning the green water like veils. He walked on a path paved with brilliant white gravel.

The bells ceased and the horn sounded again. A quiet chanting began, lilting, pleasing to the ear, drifting somnolently on the still air. Ronin strained his ears but could discern no sound from the city without the stone wall.

In the center of the garden was a large metal urn, of brass perhaps. Beside it sat an ancient man in brown robes. His wrinkled face was serene, his eyes were closed. His sparse hair was white, his beard long and wispy. He sat still as stone.

Ronin reached out and touched the bulging metal sides and felt – nothing. So pure a nothingness that it was tangible. An immutable space yawned, years falling like dry leaves, centuries passing like silent drops of rain, eons emerging, merging, sundered. And an immense quietude entered him: the thunder of eternity.

He was shaken.

He found that he had closed his eyes. When he opened them, the bells were tolling again, high in the air. He went on stiff legs through a wooden doorway and it was as if a gust of melody had transported him to another world. The air was humid with incense, the light was dim and brown as if it were ancient. Stone walls and marble pillars, a ceiling indistinguishable in the gloom.

In the distance, masses of squat yellow candles were lit, the tiny flames swaying like a chorus of dancers preparing for a performance. The incense and the tallow caused the air to take on a third dimension. Thus he moved now, feeling like the fish in the pond outside, as slowly as through water. The centuries hung upon him as taels of silver, dense and beautiful.

Then from somewhere he thought he heard a coughing, low and questioning. An animal presence. Perhaps a voice, so distant that he heard but the echo, said, *Find him.* Soft pad of paws, a scratching as gentle as the rustling of autumn foliage. *You must find him.* Echoes echoing. Away.

He looked dreamily about him. The chanting came again, pellucid, peaceful, scenting the air. Shafts of tawny light fell obliquely through the high narrow windows, lacquering the stone floor and the reed mats. He was alone.

He thought of the bronze urn and the man who sat so still beside it.

He was there when Ronin returned to the exquisite garden. Eyes closed. A statue. The fish swam lazily. The water gurgled throatily. The bells were silent.

He approached the stone wall, went through the wooden door, and as he closed it behind him the discordant noises of the city, frantic and desperate, descended upon him like a horde of locusts in the heat of summer.

145

He walked randomly, still half dazed, until he realized by the waning light that the day was almost done. He asked a corpulent merchant lolling indolently in the doorway to his store, waiting impatiently for customers, gap-toothed and sweaty, for directions back to the rikkagin's quarters. The man looked at him, his clothes, the sword at his hip, the bag of coins in his belt.

'You go to dinner, gentleman?' His breath was foul.

'Yes, but – '

'A goose perhaps. Or a fine fresh-slaughtered pig for your host.' His voice took on a wheedling tone. 'A magnificent gift, very generous and at a most modest price. Twenty coppers only.'

'Please tell me where – '

The merchant's brow wrinkled. 'If you are thinking of Farrah's his meat is not one tenth as fine as mine.' He clasped his fat hands as if in anguish. 'And the prices he charges! I should inform the Greens.'

'Double Bass Street, is it near here?'

'I would, you know, but I am not a vengeful person, ask anyone on Brown Bear Road. An honest businessman only. I mind my own affairs. Do not ask me, as many do, what goes on around the corner or' – he rolled his eyes – 'upstairs. If I told you – '

'Please,' said Ronin. 'Double Bass Street. How far?'

'If they want to do those vile things, well, who am I to say – '

Ronin left him, walking blindly down the street.

'Go to Farrah's then, as you planned all along,' the fat merchant called after him in his high whine. 'You deserve each other!'

He passed up a carpet shop along Three Peaks Street. It was crowded with customers and an army of clerks who all looked as if they were related. Next door was an apothecary's, its huge stone jar hanging above the doorway on ancient creaking chains, a dusty window filled with small coloured packets, phials of gritty-looking powders, liquids in tall tubular jars. In the centre of this display was a lidded clear glass bowl filled with a slightly yellowish liquid suspended in which was a root in the singular shape of a man. It was dusky orange-brown and had many threadlike tendrils. The thing stirred his curiosity and he went inside the shop.

It was long and narrow, dusty and tired-looking. A high wood and glass case ran the length of the shop's right wall. Within it lay neat piles of containered liquids and stacks of cartoned powders, a hundred and one items, he supposed, for headaches and stomach pains, muscle pulls and swollen feet. The proprietor stood behind a counter along the back wall.

He was small and old and stooped as if he carried his years about with him as a tangible burden. He was a sad man, with almond eyes and yellow skin as thin as rice paper, almost translucent. Long strands of hair hung down from the point of his chin, otherwise he was hairless. He was measuring out portions of a sapphire powder upon clean white squares of rice paper.

He looked up as Ronin approached.

'Yes?'

'Am I near Double Bass Street?'

'Well now, that depends.' The gnarled yellow hands continued their work.

'On what?'

'On which way you go, naturally.' He stoppered the container of powder, put it carefully away on one of a series of shelves behind him that ran all the way to the ceiling. He turned back. 'If you cut through the alley there to Blue Mountain Road, well then, you are but five minutes away.' He began to pour each mound of powder into blue glass phials. 'However, if you were to walk farther down Three Peaks Street until you reached the Nanking it would be infinitely safer.' He had two of them filled now. 'Longer but safer.' His head nodded. 'Yet' – he looked up at Ronin – 'you did not come in here merely to ask me the way to Double Bass Street.' He pointed with one crooked finger. 'Anyone out there could have told you just as well. No, I believe you came in to inquire after the root.'

Ronin did not hide his surprise. 'How could you have known?'

All the phials were filled now. One by one, he stoppered them.

'You are not the first, by any means. It is not there for decoration, though many passers-by think so.'

Ronin was fed up.

'Will you tell me?'

'The root,' he said, lining the phials up on a shelf, 'is ancient. And as with all things ancient, it has a history. Oh yes! Not a very pleasant one, I am afraid.' His nostrils dilated and he shifted several times. 'Come closer.' He nodded. 'Yes. It was you, then, who was at the temple.' He closed his eyes for just a moment. 'There is a lingering trace of incense.'

'But what – '

'I heard the horn sounding, after all.'

'The horn?'

'A visitor,' it said. 'A visitor.'

'What foolishness. It was merely a Sha'angh'sei temple.'

The old man smiled oddly and Ronin saw that his teeth were lacquered black, shiny and square-cut. He thought of the simian-faced woman in the tavern: what mysteries had she been selling, and for what price?

'Ah no.' The old man shook his head. 'The temple was here long before Sha'angh'sei came into being. The city grew up around it. It is the temple of another folk, beings gone from this continent before the beginnings of man.' He shrugged deferentially. 'Some say so, at least.'

'But there was a man in the garden of the temple.'

The smile was released again, oblique and and inferential.

'Then perhaps what they say is not the truth.

149

You know people often tell you only what they wish you to know.' The old man put a hand to his head as if it pained him. 'Such as the house on Double Bass Street.'

Ronin stared at him. 'What?'

'Take the Nanking.'

'But that is the longer way, so you said.'

'It does not matter. There is no use in your going there.'

A crawling along the back of his neck.

'Why not?'

'Because,' said the old man flatly, 'there is no one inside.'

Ronin went out the door fast without bothering to close it, weaving through the throngs of bodies, his eyes searching ahead for the alley leading to Blue Mountain Road. He almost overran it, so narrow and dark it was. The braziers and lanterns of the city were just being lit, luminescing the deep purple haze that seemed to cover Sha'angh'sei each evening.

Three Peaks Street was still dusky with the lingering dregs of afternoon so that he did not have to pause in the gloom of the alley for his night vision to become effective.

The darkness deepened and he knew at once there was trouble. There should have been at least a glow from the lanterns of Blue Mountain Road, even from around this turning just before him. He slipped his sword free. Silent and deadly now, he

150

advanced along one dank wall, went around the bend.

The smell of raw fish, putrefying; human excrement. There were hard, scraping noises. Panting. A grunt. He froze and listened intently. More than one person; more than two. That was as exact a determination as he could make. But that was all right because the adrenalin was pumping through him; his sword had been sheathed far too long. Now he ached for battle. He did not care how many men awaited him. He advanced.

Whites of eyes peered up at him as he approached at a run and he counted quickly and precisely because he knew there was little time and he had to prepare his entire body. The battle lust would not impede him because his training automatically took care of the organism. Six.

A man lay on the ground, the six over him. Brief glint of a curved blade, heavy, twisting, then the image was gone from his sight, lost in the night. But something lingered and he reviewed it because it might be important. The glint was not silvered, but black on white, wet-looking. Red is black in dim light. Blood.

He heard the faint whirring and let that guide him because he knew now what it was and they would not expect that.

Speed.

He thrust in a blur and there was a piercing scream. A chink on the stone as the axe hit the paving. He had deliberately aimed low, to open the soft viscera of the stomach and intestines to make a mess. He lifted the blade as he withdrew, flicking it, so that a fountain of black blood and wet organs spewed forth as the man collapsed.

He was already moving forward with a two-handed thrust as the second man leapt for him and the blade whistled in the air as it clove the man from shoulder to belly. The corpse danced drunkenly, dead before it hit the ground, twitching still.

The fever mounted and it seemed as if everything around him slowed as his own speed increased. He saw the axe peripherally and knew that he could not get the sword up in time because of the angle, so he let it fall and allowed the crescent blade to come at him, gleamïng, whispering scythelike. At the last instant his gauntleted hand came up, closed over the blade. The hide of the Makkon absorbed the force of the blow. There was a gasp and he saw the whites of his opponent's eyes all the way around as they opened in fear and surprise.

He laughed then, and it boomed through the close corridor of the alley, echoing menacingly off the wood and brick walls, dank and covered with slime.

The sound of running feet, the breathless air fanned, muttered voices, cursing, and the lights of Blue Mountain Road at last glowed at the far end of the alley. Ronin rubbed the scales of the gauntlet as he retrieved his sword, sheathing it.

He turned then to the man who lay twisted on

the ground. He bent on one knee, searching for the pulse at his throat.

The man coughed. He was dark-haired with almond eyes but there was a strange cast to his face that, even in this dim and uncertain light, looked vaguely familiar to Ronin. He was clad in a tight-fitting suit of dull black cloth.

'Uk – uk – uk.'

Blood came out of his mouth, black and wet in the night. His hand reached up convulsively and clutched at his neck. He coughed once more, blood and something more. Then he died.

Ronin stood up, then impulsively he bent again and opened the man's clenched hand. A slender silver necklace with something on it. He took it from the dead man for no reason at all and slipped it into his boot. Then he went down the alley and out into the confusion and flaring light of Blue Mountain Road.

Silence.

The night still and calm.

The old man had been right. There was no one at Rikkagin T'ien's quarters, not T'ien, not Tuolin, not a soldier, not a porter.

Ronin turned on the step and surveyed the street. He was absolutely alone. They had all gone. To Kamado, he assumed. Early. Not a good sign. Perhaps the situation to the north had deteriorated. If they had told him the truth; and he was not at all sure now that they had.

Abruptly, he remembered the strange root. In his haste to get here, he had not had the time to hear its history. He shrugged. Well, it was too late now, the shop would be closed. He could stop by tomorrow before he went up the mountain to the walled city to see the Council. And in any event he was hungry. He had not eaten since the morning and then only rice and tea. He went down the steps of Rikkagin T'ien's house and along the street in search of a tavern.

'Someone will come for you.'

'But – '

'No instructions.'

'All right. And the payment?'

'Now. In taels of silver.'

'Just a moment – '

'You wish to be there? You wish to see it?'

'Yes, but – '

'Then you will do as I say.'

The simian-faced woman was wrapped in a green cloak. A hairless man sat by her side tonight, narrow-skulled, flat-faced, a bright ring through his nose. He smoked a pipe with a long stem, curved downward slightly, and a small bowl. The simian-faced woman was speaking to a man with russet hair and light eyes. His skin was milk white and he sat in a peculiar position as if he could not bend one leg.

'It is too much,' said the man with the russet hair. The other man was impassive, pulling on his pipe.

The woman leaned forward and Ronin could see the sheen of her black lacquered teeth. 'Think of what the silver will buy you. The Seercus is not an everyday occurrence.' She laughed tautly. 'And I need not remind you of the restrictions. Consider yourself fortunate.' The odd head nodded, up, down. 'Most fortunate.'

They were sitting at a corner table, near enough to Ronin so that he had no difficulty in hearing their conversation over the steamy noise of the tavern.

It was a large, smoky room off the Nanking, one of Sha'angh'sei's main roads. Low wooden beams crossed the ceiling; the air was thick with wax and grease. It was, in short, like every tavern in the city.

Ronin pushed away his rice bowl, lifted his sticks, and put a last morsel of broiled meat into his mouth. He reached for the rice wine.

'Perhaps I can get a better price elsewhere,' said the man with russet hair, but there was little conviction in his voice.

The simian-faced woman laughed, a soft silvery tinkle, surprising in its delicacy. 'Oh yes, by all means. And the Greens will – '

'No, no,' said the man quickly. 'You misunderstand. Here.' He reached out a leather pouch from beneath his cloak, counted out forty silver pieces.

The woman stared at him solemnly, did not look down at the taels. The hairless man swept them off the table, his yellow hand a blur in the light for only a moment.

'And ten more,' said the woman evenly.

The man with the russet hair started.

'Ten – but you gave me a price – '

'For this ten, I will not inform the Greens.'

She laughed as the man reopened the pouch.

'The Seercus,' she whispered.

The hairless man took the coins. He pulled again on his pipe. There was a cloud of smoke. They got up and left.

The man with the russet hair ran a shaking hand over his face, reached for the small flagon of wine on his table. Drops beaded the wood as he poured.

Two men came in and sat down at Ronin's table. The proprietor wandered over and they ordered steamed fish and wine; Ronin asked for another flagon of wine.

'And how were the fields, now that you've seen them firsthand?' asked one.

'The poppies are not good.' This one had a large nose, red-veined and wide-nostriled.

'Ah, the Reds again. This time we must enlist the Greens to – '

'Not the Reds.' He was still brushing the silt of travel from his gray cloak.

'Eh?' He looked suspiciously at the other. 'This is not another of your tricks, is it? You know I agree that what the Greens ask is enormous, but we stand to lose much more if the harvest is ruined. I should well think that you would understand that by now.'

'No, I tell the truth.'

'Well, what then?'

The proprietor came over with a tray laden with

food and wine and they remained silent until he had served them and drifted away.

The man with the large nose sighed and poured himself wine. 'I wish I knew. Truly.' The fish looked at them from the centre of the table. He picked one up with his sticks, bit into the head. 'The Reds in the north have, I believe, split apart.'

The other laughed uneasily, pouring wine. 'I hardly think that is possible.'

'Still, that is what I have heard.' He began to shovel rice into his mouth with his lips close to the rim of the bowl. 'Every day, more kubaru disappear and the crops themselves are not producing as they should.'

'Well, if they are not being properly attended –'

'I am afraid that is only part of it.' He took a gulp of wine, perhaps to steady his nerves. 'It is as if the land itself has changed, become less fertile –' He began to cough thickly.

'Are you ill?'

'No, a chill only. The weather is much colder than it should be at this time of year.'

At first Ronin had been listening peripherally. He wanted to understand this complex city. To do so he had to understand its inhabitants better. Listening in on conversations seemed as good a way as any to start. It was another reason why he had chosen to go to a tavern instead of visiting one of the many street stalls selling an infinite variety of foods. But his rather casual eavesdropping became more intent the further on this conversation went. Perhaps this was the beginning; perhaps

157

he had less time than he thought. If so, it was more imperative than ever for him to gain admittance to the Council of Sha'angh'sei; to find someone who could decipher the scroll of dor-Sefrith.

Now the merchants talked of other matters, prices and the fluctuating market. Ronin paid for his meal and left. In the Nanking, he asked a boy for the way to Okan Road and had to pay for the information.

She was not there and so he waited.

It was already late. He asked for rice wine and it was brought to him by the tiny girl in the pink quilted jacket. He remembered her.

'How old are you?' he asked as he savoured the spices.

She lowered her painted eyelids.

'Eleven, sir.' So low he had to strain to hear her.

He opened his mouth again and she ran off.

He tried to relax, opening his ears to the soft sounds of silk brushing satin thighs, liquid pouring, low talking that was almost like the murmuring swell of the sea. The tawny light. He closed his eyes to slits, hearing in his mind a horn sounding, far off and alone. A gentle laugh intruded. A giggle, stifled. Perfumes drifting upon the languid air. A hint of sweet smoke from somewhere and he thought of the poppy fields. 'There is much fear in the north,' the merchant with the large nose had said. Why?

'Ronin.'

He opened his eyes.

It was Matsu. Skin white as bone; eyes like olives. Her body small and supple.

'She will be very late.' Black hair drifting over one eye. 'Please let me take you upstairs.'

She offered him her hand. Firm and warm. He stood up, rubbed her palm with his fingers. He towered over her as they went up the broad polished wood staircase to the second story. Yet he felt her support, strong and comforting. One arm was around her slender shoulders. He stroked her cheek as they rose. The yellow light grew brighter as they ascended towards the great crystal lamp. The tiny flames shivered, sparking pinpoints of light across their faces. He peered down, drunk with wine and fatigue, at the grand, deserted room with its golden couches and low lacquered tables. Even the serving girls had gone to bed by now. The room was spotlessly clean, not a stained teacup lay about, not a spill of wine, not an ash-laden pipe remained.

The tawny light streamed down endlessly, it seemed, until Matsu shut the door of the room. She did not light the small lamp on the black lacquered table next to the wide bed. The room had a high domed ceiling and across the patterned walls flowers were tossed and dripping in a summer rainfall. The curtains had not yet been drawn and through the window he could see that the moon was up, pale and ghostly but perfectly clear in the night sky.

He sat on the bed and stared out the window at the pulsing carpet of pinpoints, blue-white like rare gems and startlingly close. Matsu knelt and pulled off his boots. A part of the sky was lighter, as if a translucent scarf had been laid over the blackness of the night; a bridge of light formed by the closeness of the stars within its width. She removed his clothes and he donned the dragon robe which she held out for him.

She put him under the covers and then came into the bed, her naked body trembling from the cool of the night sweeping in from the open window, her soft skin raised in gooseflesh, and he put her head in the hollow of his shoulder, stroking her hair, his thoughts over the hills and far away.

She smoked a little, the sweet smell engulfing them as she inhaled deeply with a quiet hiss. Sounds drifted up to them from the city that never slept. A dog barked, far off, and rhythmic singing wafted up from along the waterfront. Something metallic clattered on the cobbles close by and feet pounded briefly. A hoarse shout. The rattle of a cart and someone whistling tunelessly. Matsu's eyes glazed and the cold pipe fell from her open fingers spread like the petals of a small white flower on the dark covers.

She was asleep against him, close and warm now, her shallow rhythmic breathing a soporific. At last he relaxed. Carefully, he put the pipe away. The moon was huge in the black glittering square of the window, flat and thin as rice paper. Then a cloud rode across its face and his eyes closed. He dreamed of a field of poppies shivering in a chill wind.

It was still dark when she woke him.

'She will not come tonight.'

The moon was down but the sky had not yet begun to lighten.

'It is all right.'

'Do you want me to stay?' Her voice was tiny, like a child's.

He watched her at the side of the bed, the light silk robe clinging to her firm slender body.

'Yes,' he said. 'Stay with me.'

A sinuous rustle as the robe slithered off her and she climbed into bed. Black and white.

There was silence for a time and he listened to the leaves trembling in the trees on Okan Road. Footsteps and muffled voices briefly heard. Matsu pulled the covers closer around them.

'Cold.'

Ronin felt her lithe body against him and held her close.

After a time, she spoke again. 'Do you know Tuolin well?'

Ronin turned his head to look at her.

'Not well, no.'

She shrugged. 'It does not matter. He will die at Kamado.'

He lifted himself on one elbow and stared at her.

'What are you saying?'

161

'He told Sa many things in the shallows of night. I have heard many others. Tales of evil.'

'What,' he asked, 'have you heard?'

'The rikkagin's armies no longer fight the Reds in the north. I have heard that they fight side by side now: the lawless and the law.'

'Against whom?' But he already knew.

'Others,' she said, giving the word a strange overtone, as if that were not the word she wished to use. 'Creatures. Men who are not men.'

'Who told you this?'

'Does it matter?'

'Perhaps very much.'

'My friend's husband is a soldier with Rikkagin Hsien-Do. So is his son. They spent much time in the north, near Kamado. They returned three days ago.' She clutched at him and he felt the shivers in her frame, thought of the green leaves on the trees outside. 'My friend's husband is blind now. They had to carry the son back to Sha'angh'sei. His back is broken.' Her voice came in little gusts now. 'They did not fight the Reds; they did not fight bandits. They fought – something else.' Another shudder went through her frame. 'Even the Greens are talking among themselves about the situation in the north.'

There was a thin line of the faintest grey now, visible only if he looked away because at night vision is better around the periphery. He held onto the shaking body and, from the corner of his eye, watched the line of grey widen with agonizing slowness, bringing the burden of another day.

She was still sobbing so he said, 'Who are the Greens?' Because he wanted to stop her; and because he wanted to know.

'The Greens.' She sniffed. 'You must have seen some of them.'

Two men in black in the tavern's doorway, axes at their sides, demanding payment.

'I am not sure.'

'They are,' she said, 'the law.'

He was surprised. 'I had assumed that the rikkagin were the law.'

She shook her head, her hair fanning his cheek, and the last of the tears fell from her cheeks onto the darkness of his arm as it lay along the covers.

'No,' she said quietly, calmer now. 'You must understand that the rikkagin are not native to Sha'angh'sei, or this land. Oh, they are the reason that it has grown and become – the way it is. But many are from far away. They brought their legions here to fight for the wealth of the land, the poppy fields, the silk farms, the silver, and more. They twisted the land and its people to their own ends.' She sighed a little as if she were not used to speaking so much. She moved her head against his chest; he inhaled her fragrance, clean and sweet. Her feet twined with his, their soles rubbing together. Friction warmth.

'But this is a most ancient land,' she said. 'Here there are still many who have not forgotten the ways of their ancestors, handed down carefully from father to son and daughter. A legacy more precious to us than land or silver, even after the coming of the rikkagin, the turning of the hongs.'

Her hand sought his, lightly, a feathery touch, yet it conveyed to him an intimacy most singular. 'The Greens and the Reds have been at war for all time, or so it is told; from the moment of their births there was enmity. Now each seeks to gain each other's territory.'

'What is the nature of the enmity?' he asked.

'I cannot tell you.'

'You mean you will not?'

Her eyes flicked at his face, surprised. 'No. I do not know. I doubt if they do themselves now.'

On the Okan Road, the sky was pearling the rooftops of Sha'angh'sei. A fine rain began to fall, sighing among the trees, misting through the window, blown on a gentle morning breeze. A sea horn sounded in the distance, muffled and melancholy.

She kissed his broad chest as she opened his robe, the dragons writhing. 'They are,' she whispered, 'the terrorists of tradition.' And she offered up her mouth, moist and panting.

It was the angle that made it so dreadful.

Matsu choked and turned her head away and he held her as her body convulsed.

There was nothing there and that was why the head was at such an inhuman angle; he could imagine her shock. She seemed steadier now and she turned, needing to look once more, to help dispel the shock. The head remained attached to the shoulders only by a sheet of skin glinting redly in the dismal light.

The scream had burst in on them like a thief in the night and he had unsheathed his sword and was out the door before it had entirely died away, the gilt dragons fluttering in his wake. There was noise on the wide landing from behind myriad closed doors; movement as the sleepers awoke. The scream tried to force itself out again, like a caged animal, but it was choked off and he heard instead a liquid gurgling.

He raced down the hall, toward the head of the staircase. A dull thud, leaden with finality, and he knew he had just passed the door. Matsu was coming after him, tying the sash of her robe, closing the gap now because he had stopped. Raising his sword, he opened the door, slamming it wide with his shoulder, and leapt into the room.

He saw the window first because it was directly in his line of sight and because he knew it was the room's only other egress. It was open to its fullest extent. On one side, the curtains were completely gone, on the other, the tatters fluttered uselessly. There was an increasing clatter from the hall but he ignored it. He inhaled the stench.

She was on the bed, her head at an impossible angle because everything had been torn out; throat, larynx, neck musculature. Just the frayed skin and a great pool of blood. He looked at last at her face. Sa.

He took Matsu outside into the hall, though he had to force her, because there was nothing either of them could do. He closed the door behind them.

'I have never,' said Matsu, 'seen such a death.'

The hall was crowded now, mainly with women; the men preferred their anonymity.

'Has anyone seen Kiri?' Ronin asked them. No one had.

He took Matsu back to the room of dancing, crying flowers and once there began to dress. She pulled her robe tighter about her; peach marsh with pale green ferns.

'The Greens?' he asked because he wanted to be absolutely certain.

She shook her head, hair like a thick mist, fanning out. 'No, the Greens use axes and – ' she shuddered – 'not that.'

He buckled on his belt and went to her, drawing her up to him. Her pale hands were like ice.

'It is important that I go out; and I must go now. Do you understand?' Because her eyes were clouded like the sky on the dawn of a stormy day. 'Will you be all right?' His fingers gripped her shoulders. 'You will stay with the guards?' He wanted to make certain.

She looked up into his colourless eyes now. 'Yes,' she said and he believed her. 'Kiri will soon return.'

'Tell her I was here.'

The ghost of a smile. 'Yes,' she nodded. 'I will.'

The door closed softly behind him.

* * *

166

It was a disquieting day; overcast, rain falling more heavily now, pattering against the roofs of the street stalls, and he pulled his cloak about him. It was somewhat lighter directly overhead but dark clouds scudded across the sky in the distance.

The weather had not diminished the crowds, however. Oiled rice-paper umbrellas and thick cloaks to keep out the dampness were much in evidence.

He paused at a stand on Blessant Street, for rice and tea and to inquire after the surest route to the walled city. But there was a crawling in the pit of his stomach and he found that he had little appetite. He drank his green tea and listened to the forlorn drip of the rain on the stand's meager canopy.

He took Blessant Street as far as King Knife Street, which wound around in such circuitous fashion that several times he believed that he was headed away from the incline of the mountain.

Once he saw a beggar, sprawled in the street, filthy, unmoving. It was only after he had passed the body that he realized there was no life in him. Death was ignored in Sha'angh'sei, as T'ien had told him; at least most forms. Which brought him back to Sa's death.

He had known before he asked Matsu that it had not been the doing of the Greens. The stench was still in his nostrils. But that was a time factor; even if he had been later, the smell dissipated, he would have known by the way she was killed. It was the same manner in which G'fand had died in the City of Ten Thousand Paths. The Makkon.

But why had it killed Sa? He felt that it was important for him to know, but the answer eluded him.

As King Knife Street began to wind upward, the old dust-worn shops thinned and gaps between buildings became more frequent. At first these were mere dirt alleyways into which filth and refuse had been dumped. But gradually, as he continued to ascend, they were filled with wild grass and thickets of fir trees, tall and willowy, their slender dark green tips swaying in the swirling rain.

As the incline increased so the aspect of the houses he passed was transformed. There was more brickwork in evidence here, in good repair and ornately crafted. Different styles of architecture made their presence felt.

The road was well paved now but fairly free of people and it occurred to him that here, on the way to the walled city, was the only area of Sha'angh'sei he had been to so far that was not jammed with people.

It was eerily silent. At once he missed the hubbub and jostle of the throngs, the thick swirl of commingling scents, the filth, the life and the death, the vast mysterious panoply of humanity.

In the absence of the teeming crowds, he was struck by the artificiality of the houses and he recalled Matsu's words. *They twisted the land.* For this seemed an entirely different Sha'angh'sei, at

168

once cleaner and crasser. It seemed to him that here, among the columnated houses, with their plaster and wrought-iron scalloping, the natural tones and inclinations of the land had been pushed back, held at bay along the foothills, and that here the brand of the legions of rikkagin from faraway lands, squatting, growing fat from the wealth of Sha'angh'sei's land, was very apparent.

He topped the last rise of King Knife Street and went into the chill shadow of the walled city. The wall itself was some six and a half metres high, constructed of enormous yellow stone blocks joined so cunningly that he could barely distinguish the joints. Heavy metal doors stood open to the inward side but a latticed metal grillwork gate barred the entrance.

Men in purple quilted jackets and wide black leggings stood just inside the gate. They all were armed with curved single-edged swords and short-hafted throwing axes. They were almond-eyed and their long greased hair was bound in queues.

A thickset man with a flat face and wide nose came and opened the gate.

'Why do you come to the walled city?' asked the man. 'You are a new compredore, perhaps?'

Another man drifted over in a cloud of sweet smoke. He took the pipe out of his mouth and regarded Ronin with heavy-lidded eyes.

'No, I seek an audience with the Municipal Council.'

The flat-faced man guffawed and walked away.

'They will not see you,' said the second man, pulling at his pipe.

'Why not? It is most urgent that I see them.'

Smoke swirled in the air and the man turned languidly, pointing at the trees of the walled city running in thick rows away from them, lining the quiet avenues; the large, stately buildings, flat-roofed, terraced, with carefully sculptured gardened fronts.

'Here the fat hongs and sleek functionaries of Sha'angh'sei live and build their fortunes, unseen and, for a price, safe.'

'From what?'

The black eyes studied Ronin with unwavering intensity.

'From Sha'angh'sei,' he said.

He sucked at his pipe but it had gone out. He knocked the bowl against the wall, began to refill it from a leather packet within his quilted jacket.

'No one sees the Municipal Council, my friend.' His eyes were unnaturally bright. 'At all.'

The rain beat down. The avenues were slick with wet, gleaming dully. The trees rustled in the wind, flinging moisture, and somewhere a bird sang sweetly, enfolded within brown branches and green leaves.

'Where is the Council building?'

The man with the dark eyes sighed. 'Take the avenue to the left. Second turning.' He moved into the shelter of an overhang.

* * *

The echoes of marble. The soft sighing. The prolonged susurration of whispering. The quiet click of boot soles.

The hall was cold and columnless and empty of ornamentation. Its only furniture was low, wide, backless benches of the same pink and black marble.

The hall echoed to his footsteps as he crossed the polished floor. Ahead of him, the desk.

He passed people sitting humped on the benches. There was a peculiar air about them, as if most of them had been here for so long that they had forgotten their purpose in coming. Expectancy had perished a long time ago.

The desk too was of marble, curved and thick, a heavy shield for the woman who sat behind its imposing façade. Although she had the black hair and almond eyes of the people of the Sha'angh'sei area, her face was nevertheless less delicate, with a more pronounced bone structure so that he knew that she had other blood in her. She had light eyes and a square chin which she knew gave her the appearance of strength. She spoke accordingly.

'Yes, sir. State your business, please.' She had before her a long list of names and was in the process of drawing a line through the third name from the top with her quill.

'I seek an audience with the Municipal Council of Sha'angh'sei.'

The quill dipped into the inkwell. 'Yes?' Scratch.

'I come on a matter of the utmost urgency.'

She looked up then.

'Is that so?' She smiled charmingly with small white teeth. 'I am afraid it will do you no good.'

'I am sure that when the Council hears – '

'Pardon me, but you do not seem to understand.' She wore a tightly cut green and gold quilted jacket that showed off her jutting breasts and narrow waist in a way that was severe and, because of it, sensual. Her startling sapphire nails plucked at the jacket. 'One must make an appointment to see the Council.' She brandished the list in front of her. 'It will be many days.'

'I do not think you appreciate the gravity of the situation,' said Ronin, but already he was feeling rather foolish.

The woman sighed and pursed her lips.

'Sir, everyone who seeks audience with the Council is on an urgent mission.'

'But – '

'Sir, you are in the Municipal Building of Sha'angh'sei, the seat of government for not only this vast city but the enormous area of land in the surrounding vicinity. Maintainenance is a most complex and problem-filled task. Can you understand that?' She leaned forward, her face intent. A strand of hair came loose from its binding, stroking the side of her face as she spoke. 'In the event that you do not, let me tell you that this city must feed and house not only its numerous inhabitants but also many of the outlying communities. We also must take care of the constant flood of refugees from the north.' She threw her shoulders back

172

as if it were an act of defiance; it had a double effect. She knows her job, he thought. 'Sir, through the port of Sha'angh'sei comes the bulk of the raw materials to sustain much of the continent of man. It is more than a full-time task in these evil times to keep this city running.' She finally swept a hand up, flash of deep blue, tugging the wayward strand over her ear. 'Now you can appreciate why we cannot allow the Council to be errantly disturbed. Why, if everyone who came to this building were allowed an immediate audience, I cannot imagine how this city would function.' She took a deep breath, leaning back in her chair. Her breasts arched at him, an unsubtle offering of consolation.

Ronin leaned over and stared into her eyes.

'I must see the Council today. Now.'

He did not expect her to be intimidated and she was not. She clicked her sapphire nails and two men appeared armed with axes and curving dirks.

'Would you care to have me add your name to the list?' she asked sweetly, her eyes never leaving his. They laughed.

'All right,' Ronin said, and gave it to her.

'Yes,' she said, the quill moving. Then she sat back and her pink tongue strayed for a moment between her lips. 'That is most sensible.'

The rain was heavier and they were all within the roof's brown overhang, squatting around a brick pit. Flames crackled and sparked. They were drinking rice wine when he came up. The man with the dark eyes peered at him through the smoke of his pipe; the others ignored him.

Ronin came unbidden out of the rain, shook the water off his cloak.

'The Council would not see me.'

'Yes,' said the man, 'a predictable course.' He shrugged his shoulders. 'Lamentable but what can one do?'

Ronin squatted beside the man. No one offered him wine. 'What I want,' he said, 'is a way in.'

The man with the flat face looked over at him. 'Throw him outside, T'ung,' he said to the man with the dark eyes. 'Why waste your time?'

'Because he is not from Sha'angh'sei?' said T'ung. 'Because he is not civilized?' He turned to Ronin. 'What would you give me as payment?' The flat-faced man grunted knowingly.

Ronin lifted the bag of coins at his waist, letting the fat chink of the coppers speak for him.

T'ung eyed the pouch and screwed up his mouth. 'Mmm, much too small, I am afraid.' His face assumed a sad expression. 'Not nearly enough.'

'What, then, would you want?'

'What else have you?'

Ronin looked at him.

'Nothing.'

'That is most unfortunate.' He sucked on his pipe, blew smoke lazily. It held on the humid air, a translucent pattern, a mysterious glyph.

'Wait. Perhaps there is something.' He dug in his boot. 'A chain of silver.'

Ronin drew out the dead man's chain. The silver blossom gleamed in the diffuse light. He handed it to T'ung.

The rain dripped dolefully, pattering against the overhang, making the leaves on the trees dance to its rhythm. T'ung sat very still, staring at the silver blossom. It flamed orange as he twisted it and it caught the firelight. Slowly he put down his pipe.

'Where,' he said softly, 'did you get this?'

'What?'

A brief flash in darkness.

'Tell me.'

Black blood. The scythe blade blooming silver as it swung at him in the alley.

'I want an answer.' The voice turned harsh and grating. Heads turned. The flat-faced man rose.

Too late, Ronin thought savagely. He stood up, staring at the scythe-bladed axe hung at T'ung's side. Greens.

The flat-faced man saw the silver blossom and his hand went to the haft of his axe. T'ung stood and the others, alerted now, dropped their cups and pipes and came toward him.

Ronin backed away, thinking furiously, Chill take me for a fool! Those were Greens in the alley.

T'ung was between him and the open gateway beyond which teeming Sha'angh'sei beckoned like a sweet reward.

T'ung clutched at the chain and withdrew his axe. And the others came on.

'Kill him now,' said the flat-faced man.

★ ★ ★

175

He crouched in the tangle, panting, taking deep breaths, swallowing to get the saliva back into his mouth. He listened for the sounds he knew would come, magnified by the rain. But all he heard was the rustle-drip of the soaking foliage. The sky was all but gone. The rain beat against him, running down his face. He blinked, lifted one hand across his forehead to clear his vision. He heard the sounds then.

The right arm had decided him. It was out and up, about to begin the axe's deadly descent. They had been expecting him to use his sword and to retreat defensively. He did neither. He launched himself headlong at T'ung, lifting his forearm and knocking the axe blade aside as he smashed into the body. Taken by surprise, T'ung crashed into the wall and the way was clear.

Then he was through the gate and running in an erratic zigzag through the rain, acutely aware of the axes at his back, knowing that they could be thrown as well as swung.

Boots pounded behind him and he heard the flat-faced man screaming and, farther behind, T'ung's voice, curiously calm and remote.

He heard the panting coming closer; the flat-faced man was gaining on him because he ran in a straight line, did not have to dodge.

He turned then, planting his feet and withdrawing his sword in one motion. The flat-faced man was quick and agile but he was angry and that would help. Ronin swung first and his foot slipped on the wet paving. Idiot!

Grinning now, the flat-faced man dodged the blow, came on, and the blade of his axe was a blur in the rain. Ronin was moving away when it bit into his arm with a searing white heat. Ignore. He swung his own blade in a reverse arc and the Green, not used to double-bladed weapons, was slow to react. Ronin's blade caught him beneath the arm, sinking deep into the socket. He cried out, his body jerked, and the bloody axe fell from his trembling fingers. His gaping mouth filled with water. Ronin wrenched at the hilt to free it and the arm came off. The flat-faced man shrieked and folded like a paper doll. Rain washed at the running blood. The others were coming now and Ronin took off down King Knife Street.

Through the beat of the rain he heard the boots and the echoing shouts; he kept his body low and the sounds were amplified. Then voices came to him on the wind: queries, shouts of anger. He risked some movement in order to get a visual fix. Led by T'ung, the Greens fanned out, searching for him. One was coming directly toward him.

In the end, the cart had saved him. It swerved out of a walkway blind to King Knife Street and he almost ran the owner down but there was just enough time and he missed it. It was now, however, directly in the path of his pursuers. The delay was brief but sufficient. Around the next turning, rows of houses and an explosive tangle of wild greenery, within which he promptly lost himself.

Still and calm, he remained behind his house of trees and tall ferns. Drip, drip. The rain beading and streaking the leaves. They quivered before his face. A bird fluttered in the branches above him. Crunch. The sound very close indeed and he felt the presence, separated only by the tenuous curtain of greenery. He held his breath. Perhaps – no, the branches low down swayed and began to part and he had no choice. Silently he put down his sword, then turned away from its mirrored surface, his reflection distorted by the moisture.

After a time, with Ronin's forearm jammed against his windpipe, the Green's eyes rolled up and he collapsed without a sound, his face white and pasty. Ronin crouched, listening. Still. The pinging of the rain. He dragged the Green behind a dense section of foliage, went back to where he had left his sword. He wiped it down and sheathed it, then crouched again behind the sheltering leaves until he was certain that they had gone back to the gate.

The rain had ceased by the time the shops of Sha'angh'sei built themselves around him once again on the cluttered level ground of the lower reaches of the city. Through the filth of the milling throng he pushed himself, his left arm soaked in blood and the pain a constant thing now that he attempted to clamp down on.

He passed a large group of people, wide straw hats, torn and uneven, feet bare and black with the muck of the streets, all carrying sacks and hurriedly tied bundles. Soldiers were directing them to a building farther along the street.

'Refugees,' said a soldier in response to Ronin's question. 'Refugees from the fighting in the north.'

'Is it worse?'

'I do not see how it could be,' the soldier sighed. 'This way,' he called sharply to a straggling few, staggering in exhaustion. One of them, a frail figure, fell into a puddle of brackish water. No one paid the slightest attention.

Ronin moved toward the still form.

'He is beyond help,' said the soldier.

Ronin knelt and turned the body over, wiping the black mud from the gaunt face. The mouth was slack, the eyes closed. It was a woman, young and still beautiful despite the ravages of near starvation. Ronin pushed back her stiff wide-brimmed hat, felt along the side of her neck. He opened her mouth wide and breathed into it, slowly, deeply.

The soldier sauntered over. Most of the refugees had been herded inside now.

'Save it,' he said, taking a large bite out of a tightly rolled brown stick. 'She is gone.'

'No,' said Ronin. 'There is life within her still.'

The soldier laughed, a dark and evil sound. 'She is less than worthless.' He hawked and spit. 'Unless you lack the coppers for a woman. Still she seems a poor – '

But Ronin had risen, turned, hand on sword hilt. Jaw set, muscles rigid, staring into the soldier's eyes. He said something, his voice like the whistle of a steel blade as it strikes.

179

There was a long moment when he saw the soldier weighing it in his mind. He looked for his comrades, found none.

'All right,' said the soldier. 'Do whatever you wish. It is no concern of mine. Let the Greens handle it.' He turned away, heading towards the building into which the refugees had gone.

She was taking shallow breaths now but her eyes were still closed and clearly she was seriously hurt or ill, perhaps both. He could not leave her here and, since he had been on his way to the apothecary's, he hoisted the frail form carefully on to his massive shoulder and disappeared into the hurrying masses of humanity.

The enormous jar hung suspended, creaking on its chains in the lowering light, the metal burnished. The dust seemed thicker in the shop, as if he were returning here after a century instead of merely a day.

'Ah,' exclaimed the old man without much surprise. 'So you went through the alley after all.' His long chin whiskers trembled with the movement of his mouth.

Ronin went down the narrow aisle, put the woman onto a stool. The apothecary came around from behind his counter. He wore a wide-sleeved yellow silk robe and strange shoes which seemed but wooden platforms for his feet. He glanced at Ronin, then looked at the huddled figure.

'She is not from Sha'angh'sei – '

'Yes, I can see that.' The hands moved deftly.

'She is from the north, the soldier told me. Fleeing the fighting.'

The old head shook from side to side. He touched her face, then went behind the counter, reached out packets of powders, red, grey, gold, mixed them with a milky liquid. He pushed the contents across to Ronin.

'Get her to drink that.' He turned. 'You will take her with you?'

'Yes, I cannot leave her. I am sure that they will take care of her at Tenchō.'

Something inexplicable came into the apothecary's eyes and he nodded.

Ronin pressed the hinge of her jaw and the mouth gaped open. She was still unconscious. He cradled the back of her head, mindful of the angle, and let the thick liquid dribble into her lips. Half of it went down her neck and he had to depress her tongue to prevent her choking, but he got a fair amount in her.

The apothecary returned from the musty interior of the shop and began to work on Ronin's arm, laying a square greasy pad along the wound, then wrapping it in white cloth. Over this he poured a clear liquid which seeped into the cloth and thence into the wound. For a moment the pain was exquisitely sharp. Then, almost immediately, it was gone.

There was time now, he thought.

'Tell me about the root.'

The apothecary poured more liquid, wiped at the seepage.

'It is said that it was found by a warrior.' The voice was dry and dusty like the wind of the ages. 'The greatest warrior of a people now long dead. The warrior was out riding, for he was bored. His skill was so great that none could stand against him, so that that thing which he desired most – the conquest of a powerful foe – was denied him.' He wrapped the shoulder in dry bandages.

'As evening drew nigh,' the apothecary continued, 'he came upon a glade in the high forest of his land. No other thing grew near it and a pale new moon, already lambent in the sky, illuminated the root. The glade was quite large and as he dismounted he found that cracked and weathered stone slabs were set in the earth, as if this place were an ancient burial place, but of what people he could not imagine, for time had long ago beaten the writing on the stones.'

Dust swirled in the shop, as if a wind from an unmentionable quarter had sprung up.

'The warrior went to the root and pulled it from the soil. He found that he was suddenly ravenous and he cut a piece of the root and ate it.' The apothecary was putting the last of the packets away.

Ronin stared at him.

'The warrior, so the tale goes, became more than man.'

'A god?'

'Perhaps.' The apothecary shrugged. 'If you wish. It is but a myth.'

'Not a pleasant one, you told me.'

'Yes, that is true.' The old man's eyes blinked, looked huge. 'The warrior indeed became more than man but in so doing he became a danger to the old laws because now surely there was none to stand against him. So was unleashed upon him a terrible foe. The Dolman.'

The vertigo was so severe that he thought for an instant that the tiled floor of the shop had become a river. He worked to control his breathing. Somewhere the echo of laughter.

'What was The Dolman?' It sounded like someone else's voice, far-away and indistinct.

'The ancient of ancients,' said the apothecary softly. 'The primeval fears of man. The terrors of a child alone and afraid at night. Nightmare given free rein, embodied now, substantive.'

A dry wind at the core of his being, plucking.

'It does not seem possible.' Merely a whisper in the aged dust.

'It is a most monstrous creation.'

'Where did it come from?'

'Perhaps the root?'

'Then where is the root from?'

'The gods themselves cannot know – '

'She wishes to see you.'

'Good, she has returned then.'

'She asks for you to wait for her.'

He regarded Matsu in the tawny light. The slender face, with the planes and angles of a man-made structure. Small, wide-lipped mouth, large black eyes as soft as velvet dusk at the waterside.

She wore a robe of pastel blue with brown cicadas embroidered across the body and wide sleeves. It was edged in deep gilt with a sash of the same colour. He thought –

'Wait for her here, please.' She studied the floor at his feet.

'Will you stay with me tonight?'

'I cannot.' The voice barely a whisper. He tried to find her eyes. 'Yung will see that you have wine.'

She bowed to him, a curiously formal gesture.

'Matsu?'

She went away from him, across the room of tawny light, through the buzzing conversations, the opulent silks, the exquisite bodies, the perfect faces.

These people are still a mystery to me, after all, he thought.

He found an empty chair and sat wearily. Almost immediately, tiny Yung in her pink quilted jacket appeared with a lacquered tray with a wine pot and cups. She knelt at his side and poured the wine, handed him the cup.

He sipped and she left. He savoured its warmth down the length of his throat, tasting all the spices, and he was reminded that he had not had a full meal that day.

Afterward, the apothecary had returned to the woman while Ronin withdrew his sword. He removed the hilt and produced the scroll of dor-Sefrith. Once again he studied its glyph-covered face. So many times. It stared at him blankly.

He turned. Evidently the old man had found a wound on the woman. He had tied a poultice in place on the inside of her thigh.

'Do not change the bandages even if they should become dirty. There is medicine underneath.' Then he saw the scroll and began to shake his head.

'Do you know what this is?'

He looked away. 'I cannot aid you in this.'

'You have not even looked at it.' Ronin thrust the scroll towards him.

'It does not matter.'

Ronin's eyes blazed. 'Chill take you, it does! You know of The Dolman, you alone of all the people I have met in Sha'angh'sei. You know that he exists so you must know that he is coming once again to the world of man.'

The old tired eyes stared at him without expression.

Desperately Ronin said, 'His minions are even now prowling the streets of the city. The Makkon killed this morning.'

A faint tremor began at the corner of the old man's mouth and he appeared about to crumble from misery and pain.

'Why do you speak to me of such things?' he asked in a cracked voice made thin by fear and something else. 'There is not a day in my life that I have not suffered and I have seen many days; I wish now but an end to the suffering.'

'Do you wish the death of mankind?' Ronin cried, suddenly furious. 'By not speaking of what you may know, you become an ally of The Dolman.'

'A new age is dawning. Man must look after himself.'

'Are you not a man?'

'I am unable to help you by reading that scroll.'

''Tell me then who can.'

'Perhaps no one, any more. But I can tell you this. The Dolman does in fact come and this time the world may be ground into the utter oblivion that is The Dolman's victory. It is the destroyer of all life, warrior, wielding a power beyond imagining. Already its strengthening forces are marshaling themselves in the north. Ah, I see that you have suspected this. Good. Now go. Take the woman and care for her well. Remember what I have told you. I have done all that I may for now.'

Yet what was he to do now? The Council of Sha'angh'sei would not see him for many days and he could not now return to the walled city because the Greens would never allow him through the gate. Kiri was his only hope. She knew many people, a large number of them extremely influential, for through the saffron doors of Tenchō flowed nightly the cream of Sha'angh'sei society and business; Tenchō was for the wealthy and the powerful. Among these were, no doubt, several officials of the Council itself. There leverage could be applied, if she would consent to aid him. He had to ask her now. Time was fast growing short. With each passing day the chill shadow of The

Dolman reached farther into the continent of man as his legions consolidated their strength.

Thus he waited for her, as she had bidden, sprawled in the plush chair, his scabbarded sword scraping the polished floor, drinking the clear wine – Yung had already come and gone twice more – his mind drifting, his eyes watching. The women passing were coloured reeds, pastel and slender, bending, robes sweeping in perfect folds and rustling in the gentle wind, fans and long lashes fluttering like nervous insects in the oblique rays of the sun at day's humid end as it dazzles the still water. Placid oval faces, helmets of flowing hair, the fabulous blossoms of impossible flowers, mysterious and erotic.

Two willowy girls in matching quilted jackets came for him then and led him off to be bathed and dressed and he knew that tonight would be special.

'Am I not worth the wait?' she said without coyness.

She was dressed in a formal robe of rich purple silk, like a plum sunset with threads of the palest dove grey woven into a pattern of opening flowers.

Her lips and long nails were purple and she wore an amethyst pin in the shape of a fantastic winged animal in her hair. Her extraordinary black eyes danced with diamond-point lights.

Still, she looked subtly different.

They had bathed him and dressed him in black

silk pants and wide-sleeved shirt laced with platinum thread which glittered in the light. When he was ready, they had led him to a small room and she had come in.

'Are you hungry?' she asked now.

'Yes, very.'

She laughed and it was like hot sun glancing off a naked blade. 'Well, come then, my strong man, and remember well what you have said.'

Out into the Sha'angh'sei night they went, of moist wispy fog, lavender and blue, of a thousand eyes and ten thousand knives and one million running feet.

Down the wide sweeping stairs and into a square covered carriage Kiri called a ricksha. They climbed in and the barefooted kubaru lifted his poles and set off without a word, the ride much smoother than Ronin would have imagined because it contained a peculiar rocking motion tied to the runner's gait that he found soothing.

The blazing streets of the city, aflame with the swinging lanterns and the crush of people, the smells of broiling food and boiling rice, fresh shellfish and spiced wine flowed past them in a rippling without end, a vast variegated canvas upon which it seemed all the events of the ages of man must be painted in subtle colours too potent to be real.

He breathed the musk of her perfume and stared into her eyes when he could tear his vision away from the flashing city. They were so huge that he imagined that an entire universe resided within their depths. Platinum flecks shivering and he saw with a start that her eyes were not black but the deepest shade of violet that he had ever seen.

Upward they climbed, away from the crawling delta of the port, onto higher reaches of the city where silver taels made room for spired houses, ornate balconies, sculpted stone walls, and landscaped greenery.

Trees whispered their mysterious messages and the night deepened as the intense light from the multitude of lamps drifted silently away from them, down the mountainside, the fast receding shore of an incandescent isle, remote now and unreal, just choppy splashes on the dense ocean of the night.

Just the panting of the jogging kubaru's breath, the slap-slap of his feet, soles burnished like leather, the intermittent tiny sounds of the nocturnal insects, an owl hooting high up in a tree.

Once he thought about telling her but the pale oval of her face caused his words to catch in his throat and he said nothing, but watched the platinum motes.

The ricksha stopped before a two-storeyed house of dark brick and carved hardwood, columnated, flamboyant. Slender lamps like torches stood on either side of the wide yellow-metal-bound doors.

Ronin stepped out of the ricksha and turned. Kiri came into his arms. Together, they walked up the stone steps. The doors opened inward as they approached. A rather overly dramatic welcome, Ronin thought.

Two tall men stood before them. They were
clad in black cotton shirts and leggings, armed
with short single-edged swords which hung
unscabbarded on thick brass chains at their sides.
They had eyes like slits, mouths thin-lipped and
wide, their faces peculiarly canine. They bowed to
Kiri and stepped impassively away from the doors,
allowing them entrance. They stared curiously at
Ronin as he passed them.

They were in a towering hallway the height of
the entire structure. The whole of its far end was
taken up by a forked staircase curving upward to
the second story. To the left were two closed
doors. To the right opened sliding doors of oiled
fragrant wood through which they entered a large
room, warmly furnished with satin-cushioned
chairs and plush settees without legs. The floor
was covered with an enormous rug of dark swirling patterns. The pale green walls were edged in
gilt. The room was windowless.

There were perhaps ten people arranged about
the room; less than half were women. A tall
slender man turned as they entered and a curiously
white smile split his long face. He came towards
them. He had round eyes of a pale blue and thick
greying hair which he contrived to wear very
long. Unbound and brushed, it framed his face in
such a way as to give him a startlingly leonine
appearance. He was dressed in a formal
Sha'angh'sei suit, leggings and loose shirt, in a
shadow pattern of gilt on gilt.

'Ah, Kiri.'

The voice was deep, well modulated. He smiled again and Ronin saw the semicircular arc of raised white flesh beginning at the left corner of the mouth and terminating at the side of his nose, which at some earlier time had had its left nostril sheared off.

'Llowan,' said Kiri, 'this is Ronin, a warrior from the north.'

The man turned his ice eyes on Ronin and bowed formally.

'I am most pleased that Kiri brought you.'

'Llowan is the city's bundsman. He oversees the transactions of all the harbour hongs, collecting for Sha'angh'sei, duties on each shipment coming in and departing the port.'

Again that strange smile, unnaturally extended by the livid scar.

'You honour me, lady.' Then to both of them: 'You must have some wine. Hara,' he called to a servant, who served them a sparkling white wine in stemmed crystal glasses.

'Are you really from another civilization?' asked Llowan, leading them into the vortex of figures, beginning the introductions over Ronin's reply, then, coaxed into a peripheral conversation, leaving Kiri to continue, names tumbling like leaves in an autumn wind, and he concentrated then on the faces.

'Rikkagin,' said the large man with no chin and tiny eyes like broiled insects, 'one is becoming quite alarmed by the tales being told of the fighting in the north.'

They were sitting on silk pillows on the bare floor around a low table made of a wood with grain like a stormy sea, polished to a high gloss, upon which were laid out glazed pots of hot wine and bowls of various small foods such as pieces of fish, battered and dipped in hot oil, steamed vegetables, small sticky sweetmeats.

'What of it?' said the rikkagin in a tone of voice clearly indicating that he had no wish to discuss the matter. He was a wide-shouldered man with a ruddy complexion vanguarded by a wide red-veined nose. He had a thick grey beard stained yellow around his red lips. 'This is a city of tales, Chi'en. Most of them, as I am sure you are well aware, are utterly false.'

'Yet these persist,' said Chi'en, his yellow jowls quivering. He reclined on the pillows, an ornate fan waving at the side of his sad face.

'Tales to frighten hongs such as yourself are easy to create,' the rikkagin said with some disdain. 'Do not be an old lady.'

The large man bristled. 'But the fighting is not – '

'My dear sir.' The rikkagin was frowning now, his thick brows beetling like thunderheads. 'Without the war Sha'angh'sei would still be a muddy swamp with primitive houses collapsing in the first high wind and you would be in the rice paddies with your wife earning just enough to survive. It will come as no great news to any of us here that the war is what has made us rich. Without it – '

'You speak of war,' said a thin, dour man with dark eyes and close-cropped hair, 'as if it were an object to hold in one's hand and use as one pleases.' Ronin thought for a moment, recalled his name: Mantu, a priest of the House of Canton. 'Yet war is death for thousands and mutilation, starvation, and suffering for countless others.'

'How would you know?' interjected a high-cheekboned woman, another hong. 'You who have never ventured forth from the sanctity of your region of Sha'angh'sei.'

'I am not required to do so,' the priest said acidly. 'I have quite enough on my hands with the refugees that daily stream into the city from the north seeking sanctuary and solace at the House.'

'Your piousness sickens me, Mantu,' said the rikkagin. 'Where would the Canton House be without the war? Without the great suffering, who would come to fill your cathedral?'

'Tradition would – '

'Do not talk of your tradition.'

The voice was harsh and heads turned. The man was slender and muscular, with a bony face dominated by eyes like slatted windows, black as night. He had dark curling hair and a long drooping moustache that gave him a sinister appearance. He alone at the table wore plain clothes and a travelling cloak. 'Your people came to this land before the rikkagin but as surely as they preached the faith of Canton you took from my people as much as the soldiers. The House of Canton. My tongue grows thick with rage whenever I am forced to utter that hideous name. Yours is not the religion of Sha'angh'sei.'

'Po,' said Llowan kindly, 'your people are traders, nomads from the west.'

The slatted eyes flashed like dark lightning. 'You delude yourself if you believe that there is a difference. Are not my eyes the same as Chi'en's? Is not my skin the same colour as Li Su's? They are wealthy hongs of Sha'angh'sei just as their parents were before them. They are from the south, their origins far from my people, is that what you would have me believe? Yes?' His fist hammered the table and the sound was like the crash of hammer onto anvil in the green and gilt room. 'I tell you no! Ours is a land of unlimited wealth yet my people eat half bowls of rice and, if they are fortunate, week-old fish heads which they find discarded on garbage heaps. And all the while they toil to distil the fruit of the poppy for the lords of Sha'angh'sei.'

'The tradition of the Canton House is without reproach,' said Mantu somewhat didactically. 'It has stood for many years – '

'Growing fat like the rikkagin and hongs from the sweat of our labour,' sneered Po.

'You obviously do not understand the Canton teachings and, like most men, you are misdirected,' Mantu said. 'All men crave permanence.' He lifted his arms. 'Hence they acquire many things as if in these possessions they may truly find the belief that they will not die.' The arms folded in on themselves, somehow communicating pity without condescension. 'Yet all life is transient, and man, in desiring permanence, is inevitably defeated and thus suffers; and in his suffering, makes those around him suffer.'

'Philosophy is all well and good for those with time on their hands,' said Chi'en irritably, 'but I am more concerned with what I have been hearing, Rikkagin, that the war has changed.'

'Oh, out with it,' said the rikkagin in exasperation, wiping at his beard. 'If we must listen to your prattle, best get it over with.'

Chi'en ignored this outburst. 'The tales,' he said quite carefully, 'filtering into Sha'angh'sei are that the soldiers in the north no longer fight men.'

There was a small uncomfortable silence in the room then, as if an uninvited and unwelcome guest had arrived unexpectedly with news they all dreaded yet wished to hear.

'A tale to be believed by fools,' said the rikkagin disgustedly. 'Come then, tell us, Chi'en, what these beings "other than men" are like. No doubt you have detailed descriptions for us.'

The large man's jowls quivered and his eyes blinked several times in surprise. 'No, I have told you all that I have heard.'

The rikkagin grunted and leaned forward to snag a piece of fried fish with his sticks. He sighed rather contentedly. 'Yes, it is always most enlightening to hear how the truth is twisted to serve the needs of the individual – '

Po laughed at this, a short discomforting sound like the abrupt cracking of a dry twig in a forest when one had been certain that no one else was around.

The rikkagin looked down his nose at Po and continued. 'The Reds have enlisted the aid of a savage tribe, a northern people who, it seems, are much addicted to the fruit of the poppy. From what I understand, they extract the syrup, freeze it, and then chew it.'

'What?' exclaimed Li Su. 'Uncured and uncut? It cannot be! The effect would be – '

'Most extraordinary,' said Llowan with his white lopsided smile. 'I believe we are all agreed on that point, Godaigo.'

'Quite a frightening habit, I agree,' said the rikkagin.

'I did not say that,' replied Llowan, and they all laughed.

Godaigo wiped his red lips on a silk cloth provided by the host. 'Be that as it may, it is this unusual lever that the Reds are using to induce the tribe to join with them against us.' He put his hands up. 'And I admit that until reinforcements are in place we will be rather inconvenienced. But that is all.'

'Still the tales exist,' interjected Mantu. 'It would be most appropriate if they were true.'

'What are you saying?' said the rikkagin.

'I am telling you quite plainly that I would welcome the veracity of these tales because it would likely mean an end to the war. That is, after all, what the House of Canton seeks.'

'The House seeks dominion over the continent

of man,' said Po harshly. 'And in that it shall surely fail.'

'We seek dominion over no one; you speak out of ignorance.'

'Just their souls.'

The priest smiled benignly. 'Life, my dear Po, is soulless. The essence of each man survives death to be placed in, one hopes, a more worthy body, until the final Nothingness is achieved.'

'Their minds, then.'

Mantu smiled and shrugged. 'Shall we debate semantics, trader?'

'Well,' said Llowan, clapping his hands for the servants and seeking to head off another dispute, 'I believe that it is time that we get down to the serious business of the evening. I trust everyone has brought that which they need.' The white grin.

The servants first filled everyone's glass with a cold clear wine, 'to clear one's palate,' as Llowan told them. Then they ladled out a rich steaming soup of fish stock into large enameled bowls.

Following this, new glasses were brought into which was poured a sparkling wine while several dishes of spiced raw shellfish were put before the guests.

Ronin was still thinking of what the priest had said when the servants staggered in with huge platters of meat of a bewildering assortment. Each platter had half the meat shorn in thick slabs from the white carcasses. With this was served more of the clear sparkling wine.

'Mantu,' Ronin said. 'This Nothingness you spoke of. What is it precisely?'

The priest turned to Ronin, seeming glad for the interest. 'It is the state to which all men must aspire – '

'Women also?'

Mantu was not sure whether he was being mocked.

'Certainly. Theologians use the word "man" as a shortening for "mankind."' His small mouth glistened with grease. 'Nothingness is, in essence, the total extinguishing of the ego.'

Ronin was somewhat surprised. 'Do you mean that the individuality of each person must be surrendered?'

'Is that so valuable a possession?' asked Mantu. 'It is, in the end, no different than land, a house, taels of silver, a work of art or' – he looked at Ronin – 'a sword.'

'But those are all physical.'

'Yes, but all possessions are indistinguishable and must be surrendered before the Nothingness so that wholeness may be attained.'

'And what then?'

'Why, then perfection,' said the priest, some-what nonplussed.

'But I do not believe that man was meant for perfection.'

Llowan laughed and pounded the table.

'He has you, Mantu.'

The priest did not join in the general good humour.

The animated conversations continued as the servants silently removed the dishes only to replace them with fresh ones onto which they heaped portions of steamed and fried rice diced with meats and vegetables. No sooner had this course been devoured by the guests than gleaming tureens piled with whole boiled langoustes were served with cups of rice wine.

Ronin thought then of Kiri's earlier remark and he saw that she was smiling slyly at him. Yes, I was famished, but this –

He cracked into the thin carapace. She had spent most of her time in conversation with Llowan and Li Su and he began to wonder why she had brought him here. He felt now that he was jealous of her soft whisperings and gentle touches because they were directed towards their host. He gulped at his rice wine.

Perhaps she did not own poppy fields or trade in the silver market yet she was a powerful woman, the city's leading merchant of a commodity at times more precious than either smoke or metal or silk for that matter. Was she really privy to the secrets of Sha'angh'sei? If so, she was his only way now into the Council. Yet, even as he thought again on these matters, he felt the ebbing of the urgency. As he stared at her awesome beauty, imperfect and therefore terribly thrilling, as he felt the radiance of her aura, the only imperative was his desire to master her.

The langoustes, empty red and green exoskeletons languishing now in their own congealing liquids, bits of white and pink flesh still clinging to their edges, were slowly carted away.

Hot scented cloths were brought for face and hands and then bowls of pudding, dark and creamy, custard, yellow and fluffy, trays of pastries stuffed with candied fruits were put before each guest.

'A warrior Llowan called you,' said Po, leaning over so that Ronin could hear him more clearly. 'My folk were such once upon a time.'

Ronin bit into a pastry, washed it down with more wine. He was not really interested in what this trader had to say; he could think of but one thing.

'What happened?'

'Very unprofitable.' The black eyes regarded him like those of a dangerous reptile squatting beneath a rock, suddenly magnified, unknowable in the brief moments before –

Ronin realized belatedly that he was being baited. He dipped two fingers into a pudding, cool and spicy. It did not seem to matter.

'Perhaps they were not then sufficiently adept.'

The dark eyes widened, staring madly for an instant, and Ronin's fingers closed around the hilt of his sword. Then the face relaxed and, like a thunderstorm after a long drought, Po began to laugh.

'Oh yes,' he gasped, gulping at his wine. 'I might even get to like you.' He bit into a pastry. 'But tell me, how did my people fail as warriors?'

'They do not rule this land,' said Ronin softly.

The smile was gone and the face before him now seemed incapable of expressing any happiness. The mouth opened.

'Yes, warrior. I cannot argue with that.' He sighed. 'Yet they had no choice, a small tribe from the west.' He shook his head. 'We lacked the numbers.'

'There are many tribes in this land?'

'Many, yes, scattered on the land.'

'The unification of many into one might have been a beginning.'

The ebon eyes peered at him with keen interest now. 'Do you imagine such a task to be a simple one? Words! But it takes – ' He was choked with emotion, boiling inside, an unleashed storm, and his hand clutched whitely at his glass. His voice but a sibilant whisper now, controlled and venomous. 'But there was no one. We cried out to our gods for help, sacrificed our children, rent ourselves in desperation, and how were we answered?' The unpleasant smile returned. '*They* came. The foreign priest and then the rikkagin and by then it was too late; enslavement seemed almost pleasant by comparison.'

The salad arrived in great bowls, accompanied by wedges of yellow cheese and thick slices of a heavy bread made from grain.

'Yes, it is too late now,' Mantu observed, 'because you failed to keep what could have been yours. It is ours now and it serves you ill to blame others for your own shortcomings.'

'Silence, you!' cried Po.

201

'You see,' said the priest blandly, turning to Ronin. 'An illustration of the Canton teachings. Man's craving causes suffering to all about him.'

'Words!' Po spat.

'My dear fellow.' Llowan raised a hand warningly. 'You really must learn to control – '

But the trader was already on his feet, swaying. A tall dark creature of the night.

'For too long have the outlanders plundered our land, twisted the ideologies of our people with taels of silver. Too late, is it?' He laughed. 'Now! Now the time of retribution draws nigh! Now come the days of darkness and all foreigners shall taste defeat before they are ground into the mud of the Sha'angh'sei delta!' His cloak swirled like the wings of an avian predator as he pivoted and strode from the room. In a moment they heard the door slam.

'A bitter man,' said Mantu out of the silence.

'I trust we can all forget that unfortunate outburst,' said Llowan.

But Ronin was watching the rikkagin and he did not like the look in the other's eyes.

Llowan clapped his hands and, with that, the last course was brought. Oranges, peeled and soaked in wine, figs, white raisins, and an assortment of nuts.

When, at length, the last of the dishes had been cleared away, pipes were distributed, bone-white with long stems and small bowls. Tiny open lamps were set beside each guest and Llowan commenced to carve chunks from a block of a brownish substance.

They began to smoke and it seemed to Ronin that after a time the light in the room grew dim and diffuse and there were more women around the table than before. He took little of the smoke himself but watched the others relax as they inhaled deeply. The air became thick and sweet. Kiri shared a pipe with Llowan as they continued to whisper together. He leaned over, inhaling her perfume, anger welling within him. He gripped her cool wrist and she turned as he pulled, falling into his arms because he was expecting resistance and there was none.

Her purple lips were at his throat and he felt the press of her breasts as she murmured, 'Let us not overstay.'

He felt only surprise as he watched her kiss Llowan gently on the lips.

He was rising dreamily, holding her lithe form as they moved off the soft cushions and through the sweet smoke, across the room, speaking to no one, their departure unnoticed, past the guards and out the doors into the chill startling night. He breathed deeply, freeing his lungs of the cloying scent, clearing his head. And the sweating back and jogging feet took them down the mountain-side, away from the tall firs and thickets of gardened foliage filled with the chirruping of cicadas, away from the round shining faces, lips slick with gravy and bubbling wine and lust, away from the gilt and the guards bought with precious metals.

He was silent.

She watched him for a short time as if wanting to imprint the outline of his profile on her mind.

'You are angry with me. Why should that be so? I have done nothing to you.' The call of a whippoorwill.

'Why did you bring me?'

Light on her brow and cheek like a new moon.

'Must I have a reason?'

'Yes.'

'I wished to be with you.'

He laughed shortly and she shivered a little. 'You spoke with Llowan all evening.'

'What does that matter? I am with you.'

He closed his eyes for a moment, sensing a tension springing up between them which was both unpleasant and vaguely comforting in its familiarity. *K'reen, why are you crying? You know I hate that.* Oh, you bloody fool!

Not again.

He opened his eyes, found her staring at him, the gathering lights slithering by them reflecting in her impossibly violet eyes. He smiled.

'Yes, it was foolish of me. My mind was filled with thoughts of other times. Let us forget it, yes?'

Her lips opened and she leaned toward him, the heat reaching out to him, her 'Yes' a vibration in their mouths.

Into the clearing night with a fresh sea breeze blowing, into the blazing Sha'angh'sei delta, chittering with countless people, past stalls selling rice and frying fish, silks and cottons, knives and

204

swords, past brutal brawling men, drunk and stinking, past women in pink and green parasols, white-faced, red-lipped, long-legged and beautiful, past wine vendors and money-changers hiding behind the protective barrier of their street-corner cages, past marching soldiers and screaming hongs, past thieves and pickpockets lurking in the blackness of the alleyways and drunken cripples living along the edges of the streets, past battling children and slinking dogs, past piles of refuse upon which dark figures slept and crawled, past rotting corpses kicked and stepped upon by the teeming crowd, onto the Nanking and halted now by the festival's milling throngs, the wide avenue a riot of colour and frenzied motion.

They were confronted by a giant dragon, thrice colored, undulating to the movement of the crouched figures beneath its paper hide. It eyed them mock malevolently before turning aside and following the turning of the Nanking. Children in tattered clothes danced along its writhing flanks, urging it on. There was discordant music, percussive and staccato, and much shouting as the people accompanied its slow rippling passage.

Kiri, enfolded within his arms, put her lips to his ear so that she could be heard over the tumult.

'The festival of the Lamiae is this night reaching its zenith. This creature before us is the effigy of the Lamiae, the female serpent which lives in the sea at the edge of Sha'angh'sei. It is she who turns the waters yellow by the thrashing of her immense coils, thus lifting the silt from the sea's floor. The festival annually honors her who guards our dragon gates.'

'This land is filled with legends.'

'Yes,' she said. 'So it has been for all time.'

They moved on, their kubaru seemingly tireless as they rocked gently through the endless tumbling streets filled with the sleeping and the dead, huddled families and vacant-eyed ancient men and women alone in the sputtering cracked darkness.

He smelled at last the sea as the blackness of the port quarter engulfed them, the streets slick with salt water and fish blood, the great warehouses windowless, gleaming in the silver light from the moon which had finally managed to slip its cloud cover, looming over them like vast mysterious stone monuments. The sea smell was very strong now and, when they stopped, Ronin thought that he could hear the lapping of the sea against the wooden wharves.

They slipped from the ricksha into a silent black building. He closed the door behind them and in pitch-darkness Kiri went away from him. He heard small sounds and, after a moment, a yellow flame flickered as she lit a lamp.

She led him through the rooms, four on this level.

'This is one of Llowan's harrtin,' she said. 'Where his produce is stored and where, normally, his compredore lives.'

'Llowan is a hong also?'

She laughed lightly. 'Oh yes. He is master of many poppy fields in the north.' They stepped into another room. 'Here,' she said quietly, 'are stored dreams enough for ten thousand lifetimes. Dreams of passion. Dreams of desperation.'

'What?'

She started. 'Nothing.'

They moved on.

'Look here,' she said. 'The compredore's office. He is the go-between for Llowan and the stevedores and kubaru. He runs the day-to-day shipping and oversees the storing. A most lucrative position.'

'And where is he this night?'

She turned to him and smiled. 'At Tenchō, my warrior. At Tenchō.'

The room on the second story stretched almost the entire length of the building. The far wall was constructed of a series of window doors, wooden and slatted, beyond which the spangled night beckoned.

To the left lay the expanse of an enormous bed, low, with many pillows, which took up most of the width of the room. To the right, rugs were strewn across the wooden floor boards. A massive writing desk took up a far corner. Above it was a large mirror set in a carved wooden frame. There were several low chairs made of a tough resilient reed.

Ronin went across the room and pulled at a window door. It opened, folding back on itself, and he was surprised to find that he could step out onto a wide veranda.

Below him the sea: dappled in platinum moonlight chopped to a shower of rippling shards by the undulating surface, so clear in the night that it might have been a molten pathway building itself, beckoning him to climb to the far reaches of the sky, to illimitable whirling shores. Dazzled now, he listened to the quietude composed of the gentle sea lapping at the wharves' stanchions, the creaking of the dark brooding ships at anchor, the stirrings of sleeping families on the galaxy of tasstans rocking on the waves, the splash of a fish. All these now familiar sounds made more searing to him the absolute alienness of the cosmography arched like bits of a shattered world above him.

He felt her presence behind him just before he felt the touch of her body as it pressed itself against his. Through his silk suit seeped the warmth of her skin; the contours of her breasts and thighs, at once soft and firm, defined themselves. The heat.

He turned and pressed his mouth against hers and her small tongue licked at him and the night beat on around them, the eternal lapping, the soft singing of the kubaru as they made ready for the sailings at first light, the distant cries of the festival of the Lamiae. His finger tips traced the indentations of her spine, descending slowly.

She drew him inside and the sea breeze followed them to the edges of the bed, soft and downy, upon which they tumbled as one.

Her hair whipped his face as he opened her robe and kissed the opalescent flesh. His thirst was enormous.

'Ah,' she moaned. 'Ahh.'

And the tide took him.

Floating in the loss of tension.

The window doors all folded back now so that sea and sky were before them.

'You went to see the Council today.' Her voice held a note of puzzlement.

'Yes, this afternoon.'

'And fought the Greens. That was most foolish.'

He sighed. 'It could not be helped.'

'Did you have to kill one?'

'I have killed more than one.'

She made a sharp sound.

The moon had disappeared and they had had to relight the lamp. He listened to the quiet splash of the sea for a while.

'They will come after you now.'

'I am not afraid.'

Her hand stroked his chest. 'I do not want you to die.'

He laughed. 'Then I shall stay alive.'

'The Greens are not to be taken lightly –'

'That was not my intention. I mean only that what has been done cannot be altered. I am a warrior. If Greens come for me, then I shall destroy them.'

She stared at him, her eyes unreadable. He thought he could hear the plaintive cry of a sea bird out on the water.

'Yes,' she said at last, 'I believe you would.'

Then, 'I cannot imagine saying that to anyone else.'

'Is that a compliment?'

She laughed then, a clear sparkling sound, and he reached for her hand in the night, feeling its warmth, the fingers twining in his.

She scraped a nail along his flesh. 'Why did you seek out the Council?'

He told her.

'But you cannot mean that the tales are true?'

'That is just what I do mean, Kiri.'

'But Godaigo – '

'The rikkagin was not at Tenchō this morning.'

Her head twisted so that she could see him more fully. 'What has Sa's death to do with tales of beings that are not men fighting our soldiers in the north? My men have already dispatched the murderers.'

'Murderers?' Ronin said thickly. 'Who?'

'Why, the last men with her, of course, but – '

'Kiri, she was not killed by men.'

He felt her quiver and the skin along her arms was raised in gooseflesh. It might have been the strengthening wind.

'How could you know that?'

'Because,' he said, 'I have fought the creature that killed her. It destroyed a friend of mine in precisely the same manner.'

He felt her pull away from him. 'I cannot believe that; just as I cannot believe that the war is anything but what it has always been from a time long before you or I were born.'

'Still, I ask you to aid me with the Council. I cannot see them without your assistance.'

'Why do you believe that the Council can aid you?'

'Tuolin told me of the Council.'

A cloud passed across her face, fleeting. She shrugged. 'I cannot think why he did. The Council will be of little – '

Ronin gripped her shoulders.

'Kiri, I must see them!'

'There is no other way?'

'None.'

She tousled his hair. 'All right, my warrior. Tomorrow you will be within the Council chambers.'

He drew her to him and kissed her hard, feeling her melt as her sinuous body began to writhe slowly against him. The unbound forest of her hair lifted in the wind, a tremulous bridge between their coiling muscles. The lamp sputtered and went out.

She reached under a pillow and her hand lifted, a signpost, long and white and slender, the nails as black as dried blood in the almost-light. Between thumb and forefinger a small black shape, between forefinger and middle finger, its mate. She put thumb and forefinger to her lips, inhaled, then reached out, the arm extending to him, her lips calling, calling in the werevoice of the sea bird flying lonely above the tossing waves. Fingers against his lips. A cold sensation.

'Eat this.'

211

And after he had opened his mouth, 'Do you trust me?'

But it was rhetorical and he felt no desire to reply.

The warmth suffused him, friction like a satin glove stroking yellow ivory.

Again and again her open lips, wet and shiny, spoke a kind of litany of sound and motion and form. Words were a distant concept, dim and unremembered, discarded within a far-off cave of bright light and animal smells.

The wind died and the air grew calm, ceasing its dancing. The darkness of night hung like a black velvet curtain, containing them. The atmosphere paused between breaths and he hung suspended, listening to the lapping of the waves, as clear and powerful as thunderclaps, rushing against his ear-drums in time with the throbbing of his body.

And his body changed, filled now with a delicious warmth, a sexual ecstasy suffusing his feet, climbing upward through his legs and groin and torso and into his brain, and in that moment the strength of Kiri's body moving against his became an exquisite physical sensation. Sight, sound, touch, taste, and the visions in the theatre of his mind became one while he was made aware of them as totally discrete inputs, savouring them independently and simultaneously, time stretching out before him like a new-found joyous friend, endless and concurrent. A conduit.

He ploughed the heaving seas at the prow of a mighty ship filled with warriors bent on revenge, the feeling a taste at the back of the mouth, sweet and hot. He climbed the curving neck of the high prow, carved into the sinuous head of a dragon, brandished a long sword, screamed at the wind. He was the ship, feeling the heavy water washing over his flanks, his bow cleaving the seas, sending shivering spume into the bright air, leaving white spray in his wake. Man and vessel, he was both and more.

He plunged into the sea, yellow and turgid, and felt his legs grasp the slick scaly coils. He reached down and triumphantly brought the head up, ineffably exquisite, Kiri's deep violet eyes, dark as the depths of the sea, platinum flecks like schools of flying fish, with soft seaweed hair and a face as white as snow. The coils writhed beneath him and he rode the Lamiae from out of the shallows of the Sha'angh'sei sea, past the creaming reefs, teeming with life, and out, away, away, on the great westerly currents, into the deep.

It was then that the cold terror came, a dread presence, and he was swept up like an animal in the vortex of a whirlwind. And for the first time he knew its name. From his core, which beat like an incandescent stone and which remained unmoving in the flux caused by that which he had eaten, came the sound: The Dolman. His entire being opened now and attuned, he felt it drawing near. And it was devastation; it was annihilation. A suprahuman observer, he saw the cinder of the world, blasted and lifeless, blown through the fabric of space by a firestorm of incalculable power. The terror gripped him in its fierce claw and he felt his chest contract until all the air was forced from his burning lungs. He struggled against the coming, feeling helpless. Hearing what he could not comprehend. *Thee,* howled The Dolman, the universe trembling. *Thee. Thee!*

He screamed and came off the bed, stumbling, crashing into the wall. The shutters shivered. He was drenched with sweat. Or sea water.

Kiri came after him, lovely and naked, ivory and charcoal, crouching beside him.

'It's all right,' she said softly, mistaking his reaction. 'I had forgotten that you are not used to the smoke; this was much more. I had thought to give you only pleasure.'

He put his arms around her, felt the whip of the chill night wind racing in from the water. He looked out at the black sky and willed himself to breathe deeply, oxygenating his body.

'No, no, Kiri,' he said, his voice thin and strained. 'I felt it, more than seeing. Whatever you gave me created a – connection of some kind. I felt – The Dolman is close, very close.' His voice was now a metallic whisper in the rising notes of the wind.

'And it comes for me.'

She would not let them rest and he felt the rising terror within her, as deep as an undug wellspring, although he was calm now, the intensity still with him but a shell forming, replacing the aftershock that allowed normal thought.

They dressed and went out into the narrow shiny streets. It was the time of night when the moon was down and dawn had not yet begun to pull upon the last thread of darkness. It had begun to rain and the air was heavy with an acrid active smell.

They raced the downpour to the patiently waiting carriage and the kubaru took off at his steady rocking pace, across the marshy delta of the port and into the black back recesses of Sha'angh'sei.

Lightning wreathed the sky like the twisting branches of a great ancient tree and peals of thunder echoing off the buildings' walls caused the runner to break his stride now and then.

By the storm's pale flickering light he watched the lovely profile, the eyes pools of shadow, the cheekbones whitely limned, emphasizing the face's strength and sweep.

They were in what looked to be the most ancient section of the city now, travelling down narrow unpaved streets, earth churned to mud by the rain and the fleet passage of the kubaru's soles, slap-slap, slap-slap, black water splashing in a bow wave, presaging their progress.

Small houses of board and reed grew here as if from the soil itself, dilapidated yet with a peculiar sorrowful dignity that was impossible to define. Perhaps it was merely the congruence of meagre dwelling to its surroundings that was sufficient to impart this feeling to him. Nevertheless, he understood without being told that he was seeing Sha'angh'sei as it must have been before the

Canton priests and the round-eyed rikkagin had come to the land.

The ricksha halted unbidden before the towering columns of a stone temple, squat and thick, its face slick now with rain, cracked and half covered with climbing plants.

They went into the narrow street, following the kubaru through double doors of bamboo bound in black iron. He took them through a crowd of kubaru who milled about the entranceway and who, Ronin suspected, would turn away those whom they did not wish to enter.

The grey stone floor, the arching stone walls, caught murmurings and mutterings, echoing them along their length and height like the desultory flame of a guttering candle. This temple had a completely different feel than the one Ronin had come upon in the midst of his wanderings.

'What is this place?' Ronin whispered.

Kiri turned her face towards his and he saw that she had produced a plum-colored silk scarf from somewhere and had wrapped this around her head as if she did not wish to be recognized, though who here would possibly know her he had no idea.

'Kay-Iro De,' she said, using a word that was of the ancient tongue of the Sha'angh'sei people and which had no ready translation into modern speech. It meant variously sea-song, jade-serpent, and she-who-is-without-members, and it perhaps had more meanings of which no one spoke.

'I have told you that tonight is the culmination

216

of the Festival of the Lamiae,' she said softly, her violet eyes shining. 'Yet tonight is more. Every seventh year on the last night of the festival comes the Seercus of Sha'angh'sei.' A simian-faced woman wrapped in a green cloak, a hairless man by her side gathering in the taels, her clandestine whisperings.

It appeared now that the temple was immense as they followed their kubaru down a narrow, windowless hall that seemed endless. The dank stone walls, beaded with cold moisture, echoed their footsteps. At regular intervals, stone arches were built into the passageway and from their apexes were hung iron braziers casting a dim, fitful light. At length they reached a wide stairway down which they descended. He noted with some curiosity that the hall seemed to have no other egress at this end.

They went carefully downward, their way lit now by flaring torches set into scorched metal sconces, encrusted with the detritus of the ages. Fifty steps and then a landing, peopled by kubaru who scrutinized all who passed. Down and down they went with the air becoming increasingly humid and chill, the stairs slick with moisture and slime, until he gave up counting the number of landings.

The atmosphere was thick with salt and phosphorus and sulphur by the time they reached the last landing and passed through the guard of the kubaru there. The runner motioned silently to them and they stooped, half crawling through a

217

cramped passageway, utterly dark, rough-cut from the living rock. Small creatures skittered past their feet in the wetness.

The tunnel gave onto a vast grotto lit by immense guttering torches, crackling and smoky in the damp air. Great natural columns of stone, flecked and streaked with minerals winking metallically in the light, rose up from the craggy floor into the dark reaches of the unseen ceiling.

There were so many people crowding the cavern that at first Ronin did not see that which actually dominated the place. Then, in some unfathomable shifting, the throng parted momentarily and he saw the pool.

He stepped closer, mesmerized. It was an immense oval stripped out of the floor of the cavern by some cataclysmic upheaval eons ago and the water that filled it was of the most remarkable colour he had ever seen. Not a trace of blue or brown could be seen in its shifting depths, yet surely no water could exist without at least a hint of these shades. Yet the water into which he now gazed was the most extraordinary green, halfway between a forest of firs in deep summer and the translucence of the most exquisite jade. Its depth seemed limitless. Surely it led to the vast ocean beyond Sha'angh'sei's shores.

He thought again of the simian-faced woman and her hissed words, *the Seercus,* her inflection imparting to them a mysteriousness that Ronin had supposed was merely a part of her pitch. Now he found himself at the Seercus and he wondered.

Kubaru continually poured into the grotto from several low apertures in the walls similar to the one they had used. Almond-eyed, black shining hair pulled back into queues, wearing loose suits of dark cotton and coarse silk. He felt that he was, at last, viewing the true Sha'angh'sei, naked in the arena of Kay-Iro De on this most sacred of nights. They were free now of the immense burden of the fields and of the war, of intruder and of time. The betrayals were held for this moment suspended. Ten thousand years had fallen away like so much dead skin to reveal – what? Soon the answer.

He heard chanting, far off and aloft, and the dimness gave grudging way to warm yellow light as the priests entered the grotto from some hidden doorway, carrying before them immense lanterns constructed from the whole skins of giant fish, dried, blown, and lacquered to stiffness. Various pigments had been used to cleverly reproduce and enhance the original aspect, heighten the character of each creature.

The priests wore swirling cloaks of sea-green which left their strong arms bare. They were long-skulled and yellow-skinned, hairless and quite young.

They set the fish lamps down in prescribed places and now he could see that towering over the pool, on the far shore, was a statue. It was of solid gold, carved most cunningly in the shape of an enormous dragon, its thick coils entwined about a regal throne of gold. But where he had expected a female head to be was carved a skull of semi-canine structure, with long grinning muzzle, sharp-toothed and flaring-nostriled above which large round eyes of sea-green jade sparked in the brighter light.

Kiri gripped his hand in hers and her breathing was heavy as she stared at the priests.

All were assembled now and kubaru were stationed at each entrance, he supposed to discourage intruders though in all the crowd he had not seen any glint of weaponry save his own.

One of the priests now gave a signal and incense was thrown into a wide brass brazier. Clouds of yellow steam rose into the black mists of the grotto and spices came to him on the moist air. A young boy appeared leading an animal that Ronin could not readily identify; perhaps it was a young boar. Squealing, the animal was laid out upon a stained stone slab and the chanting began again from the priests and this time it was echoed by the assembled: 'Kay-Iro De. Kay-Iro De.'

One of the priests reached inside his cloak and produced a knife with a hilt of yellow crystal. Lifting it high over his head, he spoke in the ancient tongue, words that neither Ronin nor, he suspected, Kiri could understand. Yet the meaning seemed clear and Ronin was not surprised when the gleaming blade flashed downward in a shallow arc and pierced the flesh of the animal. Hot blood spurted from the severed artery, spattering the robes of the priests. Dropping the knife, the priest reached his hand into the still trembling interior of the animal and pulled out the warm heart. This he tied with coarse thongs to the knife and cast it into the centre of the sea pool while his fellow priests set about collecting the blood of the animal in a glazed yellow bowl. With the splash a kind of sighing went up from the multitude and the chanting began again.

The priests marched silently around the perimeter of the pool toward the golden dragon on the far side and, laying the bowl of blood at the foot of the throne, each in turn bent to dip his hands into the crimson liquid. One by one, then, they climbed the huge throne and daubed the blood onto the eyes of the dragon until it dripped down the muzzle, into the mouth, staining the teeth darkly and thence from the points into the deep green waters.

Now they returned and with them was a young girl in a white robe with silver fish embroidered on it. He felt Kiri against him now, warm and trembling, as they brought the girl before the multitude. She was white-faced and beautiful, tall and shapely with black almond eyes and dark hair that came down to her buttocks. She seemed very young.

Ceremoniously, the priests washed their hands and, at another signal, more incense was thrown into the braziers so that now a green cloud rose into the thick air. Ronin felt then the heat of the throng and the denseness of the atmosphere and he was obliged to take deeper breaths to get sufficient oxygen.

Their hands still wet, the priests donned masks of papier-mâché that caused them to take on the appearance of articulated fish, scales gleaming, gills starkly delineated, round eyes staring unblinkingly. Slowly, they moved in a semicircle around the young girl and the chanting from the throng took on volume and urgency. With infinite slowness their hands lifted and unwound the robe from the girl.

Naked she was breath-taking, with wide hips and heavy breasts and firm thighs. In that electric instant, the priests' robes fell away and she collapsed to the floor of the grotto.

The chanting was all but a roar now and Ronin strained along with the others to see clearly as the priests followed the descent of the girl to the cavern's floor. For many moments the rhythmic movements of the muscular bodies moved to the cadence of the chanting, 'Kay-Iro De, Kay-Iro De,' and when the priests had finished they rose as one and servants of the temple clothed them once again and removed their fish masks. The girl lay whitely, her breasts heaving like waves upon an agitated sea, fists clenched between her legs. Kiri moaned softly next to him.

Up from a small side pool was drawn a flapping sea creature of some kind, black and sleek and gleaming. It was surely not a fish, for when the priests slew it, this time with a knife of purest green jade, the thing bled red blood as an air-breathing animal would. Again the priests caught the blood in a bowl and with it drew near the prone girl once more.

They grasped her arms and lifted her until she was standing, cradling her as they forced her head back and made her drink the warm blood. Choking and gagging, she drank and when it was all gone they took her to the far side of the sea pool and thrust her roughly upward onto the golden throne, so that her legs entwined with the metallic coils. She clung weakly to the dragon's slippery hide, her head hanging so that the face was concealed by the black forest of her tossed hair. And in no time her body convulsed and she vomited the red liquid so that it drenched the fierce head of the statue.

She shuddered and her grip upon the thing loosened and the priests' arms were retreating and, like the sticky spume that now dripped from the fanged mouth of the golden dragon, she slid inexorably from its slippery embrace into the cool green waters of the sea pool, into the bloodstained salt sea.

There was a collective gasp from the crowd and the chanting began once more from the mouths of the priests, 'Kay-Iro De, Kay-Iro De.'

The girl thrashed in the water, choking, seemingly not able to swim. Her head disappeared, then she surfaced again, mouth open in a silent scream, and with a thrash, descended into the depths.

At that moment the waters of the pool appeared to swirl as if subject to a swiftly passing current, fierce and unnatural, and the air above the water seemed to shimmer as if from some terrible heat.

Tension strung the crowd like an incipient thunderstorm and they seemed caught between an urge to press forward and an instinctive fear to pull back. As a result, they milled about chaotically as the chanting of the priests rose to the howl of a tornado, the rock walls of the grotto hurling the sounds back upon their ears.

'Kay-Iro De. Kay-Iro De.'

And now, though he could scarcely believe his eyes, a whirlpool was forming in the centre of the sea pool and abruptly the green waters darkened. Emerald mists rose from the pool's sides and salt foam fountained from its core.

'Kay-Iro De. Kay-Iro De.'

And the fountaining presaged the presence of something from deep within the sea. He saw the ill-defined shape, black and monstrous, through the imperfect lens of the water, staining the pool with its bulk.

'Kay-Iro De. Kay-Iro De.'

And now it broke the water's surface, a reluctant, elastic barrier, into the molten atmosphere of the cavern, heavy with incense and freshly spilled blood, hot with the body warmth of the frenzied people. Foam flying from the tangled seaweed of its hair, black almond eyes huge and baleful.

'Kay-Iro De. Kay-Iro De.'

Oh, surely not, thought Ronin. The black eyes within the human head surveyed the throng, the body arching upward so that within the green

224

foam and white spray of its thrust could be seen thick, sinuous coils, scaly, encrusted with algae and yellow barnacles. And within those twisting coils, a glimpse of a white broken torso, slim legs.

With a crash like the collapse of a building, the thing shot straight down, merely a ripple, dark and remote now beneath the waves slapping at the sea pool's edges. And then nothing, only the trembling of the water, limpid and deep green once again.

For an instant, all sound ceased, and had it not been for the tiny slap-slap of the diminishing wavelets, Ronin might have believed that time itself had stopped.

Kiri, shuddering, gripped his arm.

'Look,' she whispered hoarsely. 'Look.'

And his eyes lifted to the far side of the pool, at the immobile dragon. There, instead of the canine head darkly dripping blood, was the golden head of an exquisite woman with almond eyes carved of sea-green jade.

When he awoke, the sun was already past its zenith. He lay quite still for a moment, watching the bright whips of sunlight rippling like molten lead across the floor, listening to the close sounds of singing, hoarse shouts, the frenetic slap of jogging feet, the creaking of ships being outfitted, the metallic grate and the splash as a ship weighed anchor.

For a moment he floated above the receding abyss of his unconscious where rose . . .

And sat up. Slatted wooden doors through which the salt breeze blew and light streamed and he knew then that he was in Llowan's harrtin, though why Kiri had brought him back here instead of to Tenchō he could not remember. He was alone in the room. He stood up and, naked to the waist, went out into the day.

The veranda too was empty yet still he felt the complex shreds of last night clinging to the edges as if they were real and fluttering in the wind.

He looked out at the sluggish sea, clogged with vessels large and small. It was a bright, clear day with thin high clouds near the lid of the sky and he squinted in the sunshine. Below him, the activity along the long wharves of Sha'angh'sei was fierce with loadings and unloadings, the compredores calling to the stevedores, who in turn shouted at the singing kubaru, jogging under the weight of bales and barrels filled with the wealth of the city, the foods and textiles of the continent of man.

His eyes moved from the white billowing sails studding the near waters to the yellow sea farther out and, like a wave pungent with salt and phosphorus washing over him, the events of last night flooded in on him.

Kay-Iro De. Kay-Iro De.

He shook his head. Perhaps it was only the aftermath of the substance which he had taken. What had Kiri called it? The tears of the Lamiae. Merely an illusion, rising and falling like the tide. Sun dancing on the restless water, shards of liquid gold. A memory elusive and vague, as if it were part of another lifetime, lapped at the edges of his consciousness. What? A shape, dark and vast and inconstant and . . .

He heard a sound behind him and turned, passed through the open shutters into the cool room to find Matsu, serene, lithe Matsu, standing in the centre in a pale green silk robe edged in rust, leaves of the same colour falling across its surface. She held a deep blue lacquered tray on which sat a clay pot glazed grey and red and several small cups painted in the same pattern.

'I have come to take you to the Council,' she said, kneeling and setting the tray down before her. She lifted a slim arm. 'Please. Sit. I have brought your breakfast.' Her dark eyes stared up at him unblinkingly and for a moment his stomach contracted.

He ran a hand across his face and went to her, knelt, the tray a low barrier between them. He washed his face and hands from a large bowl of water which she handed him. She patted his face dry with a clean white cloth. He sat back.

'Matsu, where is – ?'

'She has much to accomplish today and it is already afternoon.'

'How is the woman I brought to Tenchō?'

She did not answer but concentrated on the ceremony of the tea, the turnings of the cup, the stirring, the pouring, all the precise movements that made it so special. He sat quietly and watched her deft hands.

At last the tea was steaming in the cup and she lifted it, an oblique offering, saying, after he had accepted it, 'She has awakened. Her name is Moeru, she wrote it for me.'

He sipped the tea and it tasted better because of the way she had served it to him.

'Has she still a fever?'

'I think not. The sweat no longer rolls off her and she is eating now.'

'That is good.' Her eyes hiding behind sooty lashes.

'She wished to remove the bandage.'

'What bandage?'

'The one high up on her thigh. The dressing is dirty.'

He put the cup down on the tray.

'Ah, no. The apothecary told me to leave it on. There is a healing poultice beneath the cloth.'

'But she says that she has no pain there.'

'Then the poultice is working.'

There was silence for a time. He continued to sip his tea. Matsu watched him, her small white hands folded on her lap. Leaves rustled as she breathed. Smells of sweat and spices and fresh fish from the wharves. Shouts and hoarse laughter. Oval face like still water, strands of hair floating in the breeze, the perfect column of the neck, slender and ivoried.

'Your friend's husband,' he asked. 'How is he?'

'Ah,' sighed Matsu, her head minutely in motion so that a wave of black hair fell over one

228

eye, across her cheek. 'It is most sad. He was knifed last night, fighting in a tavern.'

'I am sorry.'

She smiled wanly. 'It is as well he died. The war had changed him. My friend no longer knew him. He brought only sorrow to those who loved him, even his son who lies paralysed on a bed in my friend's house.'

'I do not understand.'

'His back is broken but he still has eyes with which to see. His father resented that.' She shrugged. 'As I said, it is perhaps better this way.'

'Will you have some tea?'

Matsu shook her head. 'It is for you.'

Outside, the sun beat down out of a deep cerulean sky. They smelled the gutted fish drying in the heat, a hint of cinnamon, of cloves, of coriander, and Ronin's nostrils dilated for a moment as if recalling on their own a distant and odious scent.

Then they were in the ricksha, moving off down the narrow, baking streets, past the blind faces of the harrtin which Ronin now knew opened opulently their splendid verandas onto the bund – the wharves of Sha'angh'sei and the swelling yellow sea.

Deep within the jungle of the city, the kubaru runner stumbled and fell and the ricksha jerked to a halt. Although he had been talking to Matsu and his head had been turned away, the bright line of crimson along the runner's side caught the periphery of his vision and as the two men leapt onto the

229

still rocking ricksha his sword was already withdrawn.

It was the wrong action in the confined space and the man who went for him had the advantage, the hilt of his filthy dirk slamming against the inside of Ronin's wrist with a quick flick, the sword clattering to the muddy street. A professional, Ronin thought, and he did the only thing he could do, grappling, tearing the momentum so that they both fell to the ground.

He inhaled the stench of the body and the foulness of the breath as the man slashed the dirk at his throat. Saw the yellowed stumps of teeth, holes in the gray gums, images flashing across his vision path as the head whipped and the shoulders twisted and the blade blurred into the soft earth just past his neck.

Elbows in and up, using the heavy bone structure, and the man's jaws clashed together with a crack as Ronin hit him. He had the good sense to scramble away then so that he could regain his advantage.

He let Ronin get up before he came towards him, confident because Ronin was unarmed. He was small but very powerful with broad shoulders and lean hips and thick muscular arms. He had a wide flat intelligent face, dark cunning eyes. He was bald save for a long queue of dirty blue-black hair. He was missing an ear.

He was clever and ignorant at the same time. He feinted, the blade of his dirk appearing to whip towards Ronin's neck, canting downward at the last instant, reaching to slit his stomach. Using the man's momentum, Ronin stepped into the thrust, grasping the extended arm, and leaned back, his hip and groin beneath the man's buttocks, a solid base as he planted his feet and stiffened the muscles of his legs. He lifted his right foot, slamming the sole of his boot down onto the stretched knee joint. Resistance was minimal. The kneecap shattered in a shower of white and pink and the vulnerable thighbone cracked as if it were a dry twig. The man screamed and collapsed and Ronin reached for his fallen dirk.

'Stop right there,' said a voice.

Ronin turned and in that instant remembered the second man. He stood now several paces from Ronin with Matsu drawn to his side, his dirk at her throbbing white throat, so perfect, like ivory. The blade grazed her windpipe for emphasis. He stared into her eyes, saw in their darkness no fear. What then?

The second man shook his head sadly.

'You should not have done that.' He was large, very tall, with a grizzled head and long greasy hair. He had a high forehead and the eyes of an animal. Ronin froze. 'What shall I tell his woman and her children? How will they eat? Now I will take your money and the woman.' His feral eyes flicked at the man, broken and unconscious in the muddy earth, came back to Ronin. 'She will fetch a high price at the Sha-rida.' Matsu gasped in pain as the blade bit into her throat.

231

'Sha-rida?' said Ronin, edging closer, wanting to keep the man talking.

'Outlander. Fool to travel these streets in a ricksha. The scent of your money precedes you.' He smiled mockingly. 'Yet I salute your foolishness because you are my living. Long may it last. Do not come closer,' he snapped suddenly. His voice was now cold and hard. 'The woman will be breathing through the hole in her throat. You are not that foolish, I trust.' The man pulled Matsu in front of him and his blade caught the sunlight in a dazzle. 'Now come, let us not drag out this encounter. Toss your money to the ground.'

'All right,' said Ronin. 'Do not harm her.' Because he was close enough now and Matsu was in the correct position. He had deliberately moved because he wanted her in front of the man, where he could look at her, read her expression. He needed that advantage. His sword was out of the question. She would die before he got halfway to where it lay.

His shoulders moved minutely, slumping in an attitude of defeat. Back within the depths of the Freehold and his Senseii, the Salamander was before him, saying, 'Provide your foe with clues. He will be trained to look for the key to victory through the tiny betrayals of your body. So you must give him that which he wishes to find.' These men were sufficiently adept.

His hands were at his belt, slowly unknotting the cord to his bag of coins. He stared at Matsu and she read what he wished her to know, written in his colourless eyes.

The bag hit the soft ground with a heavy chink and the gauntleted hand sped across the short space without warning. The hesitation, the merest split instant caused by Ronin's attitude of defeat and the visual and aural distraction of the bag of coins dropping, was sufficient. Ronin grasped the blade just as it commenced its inward stroke. He wrenched at it and the metal snapped. At the same time, Matsu twisted her body, swung her arm, and her fist hit his stomach. Then she was away and Ronin was closing with the man.

He went for the throat and the man blocked him, turning as he did so, taking Ronin down. There was pressure against Ronin's windpipe and he had to force his breathing. The man's fist smashed into the side of his head and the grip tightened on his throat. He felt the urge to retch as his body rapidly used up the last of the oxygen in his stilled lungs. He fought to breathe, could not, and so turned his attention to bringing up his right hand. It was caught between their bodies and he worked at freeing it while he began to strangle on carbon dioxide. The man's attention narrowed as he increased the pressure and now the hand was free; bring it up, through the maze. Groping, he found the open spot on the side of the neck, jabbed with his thumb.

The man could not even scream and Ronin was up, his lungs heaving in great bursts of air. They were on their knees in the mud and slime and the man was recovering and there was no time to reconsider, the organism out to survive. Ronin's fist, sealed within the hide of the Makkon gauntlet, smashed into the lower end of the man's sternum. The bone cracked, splintered, the force of the fist plunging it upward into the heart. Blood and viscera fountained outward, drenching him as the face before him, drained and white, bobbed like a berserk marionette. The jaws snapped shut spasmodically, biting off the end of the lolling tongue.

Ronin stood and kicked at the body, looking around, but there was only Matsu staring at the ruined corpse.

She started then, looking at him. She went and got his sword and he sheathed it as she bent to pick up the bag of coins. Then she went to the slain kubaru and ripped off his damp shirt, returning to Ronin and wiping the pink foam from his face and chest and arms. She reached out and touched the strange scaled gauntlet, horny and unreflective, glistening now, beaded with dark fluids.

'What is that?' she whispered, stroking the hide.

'A present,' Ronin said, watching the thin line of red across her throat where the dirk had crossed the delicate flesh. It stood out like a tear on a shadowed cheek. He licked his finger, wiped it along her neck. Her eyes closed and she shuddered. 'It was given to me by a little man who walks with a limp, whose companion is a singular creature. It is made from the claw of the thing that killed Sa.'

She seemed not to hear him. 'I could not believe

that any man could do what you have just done. Was it the gauntlet?' Her fingers dark now with the viscous liquids.

Ronin wiped her hand and the gauntlet on the sodden shirt, then threw it from him. He shrugged. 'Perhaps, in part.' He reached for her. 'Now we must finish our journey. The Council awaits me.'

The dark eyes lifted, looked at him strangely. Then she nodded and they set off through the labyrinthine streets, finding at length the Nanking and then, a short time later, a narrow winding road with no name that Ronin could see.

'I came a different way the last time.'

'I have no doubt. But it is not prudent to take King Knife Street, is this not so?'

He laughed then. 'Yes, Matsu, it would indeed not be wise. But what about the Greens at the gate?'

She smiled. 'There are many entrances to the walled city.'

The climb was steep this way. No houses lay along the road, only giant firs and lush green-leafed trees. The earth was thick with small plants and wild flowering bushes.

Soon the shadow of the great wall blotted out the warmth of the sun and they stood in the cool dimness while Matsu spoke in low tones to the Greens who guarded this gate. The metal door swung open and they went through. The Greens ignored them, returning to the absorption of their dice game.

Within the perfectly linear corridor of the carefully tended trees he asked her, 'The Sha-rida, Matsu. What is it?'

She laughed nervously, the sound like shattering crystal in the quietude, and he heard the sighing of the trees before she said, 'The Sha-rida is a tale told to frighten outlanders.' But he saw the look on her face and did not quite believe her.

'Tell me then,' he said lightly. 'I am not easily frightened.'

Her eyes swept his face and she tried a smile but did not quite make it.

'It is a market, a special kind of market, which, it is said, moves from night to night, through the black alleyways of Sha'angh'sei, opening only after the moon has left the sky.'

'A flesh market,' said Ronin. 'Slave trade.'

She shook her head. 'No. There are many of those in the city. They conduct their business during the day.'

'Well then?'

'It is true that the Sha-rida deals in human flesh, but only the most beautiful women and men, young and healthy.'

'Towards what end?'

They walked in silence for a time. The cicadas were singing among the trees and birds called in staccato rhythm above their heads. The avenue stretched before them, white and empty, as if it were some giant's plaything abandoned now for some newer and more elaborate toy.

'Towards, it is said, a hideous death.' Her voice

was like the first touch of autumn's winds. 'The buyers wish only to observe death and the act of dying, and the more they indulge themselves, the more bored they become and the more monstrous the forms of dying they conjure up.' She looked at him. 'Even in a city such as this, such a thing does not seem possible.'

'It is only a tale.'

'Yes,' she said. 'That is all.'

Their footsteps shattered the silence of the hall and the still air eddied softly in their wake. The woman with the light eyes and jutting breasts was at her post behind the heavy marble desk. Two Greens, armed with axes and curving dirks, stood watch outside heavy wooden doors with iron rings in their centres.

'Yes?' she inquired, lifting her head. She did not seem to recognize Ronin. He was about to say something when Matsu squeezed his arm.

She spoke to the woman who said, 'Ah,' softly as she listened, her eyes on Ronin.

'Ah.' Her lacquered nails scraping across the cool desk top like articulated insects. 'No, I am afraid – ' But Matsu cut into her prepared speech and they stared at each other now, a test of power that encompassed more then mere wills. The woman licked her lips with her bright tongue. 'Well, I – ' Matsu spoke at length and the woman's face came apart, a subtle thing which he observed with some wonderment. 'Yes. Yes, of course.'

237

She signalled to the Greens who turned and, pulling on the iron rings, opened the doors.

At last, Ronin thought, as they went forward. An audience with the Municipal Council of Sha'angh'sei. They went into the Council chambers. He was already unscrewing the hilt of the sword. An answer to the long riddle. An end to the uncertainty. The way now open to defeat. The Dolman and his hordes. The doors closed behind them. His hand stopped as it was about to pull forth the scroll of dor-Sefrith.

He whirled on Matsu.

'What insane jest is this?'

'There is no jest.' Calm. The black eyes steady.

'Then surely this is the wrong chamber.'

'You can see for yourself that this is the Council's chamber.'

It was a high-ceilinged, windowless room dominated by an immense ornate table around which were placed at regular intervals high-backed wooden chairs, richly carved, regal. Save for the two of these, the chamber was empty.

'Why did you bring me on a day when the Council is not in session?' he demanded.

'If it were not in session, the building would have been closed.'

Ronin's temper broke and he shook her by the shoulders.

'Are they ghosts then that I cannot see them?'

'No.' The voice as distinct in the room as a bird call in high summer. 'It is quite simple.'

His hands moved. 'Matsu, I will break your neck – '

'The Municipal Council of Sha'angh'sei does not exist.'

The dragon stared at him quizzically. From the chair, its golden eyes sparked in the last oblique rays of sunlight. Its head was erect but its body was distorted, foreshortened by the folds. Ronin crossed the room and, removing his shirt and weapons belt, donned the robe as Matsu had bidden him. The silk moved in the breeze from the open window and the dragons writhed.

Day was almost done. They had not spoken on the journey back to Tenchō. Although he had been hungry and although they had passed many street stalls filled with a variety of fragrant foods, he had denied himself that pleasure, preferring not to delay the explanation. He had spent too long seeking an answer only to find other riddles.

He had raged at Matsu, threatening to tear the chambers apart, to destroy the Greens outside the door. She had merely stared at him and asked that he return to Tenchō with her. 'The answer is there,' was all that she had said and had waited him out.

Eventually he had given in. He had no choice.

Clouds were piling up to the west, darkening the lowering sun, turning it from orange to deep crimson, a half-seen oblate, bloated and veiled by the oncoming weather. Another storm approaches, Ronin thought, sliding the dragons over his torso. The silk felt cool on his flesh.

Matsu came to him beside the window and tied his sash in the formal manner. She had changed into a crimson formal robe, the colour more vivid than was usual for her. Deep brown reeds on the body, the wide sleeves plain, bordered in deep red.

She studied him for a moment in the twilight, the fast-disappearing sun now a dusky ruby glowing between the buildings on Okan Road. And the strange light, burnished and intense, drew all the colour from her face, causing her to appear pale, shadows building in layers around her eyes, across the hollows below her cheeks. The skin was perfectly drawn, not a line, not a blemish marred its satin surface. She stood quite still, all light and dark, and he felt compelled to reach out and touch the face to assure himself that it was indeed flesh and blood, warm and pliant, that he was not staring at some fantastically conceived and crafted mask. Her lashes dipped for an instant and her lips parted as if she were about to say something. Then her lids rose and her slim hand moved startlingly, passing through the light, then black shadow, as she reached down for his hand. And she managed somehow to turn that simple gesture into a tender caress as she led him wordlessly from the room, into the dim corridor, the great lamp not yet spilling its tawny light.

Down the curving stairs in a wide arc and into the rear of the house where he had never before ventured. They went out the back, swiftly, silently, through a small wooden door with a large iron lock and, instead of the expected crowded street, Ronin found himself in a spacious garden, lush and green with the plumage of ripe foliage.

Amid the artful jungle of greenery stood a pair of four-legged creatures, saddled and harnessed. They snorted and pawed the earth as Ronin and Matsu neared them so that their attendants were obliged to pull on their bits and talk to them soothingly in meaningless words.

'These are not horses,' said Ronin and Matsu smiled.

'No. They are luma. Steeds from the far north, very powerful and quite intelligent.' She shrugged. 'Horses are quite stupid. They are fine for warfare and that is where they are primarily used. In any event, the luma are quite rare.' She lifted one arm. 'This one is a present from Kiri.'

The animal was a deep red-brown stallion with a thick red mane. It had a long tapering head with flaring nostrils and erect triangular ears. Its eyes, round and large, were a deep blue and, between them, thrusting from the thick skull, were three stubby yellow horns in a vertical row like a miniature trident. The luma had no tail but the lower reaches of its legs were streamered with silky red hair.

Slowly, Ronin approached it. One large blue eye followed his progress with curiosity and, as Matsu had told him, intelligence and when he reached out to stroke its head it snorted and pushed its muzzle against his hand.

241

He mounted the luma and Matsu leapt onto her own, a grey mare with a pure white mane. He saw that a double slit in her robe allowed her to sit astride the luma without difficulty.

They rode out from the dense garden, the attendants opening thick iron gates, the lumas' hoofs resounding against the cobbles and the close walls of the city's streets like pounding hammers, and blue-white sparks flew in their wake.

The dragons along his arms rippled in the wind, seeming to come alive, dancing across his body to the music of their movement. Matsu, riding just ahead of him, cried out frequently, guiding her mount and warning the crowds clogging the streets. Dark figures scrambled hastily from their path, pointing and murmuring, their words jumbled and lost in the swift passage.

Into the dark labyrinth of the delta, the port area less jammed with people but with narrower, twisting streets. Then, all at once, they broke from the confinement of the alleys of the bund, purple and black and deep red in the last of the sun, a minute crescent now against the unmarred horizon as it heaved its bulk into the welcoming embrace of the singing sea.

Along the wooden boards of the bund they raced, the kubarus' songs a spice on the salt air. He inhaled the scents of the sea, pungent drying fish, the cloying sweetness of the poppy's syrup, and the violet faces of the harrtin with their wide verandas, impassively observing the end of another day, swept by them in majestic array.

Until, abruptly, they were alone on the sand, the curving, darkling beach stretching before them in exultant desolation, and Ronin's luma lifted its head in an unmistakable sound of pleasure and triumph, calling, galloping, galloping, the sea to the left now cinnabar solid in the last of the red light, and he felt a tremendous jolt of adrenalin, as if he were joining battle, and his heart thudded and, as his steed leapt over a dark dune, its crest as sinuous as a snake, he unsheathed his sword and lifted it towards the cold pinpoints of light just becoming visible and he thought, Let The Dolman come. I welcome now the Makkon's freezing embrace, for surely I am its nemesis, I am its slayer.

And he rode on into the deepening dusk with Matsu at his side, her shadowed face impassive, thinking her unfathomable thoughts.

When the hazy golden lights of Sha'angh'sei were but a smear behind them, Matsu broke off and called to him, into the singing wind rolling in off the turbulent sea, alive with green and blue phosphorescence.

'I must leave you here, Ronin. Ride on. The luma will take you unerringly.'

'But what – '

She was gone, had already wheeled her mount, its hoofs but a whisper against the sand in the night, and he shrugged, dug his heels into the luma's flanks as she had instructed him, and it leapt forward. He concentrated on its power, the concordant rippling of its muscles, the thin film of sweat slickening its rich coat, and then it was slowing, snorting and bobbing its head as if telling him of something ahead.

He peered into the darkness and heard the luma's prancing steps before he saw its silhouette looming up before him. All at once he was close enough to see that it was of a deep saffron with a black mane.

Astride it sat Kiri. The lustrous violet eyes stared back at him. She flicked her head and he saw the unmistakable lines of her proud face. Her long dark hair was unbound, streaming in the wind. It was held back from her face by a narrow band of yellow topaz. She wore a pale yellow robe with golden flowers embroidered upon it in the most intricate pattern. It was different from all the others he had ever seen but he could not tell why.

'Kiri,' he said almost breathlessly, the wind moaning between them, 'I thank you for this present. It gives me great pleasure to ride.'

She smiled. 'It suits you well, the luma, and I am told that it welcomed you immediately; they are not easily tamed, the luma.'

'Yes, but how in –'

'Come!' she called over the shifting sand, pulling on her reins. 'Ride with me, my warrior.'

And over the undulating dunes, by the shore of the crashing luminescent sea, they flew, chill white spray thrown up by the lumas' flashing hoofs, sparkling their hair and faces. Her feet were bare, digging into the creature's flanks, spurring it on.

'Kiri,' he called. 'What of the Council? What trick have you played on me?'

She shook her head, hair like a vast fan. 'No trick. Only the truth.' Her pale face turned to him. 'If I had told you, you would not have believed me.' The sea crashed around them as they sped into the yellow surf. He could hear the jangle of the bits, the creak of their saddles very clear on the cold air. 'The Council is an elaborate myth. It is best for the people to believe that a body rules their lives and governs the city. But the truth is that no such Council could exist here and survive. Sha'angh'sei would not tolerate it.'

'You talk as if the city were alive.'

She nodded. 'There is no other place in all the world like it. Yes, a Council of the factions makes sense here only as thought. In reality, they would tear each other apart.'

'Who sees the people who wait for audience in the walled city?'

'They see me, when they see anyone at all.'

He stared at her, back erect, hair billowing, eyes like wells out of time.

'You? But why? Do you lead a faction within Sha'angh'sei?'

She laughed then, deep and long, a delightful sound, the wind carrying her melodious voice into the reaches of the night.

'No, my warrior, not a faction.'

Surf sprayed along the lumas' flanks so that they gleamed in the phosphorescence. She dug her heels into her mount and she sped ahead, over the sighing dunes, their white crests shifting, and he took the water route, cutting across a crescent cove, the sea flaring outward like wings in his wake. The stars seemed very close at that moment.

He broke from the surf, his steed's coat fire red now, as deeply crimson as a hurled torch, hearing her startling cry, 'Not a faction, oh no. Only one can rule. Into one's hands is delivered the ultimate power.' Her face a platinum and onyx helm in the cold light. 'It is I, Ronin. I am the Empress of Sha'angh'sei.'

The night was an expert shroud. Somewhere, water dripped dolefully. The lamps were unlit and no one came to relight them. A strident argument raged from an open window on the second storey overhead. There was a slap and a brief cry. Silence. He crouched in a doorway, cloaked in shadow, still and watchful. A dog howled and he heard the pad of its paws. The sharp odour of sweat as two women reeled by, laughing, their robes held together by unsteady hands; the momentary glow of white skin. Then the street was quite deserted.

The gates opened at their approach and he inhaled the humid perfume of the green velvet garden, black now in the night, for only after they had dismounted and their glistening luma were led away, snorting and prancing, was a tiny torch lit.

The lushness was overwhelming after the barren beauty of the white sand and black sky. He breathed the jasmine air, listened to the myriad rustlings all around him.

Yellow insects dancing in the torchlight as she moved towards him. The silence was startling and he put a hand out to stop her. After a moment the nocturnal noises commenced again.

She took his hand, her face a pale oval, wreathed by the trembling forest of her hair, and they walked across the grass, through a maze of hedges reaching far above their heads, past whispering firs, scented and jewelled with dew, to the other side of the garden. She dropped the torch and smothered the flame. They were in total darkness and the small sounds were suddenly amplified as vision went to nil. His pupils expanded. They stood before a blank stone building. A recessed door stood ajar and she bade him enter. He turned on the threshold.

'Kiri, why did Tuolin suggest I seek out the Council?'

She shrugged. 'Perhaps he wished to give you hope.'

'But there is no Council.'

'I hardly think that Tuolin would know that.'

'Are you sure?'

'Reasonably. Why?'

'I – do not know. For a moment I thought – '

'Yes?'

'Why should he leave so unexpectedly?'

'Soldiers are governed by their own time. He left because he was summoned early.'

'Of course. You must be right.'

He turned. They were in a black corridor.

'Walk straight ahead,' she said from behind him. 'There are no turnings.'

Still he kept his eyes moving.

'The woman you brought in is much better. She is up and wanting to help the girls. Her recovery has been remarkably swift.'

'What has she told you?'

'Nothing.'

'Nothing at all?'

'She is mute.'

'I would like to see her.'

'Certainly. Matsu has told her about you. She wants to thank – '

He staggered and almost fell, the breath lost inside of him, sucked away. Before him was light, an abrupt end to the blackness, and what he saw was an immense hall built all of streaked marble, yellow and pink and black, the arched, gilt roof supported by twelve pillars, six on each side. The muraled walls were dusky in the light from golden braziers hung at intervals, watery and flowing in their depiction of strange, beautiful women and men, golden-skinned, sapphire-haired, tall and lithe. He blinked and forced his lungs to work.

'What is it?' Her hands on his shoulders.

'I have seen this place before.' Voice thick and furry.

'Oh, but that is impossible. You – '

'I have been here before, Kiri – '

'Ronin – '

'Will be here again, I know that now. Believe me, I know this place. In the City of Ten Thou-

248

sand Paths, in the house of dor-Sefrith, the great magus of Ama-no-mori – '

He had waited long enough. He went cautiously across the street, from shadow to shadow, and when he stood beneath the stone jar his sword was out.

He went in quickly and silently, leading with his right shoulder to present the smallest target. The stench of the shop's supplies of potions and powders was heavily in the air and he knew even before he looked that the bottles and jars and phials were lying smashed on the floor, their mysterious contents spilled darkly, lying in small mounds and thick streaks, mingled in arcane combinations, drifting on the night wind.

He found the apothecary against the side of the counter in back, spread-eagled, the blade of an axe protruding like an obscene growth from the frail chest. Ronin tried to pull him down but the blade had gone entirely through him, impaling him to the wood. Ronin pulled at the haft and it came away, the body sliding limply down into the dry rivers of powders littering the floor.

Ronin stared at where the old man had hung. Along the wood were two dark streaks in the shape of an inverted V, as if he had been trying to write some message in his own blood as it gushed from him, life ebbing away.

The last hope gone now, the scroll useless and nothing to stop The Dolman, the death of man assured, and his blade was a silver arc and he felt the bite and heard the scream at the same instant.

He hacked through both legs and an axe fell heavily to the floor. Creakings as of weight on the floor boards and there was movement all around him. He whirled and thrust obliquely, short and chopping, the blade biting deeply, then, reversing the momentum of his thrust, used the opposite edge to slice into another man's neck. Hot blood spurted at his face and he moved away from the bodies dancing frenziedly as they died.

They rushed him now, lunging for his sword arm, and he swung, fingers dismembered, hands split like butchered meat, but there were far too many, they were taking no chances, and at length they had it and pulled him down to the airless floor. Forearms along his windpipe. He struggled but his hands and legs were pinioned and, lungs labouring, finding no oxygen, he began to tumble down an endless escarpment of sand into a black land where sickle-bladed axes grew like uncut wheat from crimson corpses.

'We are not greedy souls.'

Tourmaline hung in the smoke.

'We are what we must be.'

Red green brown, its facets winked dully in the pearled glow.

'What history decreed we become.'

The blue haze, frozen, rose and fell like the swell and suck of the sea.

'Pawns.'

There was a raucous burst of laughter bubbling like the release of water under pressure.

'Oh my. Oh my.' Voice deep and heavy.

Tourmaline dancing in multicoloured splendour, a miniature sun upon the convex surface.

'Yes. We are the result of an unforgiving past. Hurled this way and that by the necessities of our land. Did we arise before the need for us had arisen? Could we?'

Tourmaline sun shaking against its quivering sky.

He had fat cheeks and heavy jowls which wobbled when he laughed. Wide flat nose, cheekbones lost in flesh guarding long almond eyes of a cobalt blue. No neck, his billiard head stuck to his massive shoulders and bare chest, deep green robe open to the waist. His mouth was small and delicate.

'We were formed from the minds of our gods, in centuries too distant to calculate, for the protection of our people, to guard the wealth of the land.'

He was sitting in a wicker chair, its high back curving up and out like the questing necks of some monstrous and headless creatures, mindless twins.

'To destroy the Reds!'

A massive arm lifted, fell to the wicker with a sharp snap.

'To undermine the power of the rikkagin. To take vengeance on all who come within our precincts seeking only wealth. Thieves and worse. Murderers.'

The cobalt eyes shifted their focus.

'Our price is high, yes; and it is met every hour of every day and night within the borders of Sha'angh'sei. We are paid to protect those who live like frightened ants within the walled city. Yet the walled city is ours if we so wished. The fat hongs deliver up to us the tariffs we request. The rikkagin, who grow rich on the war to the north, pay us taels of silver on the last day of each month – ' The eyes flashed. 'How I hate them! How I work to defeat them. It is not enough to take their money, no, not nearly. Infiltrate, am I not correct?'

There was a noise. The eyes peered down in front of him.

'Has he heard, do you think?'

He made a motion with his hand, a flicker of movement, and Ronin was drenched with sea water, chill and fecund with microscopic life. The salt burned in his wounds but it cleared his head. He groaned again.

'We wish you to be fully conscious,' said the immense man.

Ronin broke his bleary gaze from the tourmaline around the man's neck. He was in a room whose walls were constructed of bamboo, coated in a clear lacquer so that they gleamed in the low lamplight. There were no windows but overhead a skylight was open to the clear night.

'You have caused us many deaths, brought grief to many women and their families.' He sighed. 'We are the Ching Pang. The Greens.' His hands reached into his robe. Something sparkled in the air and dropped in front of Ronin. 'There.'

It was the silver necklace he had taken off the dead man in the alley and which T'ung had taken from him at the gate of the walled city. He stared at the tiny silver blossom, wiping the salt water from his eyes, and for an instant he fancied he heard the tolling of far-off bells, the muted call of a horn, seeing again the lazy fish in the perfect garden of that mysterious temple, lost now within the maze of Sha'angh'sei. Eternity.

'Tell us who you are. Who sent you to Sha'angh'sei?'

Ronin coughed, put his hand up to his throat. He swallowed experimentally.

'Not the Reds, surely. They know less of the sakura than we do.'

'I know nothing of this necklace.'

'That is a lie. You attacked Ching Pang in the alley, trying to save your friend.'

'Who?'

'The man in black.' The voice was patient, an uncle speaking to a mischievous child.

'I saw someone being attacked by many men. I went to help him.'

The immense man laughed.

'I have no doubt. Stupid to expose yourself to us so openly. You underestimate us. Why were you sent here?'

'I came to Sha'angh'sei to seek the answer to a riddle.'

'Where did you come from?'

'The north.'

'Liar. There are savages only to the north.'

'I am not of this land.'

'And the sakura.'

'I do not know what you want.'

The immense man looked with pity upon Ronin and then lifted his eyes.

'T'ung, it is time for you to do what you must do.'

'Shall I kill him first?'

'No, but be content, that will come later.'

'I want him.'

'Yes, of course you do. But first you will take him with you.'

'But – I – '

'Let him witness it.'

They moved stealthily through the twisting, refuse-strewn alleys of the city, deep in shadows where no night lanterns shone, where the sweet smoke drifted through the air and the rattle of gaming dice was an intermittent atonal tattoo.

He went with four of them. T'ung and two other Greens garbed in deep blue, axe blades sheathed in black fabric so as not to reflect. They had with them a man with lustreless skin and bright burning eyes, whose body trembled with fear and who ceaselessly implored them to spare him. His hands were bound to a short bamboo pole behind him.

T'ung, ever by Ronin's side, had whispered to him, 'If you attempt to cry out, I will stuff a rag in your mouth. This is Du-Sing's order. I would slit your belly now, if I could. But I am a patient man. My time will come when we return.'

The shadows were endless as they moved silently through the replicating alleys in the night. A dog barked throatily. There was the sound of someone urinating against a wall close by, curiously distinct. They heard distant laughter, the thrumming of nocturnal hoofs, a tense and enervating noise. They walked through the litter of the tiny animals who screeched briefly at the disturbance.

'Where are we bound?' said Ronin, careful to keep his voice down.

T'ung smashed him just above his ear.

He called softly to the Green leading the way and they turned to the right, into a dimly lit street, residential, a fairly wealthy area.

They approached a house and one of the Greens produced a bowl of rice from beneath his cloak. The man's eyes bulged at the sight and the other Green was obliged to hold him.

Carefully, ritually, the first Green set the bowl of rice onto the street directly in front of the steps leading up to the front door. Then he rose, produced a pair of sticks, bent again, setting them beside the bowl. He turned and, bowing to T'ung, went and stood beside Ronin.

Swiftly T'ung moved to the side of the squirming man, slammed his fists into the hinges of his jaws so that they gaped open in reflex. His left hand moved into the mouth, the fingers expertly grasping the slippery tongue while the right hand flashed upward. The glint of naked metal. The man was about to gag and the blade had already slashed through his tongue. Blood spurted, black in the dimness of the street, and the man's head whipped about. Terrible guttural sounds issued from him like an animal pathetically attempting to mimic human speech.

Again the dagger rose and flashed forward and the man's head recoiled horribly and the mouth redoubled its efforts to scream. The Green gripped the dripping hair and the blade came up for the third ghastly time. Then the Green let go of the head and it bounced back and forth as if on a spring. The maimed face came up and stared sightlessly at Ronin, two black holes, wet and shiny, running with blood and ribbons of viscera.

T'ung nodded and the Green unsheathed his axe, arcing it down, severing the tendons at the backs of the man's knees, so that the body folded in on itself and he was forced to kneel in the dust of the street. He fell over into his own blood.

T'ung bent and arranged the tongue and eye-balls on their bed of rice as if they were savory delicacies to be consumed by the most discerning of gourmets. When he had finished, the Green placed the body of the man next to the bowl and sticks.

The Green who stood beside Ronin handed T'ung an immaculate yellow silk cloth as he came up. T'ung wiped his hands.

'He knew many things,' he said to Ronin when

he was quite close. He handed the cloth back. 'But he said them to the wrong people.'

He shoved Ronin and they all vanished into the alley from which they had moments before emerged and were swallowed up by the Sha'angh'sei night.

'You see how unfortunate it is,' said Du-Sing. 'We who are the protectors of Sha'angh'sei must rule it by fear. It is an imperative of this city, a given rule, if you will, which we view simply as another fact of our existence. There are no two ways about it. Fear cuts through all boundaries. If you say to a kubaru, "Tell us what we wish to know or we shall be forced to cut off your foot," why then he will respond because, without his foot, he cannot work the poppy fields and thus feed his family. Similarly, if you say to a rikka-gin, "Tell us or we shall cut off your sword hand," what do you imagine his answer will be?' He laughed, his fat face jiggling.

Then Du-Sing's face took on a sorrowful edge. 'It is the hongs and the rikkagin and the Canton priests spewing their soulless filth who rob the people of Sha'angh'sei. Yet it is the Ching Pang which gains the reputation of thieves, murderers, and evil men.' His fat hands clapped together. 'Nothing could be further from the truth!'

'Is that justification for what T'ung and these others just did?' asked Ronin.

'Justification?' cried Du-Sing. 'We require no justification here. We do what must be done. No one else will do it. And this city must survive. Through us it does.' He settled himself more comfortably in his wicker chair. 'You were shown that as a moral lesson. You are drawing breath now under our sufferance.' He drew out the silver necklace. 'Where is yours?' he snapped suddenly.

'I have only seen that one,' replied Ronin.

'Did you bury it, perhaps?'

'I have only seen that one.'

'Is your mission in Sha'angh'sei the same as the other's?'

'I never heard of this city until I was fished out of the water.'

'Is that where you met the man?'

'I never saw him before – '

'There are many ways to induce the truth from you and T'ung knows them all. I need not remind you how eager he is to have you all to himself.'

'The truth has already been spoken.'

'Spoken like a true hero,' said Du-Sing sarcastically. 'Are you so stupid as to believe that we lack the skills to break you?'

'No. You will eventually find a way and then I shall be forced to tell you a lie so that you will kill me.'

'The truth is all that we require.'

Ronin laughed shortly. 'That and my life. I am not a kubaru or a fat hong whom your threats can affect. I am not of this city. I do not hold you or the Ching Pang in reverential awe as all do in Sha'angh'sei. You are nothing to me.' He stared at the deep blue eyes, which had not blinked for the longest time. 'And besides, this is all academic. Tomorrow's handwriting is already on the wall. All your carefully built networks of power will be for nought if The Dolman cannot be stopped.'

T'ung stirred behind him. 'Such foolishness is –'

A flicker of Du-Sing's heavy hand stopped him. The blue eyes blinked and within the instant Ronin thought he could detect a hint of some emotion quite foreign to Du-Sing flickering uncertainly in those depths.

'He knows of the Bujun,' said T'ung. 'I know it. He can tell us –'

'Silence!' roared Du-Sing. 'Fool! Do you wish your tongue ripped from your mouth?' He made a great effort to calm himself. 'Have Chei send in four men,' he said after a time.

T'ung went to the door and spoke softly to a Green standing just outside. When he returned, Du-Sing looked up at him and said: 'Now give him his sword.'

Ripple like liquid silver. One, then two in the lamplight. Cold and hard and honed. Whistle of curved blades swinging through the air, the hot pungency of sweat and animal fear. Ripple along the periphery of his vision. Light squirting across the double edges of his long blade causing his heart to soar, the adrenalin pumping again, the brain thinking in rapid-fire bursts. Double. Thrust and reverse.

They did not understand, their style was different and adaptation takes time. He did not give it to them. A blade scythed upward at him and he deflected it out and away, reversing simultaneously, his own blade biting into the flesh of the Green behind him on the vicious downswipe. The man cried out as the blood spurted from his side. He stumbled and fell.

Ronin whirled as he felt an axe nick his shoulder, ripping into his robe. His sword thrust forward, scraping along the curving blade, and blue sparks flew. He parried two more blows before lunging in under an oblique swipe, thrusting with the point, spitting a Green through the mid-section. The man went to his knees as Ronin withdrew, his shaking hands clutching at the ooze, trying vainly to stem the flow. The stench of death thickened the air.

He was out of position now and the third man slammed his blade against Ronin's sword and it all but flew from his hands. The axe came at him again and he went to his knees in parrying the jarring blow. His sword flashed again and again but he could not regain his feet, so profuse were the slashes raining upon him. He waited patiently for an opening and when it came, an instant when his opponent reached back to deliver the killing blow which would break through Ronin's defense, he used his blade vertically, driving upward with all his strength. He caught the man under the chin, the tip biting deep. He jammed it in, through the throat and into the brain. The body jerked, arms flying out wildly as if the man were attempting to fly. The mouth gaped open and bits of pink and grey spattered out. The corpse convulsed as if trying to throw off a tremendous weight and the axe skittered along the floor.

Ronin ripped his sword through the head and dropped, rolling across the room until his back was against a lacquered bamboo wall. The fourth man moved towards him but T'ung caught him by the arm and, staring at Ronin, said, 'He is mine. Stay away.'

T'ung advanced on Ronin then, crouching, his gleaming axe blade swinging. He came in low, aiming for the knees, wanting to cripple first and then kill, and Ronin got his own blade down barely in time. As it was, the sickle came away with skin and a film of blood.

T'ung feinted right, came in on the left. The blow was deceptively sluggish and he got in behind Ronin's guard, the crescent of sharp metal rushing towards the collarbone. Ronin was in no position to block the attack so he swatted at the axe with his gauntleted hand.

The blade made contact and T'ung's eyes widened as, instead of slicing through flesh into bone, it was deflected harmlessly.

Ronin saw the look and immediately dropped his sword, lunging for T'ung with the gauntlet. Light spun off the scales as his hand went in. He slammed the right arm to get the axe out of the way and his fist hammered at T'ung's windpipe.

The eyes bulged, the tongue came out in reflex and the axe dropped.

T'ung tried to get his hands inside Ronin's arms so that he would have the leverage but Ronin would not let him. The gauntlet, balled into a fist, slammed into T'ung's face and his cheekbone shattered. He screamed and his head twisted. His hands scrabbled along the floor for his axe. The remaining Green moved to give it to him but stopped at a motion from Du-Sing. Again Ronin smote him, visions of the dark alley and the pleading and teeth cracked under the force of the blow, the lower jaw smashed and hanging, eyeless sockets like the gates of hell and a mouth that could not speak, and he drove in again with a kind of black joy and the nose a pulpy mass spread over the crimson face.

Then he was rolling off and grasping the hilt of his sword all in one motion, moving in on the last Green, the balanced weight in his right hand like holding lightning.

And now he moved in, the blade a humming instrument of destruction, hacking at his opponent with the blood singing in his ears and his vision pulsing with the power welling up, shooting through his arms, his skin gleaming with sweat and sea salt, rippling as if a serpent reared beneath his skin.

Terrified, the Green retreated, and then he stumbled, his axe coming up centimetres to the right of where it should have been, and Ronin's blurred blade, pulsing platinum along its length, screamed

262

downward and clove his head in two. The body leapt into the humid air like a speared fish and he whirled, the blur a halo of death surrounding him.

One step, two, the corpse jerked as if it were still alive and as it crumpled to the slick floor Ronin scooped up the fallen silver necklace. He raced for the door and, picking up momentum, crashed into the Green just outside, sending him flying.

Chei came through the door, axe over his head.

Du-Sing made a brief gesture. 'Leave him.' And then, after a moment, 'Close the door and come here.'

Chei went through the carnage, stepping carefully across the outflung corpses, thinking of the dangerous man. Crimson dripped along the shining bamboo, beading like bright tears of pain.

Du-Sing rubbed at his eyes with his thick hand, waiting for Chei's return.

'Summon a runner,' he said slowly, 'and an escort of three Ching Pang. Our best. You will go with them.' He stared at the man in front of him. 'I wish you to take a message to Lui Wu.'

'But, Du-Sing, you cannot mean that you will now – '

'Yes. That is precisely what I mean to do. I am contacting the taipan of the Hung Pang.'

'The Reds,' breathed Chei, and there was only wonderment on his face as he gazed upon the cold blue eyes of Du-Sing.

He was not running from the Greens. It was not in his nature and, too, he felt that somehow they were not a danger to him now. Not after what he had seen in Du-Sing's eyes. The man knew of The Dolman, or at least that the war to the north was no longer what it had been for so many centuries.

Nonetheless, he ran through the torpid Sha'angh'sei night, down back streets filled with slumbering families and roaming yellow dogs, skin ribboned with jutting ribs, through the wider thoroughfares where nocturnal revellers staggered and moaned and vomited, sodden with drink and lust and the smoke of the city's notorious pleasure houses, coughing and shaking as with a fever, kissing, pressed together against filthy brick and wood walls, fighting with bleeding fists and crusty knives, locked within the penultimate stages of arguments whose beginnings had already been forgotten. A woman screamed somewhere in the jasmine night, a piercing shriek abruptly cut off, and at last he knew that it did not matter where the sound came from.

And he ran on, his lungs on fire, his legs pumping on their own, desperation sweeping over him as he headed toward Okan Road. His mind was filled with a succession of minute details, words and events and hints which he had absorbed but which had been floating in the back of his mind. Separately, they were meaningless, yet as pieces of a whole they held a terrifying imperative. Oh, Kiri, like a song in his dazzled brain, as he slipped through the crowded labyrinth of streets.

And at last Sha'angh'sei came alive for him, a glowing throbbing entity with a corporeal existence of its own. As he rushed through its sinuous entrails, filled with naked thighs and almond eyes, thrusting breasts and canted hips passing him by, pouting lips, drowsing children and petty thieves sharing the same oblique bars of shadows comfortable in the blackness, he felt its presence like a lover's body, hot and moist, exciting and frightening, possessive and insatiable, and the mingling of triumph and terror was overwhelming within him.

The Okan Road was perfectly silent in the unlight of predawn, the tall trees still and calm, the night sounds of the city seemingly far away, as if they belonged to another time, some dimly perceived future perhaps, voices chiming in the slow changing of the centuries.

Up the gracefully curving stairway he flew, reaching the top and pounding on the massive yellow doors. When they opened, he clutched at the wide-eyed woman, panting, 'Kiri, where is she?'

She recognized him of course and stayed the guards who would otherwise have attempted to restrain him, taking him to the room of tawny light and then leaving him hurriedly.

He prowled among the settees and tables, searching anxiously for some wine, but as usual it had all been put away. He turned as the woman came down the staircase.

'She will be with you.'

Relief flooded him and he allowed himself to relax somewhat and he opened up his breathing to oxygenate his system.

Then she was on the stairs, slender and lithe, black hair falling around her, and for a moment she seemed to be someone else. Then he gazed into her violet eyes, platinum flecks swimming in their depths.

'What has happened to you?' She came down the stairs quickly, with an economy of movement. 'Are you hurt?'

He glanced down at his torn and bloody robe.

'Hurt? No, I do not think so.' He looked up. 'Do you know Du-Sing?'

She stared at him. 'Where have you heard that name?'

'Greens were waiting for me at the apothecary's. They took me to him.'

'Yet you are not dead.' She looked surprised. 'He thought you had information. But what kind – '

Ronin sighed. 'In the alley that evening when I fought the Greens, remember, I told you – '

She waved a hand, flowing lavender along her nails. 'Yes, go on.'

'I took a silver chain from around the dead man's neck. It was an impulse only. That was the basis of my altercation with the Greens at the walled city.'

'You showed it to them.'

'Like a fool. Trying to buy my way into seeing the Council.'

'It would be funny if it was not so serious.'

'Yes, well – '

'What is the chain's importance?'

'It holds a silver flower. The "sakura," Du-Sing called it.'

'I – '

He held up a hand. 'I will show it to you when there is more time. Right now I must see the woman I brought to you. Moeru.'

'But it is so late. I do not want to wake her.'

'Kiri – '

She smiled. 'All right, but then you must tell me what Du-Sing wanted. And about the man in the alley – '

'Come on,' he said.

She led the way upstairs into one of the rooms along the dim corridor. They went in and she lit the lamp on the wooden table beside the wide bed.

She was quite beautiful, he saw now. Stripped of the filth and mud and pain, dusky face in repose, with days and nights of food and rest behind her, Moeru was lovely. Her long oval eyes and wide mouth gave her face the openness of innocence, a child asleep in a distant land.

Kiri bent over her. Her eyes came open and she stared at Ronin. He saw the wild open sea.

'This is the man who saved you, Moeru. Matsu told you about him.'

The woman nodded and reached out a slim hand. They had cut and polished her ragged nails and they had already begun to grow shiny and translucent with clear lacquer. She touched his hand, stroked the back of it. He watched her mouth, but the coral lips did not move. Mute from birth, he thought.

'Moeru, I must ask you to do something for me. It is very important. Will you do it?'

She nodded.

'Pull down the bedcovers,' he said.

Kiri watched him silently.

Moèru did as she was told. She was naked. Skin like burnished gold. Perhaps a trace of olive. Her body was as beautiful as her face, firm and rounded and sensual.

'Has the bandage been changed?'

'You asked Matsu that it not be,' Kiri said.

'Moeru, I will take the bandage off now.'

The long blue-green eyes regarded him placidly. She opened her legs.

Ronin reached between them, fingers on her warm thigh. A muscle jumped under her skin at the contact. He pulled carefully at the dirty fabric, a bulge against her inner thigh. He looked at her legs. Apart, they formed the configuration of an inverted V. He lifted the bandage from her thigh. Beneath it, nestled within the cloth, was the man-shaped root.

Moeru stroked her thigh where the bandage had come off, then covered herself.

'She had no wound under the poultice, Ronin,' said Kiri.

'Yes, I know. The old apothecary used that as a ruse to hide this.' He showed her the root.

'What is it?'

'The root of all good,' he said with a laugh. 'Or of all evil.'

The scream came then, filled with terror and something more, and he bolted out the door with Kiri just behind him. Down the hall he ran, his ears questing ahead for sounds of scuffling. Then he smelled the stench and felt even through the closed door the unutterable cold.

He stopped.

'No,' moaned Kiri. 'Oh no.'

And he did not understand until he had flung the door open and was already within the room. Then the enormity of his error hit him and he cursed aloud and, brandishing his sword, slammed the door shut behind him. Kiri pounded on it from the other side. He ignored her, concentrating on the thing in front of him.

It was over three meters in height with thick powerful legs, short, twisted, hoofed. Its upper limbs were much longer, with six-fingered hands tipped by curved talons.

Its head was monstrous. Baleful alien eyes, the orange pupils no more than vertical slits below which protruded obscenely a short curving beak opening and closing spastically. The creature pulsed unsteadily, its outline ebbing and flowing. A tail whipped behind it.

It turned to look at him and a short eerie cry broke from its beak. It threw the remains of what

269

must once have been a man at him, a broken pink and white husk.

Ronin moved easily out of the way but it had Matsu and his stomach contracted again because he should have known. He had been with Matsu, not Kiri, that night when the Makkon came to Tenchō and killed Sa. *Thee*, The Dolman had called in his mind. *Thee*. Thus had he raced to return to Tenchō, less concerned with Du-Sing and the Greens than he was with the revelation that the Makkon had been searching for him that night and that it would surely return soon. He had thought only of Kiri, with whom he had been so much lately, and now he saw the look in Matsu's eyes and his heart cried out in sudden pain.

His lips moved, calling softly her name.

The Makkon cried out again and its taloned fist slammed into her hip and she screamed in pain as her pelvis cracked and white bone pushed itself through her soft flesh.

'Matsu.'

Ronin rushed the Makkon now, nauseated by its awful stench, his unprotected face already beginning to numb from its unearthly chill. He yelled reflexively as the pain raced through him, his blade sliding off its scaly hide.

The hideous beak opened and a peculiar sound filled the room, a dreadful laughter, and the thing brushed Ronin aside with a lightning motion, moving towards the open window and the were-light of predawn.

The whistle came then, high-pitched and piercing, echoing in his mind, and the Makkon fell silent. The sound came again, insistent now. The Makkon screamed in fury, wrenched at Matsu's arm, ripping it from its socket, and as Ronin advanced, still dazed from the mighty blow, the thing reached up and slowly, deliberately, tore her throat out, all the pale flesh of her body running red now, and the Makkon threw her at him finally as it went swiftly out the window.

Ronin staggered as she came into his arms. Too late, he thought numbly, why did I not think of the gauntlet? He stared down at her crimson corpse, oblivious to the renewed pounding at the door, did not even turn around when it splintered and flew open.

He knelt in the centre of the room, a cold wind blowing over him, cradling all that was left of Matsu. Only when a shadow dropped across his face did he look up to behold Kiri in breastplate of deep yellow lacquered leather, high polished boots, and light leather leggings.

She went straight to the window and looked out. She gasped as she saw through the dawn's deep haze the hideous orange beacons, pulsing, the snapping beak with its thick grey tongue.

The Makkon screamed again.

And Ronin, clutching the chill frame to him as if he could prevent the life from leaking from her, thought of the night he had held her close, feeling the delicious warmth seep into his body, listening to her speak as he watched the slow wheel of the stars in the glowing heavens. Again and again, bound upon a tortuous circlet. Are my feelings so well hidden? Ah, Chill take me.

Surely, he thought, I am a doomed man.

4

Hart of Darkness

'Strange,' she said, reining in her mount.

To their right the sky was pearled lavender, the sun still but a ghost ascending behind the morning's thick haze. To the north and west it was not yet light.

Their luma snorted and stamped at the earth, eager to be galloping before the wind again. Sha'angh'sei was a sprawl at their backs, a dirty smudge stretching, entangled, to the sea.

They were on a hill burned brown by the sun which overlooked the wide snaking river whose mouth Ronin had glimpsed when first he sailed into port aboard Rikkagin T'ien's ship. It was deep, turbulent in spots, quiet and sluggish in others. It ran out from the edge of the city at seaside almost due north. The Makkon was following its path and they it.

'What is it?' asked Ronin.

She turned to look at him, her long hair trailing across her face.

'The autumn wind is blowing,' she said.

He felt the strong gusts, chill and damp, plucking at their cloaks, shivering the lines of tall slender pines.

'What of it?'

There was a curious cast to her face caused perhaps by the oblique light.

'It is,' she said softly, 'the season of high summer.'

'You are going after it and I am coming with you.'

He was about to say no but he saw across her visage the play of stormy emotions. She was beyond weeping, her face a white mask of hatred.

'I want to tell you something – ' His chest hurt as if he had been struck down.

'There is no need.' The sound of bitter tears, the clash of gleaming metal.

'I do not understand. You cannot know – '

'I can and I do.' She turned to the window, the budding light strange and spectral still. 'Matsu was more than sister to me. More than daughter.'

'What then?'

'If I told you, you would think me mad.'

They sped through the new day, the light quickening around them like molten metal, the winds of autumn whipping at their cloaks. Kiri's unbound hair swept behind her like the tail of some mythical creature, half animal, half human.

Over the bleak countryside they raced, past the long level fields of marshy plants in precise rows down which myriad kubaru women and men in wide-brimmed straw hats, skirts gathered and tied about their waists, waded, bent almost double as they plucked the raw rice. Along the shooting waters of the river as it sliced ever northward toward the death and destruction of the war, its banks wide and brown with mud and silt, precious minerals thrown up to nourish the far-flung fields.

After the Makkon they flew and Ronin, glancing at Kiri, the noble profile with its firm nose and high cheekbones, failed to notice the movement behind them, as a pursuing luma kept pace with them.

By midday the land had swallowed them and all vestiges of civilization, all habitation and settlement, seemed a thing of the past. The remnants of the alluvial delta which was the source of much of Sha'angh'sei's material wealth had long since dropped away. The terrain became increasingly dry and rocky, undulating in ever higher waves, like a storm-tossed ocean.

There was little vegetation now. Brown and green plants, scraggy and deformed, grew here and there among the chunky rocks, hanging on tenaciously for whatever nourishment they could find. The earth was drier and coarser and ran before them in a gentle incline, rising higher the farther they got from the sea.

Once, to the east, they spied a long line of soldiers marching northward, a supply train of horses to the rear, horsemen to the front, kicking up long plumes of dust. They spurred their mounts onward and soon left the column far behind.

Sun still shone to the south but overhead and to the north billowing grey clouds were roiling.

'Tell me now what Du-Sing wished from you.'

275

Ronin shrugged. 'He wanted something that I could not give him. I know nothing of the sakura.'

'And what of the man in the alley?'

'He had been struck by Greens, perhaps four of them, maybe more. I went to his aid.'

'What did he look like?'

His head came around and he thought, Ah.

'Now why would you ask that?'

'It is a natural question.'

He shook his head. 'Not really.'

She smiled. 'All right. I have a reason. Will you tell me now?'

He contemplated her for a moment, watching her hair brush her cheeks. It reminded him of Matsu. Her hair would –

'He – did not look like the Sha'angh'sei people and he did not look like my people. But it was difficult to see because of the light – '

'His skin was yellow?'

'Yes.'

'And his face?'

'Black eyes. High cheekbones.'

'Let me see the chain.' She took it, saw the silver blossom.

'Bujun.' Her breath an explosive sound.

'The Green, T'ung, mentioned that word and would have gone on but Du-Sing cut him off.'

'Yes, I imagine he would.' She gave the necklace back to him. 'The Bujun are the lost race of man, purportedly the greatest warriors and the elite magi during the ages when sorcerous elements formed the primal elements on the world. The sakura is their symbol. It is a flower which is said to grow only on their isle.'

'What happened to them?'

'No one knows if they actually exist. The stories of the Bujun dropped away sometime during the sorcerous wars. Perhaps Ama-no-mori was destroyed –'

Ronin started.

'Their island is called Ama-no-mori?'

'The floating kingdom, yes.'

'Kiri, the scroll I possess is written in the hand of dor-Sefrith, the most powerful magus of Ama-no-mori.'

'Who told you this?'

'A Magic Man from the Freehold. He had been studying ancient codices which told of the scroll. It was confirmed later by a man I met in the City of Ten Thousand Paths, Bonneduce the Last. Dor-Sefrith is Bujun, there is no doubt.'

'Then the man in the alley was Bujun also. They still live!' Her violet eyes flashed. 'No wonder Du-Sing was so anxious to learn of your involvement. The presence of a Bujun in Sha'angh'sei indicates that their interest in the continent of man will cause the balance of power to change. He wishes the Ching Pang to stay ahead of the Hung Pang.'

Ronin nodded.

'Yes, at first. Now I believe he has other concerns; the same as ours.'

'What do you mean?'

'Du-Sing could have had me killed at any time, yet he did not. All right, it is obvious that he wanted information from me. But he is a shrewd man and at some point he realized that I knew nothing of the sakura – '

'Why should he believe that?'

'I do not think that he had a choice and he knew it. I told him the truth and he was aware that I would not break. I told him then about the coming of The Dolman. And he knew, Kiri!' He slapped the pommel of his saddle. 'The fox knew! You know better than any save Du-Sing himself how extensive his network is. Every caste in Sha'angh'sei is involved with the Ching Pang. He has ten thousand eyes and ears within the city and without. He knows that the war in the north is no longer against the Reds; he understands the rikka-gin's anxiety. They fight that which is non-human. You have already seen the Makkon and what it can do to human life. The traditional lines of enmity which have guided the fates of the Greens and the Reds, and thus Sha'angh'sei itself, have broken at last. The forces of The Dolman have come to the continent of man.'

They had been travelling along a high plateau and this gave now onto a gorge of red rock and dry dust, their luma leaving a vapour trail drifting high above them as they descended. On the plateau behind them came the sky-blue luma, carrying its slim passenger.

They were well into the gorge now. Far to the right, atop a low bluff beyond the perimeter of the red defile, a last row of green pine trees swayed in the gathering wind. Above them, a flock of grey

and brown birds flying high moved swiftly southward before the oncoming clouds. Ronin thought
that he could hear them calling to each other in
shrill cries of longing, but perhaps it was merely
the wind shivering the lonely pines. The desolation
of this land lent their presence the symbolic
strength of eternal guards at the outpost of man.

They wended their way through the gorge,
around huge boulders and stratified shelves of
crimson shale until, at length, they found the way
rising again onto another plateau.

They reined in and Ronin dismounted, stroking
his steed's long neck as he went around it to look
at the tracks. It danced impatiently as he knelt,
fingers moving in the dust. Unmistakable. The
hoofprints of any lesser creature would have been
at least partially obliterated by the wind-swept
dust. But the signs of the Makkon's passage could
not be so easily obscured. At least if it wished to
leave a deliberate trail. *Thee*. An echo in his mind.
Thee.

'Are we gaining?'

He shrugged. 'If it wants us to, then we will.'

He leapt upon his luma and they took off over
the plateau, riding easily, giving their mounts their
heads so that they galloped full out. The creatures
seemed indefatigable, happiest when they pushed
themselves to their limit.

'I would choose the place of battle this time,' he
called to her over the rushing of the wind and the
hard jangle of their riding gear.

'That may not be possible.'
'I know that better than anyone.'

They were aware that the sun was about to set only when the light abruptly began to fade. It had been diffuse for most of the day, grey and vitiated by the thick tumultuous cloud layers that now enveloped all the sky for as far in every direction as they could see.

The land was colourless and shadowless and they had had for some time the peculiar and disquieting sensation of travelling across an endless dreamscape, that they moved not in kilometres but rather in spirit farther and farther from the familiar world of man into the realm of another kind of life that was both more and less than they.

It was dark in the north already when they reached the far edge of the plateau and so rode downward into a vast valley completely engulfed in shadow. They had descended perhaps halfway when Kiri gasped and strained forward in her saddle. She pointed wordlessly ahead.

Below, rushing toward them as they sped over the rubble-strewn slope, was a field of waving flowers, as white as bleached bones. Then the sweet smell flooded over them like a sticky cataract and they were within the meadow.

'Poppies!' Kiri breathed.

The luma shook their heads and called to each other and they lifted high their legs, careful now because they could not see the earth.

It was a sea through which they plunged, rustling with an infectious insistence, white crests and blue troughs caused by the rippling of the blossoms as the wind swept across their illimitable faces.

At that moment the sun broke through a rent in the clouds at the edge of the sky to the west and the sea was stained a lurid purple. That same singular light illuminated before them a hulking shape, rising up as if from the floor of the ocean, a fearsome apparition with lambent orange eyes.

Its outline pulsed as it waded heavily toward them, its long arms swinging, the talons cutting dark swaths in the purple sea. The luma screamed in fear and reared, kicking out their forelegs. Their eyes rolled in their sockets and Kiri yelled to him, 'Dismount! Dismount before it throws you!'

Into the waving poppies they dropped, up around their waists, Kiri's curving sword already out. He waved her back.

'Your blade will hurt it no more than did mine.'

She did not glance at him.

'I must kill it.' Voice like frost as she advanced on the Makkon.

Ronin grabbed at her, held her tightly, his face very near hers. She struggled in his embrace.

'Hear me, Kiri. I know how you feel. The Makkon slew my friend. I have fought it before. Mere metal and muscle are useless against it. It is not of this world and therefore not bound by its laws.' Still she stared over his shoulder at the shambling monstrosity coming towards them.

'Too many have already lost their lives. G'fand, Sa, then Matsu. You will not be the next.'

Her violet eyes were glowing coals in the dusk as she looked at him at last.

'This is not a time for reason; that has fled for all time.' With an effort she broke away from him but he still stood between her and the Makkon. 'I am already half dead,' she cried wildly. 'Oblivion will be heaven if I can take that foul thing with me!'

She came at him and he hit her then, swiftly and compactly and without warning, striking her along the jaw. Just a ripple of movement. He caught her as she fell, thinking, At least you will not die, and gently laid her down in the purple poppies. They danced, whispering, above her still form.

'You cannot kill it,' he said sadly. 'And you also mean something to me.'

The long sword was a heavy weight around his waist, threatening to pull him to the ocean's floor, and he turned, watching the stumbling rush of the Makkon as he unbuckled the belt. The sword fell beside Kiri.

The creature screamed as it recognized him and he heard the luma away behind him calling nervously to each other as he went out to meet it, out from the shallows into the depths of the sighing sea, the strange blossoms caressing his legs, the rich sweet aroma mingling now with the choking stench of the thing.

He came in under the swift sweep of its arms,

his gauntleted hand held before him like a shield. He leapt at the last instant so that his balled fist smashed into its cruelly curved beak. The Makkon howled and he thought that his eardrums had burst. They were hot and blood began to leak from them because of the vibrations but he had opened the beak and was fighting now for leverage in order to force the gauntlet down its throat.

The howling increased in intensity and he was forced to close his eyes to the terrible slitted orbs which hung before his face like hateful crescent moons in an inimical alien sky.

But now as he struggled for purchase on the scaly hide, needles of pain shot through him like shards of broken glass and tears welled up in his eyes, coursing down his cheeks. The cold was so profound that his legs were already numb as they attempted to climb the alien musculature. He began to shake with the pain and his resolve weakened. The beak ground down against the gauntlet and unless he kept up the thrusting pressure it would slip out and he would be as good as dead. Slowly and purposefully it had stood there and torn out her throat, ripe flesh that he had kissed and stroked ruptured now and gouting red and bits of it flying in his face, the taste of her blood, salt and sticky with spume like sea water, and what are we anyway but salt and phosphorus and water like the ocean? And the hate burned at his core and its heat glowed and grew as he banked the fire with the images, forcing himself to remember the details, her blood in his mouth in an abrupt spray, and he yelled silently, bringing the killing power together within him, and he reached up with his arm, though the pain still shook him and water was in his eyes, forcing the gauntlet farther inside.

Then the Makkon's arms came up across his back, the talons seeking his flesh, trying to pry him from its maw. There was no longer air in his lungs and he subsisted from heartbeat to heartbeat, time taken, molded like putty in some monstrous claw, perverted and realigned so that it no longer bore any resemblance to the concept which ruled his world. His heart pounded and he was Outside, his stomach churning in nausea, his back aflame with pain, his legs hanging uselessly, a cripple, and still he persisted, though the numbness now lapped at his brain, an unstoppable crimson tide, and still he strove, long after his last inhalation, his lungs deflating, pulse surging vainly – And he took the last step, all thoughts but one gone, out into the deep.

From his hip, up through his massive shoulders and along his arm, as unyielding now as a forged metal blade, pushing solely by instinct, reasoning at an end, berserk at last, reduced to pure matter, elevated to pure matter. *Survival!* It bellowed through his brain like a firestorm, battering behind his blind eyes, and a warm rain now washing the lining of his body, emanating from his core, the central vortex of which he mercifully had no understanding, and blue lightning ringing the sky above him, gyring across the opening heavens, something feeding him now and, though he was past knowing it, the shaking fist enclosed within the sanctity of the Makkon gauntlet, scales bright with alien saliva, finally slipped past the spasmodically working tongue, breaching the roof of the creature's mouth, driving with inhuman power upward into its eye cavity.

The vibrations became intolerable and he burst apart then into ten thousand fragments, his hot red flesh drifting upon a cool wind which gusted upward in a tenacious spiral, the serpentine breaching the roiling lavender clouds, away, away . . .

First it was the sweetness and then the darkness.

Night had fallen.

He attempted to rise but he seemed incapable of any movement. All about him the susurrations of the poppies. Above him the nodding bell petals.

He rested, concentrating on his breathing, his mind turning over with curiosity each of his senses. Sight, sound, taste, smell, touch: life.

At length able to move his fingers, then his hand, finally his arm. He attempted to sit up. No movement. He explored, found that he could not feel his feet. It was his back then, where the Makkon had enwrapped him.

He called to Kiri but his voice was a quiet croak in the restless meadow. His throat was dry. He heard movement, above and behind him, and he called out again as loudly as he was able and there was a snort, hesitant, questioning. The sounds of the poppies parting, stalks whooshing, and he longed to look but could not.

A long head and wet muzzle were abruptly over him. His luma. Its blue eyes looked at him with intelligence and he whispered to it softly, wordlessly, a crooning singsong as he had heard its attendant talking to it in Kiri's jeweled garden. The luma moved closer, extending its muzzle. He heard its hoofs very close and felt the columns of its strong forelegs almost touching his head. It opened its wide mouth and licked at his face and then lower so that he could drink its saliva. Then it rested its head against his while he spoke to it again, stroking the side of its head, reassuring it.

After a while he slept and the luma stood over him, watchful in the night, its wide nostrils flared for first scent, its triangular ears twitching to pick up any movement. Several times it called to the mare who stood some metres away, over Kiri's sleeping form.

The luma guarded them through the night. But no one came.

And only Ronin heard, deep within his being, below the dreams that played across his mind, the confused jumble of echoing voices, calling, calling in some desperation now, *Have you found him? You must find him. Yes, I will. But if he does not have it? We are truly lost then. Even if I find him, the Kai-feng still comes. There is little time then, even for us –*

Abruptly, borne on some desolate wind, the voices drop away from him.

* * *

The blue morning light woke him. Above him stood the roan luma, its coat a glowing red in the sun's first oblique rays. It shook its head and stamped the poppies beside him. The exhalations from its nostrils were white clouds in the chill air.

Ronin reached up, grabbing for the swinging stirrup, pulled himself hand over hand until he stood on his feet, testing his legs and back. The numbness was gone but his co-ordination was off and he leaned on the luma for a moment, gathering his strength. He walked with its help across the white and blue field to where the golden luma stood over Kiri.

She was still asleep deep within the rustling sea. A large purple bruise swelled along the left side of her forehead.

She awoke as he bent over her and he stepped quickly back, half expecting her to unsheathe her blade and cross swords with him. She was, after all, the Empress of Sha'angh'sei and he had struck her. But she was quite calm.

She broke out food from her saddlebags, feeding the luma before she would eat herself. She offered some to Ronin.

'Against your strong advice, I rushed the Makkon,' she said ruefully. 'You did not hit me that hard. When I looked it already had you and I struck at it with my sword.' She gave him a small smile then. 'I did not believe you, I suppose. I thought, well, you are a warrior and – the rikkagin do not approve of women warriors; they are frightened, I think.'

Coming against him in the metaled ellipse just below the crust of the surface, his equal perhaps as warrior, who knows, no one ever will now.

'Now you know I told you the truth.'

'Oh, but yes!' She reached up and gingerly touched the bruise. 'It slapped me, just a backhand swipe of its claw. I have never felt such power. I was flung a good distance away. That is all I remember.'

Ronin chewed on his food. 'I wounded it,' he said.

'But how?'

He lifted the gauntlet so that the strange scales caught the light of dawn.

'With this! Its own hide.' He laughed then. 'Thank you, Bonneduce the Last, wherever you may now be. A better gift you could not have left me.'

He went to pick up his sword and as he buckled the belt around his waist she said, 'What now? Where has it gone?'

'Impossible to say. Too much time has already passed for us to attempt to continue to pursue it. Do you know of Kamado?'

'Of course.'

'Can you guide us there?'

'It lies north, along the river. I do not think that we shall have a problem finding it.'

They rode hard due north, keeping the snaking river on their left, and it was not long before they encountered soldiers streaming northward in long lines, columns bristling with weaponry and machines of war.

They joined this caravan for the last part of their journey, riding swiftly by the soldiers' sides.

Flags fluttered in the wind, the men in leather jerkins and metal helms, armed with long curving swords and bright, finely tipped lances. There were archers, their immense longbows strung vertically on their backs, and cavalry, acting as outriders and scouts, protecting the column's flanks. Metal clanged and jangled and the wooden carts, laden with food and spare arms, creaked under their heavy loads.

They moved up gradually until they reached the horsemen of the rikkagin's retinue who directed them to their commander. He was a sharp-faced man with a long queue and many scars along his desiccated cheeks.

'Are you bound for Kamado?' asked Ronin.

'All are bound for Kamado these days,' said the rikkagin darkly. 'Or away from it.'

'Do you know the Rikkagin T'ien?'

'By name only. There are many rikkagin.'

'I have heard that he is at Kamado.'

The rikkagin nodded. 'Yes. That is my understanding also. You may ride along with my men, if you wish.'

'Thank you.'

They rode in silence for a time, listening to the wind and the creaking of leather, the clop-clop of hoofs in the dust, the clash of metal.

'You have been to Kamado before?' asked Kiri.

The rikkagin turned his bleak gaze upon her.

'Too often, lady. We were not due back there for another fortnight but the enemy grows stronger each day and we must return now. From whence they come, I cannot say. Nor can anyone else, though we have made strenuous efforts to find out.'

'You have learned nothing?' said Kiri.

'Nothing at all,' answered the rikkagin. 'For none of our scouts have returned.'

They caught sight of Kamado just past midday, its dun-coloured walls, thick and high and crenellated, dominating the huge hill on which it had been built long ago. The wide river crashed along the left of the fortress and, to the north, it was possible to make out the verdant splash of a forest.

It was truly cold now and the sky had been lowering as they moved farther north. A fine rain had sprung up a short time before but it was freezing, turned to sleet by the unnatural weather, and it hammered now against the soldiers' helms, caked the mounts' hides.

They had broken the crest of a rise and, across the last gentle valley, the yellow outline of the great fort had come into sight, rising like a spectral city in the wilderness of the bleak landscape.

The stone walls rose upward, an extension of the dusty hill, wider at the bottom. It was roughly circular, with newer extensions to the east and west, rectangular bulges which gave it a peculiar look.

Massive metal-bound doors faced them, guarded by wide outcroppings of the walls along which soldiers constantly patrolled. To the west, the hill dropped away, sweeping down to the water. A wooden bridge with two stone pillars spanned the river at that point. On the far shore, a multitude of tents and pavilions could be seen among which strode many soldiers, some leading horses. Cooking fires were already being started in several places.

The rikkagin halted the column and sent a rider ahead to inform the citadel of their arrival. The man spurred his mount up the slope of the hill, through the thickening sleet, calling out to the guards on the ramparts.

After a brief time he turned in his saddle and signalled the rikkagin who, spurring his horse forward, ordered the column to move out.

With an enormous clash of arms and booted feet, the soldiers marched to the war, trudging in a tired procession through the huge gates of burnished bronze, dwarfed by the towering walls, into the dark and dismal depths of Kamado, the stone citadel.

It was a city unto itself, constructed expressly for the agonies of war; not petty raids or vengeful strikes but centuries of sustained conflict. There was no way of determining this by observing it from outside, where all that was visible were the awesome stone fortifications four and a half metres thick so that men could walk atop the walls, safe behind the stone crenellations. And perhaps this was artfulness also, for it gave no hint at all of the citadel's interior.

Kamado was so vast and so complex in construction that, seated atop his luma just inside the southern postern, Ronin could not discern the far northern limits of the fortress.

Long two-story buildings formed the immediate southern area of the citadel. The walls facing outward were windowless and constructed of stone so that they could not burn should any invader choose to rain liquid fire into Kamado's streets. They were blank, featureless, save for the stains and scars of the years.

However, their appearance changed as one went between them, down the angustate streets. Their inward faces were of wood, with wide beams carved in the shapes of the ancient gods of war, fierce women in high curving helms, attended by dwarfs with curling beards and rings in their noses, from whom the warriors of yore sought advice and favours to assure victory.

Certainly, from this evidence alone, Kamado predated the building of Sha'angh'sei which, Ronin had been told, had sprung up largely because of the rikkagin from other lands. Who then had constructed this fantastic monument to battle? Surely not the Sha'angh'sei people.

All about them as their luma danced gingerly down the dirt streets, the corps of the conflict were to be seen preparing themselves for battle. Grinding wheels sharpened axes and scimitar-bladed swords in a shimmering cascade of cold blue sparks, archers stringing their bows, fletchers gluing feathers to thin wooden shafts that would soon, in their diligent hands, become arrows. Soldiers doubling as stable hands fed and watered horses, wiping at their lathered flanks. Men trotted by them, relief for the soldiers manning the battlements. Up narrow stone stairways they clambered, reaching at last the topmost ramparts.

All about them too were the wounded, a pain-filled world of blood and bandages, of the one-armed and the one-legged, of the eyeless and the scarred. They lay, backs against the wooden pillars or curled in the dust in front of their lost gods of war, who looked down upon them, arrogant and uncaring. Perhaps their rikkagin had not gone before these deities with sufficient humility, perhaps their sacrifices were not great enough, or, more likely, the time of their power had long since been swept from the face of the world. Alone and forgotten, they yet looked out mutely on a domain no longer theirs.

Ronin stopped before one group of wounded men and asked for directions to Rikkagin T'ien's quarters.

They moved on, through inner gates and circular courtyards, along straight avenues and around stone buildings, and at length dismounted before a wooden-fronted barracks. They turned, hearing voices and the heavy tramp of boots.

He saw Tuolin first, his blond hair and height unmistakable in the crowd of soldiers.

All right, bring him out here.'

A group of soldiers with drawn swords emerged from the barracks. Ronin strained to see whom they held prisoner. Slowly, he drifted towards the men, circling to get a better angle. He stopped short.

The man the soldiers escorted, hands bound behind his back, was Rikkagin T'ien. Light gleamed along his hairless head. He stared straight ahead.

At Tuolin's command, T'ien and his guards halted.

'You are Ching Pang, do you deny this?'

'No.' Eyes straight ahead.

'You are a spy.'

'I am Ching Pang, that is all.'

'All?' echoed Tuolin sardonically. 'The Ching Pang wish us destroyed.'

'We wish only for the freedom of the Sha'angh'sei people.'

'And what would they do with this freedom?' Tuolin said contemptuously. 'Return to the mud and bamboo hovels of their ancestors?'

'Our ancestors were great once. Greater than your people ever dreamed of becoming.'

Tuolin turned abruptly away and, as if that were a signal, the soldiers surrounding T'ien slashed at him simultaneously and in an instant he was but so much dead meat.

'I do not understand .this,' Ronin said to Kiri. 'Rikkagin T'ien a Green?'

'What are you talking about?' She glanced at him. 'The Rikkagin T'ien comes towards us now.'

'That is Tuolin.'

'Yes,' she nodded. 'And Rikkagin T'ien.' She noted the look of puzzlement on his face. 'All rikkagin take a second name at the end of their training.'

'Then who was the man Tuolin just had executed?'

'Lei'in, the rikkagin's chief adviser.' She seemed amused. 'And a Ching Pang; Tuolin must be furious.'

Ronin was about to tell her of the ruse T'ien had used on him but thought better of it. He wanted to think it through himself now. He recalled the events aboard the rikkagin's vessel. He had not been disarmed when he was brought aboard; he had been kept at ease. When they judged him well enough, he had been interviewed by Lei'in masquerading as the rikkagin. He had been tested. Only then had he been allowed abovedecks into Tuolin's presence. Yes, it made perfect sense now; war breeds its own form of paranoia. It all fitted now, the assassination attempt on the ship, his night out with Tuolin.

The big blond man had seen them now and he seemed unsure whether to scowl or smile, finally opted for a neutral look.

'Did you find the Council of assistance?' he asked Ronin.

'I – never got to see them.' Ronin remembered Kiri's warning that Tuolin did not know.

'What a pity,' he said without much conviction. He turned to Kiri. 'I almost did not recognize you.' He glanced down at the sword scabbarded at her left hip. 'Can you actually use that or is it for show?'

'What do you think?' Kiri said.

'I think I prefer to see you at Tenchō,' Tuolin said quite calmly. 'I distrust women on the battlefield.'

'Oh, why is that?' She was struggling to control her anger.

'They never seem to know which way to go.'

'I do not understand you at all.'

He shrugged. 'There is nothing to understand. Fighting should be left to those who can do it best. End of discussion.'

He turned his attention back to Ronin as if she did not exist. 'Why are you here?' He began to walk towards the barracks and they went with him.

'That depends.'

'Oh, on what?'

'On whether you think you can trust me yet.'

Tuolin threw his head back and laughed.

'Yes, I see.' He wiped his eyes. 'I think we can safely say that your time of trial is at an end.'

They went up the wooden steps and into the interior. It was dim and cool. The low ceilings were beamed and dark with smoke residue. The furniture was sparse and utilitarian. In the main room of the first story a fire burned on a large stone hearth.

Tuolin led them through this space, filled with

soldiers, into a smaller back room, windowless, with a desk of scarred wood, several hard chairs, and a low cabinet against the back wall. At some time previous, the doors had been removed. The rikkagin sat down behind the desk and reached into the cabinet. He offered them cold wine, which they drank.

Ronin wondered briefly about the rikkagin's changed attitude toward Kiri, then put it out of his mind.

'Sa was killed, then Matsu, by a creature whom I had fought in my own land. It came north out of Sha'angh'sei. It was waiting for me in the poppy fields half a day's ride south of here.' He paused. 'You do not seem surprised.'

'My friend, many things have transpired since first we met. I have seen many sights, battled foes I could not have dreamed of in my worst nightmares.' He gestured at the walls. 'We fight nonmen.' He sighed. 'Not many here remember the things spawned by the sorcerous wars.'

'I do not think that these creatures are connected with that time.'

Tuolin drained his cup and poured himself more wine without offering them more. He waved the cup. 'No matter. These men are not cowards; for most, fighting is all they know. But they are used to foes who bleed when they are cut; give them an enemy that they can see and kill. But this – ' The wine sloshed over the cup's rim and onto the desk. He ignored it. 'We are losing this battle.'

Ronin leaned forward. 'Tuolin, this creature,

the Makkon, is an emissary of The Dolman. Do you remember? I told you – ' The rikkagin waved his cup at him. 'There are four Makkon and it is imperative that I kill at least one before they can all gather.'

'Why?'

'Because when the four come together they will summon The Dolman and then, I fear, it will be too late for all of us.'

'You have already fought one of these – Makkon?'

'Yes, more than once. But this last time I was able to injure it. With this – ' He held up the scaled gauntlet. 'Tuolin, it cannot be harmed with ordinary weapons. But this is made of its own hide. I hurt it but it almost killed me.'

The rikkagin ran a hand over his eyes and Ronin became aware of the new lines of fatigue etched into his face.

'The Makkon is likely here then.'

'I must find it,' said Ronin.

'All right.' Tuolin pulled at the ivory bar which pierced one ear lobe. 'We must cross to the field encampment. There we will be most likely to find news of your Makkon.'

'I am pleased that you believe me.'

The big man sighed. 'I have spent too much time with the dead and dying not to,' he said wearily.

The dusty streets of Kamado were filled with the din of hoarse shouting, the clang of iron against heated iron, the snort and stamp of war horses, the moans of the injured, the tramp of booted feet.

They went out through the southern postern, escorted by soldiers as far as the bridge.

Dark thunderheads were piling up in the north-west, writhing their way rapidly southward. The wind had died and the air was leaden and chill. The moist land steamed whitely.

They moved as swiftly as they could across the wooden planks, hands gripping the rope sides. Ronin peered down into the frothy depths, catching an occasional glimpse of glistening black rocks and sleek leaping fish.

To the south, the land was brown and barren, as if blasted by intense heat. Off to their right, almost due north, lay the encampment with its rows of tents and bright pavilions, lines of tethered horses and bright flickering fires, like silent insects, around which the shadows of the soldiers darted.

The encampment was on the near edge of an undulating meadow of high green grass perhaps a third of a kilometre wide, beyond which began the first low bushes and wide trees of the forest Ronin had seen as they approached the fortress. Now, as they neared the far shore, he could see that the forest was immensely thick, the tree trunks so tall and the numerous branches so heavily foliaged that it appeared to be a solid wall of green.

Soldiers met them as they stepped off the bridge. Tuolin ordered them to take them to Rikkagin Wo's pavilion. They went into the high grass. Fireflies swept the twilight with minute arcs of cool light. The meadow rustled in the wind and cicadas chirruped. Everything was steeped in deep blue except the far-off forest, cloaked in black shadows, pooling and impenetrable.

The pavilion was striped bright yellow and blue, its canvas walls quiescent now as what little breeze there was died. Lamps were being lit throughout the encampment. Wood smoke and charcoaled meat were the dominant scents which came to them.

Within, it was warm and bright from a multitude of lamps. Shadows danced along the insubstantial walls as soldiers went to and fro, preparing for battle. An almost constant stream of runners came and went, depositing and receiving coded messages on slips of rice paper.

Tuolin led them a seemingly circuitous path through the disciplined confusion towards a tall man who broke abruptly into their field of vision. He had dark hair which he wore long and loose and a thin pinched mouth. His chin thrust forward. He turned and gazed at Tuolin as they approached.

'Ah, T'ien, has Hui arrived with his troops?'

'Yes, just before sunset.'

'Good. We need every man.'

Rikkagin Wo took a slip of paper from a runner, went a few paces away, nearer a light and farther from them. He read the message, went to his desk, and wrote several characters with his quill. He gave the slip back to the runner, who left.

He turned back to Tuolin. 'We lost another patrol this afternoon.'

'Where?'

'Due north. In the forest.'

'How many?'

'Thirteen. Only one came back.' Wo looked disgusted. 'And he is no good to us. Raving like a lunatic.'

'What did he say?'

Wo took another message. He did not look up. 'I cannot remember. Ask Le'ehu, if you wish. I would not bother myself.'

Tuolin, with Ronin's urgings, sought out a heavy squat individual with his black hair in a queue, fat cheeks and long glittering eyes.

Le'ehu drew them to the side, against the canvas, where few passed close to them.

'He is gone now, the last soldier.' He paused, his eyes on Ronin and Kiri.

Tuolin patted his arm. 'Go on, these two will not pass on what you say.'

'All right, it is just that' – he rubbed at his upper lip, which had begun to sweat – 'I killed him, you know, in the end.' The glittery eyes glanced quickly around. 'I mean he was dying anyway and he pleaded with me. He could not bear to live another moment, after what he had seen – '

'What attacked the patrol?' asked Ronin.

Le'ehu looked startled. 'How – how did you know? How did he know, T'ien?'

'Know what?' asked Tuolin.

'He knew a "what" attacked the patrol.'

'Did the man describe it?' asked the blond man patiently.

'Yes, curse him. I will not sleep this night. It was huge with great claws and a nightmare face. It ripped out their throats, he said.'

'The Makkon,' Ronin said and Tuolin nodded.

'In the forest?'

'Yes.' The man tried to swallow. 'Over the meadow's ridge, perhaps a kilometre into that cursed place – '

They were silent, waiting for him to continue. Le'ehu stared over their shoulders at the fluttering shadows along the far side of the pavilion.

'What else?' Tuolin said very gently.

'It was not of that creature that he talked before he died.' The words came out of him reluctantly now, as if by saying this aloud he might conjure up terrifying creatures. 'Something came in that thing's wake.'

'Another one?' asked Ronin.

Le'ehu's head snapped around. 'Another – ? Oh no. No, it was. I do not know, something else. There was whirling fog, he said, and blood raining in the melee. He caught a glimpse only – '

'And,' prompted Tuolin.

Le'ehu swallowed again.

'Rikkagin – he said it was the Hart – '

'Oh, come on,' Tuolin snorted.

'Rikkagin, he bade me kill him,' the squat man said miserably. 'I do not think that otherwise – '

'The Hart is but legend, Le'ehu, a foul – '

'What legend?' asked Ronin.

'The tale is told,' said Tuolin, 'of the Hart. He is half man and half beast.'

'That is all?'

Tuolin stared at Le'ehu, who winced at his words. 'Some say that he is evil incarnate. And others suggest that he was once a whole man, transmogrified, forced now to serve a sorcerous liege, fighting those who are really his kin.'

'Whatever is truth,' said the squat man, 'that soldier believed that he saw it' – he turned his head – 'out there. In the forest.'

Ronin turned to Tuolin.

'I care not for legends. The Makkon is my only concern. At first light I must go into the wood and destroy it – '

Le'ehu's eyes bulged. 'Surely you must be mad. The Hart – '

'Be silent,' snapped Tuolin. 'We are confronted with enough real monstrosities without you fabricating nightmares.' He swung his gaze toward Ronin and his tone softened. 'You cannot mean to go alone. I will accompany you.'

Ronin shook his head.

'You will not be able to help. I require but two men who know this area. When I find it I will send them away.'

The big man put a hand on his shoulder.

'My friend, I have done many things for you. Fished you out of the sea when you were half dead, introduced you to Tenchō. It is time now to repay me. I want to see this Makkon for myself.'

303

His grip tightened. 'I must know the enemy, can you understand that?'

Ronin searched the cerulean eyes and nodded. 'Yes, that is something that I can accept.'

Le'ehu stared from one to the other, backing off.

'You are both mad! You – '

A stifled yell. The clash of metal against metal.

They all turned at the sounds. Boots pounded outside and there came now confused shouts.

'Quickly,' Tuolin said. 'Outside.'

The heavy darkness of the massive forest seemed to have pervaded the meadow. The fireflies were gone. Above the waving grass now rolled an oncoming tide of black shadows.

They came swiftly and silently, without the telltale gleam of metal. Somehow they had pierced the perimeter of the encampment without an alarm being sounded.

They were like tree trunks, dark, with wide shoulders and thick legs. Their long beards and wiry hair were greased and plaited. Their faces were moon-shaped and perfectly flat as if evolution had decreed to their ancestors that the protrusions of nose and cheeks and forehead were superfluous. They seemed more animated creatures from the wall paintings in Kiri's palace then true men. Yet they were real enough, brandishing wide scimitars of an unreflective metal that was almost black with bell-shaped fist guards.

Behind them loomed other shadows, coalescing slowly in the dark, impossibly tall and bony, their skin pallid gray, their faces desiccated and fleshless, their skulls gleaming in their nakedness. These creatures strode behind their fellow warriors, swinging heavy short chains ending in fanged iron spheres. Ronin caught the sound of their brief hissing arcs in the close air.

Tuolin unsheathed his sword as did Ronin and Kiri. All about them were confusion and disarray as soldiers scrambled for their weapons. Fires guttered and flickered out as if by a strong wind, although the air was calm.

Mist rolled in, sweeping through the meadow and into the encampment, and there was a choking stench as the enemy advanced, the first wave already past the hapless outer patrols. The scimitars swung darkly in whooshing arcs, cleaving a hideous harvest in this sorcerous high summer.

Still within the long grass, the gaunt warriors whirled their chains, the deadly globes hissing in the night like locusts, crushing flesh and bone indiscriminately, and the groans of the dying mingled with the wet slap and crunch of the reaving.

Ronin leapt forward with a cry and his blade swept to and fro in mighty two-handed slashes, ripping into the torsos of those wide men closest to him. They squealed and backed into each other, bewildered, and he stepped into their midst, using oblique blows now, slicing into the juncture of neck and collarbone of one warrior, withdrawing his sword and, in the same motion, decapitating another.

Beside him came Tuolin and Kiri, hacking at the

warriors as if they were wild foliage. He concentrated, moving slowly forward, his blade singing its fiery song of death, gleaming, running with blood. He hammered at them without letup, his heart thudding in his chest, his arms electric with the power of the destruction he was reaping, no longer conscious of the peripheral sights and sounds of the night; he was intent, content as he hammered at them, severing bodies which convulsed and spurted their liquids hotly about his swaying form. His muscles rippled and glistened with a fine film of sweat, beaded with sprays of his enemies' blood and entrails, and he grinned in savage delight. He clove a warrior from shoulder to ribcage on a forward swing, slashed into the mid-section of another on his backward arc.

Near him, Kiri was nearly disemboweled as she watched, horrified and fascinated. She parried at the last instant and turned her face away from him, working at her own task.

At their backs, they heard Rikkagin Wo's voice lifted in sharp command. Men ran everywhere, attempting to form themselves into defense lines, but it seemed useless; the warriors moved inexorably forward. The mist rolled past them and over the soldiers, burning their calves with cold. And more of the gaunt warriors appeared as their shorter compatriots fell beneath the swords of the soldiers. These were destroying the rikkagin's men with terrifying expertise. They carried round iron shields in addition to their weapons, which seemed much too heavy for any man to wield effectively yet these warded off most of the soldiers' blows while, with their other hands, the fanged spheres described their tight orbits, exploding with terrible impact.

Ronin felt himself engulfed in a dark tide, no longer an individual, another piece of floating flotsam carried along by the undertow. He fought and the warriors fell before his blurred blade like wheat before a scythe but always there were others to take the place of the fallen, as if in each individual's death two more were created.

Onward he waded, the footing unsure and gluey with the innards of the fallen as he made his laborious way out into the meadow to meet the gaunt deathhead warriors. Tuolin and Kiri were just behind him. The rikkagin's great blade lifted and fell and in his left hand was the emerald-hilted dirk with which he slashed and parried. For her part, the Empress was using her sword with consummate skill. Her breastplate was shiny, sodden with blood and splattered gore, her black hair had slipped its bonds and now whirled about her, a dark mantle.

With an enormous swipe that ripped apart a barrel chest, Ronin went through the outer fringes of the wide warriors and for the first time in many moments there was space around him. The still air was alive with the harsh whisper of the globes. The last of the soldiers went down, his head smashed open like a ripe fruit, and he peered into the roiling night at the grinning faces, as white now in the guttering firelight as the pallid poppies.

Their sunken eyes were featureless holes with no discernible trace of iris or pupil; their heads turned on their spindly spines as they looked about them.

Ronin lifted his blade and went in quickly, driving it down in a blur, through the collarbone of one of the warriors. The neck was severed and the head flew from the bony shoulders. There was no blood but a shower of gray dust which plumed momentarily, spitting shards of vertebrae from its periphery. The decapitated torso came at him, its arm still lifted, the fanged globe whirring, and he was obliged to duck the blow that came. A hissing passed over him as he crouched and the creature, shuddering now, stumbled on its nerveless legs and collapsed.

At that moment he felt a titanic wrench and his blade went spinning to the sodden ground. He lurched forward and almost fell on top of the gaunt corpse. He turned, saw another deathhead warrior whipping back the globe that had slammed into his sword. It advanced upon him, the deadly sphere a menacing blur.

The creature leaned back and the globe came at him with such speed that its fangs grazed his cheek even as he jerked away. He risked a glance downward, saw that he was too far from his sword to risk lunging for it and the gaunt warrior was circling so that he was now between Ronin and the weapon.

Ronin turned his body sideways, waited for the next swing, counting to himself so that the timing would be perfect. The globe glistened as it came at him and he was away, counting again to be certain of the rhythm. He timed his dive to coincide with the peak of its arc away from him to give himself the maximum amount of time.

He hit the ground and rolled onto the warrior he had just slain, his fingers scrabbling along the moist earth for the chain and globe. The long grass made it difficult to locate but his peripheral vision had picked up where it had fallen when the warrior fell and now he had it and he was rolling. He regained his feet and went down immediately to avoid the globe.

Whir. The other's weapon was circling again and he swung his own globe, gaining momentum, but the fangs loomed at him without warning and he had time but to throw up his globe reflexively. The chains clashed, momentum taking the globes and whipping them around as the chain entwined.

The gaunt warrior pulled viciously and Ronin, caught off balance, was jerked forward, slamming into his adversary. The skeletal figure bent and the head darted towards him, the mouth opening impossibly wide. Filed yellow teeth, long and ragged, snapped hideously at his face and he writhed away just in time. The clashing jaws pursued him as he attempted to disengage himself. But to break free now was to lose his only weapon. Snap, snap. The neck, long and willowy, brought the fangs at him again and again.

Still holding onto the chain, Ronin brought his left hand up and balling the Makkon gauntlet into a fist, he smashed upward into the working mouth. Shards of fractured teeth rained upon them both and Ronin punched once more and the thing let go his weapon, bringing his shield up with both hands.

Ronin whirled the spiked globe and aimed it. The bony skull caved in, the entire left side crushed, and the thing went down on its bony knees. Ronin hit it again and the warrior keeled over as its knees splintered and the bones in its legs cracked.

Ronin ran for his sword then, dropping the chain and globe and, grasping it, turned back into the fray. The soldiers were dying under the assault of the deathhead warriors.

He heard Tuolin's shout and, looking around, he located the tall rikkagin. He moved off in this direction, dodging hissing spheres. He saw Kiri fighting at Tuolin's side.

'We cannot hold against them, Ronin,' he panted as he hacked at a skeletal figure. 'The encampment is routed, I fear. We must find Wo and marshal the remaining men in a retreat to Kamado.'

Ronin looked about them. The gaunt warriors were advancing steadily and were now within the perimeter of the pavilions. The moans of the dying were in his ears as he retreated with Tuolin and Kiri back to the pavilions, slashing at their foes with each step. Firelight blazed up briefly and he saw a tent bursting into flames. There were screams from soldiers trapped inside.

The night was streaked with yellow and orange

and heat danced in waves, alternating with the chill. The earth steamed whitely until they could no longer see their boots. Kiri slipped and fell over a body, her head cracked against a skull, and when she lifted her face, her forehead was black and shiny with blood. Ronin lifted her, her hand grasping his arm, and they went on, through the narrow dark lanes between the canvas walls, ducking flames, hacking at the wide warriors who blocked their way. The ground was muddy with viscous liquids and soft things squished under the soles of their boots. More pavilions began to smoke and crackle with flame.

Just ahead of them, the green canvas wall of a pavilion bulged and ripped open, three men tumbling through, slashing at each other. A wide warrior hit the ground at a bad angle and his neck snapped. At the same instant a deathhead warrior swung his globe, smashing the breastbone of the soldier, who moaned and folded in upon himself.

Ronin's blade struck off the head of the gaunt warrior and the skeletal body crashed backward into the pavilion's interior.

They went on, Tuolin leading them now, searching through the frenzy for the yellow and blue pavilion, picking their way through the grisly litter strewn across the earth like stinking loam.

It was already in flames when they reached it, sheets of orange sparks cracking open the night. They swept aside the burning walls and went in, finding Rikkagin Wo armless, his shoulder sockets crimson. White bones protruded pinkly. One side of his head was a pool of blood and pulpy matter. His face was untouched.

Tuolin took them out of the burning pavilion. A shower of bright sparks fell along their shoulders. Outside, the night had heated up. Flames crackled everywhere. They ran into a pack of the wide warriors and slew them. They backed away from Ronin and he went after them, back into the torched pavilions, and Tuolin was obliged to take him by the shoulder and turn him around. More of the deathhead warriors were arriving.

'We have lost the field this night, Ronin,' he said. 'We must return to the fortress.'

They went out of the encampment, the earth once again firm beneath their feet, along the black and deserted road leading to the bridge. Blood rolled off them like black rain. They were numb and sick at heart. Onto the bridge, the screams and crunchings following them like living creatures. No other sound could be heard. No insect trilled; no bird called to its mate.

A wind had sprung up from the northwest, chilling, plucking at their sodden cloaks, twanging the ropes on the bridge. Below them, the water whooshed by, pale, ribboning in the gloom, swirling against the black rocks.

It was quieter now and the night lit up as they passed a stand of tall firs and the illumination of the flames reached them again. And Ronin was swinging all at once at the shadows looming greyly between them and the sanctuary of Kamado. They had been waiting for retreating soldiers, standing in the shadows midway across the bridge. Only the flickering firelight had betrayed them and the night was abruptly filled again with the hiss and whir of the fanged globes. One gaunt warrior swung into Tuolin's side before he had a chance to react. Ronin heard his sharp exhalation like a dull explosion as he swung in a short oblique arc, severing the chain. The rikkagin clutched at his bleeding side, leaning on the guide ropes along the bridge's edge. His legs began to buckle and blood oozed through his fingers.

Kiri moved in front of the big man, slashing within the guard of a warrior, her blade sinking into its narrow chest. Its head weaved on its long neck and it threw its shield at her. It slammed into her shoulder as she attempted to twist away, caroming over the side of the bridge, its flight a dull booming in their ears. She staggered and her guard came down and the wounded warrior launched his globe.

Two of the warriors pressed Ronin back, attempting to split him off from the other two, but he counterattacked, his blade blurring whitely, lashing out at the two globes filling the air around him like flying creatures.

Tuolin was panting, his face a pale mask of pain. He tried to lift his blade. Sweat broke out on his face with the effort.

Near him, Kiri pressed her attack, rolling to avoid the warrior's blow, leaping up and slamming her boots into its stomach. She swung at him, two-handed, her feet wide apart and planted firmly, swinging up, from the hip, the power travelling into her shoulders, along her arms, the momentum flashing the blade in the night. It clove into the warrior's skull, down from the cranium into the blackness of its eye, crashing at length into the roof of its mouth. The skull flew apart like a shell, the bone fragments whirring and pattering around her. The body folded and went down heavily.

She turned then, eyes flashing, and in one long beautiful sweep of her sword cut through the torso of one of Ronin's foes. The head swivelled even as she began to withdraw the blade and the gnashing mouth reached for her. Startled, she stepped back and almost fell off the slickened verge of the bridge. The teeth clashed together as the torso fell at her feet.

Ronin swept aside the whistling sphere, timing it perfectly so that he deflected its flight back into the warrior's face. As it jerked desperately away from the oncoming globe, its head whipped directly into the path of Ronin's extended blade, flying apart in a grey flurry of bone and dust.

Another deathhead came at Kiri and she calmly cut its legs under it. Ronin saw her wince with the blow. With a second swipe, she sent the collapsing body over the brink, a bony blur cartwheeling out of sight. But she was spent now, the blow from the heavy iron shield taking its toll, and she stood, gasping, leaning on her sword while her thighs trembled with fatigue.

Ronin heard a grunt and swung around. The

last of the gaunt warriors had taken his severed chain and had wrapped it around Tuolin's neck, the silvered links biting into his flesh. The inconstant light of the flames played over their struggling bodies, the one wiry and stooped now, yellow as old bone, the other twisting in pain, dark with running blood. The rikkagin's eyes bulged and his empty hands scrabbled uselessly at the metal links tightening about his throat. Blood pooled at his feet.

Ronin leapt at the thing, grasping its wide shoulders, attempting to wrest it away from Tuolin. The head swivelled and the jaws gaped, snapping at him. He raised his sword but he lacked the room to use it and he could not step away and attack the warrior for fear of cutting the big man.

The creature's head snaked forward while he was thus debating and caught the blade in its mouth, the teeth gripping it so that Ronin could not pull it away. Still the warrior heaved on the chain and Tuolin sagged, choking on his own exhalations as his lungs vainly strove for air. His knees buckled and the deathhead warrior pulled mightily on the chain, the grinding sound of the links tightening unnaturally loud in the night.

Only Ronin's left hand was free, his right was trapped on the hilt of his blade and he dared not let go. He brought the hand up, using the thumb at his opponent's neck, pressing in through the small space under his horizontal sword. Just above the base of the neck, he located the triangular soft spot and lunged inward, puncturing the throat.

315

Fetid gas swirled at him and he gasped, turning his head away, ripping upward along the stalklike neck with his thumb. The long teeth rattled against the smooth metal of his blade and the grip of the powerful jaws loosened as the thing tried to regain its breath. He drove inward then, using the full weight of his body through his right hand, and the keen edge of his blade swept before him, unstoppable, shearing through the warrior's skull.

Ronin slammed the corpse aside, working frantically on the chain still tightly bound around Tuolin's throat. The bony hands refused to relinquish their hold on the links, though the body was half slumped over the side of the bridge. And Ronin pried at the fingers, staring into the rikkagin's pinched face. His skin had a blue tinge around the eyes.

Kiri was there, then, using a small curved knife to slash at the clenched bones, shearing through the knuckles until one by one they came apart. With a harsh grate, the links slid back slowly as Ronin forced the chain from around the big man's neck. He caught him as he fell.

It had begun to snow, the large white flakes sheeting down obliquely, dusting the corpses on the bridge, their faces white masks already, sparkling in the flickering glow from the encampment. They hissed in the flames and Kiri shuddered, thinking of the spinning fanged globes.

She turned, holding her left arm to her side, tucked in, using her hipbone as support for the weight to ease the pain in her shoulder.

Ronin sheathed his sword and scooped Tuolin into his arms.

'Now, Kiri,' he called, pushing her before him. They sprinted across the remaining expanse of the bridge and onto the high road stretching uphill to Kamado.

They were met by soldiers who escorted them to the towering walls, calling to the guards at the postern. The metal-bound gates creaked open just enough for them to slip through. Then they swung shut with an echoing clang.

There was an immediate tumult around them. Ronin delivered up the rikkagin into the hands of his men, his neck torn and black with terrible marks, his shirt and leggings dripping blood; they bore him away to his barracks. Ronin followed, his arm around Kiri as she struggled against unconsciousness. He declined the soldiers' aid but when he stumbled they took her from him and two of them lifted her up the barracks steps and through the entrance. Ronin sank down on the steep steps, too weary to go any further.

After a time a man came out of the barracks and sat down beside him.

'He almost died.'

He was tall and wide-shouldered, with greying hair and a full but close-cut beard. His nose was long and curving; his eyes were black.

'T'ien's own physician is inside if you need attention.'

'I am tired,' said Ronin. 'That is all.'

'Perhaps he had better see you anyway.'

He called for the physician, who came out and grunted when he saw Ronin. He was the one from aboard Tuolin's ship. While he worked, the other said, 'Good for us that he did not die, eh?' Then, more softly, 'What is your name?'

'Ronin.'

'I am Rikkagin Aerant.'

Ronin leaned his head against the wooden banister. The ancient gods of war, carved into the columns, looked blankly out at the darkness.

'You saved his life.'

'What?' There was a stinging along his shoulders.

'Tuolin told me that you saved –'

'Do you always call him by his other name?'

'We are brothers.'

Ronin turned his head. 'You hardly look it.' The physician finished tying the bandages. He went back inside.

'We had different fathers.'

'I see.' He thought of nothing.

'I can help you.'

Ronin ran a hand over his face. 'How?'

'Tell me what happened.'

Rikkagin Aerant nodded his head as Ronin related the events in the encampment.

'Best that Wo is dead, truly. His mind was closed to this war; he was so used to fighting Reds and the northern tribes that he could not see that the war had changed.'

'How could he explain the warriors who do not bleed?'

Rikkagin Aerant shrugged. 'The military mind can rationalize any situation. He lacked imagination.' He brushed at his leggings. 'Pity. He was a fine leader.'

'He was unprepared for that attack.'

'Yes. I would dearly like to know how they got through the perimeter so easily.'

'Tuolin told you – '

His face was bright in the torchlight. 'Yes. I have seen this thing which you have fought.'

'You told Wo?'

Rikkagin Aerant laughed shortly. 'I told no one but Tuolin and even he – ' His eyes were like cool crystal, they were open and keenly intelligent. 'You know, even brothers do not love each other all the time.'

'He wanted to go with me.'

'He will not have that now.' Several sentries ran by, their boots echoing against the wooden walls. The snow had ceased for the moment, but the sky was low and the air felt heavy and damp. 'It is best that way.'

'Do you wish to go?'

Rikkagin Aerant turned his head away. A dog barked along the next block of barracks. 'I do not know. But it does not matter. I am needed here. I will send you two Reds. They were born in this region.'

'All right.'

He stood up, his eyes dark and unreadable as he stared down at Ronin.

'Perhaps you will return.'

He went off down the muddy street.

Snow fell quietly along the ramparts, dampening the scrape of the guards' high boots against the stone. It pattered about him, obscuring the last dying embers sparking in the ashes of the encampment, a wan carpet humped along the earth, hiding the bodies of the fallen combatants.

It was still in Kamado save for the crunch of an occasional group of soldiers on patrol. Soft voices floated up to him for a moment and then were gone in the hissing of the snow. He pulled his cloak closer about his shoulders. The pain there was lessening. He willed his mind to be blank, not wanting to anticipate.

He saw Kiri walking along the ramparts, searching for him. He called wordlessly to her.

'How is your shoulder?' he asked.

'Better.' She sat beside him. 'The bone was knocked out of the socket. He is very good.' She meant the physician.

He nodded into the night.

She put a hand along his arm, ran it upward. 'There is a room in the barracks.'

'I do not think so.'

'I will return to Sha'angh'sei at dawn. I must talk to Du-Sing. The Greens and Reds must unite now.'

'Yes.'

'And you must go into the forest at first light.' Her breath ran in warm white puffs against the side of his face. 'Why not?'

He looked into her face. 'You have changed.'

He did not know what he expected to see there but he was surprised. She looked humiliated, her cheeks flushing pink.

'Of course. Matsu is dead. I am half a person now, not fit to be with.' She got up and went away from him, along the white escarpment of the high rampart, disappearing down the steep stairs.

Dawn was a blood-red smear, burning coldly through a long rent in the massed grey clouds, pink-edged and pearled now in the east where the bloated oblate disc of the sun rose with agonizing deliberation.

He watched the light come into the world, atop the southern rampart where he had stayed all the long night. The snow had stopped falling just before first light and this day seemed somehow more natural than the last.

Ronin stood up, breathing deeply the chill air, and stretched his cramped muscles. He peered southward along the barren trail, completely white now. Higher up the snow was pink. He could pick out no imprints and the sparse foliage and his angle of elevation made it clear to him that the way was clear back to Sha'angh'sei.

He went down to the barracks. Two short men with long queues and black almond eyes waited patiently for him. A soldier came down the steps with a steaming cup of tea. He took it gratefully and sipped it, savouring its warmth and spice. He declined the bowl of rice.

Kiri was already at the stables. She saddled her luma silently, running her hand constantly down its flanks. His luma snorted and beat its hoofs against the earth as he came in. Straw floated through the air.

She mounted the animal and it pranced in its desire to be away. She pulled hard on the reins to keep it in check. It called to the roan, a plaintive farewell touched with the exultation of the wind and the road, and Kiri pulled again on the reins.

She took the luma out from the stable, Ronin at her side. They went along the quiet streets, the mount's clop–clop muffled by the carpet of snow. The luma's head bobbed as it sniffed the cold air, plumes of smoke shooting from its wide nostrils. Its ears twitched and Kiri spoke to it softly, a singsong litany.

At the southern postern she drew up and he pulled her down to him, kissing her cheek.

'Kill it,' she said in his ear with a sob. 'Kill it before I return.'

And she dug her boot heels into the luma's flanks, rattling the reins, and it leapt through the parted gates, a saffron streak, out from the citadel, onto the long white road home.

The silence was like a clap of thunder, lapping at his eardrums with an unnatural proximity. Deep in the forest, the snowfall was but a light dusting because of the canopy of thick branches overhead. He was struck by their austere beauty, frosted white across their interlacing upper surfaces, the spreading undersides a deep green shading into black among the blue shadows.

The quietude was extraordinary. If he ceased to move, he could hear the hissing of his own breath and, somewhat farther away, the inhalations and exhalations of the two Reds.

With a shivery rustle, a miniature snowslide fell from a branch and Ronin instinctively looked up. The wide green bough with its sweet-smelling needles bobbed and a flash of deep scarlet flew off in a flutter.

They were in a minute clearing but even so the sky was entirely obscured. Within the tall stands of pines, beds of fragrant brown needles cushioned the forest floor. The frozen earth was hard near the ancient twisting oaks with their entwining networks of branches and the profusion of oval leaves.

They moved deeper into the forest, Ronin carefully imitating the Reds' slow, deliberate movements, creating a minimum of disturbance. The way was so entangled that more often than not they were forced to go single file, turning their bodies sideways in order to move through the narrow gap between the trees.

He became aware that they were on an incline and, as the way became steeper, granite outcroppings began to appear. Soon they crested the rise and the forest floor fell away from them. Off to their left, they could make out the clatter of a stream. Black birds flew among the laden branches, calling in shrill staccato cries, sending occasional showers of powdery snow onto the earth about them. There was little underbrush, only green moss and a greyish-blue lichen which clung to the rock faces.

They saw no tracks that morning and Yuan, one of the Reds, sent his companion off on a tangent.

'Perhaps we will have better luck this way,' he said to Ronin.

They went ever north, the forest unchanging in its denseness. Once Yuan halted and pointed to their right. Ronin saw a red fox, long tail sweeping the ground as it ran from them.

Just past noon the Red signaled to him and, crouching, he moved from tree to tree as silently as he was able until he was next to the kneeling man.

Yuan whispered in his ear and Ronin looked through a stand of thick oak. There was movement and he inched closer, changing his angle of vision. On the other side of the trees were perhaps a dozen of the gaunt deathhead warriors, shields on arms, fanged globes swaying at their hips as they marched. Beside them strode a score of more men with straight black hair combed back into a queue. They had black almond eyes. They were armed with the single-edged curving swords and short-hafted axes identical to Yuan's. Another man came into view and he started. Eyes like stones magnified in still water, long drooping moustache.

He would not forget that face. Po, the embittered trader who had walked out of Llowan's dinner party.

Ronin touched Yuan on the shoulder and they moved back from the oaks.

'Who are the men with the tall ones?' Ronin asked softly.

'Reds.'

'Why are they with the enemy?'

'They hate the Greens. That is an old hate. The tall ones promise them power in Sha'angh'sei where the Greens are supreme in exchange for their aid here in the north.'

'They would battle their own kind; join forces with those that are not men?'

'Power is strange, is it not?' said Yuan.

'Yet they will die along with us, if this enemy is victorious.'

The other stared at him. 'Do you think that you could convince them of this?'

Ronin thought of Po's outburst. He shook his head.

The afternoon waned as they searched vainly for any trace of the Makkon. Near dusk they gave it up and Yuan led them back to the clearing where they had arranged to rendezvous with the other Red.

'We can only trust that Li had better luck,' said Yuan.

The clearing was darkling when they arrived, the snow blue, the shadows bluer still. Across the small open space a tree loomed in the dusk, lumped and misshapen. Yuan went and stood in front of the tree. Ronin went slowly after him, his eyes raking the shadows.

At perhaps the height of five meters from the forest's floor a branch had been torn from the tree, leaving a long ragged stump like a spear. Upon this makeshift stake Li had been impaled through back and breastbone, as if he had been hurled there by a titanic force.

Without a word Yuan unsheathed his sword and swung it over his head, shearing through the branch behind Li. He fell heavily to the ground, his legs crumpled under him, his eyes open, staring wildly. The snow was dark where he half sat, back against the old tree trunk.

The ground was too hard to bury him so they moved north, making camp shortly. Yuan gathered dry wood and set about making a smokeless fire.

Ronin took the first watch. The pale firelight danced against the blue expanse of snow and black trees. Shadows ran to and fro. Just outside the ring of light, he heard the small skitterings and soft susurrations of the nocturnal animals.

If he leaned to his right he could just make out the crescent moon and its attendant star, bits of glittering platinum, cool and remote, through a tiny gap in the forest's canopy.

Something howled, a snow wolf perhaps, and the forest chitterings ceased momentarily. But the sound did not come again and gradually the tiny myriad sounds sprang up once more. An owl hooted and, unseen, a bird flapped its wings above his head.

Near the end of his watch it began to snow, a fine dusting filtering down upon him and Yuan through the maze of branches, leaves, and needles.

He woke the Red, who stretched, yawned, and went to put more wood on the dying fire.

Ronin fell asleep instantly, a long dreamless flight until the blackness gave way to a flickering crimson and it seemed to him that the sky dripped blood. He heard low voices, far away yet so close that the individual words seemed to reverberate upon his eardrums. *Not yet? There can be no more delay. You know as well as I what must transpire before I can find him. Yes. All right. I am already in place; the vessel is prepared. I will get him there, be assured of that. I am assured of nothing now; time flows past too quickly: the Kai-feng comes. But we are Outside. Yes, but we must depend on those who are not; our time is ending.* He fell away from it and opened his eyes. He heard the soughing of the branches in the wind, a whippoorwill's mournful call. He turned his head. The fire crackled, the embers glowing orange and white. Yuan sat, arms around his knees to keep out the cold, staring out into the forest's shadows.

Ronin closed his eyes and went back to sleep.

The chill blue light of dawn woke him. He remembered the voices and for an instant, disoriented, thought that two men had been by the fireside.

The fire was out, the ashes gray and cold. Yuan

sat in the same position, staring into the trees. Ronin crossed to him, reached out a hand, and paused. He crouched down. The Red was dead. There was a black hole through his heart. Something had gone swiftly through him from chest to back. He might have been gored by a wild animal. He had not moved during the night.

Ronin went away from the campsite, swiftly and without a sound, moving north, farther into the forest. His spine tingled.

Snow began to fall again, harder now, deadening sound and limiting what visibility there was in that maze.

A wind arose, plucking at his cloak and swirling the snow into his face. He thought then that he heard a horn sound, plaintive and far off.

Mist steamed from the forest's floor, pearled and thick. Now all sound, all sense of direction was blotted out. His boots were silent along the ground but he heard the hammering of his heart. Oblique bars of grey light slanted down, illuminating the translucence of the mist, and abruptly he was lost in a wilderness of smoke and vague shadows.

The minute sounds of the forest were gone now and with them the small comfort of being with other living creatures. He felt cut off, as if he no longer trod the world of man.

The snow fell silently, mingling with the syrupy mist. He went cautiously forward with one hand held before him like a blind man to guide him around the tree trunks which loomed in his path, visible only at the last moment.

His sense of time slipped away. He no longer knew whether he had been marching for hours or days, whether the sun shone above the roof of his world or whether it had set.

He opened his mouth, letting the snow melt and slake his thirst. With that, he was suddenly aware of his hunger. He began to search the forest for game but he saw nothing. No animal, no fruit-bearing bush or tree. His hunger grew, gnawing at him. He pushed on.

At length he stumbled over an exposed root and he knew numbly that he must rest. Exhausted, he sat with his back against the trunk of an old pine. Its scent was all around him. The brown needles were soft beneath him. His head nodded on his chest but the hunger would not let him sleep.

It seemed darker now, the diffuse light flickering at the periphery of his vision. He became aware of a bulge under his belt. Half asleep, he fumbled with his fingers, found something. It was spongy. Food. He looked down at it but the uncertain light made it impossible to see. He took a bite, then another, chewing thoughtfully. It tasted slightly bitter. It was only when he had finished that the mist seemed to clear from his mind and he knew that he had eaten the strange man-shaped root from the apothecary's in Sha'angh'sei. An immense urn, fish swimming lazily, gossamer fins waving in the current, the feel of the curving side

– Eternity. He shrugged. He felt a renewed strength already. All he needed was –

At that moment he thought he heard a distant call, like a shout of triumph, and he stood up, about to move in that direction, when he heard a more immediate sound behind him. He turned.

The mist was thicker now, the pearl grey glistening in rainbows at the edges of his vision.

He faced a shadow, distinct from those of the trees, within a line of vast ancient oaks, within the deep blue of their shade. He took a step forward, sure now that the Makkon had found him. His hand went to the hilt of his sword by force of habit. It would do him no good against the creature.

The figure stepped out from the shadows, a minute snowfall fluttering about its shoulders as a branch was disturbed by the movement of its head. Shivering, the branch turned from white to deep green.

The sound of Ronin's sword unsheathing was an unnaturally sharp rasp, its volume shattering, for he looked upon a visage so strange as to drive all thought of the Makkon from his mind.

Ronin stared at the Hart.

He was over four meters tall, with wide shoulders and long, slender arms, thick-thighed legs. He was dressed in leggings of the deepest black, a peculiar, dense shade that was difficult to focus on. He wore a mail shirt lacquered the same color, dull and unreflective. A cloak swirled out behind him to the forest's floor. He had a massive black

330

metal belt strapped across his waist and from it hung two scabbarded swords, one so long that it almost scraped the earth, the other shorter than the traditional Sha'angh'sei weapon. Ronin stared at these for long moments, wondering why they were so familiar. He was certain that he had never seen their like before and still –

His eyes were drawn irresistibly to the head yet with a reluctance that he found confusing. He was not afraid of death but he was terrified now. There was shivering inside himself, not at all a physical thing, as if someone was plucking the cords of his nerves at the core of his being and there was a terrible laughter from somewhere within him, a chill and ghastly rending. His stomach contracted.

The immense head emerged into the uncertain illumination of the mist. Shadows fluttered behind it. It was dominated by a long muzzle with wide wet flaring nostrils and, below them, a huge mouth with large square-cut teeth. The swivelling ears were triangular, furry and, beside them, growing out from the canted forehead, were two enormous antlers, curved and treed.

The entire head was covered in deep black fur, rich and glossy. His gaze moved along the pelt until he looked into the Hart's eyes. They were not round like an animal's but rather oval, the intelligent eyes of man. They were piercing, pigmented with a cold colour that had no analogue on this world.

The Hart opened his lips and something screamed through Ronin's brain so that his knees buckled and he dropped his blade, falling before the creature. There was maniacal laughter and beyond that a horrified voice was screaming *Get up! Get up and slay the beast, for beast is all it is!* But his arms would not respond and his fingers were numb as they clutched the soft pine needles of the forest's floor. *Destroy him before he destroys you!* He tried to vomit but nothing would come up. His head bent to the snow, the cold like flame against his forehead as the Hart moved farther out from the cerulean shadows. His high boots crunched the snow, echoing among the trees. The wind rose steadily, howling through the maze of branches like a hateful child. Ronin felt rooted to the earth, another tree in the forest, gravity sucking at him.

One strange horny hand moving to his side, the Hart withdrew the long sword, its blade a deep black onyx, translucent, forged by ancient anvil. There was a sighing as the leaves trembled, whispering his name: *Setsoru*.

The Hart came to rest before Ronin's kneeling form and, reaching down with his free hand, he gripped the hair, pulling the head back so that he stared into Ronin's face. The immense sword was held high, flashing through the mist which curled about them. And then the Hart looked down. He stared into Ronin's colourless eyes. The animal lips pulled back in a snarl and his own eyes rolled in their sockets. The antlers shook the snow from the branches overhead. Hatred and fear swam in his visage and the onyx blade trembled.

No! the Hart screamed. The wind howled.

There was a voice in Ronin's mind; his ears heard only the gathering wind.

And in that instant of hesitation, when both figures, locked together, seemed incapable of movement or cohesive thought, there came a fierce growl and a frantic blur of lithe motion. From out of the swirling mist streaked a shape, huge jaws agape and slathering forepaws extended. Their curving talons raked at the Hart's throat. Still distracted, his face a hate-filled mask, he could do little more than throw up his free arm to ward off the unexpected attack. But the creature held on tenaciously, the jaws snapping, the claws raking at the exposed pelt again and again. The body thrashed powerfully.

The Hart's mouth opened and from it emerged a terrifying scream of rage and confusion which echoed in Ronin's mind like a crack of thunder. He gave one last swipe at the creature with the hilt of his sword and, with amazing swiftness, he bounded into the maze of pines and oak, vanishing instantly.

The attacker was still now, sitting calmly in a bed of pine needles near Ronin's prostrate form, licking quietly at its forepaws.

You have found him then.

As you knew I would. The attacker's head lifted. He was perhaps two metres long, a four-legged animal with a tough scaly hide along his muscular body and powerful legs. He had a furred head with a long wicked-looking snout filled with sharp teeth. His eyes were red and quite intelligent. His wire-thin tail whipped back and forth, rustling the needles.

Hynd, did you . . .?

Yes. The intelligent eyes looked at Ronin. *The luma is waiting at the edge of the forest.*

Excellent. Is she still there?

Yes. She will come. Is that good?

It is what must be. The disembodied voice somehow conveyed a shrug. *The Makkon is being otherwise occupied but I do not know for how long.*

I understand.

The creature stuck his snout down and began to push at Ronin's head, directing the cool snow onto his face.

He awoke, blinking, seeing before the green and white trees or the glint of his fallen sword the friendly face of Hynd. Hynd, the cruel-visaged but wondrous companion to Bonneduce the Last, the mysterious small man whom he had encountered in the City of Ten Thousand Paths, who had made him a gift of the Makkon gauntlet.

He sat up, still half dazed. The pearled mist was receding. Golden sunlight streamed down in fluttering bars through the forest's canopy. He rose and, sheathing his blade, allowed Hynd to lead him through the tangle of trees. The forest's floor became less rocky and softer as the ancient oaks gave gradual way to stands of willowy pine and blue spruce. Unerringly, Hynd led him to the eastern fringes of the forest. They broke through the last stand of trees, pushing aside the smaller ground foliage which formed the verge, and Ronin saw his luma, its coat glowing crimson in the light. He saw the sky, a rich blue, evening already in the east.

Beside his luma stood another, smaller, its coat sky blue. Astride this sat Moeru. He went to her. Hynd loping easily at his side. She smiled and touched his face with her small pale hand. Her long black hair whipped about her, covering one eye. Just like –

'Moeru, how did you get here?'

She looked down at him, drew in the dust coating her saddle two dots, moving, one behind: riders.

He gripped the quilting of her riding jacket.

'Why did you follow us?'

She laid a finger along his collarbone, tracing down the contours of his chest. Her clear nail scraped against the fabric.

Abruptly, he felt a wave of dizziness and he leaned his head against the cool leather of her saddle. The riders disappeared. He felt her hand on his neck, stroking. His head cleared. She wiped the dirt from his forehead, licking her fingers.

Ronin felt a pulling at his pants leg and he looked down. Hynd growled. He knelt, stroking the strange plated hide.

'It was you I heard searching for me?'

Hynd coughed softly. He swung his snout at Ronin's luma.

'Where do you take me, then?' It was a rhetorical question.

He stood up, went to his steed. He paused with

335

one foot in the stirrup. 'What of the Makkon, Hynd? I must slay it or we are all doomed.'

The creature growled again, low in his throat.

'I must follow you, I know.' He glanced down at Hynd. 'And how did you find me, I wonder?' There was no answer.

He swung up across the saddle and gathered in the reins. The luma snorted and reared, calling, and Hynd loped up an incline heading east. Ronin pulled on the reins and his luma wheeled. He dug his heels into its flanks and took off, Moeru beside him, into the darkling east, away from the forest of bowing pines.

The land gradually fell away from them as dusk gave way to night. They galloped along a winding path, the terrain now filled with outcrops of rock against which dense scrub foliage flourished in wild abandon. Yellow blossoms studded the earth in great patches.

Abruptly, they were struggling up a steep incline and he soon realized that they were winding their way up the slopes of a mountain. The flowers disappeared as the way became increasingly precipitous. Here and there the black outline of a stately pine broke the skyline, but the farther they climbed the sparser the trees became until all flora was gone.

The night sky was filled with dense turbulent clouds with vaguely phosphorescent undersides sliding through disturbing hues. Ronin watched them pile and shape themselves as he felt the luma's powerful musculature working under him in fluid cadence and co-ordination.

Through the chill darkness they swept, the animals tirelessly galloping at full speed. The luma rejoiced in their kinetic flight, perhaps drawing energy from the journey itself, for it seemed to Ronin that the farther they went the stronger the mounts became. They were guided by Hynd's bounding body, calling to him or to each other.

It began to snow in cold driving bursts, the wind like a cruel knife, ripping at body and face, shoving them, moaning through the boulder-strewn mountain pass along which they continued to climb. The air became frigid and the snow turned to hail, pattering onto them, bouncing off the granite, the frozen earth, matting the luma's coats, ringing like metal off Hynd's armor plate.

Once Ronin glanced behind him. The plain from which they had ascended was still visible and he saw the spread of fat flames streaking the velvet of the night and he heard deep rumblings that were impossible to fathom. And it seemed to him that he saw the dark shadows of moving men, marching to a deep drumbeat, and the arcane structures of a full array of the machines of war, inventions to kill and maim, mutilate and cripple. It was raining fire, the continent of man shaking with the movements of war. Breath left him and, his eyes half closed, he dug his boot heels into his steed's flanks, following the lithe form of Hynd as he loped easily ahead. Then immense projecting rocks blotted out both sight and sound as they raced around a turning, adrift among the restless sleeting clouds.

His eyes flew open at the sound of a high shriek beside him. He drew up, calling to Hynd, who was already doubling back. He peered into the gloom, saw Moeru on the ground pinned beneath her luma.

He dismounted and went to her. The luma cried out and he saw that its left foreleg was broken. He bent down and carefully pulled her free; she seemed unhurt. He withdrew his blade and swiftly cut the luma's throat.

Sheathing his sword, he mounted his roan and, leaning over, drew Moeru's slim form up behind him. She wrapped her arms around him. He felt her warmth, the press of her breasts, the quickness of pulse at the back of his neck, the rhythm of her breathing.

All through the night they climbed the mountain and, as the coming sun commenced to stain the eastern horizon, they reached the summit. Ronin reined in for a moment to take in the mounting light. The mountain's eastern slopes were spread out before them, leading far below onto a plateau of geometric fields and meadows, dotted with the deep green of several forests, which descended gradually to the sea, sparking and glistening as the red sun inched over the horizon. It lacquered the sea crimson, flat and shining like burnished metal.

Then they were making their zigzag way down the mountainside and by dusk they were on the

verge of the plateau. They raced across the undulating carpet of grass. There was no trace of snow
here and the sky was clear, a deep blue, dark
already near the eastern horizon where the sun was
first to come and first to leave.

Hynd led them a winding path as the grasslands
gave way to cultivated fields, sodden and deserted
rice paddies on the edges of which stood ramshac-
kle wooden houses on stilts, roofed with paper,
tiny lanterns hanging from their front doors like
glossy insect eyes in the gathering darkness.

Several times Hynd guided them into the shallows of the dripping paddies, the water sloshing
around them until they stood perfectly still, Ronin
stroking his luma's neck so that it would not call
out, as distant rumblings became the urgent thunder of many horses' hoofs, scattering clods of dirt
and grass as they passed in long lines.

At length the rice fields ceased and they flew
past groves of trees hissing in the night. They
were on dry land again, picking up speed, Hynd's
instincts superb.

And now they ran with the wind, due east, the
land flat with only low brush to break the monot-
ony. Hynd bounded forward as if sensing that the
end of their journey was near. The luma snorted
and took off after him and Ronin, drunk with the
speed and the repetitive rhythmic movement of
the long ride, still not recovered from his singular
encounter in the forest, held on now, allowing his
mount to take him, no longer contemplating the
journey's end, Moeru's cheek a gentle weight on

..er, no longer caring whither he went,
..ing only for it to end now or for it never to
end, numb, spent.

Thus, led by the strange hybrid that was part
crocodile, part rodent, and something far more,
riding a sweat-streaked crimson steed, with a
woman he barely knew clinging to his back, he
rode into the small port town of Khiyan,
exhausted and bleary-eyed, half starved, his lips
puffy from thirst and his face black with travel,
past startled early risers, for it was just before
dawn. They pounded down the slick cobbled
streets, past wooden houses with slanting roofs
and stone chimneys from which thin trails of
smoke were already rising into the cool salt air of
morning.

Gulls wheeled in the sky, skimming low off the
water, crying into the sunrise. And at last Hynd
led them onto the waterfront, to a tavern with a
swinging wooden sign hanging above its open
double doors, its black lettering too worn by wind
and rain to make out. The crescent webbing of
fishing nets was strung along one wall.

At the side of the door stood a short man with
white hair held back from his face by a worn
leather band, a grizzled beard, and deep green eyes
set wide apart on his lined tanned face. He was
dressed plainly in a creased leather jerkin over
which was hung a chain mail vest. He wore brown
leggings and low boots of a soft leather. He came

away from the door to greet them when they are
up. He had a discernible limp when he walked.

'Ah, Ronin,' said Bonneduce the Last. 'How
good it is to see you again.'

'The continent of man is under siege from all sides
now.'

'But Kamado is the main thrust.'

'Yes. I believe that the Kai-feng will be won or
lost there.'

'I have heard that word before – '

'It is the last battle of mankind.'

'But the key is the Makkon. To destroy one is
to stop The Dolman from appearing on the
world.' He gulped down a piece of meat, poured
more wine for Moeru. 'Why then did you have
Hynd take me away from it?'

'Because,' Bonneduce the Last said slowly, 'you
cannot yet defeat the Makkon. If it had got to you
in the forest, it would surely have destroyed you.'

'How do you know?'

'How did I know that it would slay G'fand in
the City of Ten Thousand Paths? The Bones.'

'You knew, yet you let us go?'

'You would not have let me stop you.'

They sat in the dim interior of the tavern, near
the front windows and the open doors which faced
the wide wharves of Khiyan. Tall ships with
square-rigged sails as white as snow lay at anchor,
their fittings creaking. Longboats laden with men
and stores made their way across the short expanse
of water from dockside to the lee of the ships.

341

...men passed by the doorway, began to
...down the nets from the side of the tavern.
There was laughter. The owner of the tavern went
out from behind his bar and stood talking to the
fishermen.

Within the tavern, the stone hearth along one
wall was spitting flames upward into the lower
reaches of the blackened chimney but it was still
too early for the place to have become smoky. The
wood rafters were dark with an accumulation of
charcoal and cooking fat.

Bonneduce the Last had granted Ronin three
hours of sleep in a small room on the second floor
with leaded windows overlooking the docks and a
high goose-down bed onto which he fell without
a sound and not even the harsh cries of the sailors
along the short embankment outside disturbed his
slumber. The little man had shown Moeru to the
adjoining room. She was up before Ronin, gently
shaking his shoulder to wake him when she heard
Bonneduce the Last's limping step on the stairway.

'Where are they?' Ronin asked suddenly.

Bonneduce the Last reached into his leather
jerkin with a thin smile and produced the seven
geometric shapes, carved, so the little man had
told him, of the teeth of the legendary giant
crocodile. Strange glyphs were etched into every
face. The Bones.

'What do they tell you?'

'The Kai-feng has commenced, Ronin. All are
now committed to playing out their parts in the
last struggle. Even Hynd and I.'

342

'Even?'

The little man's face darkened. 'By this battle will mankind stand or fall. A new age is dawning, Ronin, and no one can say what it will bring.'

'Not even the Bones.' It was not a question.

'No man, no being, may know the balance of power now.' Hynd stirred at his feet. His forepaws twitched. Ronin glanced down at him. Perhaps he dreamed, as Ronin had, of grasslands flying by under his feet, racing with the Hart, transmogrified, his great treed antlers now a gleaming helm. 'Thus, with all the glistening lines to the future severed, are the blind forces arrayed. Thus is the struggle for power made complex; thus is the winning worth the suffering: thus' – he reached down and stroked Hynd's plated back – 'I know no more of this battle's ending than do you.'

Thoughts of the Kai-feng and the Hart, inexplicably intertwined, filled Ronin's mind. Then he put these questions aside, raised his gauntleted fist.

'I have cause to thank you. Your gift has aided me often.'

Bonneduce the Last smiled. 'I am pleased then.'

From somewhere, Ronin thought he heard a sonorous ticking like that he had heard in the little man's house in the City of Ten Thousand Paths. He poured more wine.

'You must tell me how Hynd found me.'

'Yes, of course. I thought you knew. It was the root.'

'You mean eating it.'

Bonneduce the Last nodded. 'Once you had

of it, it was only a matter of time before
we it –'

'But how could you know – '

'Circumstances.' He rubbed at his short leg. 'In any event, our connection is now stronger and that is important –'

'But –'

'You did not question the Makkon gauntlet,' Bonneduce the Last said carefully. 'Do not question this. It was the penultimate step in the ending of the Old Cycle.' He held up a hand as Ronin was about to voice another query. 'There is no time now. Three of the Makkon are already come to the continent of man and the fourth is very near.'

'What of the scroll?'

'I was just about to tell you,' the little man said sharply. 'You must sail,' he said, 'for Ama-no-mori.'

There was silence for a time. Across the room the flames licked along the huge logs in the hearth and, with a soft crash, the bottom one split, eaten through. Sparks sailed upward. Outside, along the docks, the calls and songs of the sailors outfitting their ships for their sea runs seemed dim and remote. The sunlight streamed down in molten bars, warm as honey, far away.

Ronin stared at the seamed face.

'You know where the isle lies?'

The little man nodded. 'I have plotted your course. The knowledge you seek, the knowledge which mankind needs, no longer exists on the continent of man.'

'The Bujun – ' said Ronin.
'Yes.'

The air was warm and gentle as the air of summer should be. The aged sun seemed to burn stronger here. Yet it was not possible to forget the strife destroying the continent of man beyond the blue hazy slopes of the mountain in the west.

Ronin's face was grim as he strode along the foreshore and out onto the docks. Bonneduce the Last and Hynd loped along. He held Moeru by the hand.

The little man pointed and, shading his eyes from the sun, Ronin followed his hand outward and saw the two-masted vessel lying off the shore. Its square sails were unfurling and men climbed its rigging, preparing to weigh anchor.

'The *Kioku*,' said Bonneduce the Last. 'Your ship.'

'Mine?' Ronin stared.

'You are its captain. The crew is already picked and on board.' He put his hand on Ronin's shoulder. 'You sail on the tide. Now.'

Along the quay, a longboat had heaved to and its crew waited patiently as it rocked in the gentle swells. Ronin let go of Moeru's hand.

'Take care of her.'

But Bonneduce the Last shook his head.

'She sails with you, Ronin.'

He looked from the little man to the woman beside him. Perhaps it was the light, but he thought that her eyes were different, not at all like the eyes of the people of Sha'angh'sei. Within them, some far-off, storm-tossed sea.

'Yes. Perhaps it is better this way.'

Bonneduce the Last glanced out to sea.

'It is the only way.'

They climbed down to the longboat and sat in the midship seats, facing the bow.

'I wish you could come,' Ronin called out.

The little man's hand scratched at the fur along Hynd's neck.

'We have much to do and other places to go. I trust your journey will be successful.'

'Will I see you again?' Ronin called. But the longboat had already pulled away from the dock and the wind swept the little man's reply away into the dazzling sunlight. And they moved out from the shores of the continent of man.

The *Kioku* weighed anchor as soon as the longboat had delivered up its passengers and had been hoisted aboard. The white sails billowing in the freshening wind, the ship headed into the morning sun.

Ronin stood on the high poop deck at *Kioku's* stern watching the creaming water wash along the sleek flanks of his ship as it headed out into the deep, towards Ama-no-mori, towards an uncertain and enigmatic future. *Thus, with all the glistening lines to the future severed, are the blind forces arrayed*. Even the Bones useless now. Moeru stood by his side as the last gulls wheeled about the masts of the ship before sheering off and returning landward.

And so entranced was he by the enormous vista of the swelling open seas, by the anticipation of at last seeing the mysterious fabled isle of Ama-no-mori, the end to his long and arduous journey, that he failed to recognize or even notice the visage of his first mate, now hideously disfigured and scarred about his twisted mouth, which had no lips, no jaw. Had he taken more care he would have seen within that bizarre mask of pale white flesh the writhing of controlled loathing burning like cold flames in the black eyes so well known to him. But his mind, filled with new and arcane visions, was very far indeed from the unguided ship arcing away from him on the vast uncharted ice sea so long ago; far from the Saardin he thought dead, who now stared balefully up at him from the *Kioku*'s gleaming foredeck, contemplating his terrible agonizing revenge.

Weaveworld
Clive Barker

Weaveworld is an epic adventure of the imagination. It begin
with a carpet in which a world of rapture and enchantment i
hiding; a world which comes back to life, alerting the dar
forces from which it was hiding, and beginning a desperat
battle to preserve the last vestiges of magic which Human
kind still has access to.

Mysteriously drawn by the carpet and into the world
represents are Cal Mooney and Suzanna Parrish, two youn
people with no knowledge of what they are about to liv
through and confront. For the final conflict between th
forces of good – the Seerkind – and of evil, embodied by th
terrible Immacolata and her ravening twin wraith sisters, i
about to take place.

Weaveworld is a book of visions and horrors, as real as th
world we live and breathe in, yet opening doors
experiences, places and people that we all dream of, bu
daren't hope are real. It is a story of quest, of titani
struggles, of love and of hope. It is a triumph of imaginatio
and storytelling, an adventure, a nightmare, a promise . . .

'Graphic, grotesque, and yet compellingly readable . . . i
energy is unstoppable.'   *Washington Po*

'A powerful and fascinating writer with a brilliant imagin
ation. *Weaveworld* reveals Clive Barker as an outstandin
storyteller.'   J. G. Ballar

ISBN 0 00 617489 2

The Rainbow Abyss
Barbara Hambly

A brilliant new fantasy by the best-selling author of
the Darwath Trilogy

Jaldis and Rhion make a scant living, like most freelance
wizards in a hostile universe, from luck spells, love-potions
and fortune-telling. Love and magic are dangerous practices:
combining the two can be lethal, as Rhion discovers when he
sells a love-potion to the wrong woman. Before long, the
wizards are running for their lives, leaving a rare and
dangerous spell unfinished.

Years pass before Jaldis can repeat the spell: to open a Dark
Well across the Void. From the Well he hears a voice crying
for help: magic in their world is being destroyed – they need a
wizard to save them . . .

'When the author is Barbara Hambly, prepare for something
special.'   *Locus*

The tale is concluded in *The Magicians of the Night*, also
available in Grafton paperbacks.

ISBN 0 586 21300 7

HarperCollins Paperbacks – Fiction

HarperCollins is a leading publisher of paperback fiction. Below are some recent titles.

- ☐ RED SQUARE Martin Cruz Smith £4.99
- ☐ THIEF OF ALWAYS Clive Barker £3.99
- ☐ BELLADONNA Michael Stewart £4.99
- ☐ NIGHT OF THE HAWK Dale Brown £5.99
- ☐ MORNINGSTAR Peter Atkins £4.99
- ☐ DEEP BLUE Gavin Esler £4.99
- ☐ THE TIGER OF DESIRE John Trenhaile £4.99
- ☐ THE ANIMAL HOUR Andrew Klavan £4.99
- ☐ EVIDENCE OF BLOOD Thomas H. Cook £4.99

You can buy HarperCollins Paperbacks at your local bookshops or newsagents. Or you can order them from HarperCollins Paperbacks, Cash Sales Department, Box 29, Douglas, Isle of Man. Please send a cheque, postal or money order (not currency) worth the price plus 24p per book for postage (maximum postage required is £3.00 for orders within the UK).

NAME (Block letters)_____

ADDRESS_____

_____